THE WOMAN EVERYBODY WANTED

Who was Mollie Binning?

To Hollywood reporters, she was the hottest discovery since Marilyn Monroe. To the "beach bums," she was a reckless, free-living woman always looking for a good time. To "M.Z.", her producer, she was a love affair complicating his new picture—yet he could not resist her.

The other men in Mollie's life included Dr. Myron Sontag, psychologist, who knew the secrets of her past, and sculptor Beppo Kubelik, who pursued female beauty more as a Don Juan than an artist.

"Mr. Longstreet lets the reader have it straight . . . a coldblooded, often brutal portrait. He has been part of the motion picture world, and he has the yarn-spinning knack. Sparkling flashes of vivid writing and sharp perceptions. Entertaining."

—San Francisco CHRONICLE

A NOTE ABOUT THE AUTHOR Stephen Longstreet was born in New York City in 1907 and grew up in New Brunswick, N. J. He attended Rutgers and Harvard Universities and was graduated from the New School of Fine Arts.

His widely diversified career as artist, author, critic, and playwright has included writing and drawing for such magazines as THE NEW YORKER and THE SATURDAY EVENING POST, helping to edit SATURDAY REVIEW, TIME MAGAZINE and GOURMET, the publication of several novels, the production of plays and motion pictures, and a number of one-man shows of his paintings.

In 1948 he received the Billboard Magazine Award for the best play of the year, HIGH BUTTON SHOES. He is the author of several distinguished novels, among them, THE PROMOTERS.

From The Reviews

A Novel of Hollywood

The Beach House

STEPHEN LONGSTREET

Author of "The Promoters"

POPULAR LIBRARY · NEW YORK

POPULAR LIBRARY EDITION
Published in December, 1957

Copyright, 1952, by Stephen Longstreet
Library of Congress Catalog Card Number: 52-6630

Published by arrangement with Henry Holt and Company

Henry Holt edition published in June, 1952
First printing: April, 1952
Second printing: June, 1952

A selection of the Fiction Book Club for December, 1952

For John Collier
and Christopher Isherwood

Lines from "The Second Coming," in *The Collected Poems of
W. B. Yeats,* used by permission of The Macmillan Company.

> *"Are they shadows that we see?*
> *And can shadows pleasure give?*
> *Pleasures only shadows be,*
> *Cast by bodies we conceive . . ."*
>
> —SAMUEL DANIEL

BOOK ONE

"There is no abstract art. You must always start with something. Afterwards you can remove all traces of reality . . ."

—PABLO PICASSO

1

WHAT the hell, Mike Zelsmith thought, here he was falling and twisting through the expanding universe, out here in outer space, just the way the science-fiction boys said it would be. And the big blue star was always in his eyes, the blue ghostly glow of it and him falling and moving here among the star life with no sound, and no feeling of being alive. It was bigger and darker and more fearful than he had ever imagined. He looked over his shoulder and there was the curved body of the debris of his life. All the props and projects, and the shapes of Alice and Mollie, and all the collected possessions a man piled up around him. They were following him, a long tail of objects, and the blue star, the bright star, never out of his eyes. No matter how he turned or struggled it burned in his eyes . . . And then with a merging of images he came awake suddenly, feeling wet, sucking in the sterile air of the air conditioning. He knew at once he was on a train, and he saw that the blue star was the heavy glassed night light set in the ceiling of his compartment, the Super-Chief road bed roaring under his back.

Mike Zelsmith sat up and shot high the heavy window shade. Running past his clearing vision was the lime-colored early dawn of the mountain desert. They had come in the night out of Nevada, and now they were climbing down into California, the train twisting and turning, following like a sure-footed mule the way down, down . . . He could see, when they went around a bend, the whole train ahead of him gliding down into the decomposed granite hills, and the yucca plants and the stains of iron oxidizing on the stones cut apart for the right of way. The deli-

5

cate, intricate thinking and feeling that few understood in him began to tick . . .

He sat, quickly coming into consciousness and into focus, taking up the cables of his problems and his projects. The little adobe huts, the tin-roofed garages, the long white bone of a highway, all went passing by his vision. It was an arid, yet to him, beautiful landscape. Each time he came back to California it always became real to him. Away from it he often wondered if any of it existed as he imagined it. People were so harsh to it elsewhere.

He went to the washstand, steadying himself to the rolling train on his heavy powerful legs, and turned on the light on the mirror. He had never liked his face—a face lacking finish—and he liked it less this morning. The big broken nose, the wide practical features. He put on the heavy black-rimmed glasses that had failed, somehow, Alice said, to make him look even a little like the late Leslie Howard, and he grimaced into the mirror.

While he shaved, his mind had come fully alive, had become the busy, probing tool he expected—and he was again in the middle of his projects and would not think of himself again that day, at least not that part that would gnaw at his ego. He must see the bank and snarl his way into the money he needed for the new production. He must decide about Mollie, and then when Alice got back . : . well *that* could wait. He was thinking of his project and as always it began to build into intricate detail, fine values. And he saw it grow and take on that thing he never could explain, because he never knew just what rang the bell inside him that told him he had reached it, had brought to a climax a work of art.

He changed into a heavy gray suit, single-breasted, and into his new English shoes, and as he knotted the solid dark blue tie he saw the day had come fully up. It was a yellow-and blue-shadowed world outside. Tight, knotted breakfast smoke came from the huts of the railroad workers. Cattle shot past on the slant, and there were miles of wire fence.

Mike Zelsmith suddenly remembered when he was a boy and Papa was dead and they sent him East by train to be with the family—a family going downhill. But before that the family had been big and sprawling, and rather careless with their health and itching for money, like any other family. They had been here a long time, the Zelsmiths. When Mike came to know what was what around him, they were

6

all cluttered around the Jersey seashore resorts, playing at real estate and combing out their pride with the long hair of their women; the women were very proud of their long hair. Mike could remember it all when he wanted to: the big house, full of bad taste and fumed oak, and solid plumbing comforts that often didn't work, and the layers and layers of old wallpapers that seemed to be the only thing that held all the family histories together.

Uncle Ben put wax on his mustache and Aunt Rose gave card parties and sipped wine and Mike played on the shoreline stepping on the crackling seaweed pods and getting sand in his hair, while far out at sea the ships passed all the time. His body was very brown. In the late fall they had clambakes, and the lobsters tasted wonderful, and the jelly they made down in the old kitchen smelled so it took months to get the grape odor out of the bed linen.

Everyone liked the children and brought them damp containers of goldfish from the city, and a mean-eyed pony came one spring and had to be sold after he had kicked little Alfred in the head. Alfred never was very bright after that and grew up loving dogs and hunting guns until he had an accident crossing a wall, and they buried what the shotgun had spared.

Mike used to lie in the clover field behind the house, smelling the hairy-legged bees at work and the reek of sea kelp from the ocean front and listening to the click of glasses and the card players in the hot afternoon, talking of minor scandals. Later the smell of horses would mingle with the sound of approaching hoofs, and that meant that the uncles were back from the city biting the necks of good cigars (Mike collected the bands). Supper was laid in the big dining room and everyone ate a lot, in shirt sleeves, and the elders picked their teeth behind crisp napkins. The early Country Gentleman corn and wedges of watermelon and the good Spode china filled with coffee brewed in a big white pot that came to the table on a polite knitted pot holder.

Mike grew that year and the next year with the smell of sea and the scent of meadow grass. When he went to the city and sniffed it he didn't like it. But the boat trips to Europe later with the uncles were very fine, smelling of vomit and pea soup and new leather luggage and the odor of tar and sailors' sweat.

His boyhood was the apple orchards or the dusty barn, and the road the huckleberry pickers took, and the disgrace

7

of being caught stealing a book, and the ache in one's heart when the younger aunt died (the one who wore her hair longest and had white arms and smelled as delightful as shoe polish and put body powder on her shoulders). It was the painful stiffness of little girls, the starch and urine of dancing classes, the taste of beer for the first time, and the ache of the groin in swimming when he dove deep down into the cold blue, and the world was a dull roar far away and everything looked like Uncle Ben's William Blakes, and they made him dry his hair in a rough sun-hot towel, and the walk across the meadows where the cows were (and how it felt under his bare feet when he stepped into it). They made him play the piano and remember English kings, with dates. Going to Europe to visit the other aunt helped. She had given him books. Too soon it was all over and back to California and Mama.

Mike came back to the present and his problems. The cattle fencing was still crossing his vision, like TV static. He remembered that John Fennel was on the train. It was risky bringing a writer over from London. But he couldn't depend any more on being able to excite and project the local talent into getting what he wanted. Besides, he liked John, he liked the way he talked, and they said he was a hell of a writer. The critics ought to know. Mike respected men who did great work in their own field. He would have breakfast with John and begin to explain how he worked and what he wanted. That was hardest; getting them to understand.

He grinned into the mirror—what a hell of a face, power, sure, and a lot of sensual vitality, but Jesu, why couldn't he have been born pretty like Walter Chase? He shot his cuffs into place, touched for luck the big robin's egg blue cuff links that Alice's father had given him. He made a mental note to get over these little silly ideas about luck. It was one of his good days, like they had all been in the old days, in the times and places when the bell kept ringing. He loved the world and all its people, and best of all he loved the idea that what he was doing was a work of art, and to hell with the mugs who said, "Who cares as long as it makes a buck?"

The diner was still almost empty. Mike ordered scrambled eggs, corned-beef hash, fresh fruit, and coffee.

John Fennel sitting across from him had orange juice and a cup of tea and part of a muffin. John Fennel was tired by travel. He smiled and said, "Mike, I never had an idea it was such a big country."

"Sure. I always wonder why we forget that."

"I'd have come back sooner, if I had remembered it like this."

Mike attacked his corned-beef hash with relish. "We'll make an American of you again. Just watch."

Fennel smiled and looked out at the highway on the ridge above. "Somehow in Europe California isn't thought of as part of America . . . It's a dream country to most people, all oranges and oil millionaires lying in the sun, and girls with cute behinds in bathing suits."

Mike grinned and went back to finishing breakfast. His mind was figuring, adding, and planning. Vacation was over. He looked at the heavy Swiss watch strapped to his wide hairy wrist. "Better get ready, John, we're getting off soon."

"I could use dry land, steady dry land," John Fennel said. "It's worse than traveling by ship."

"Goddamn train is a beaut, isn't it?"

"It's a space ship."

Mike frowned. "I dreamed I was floating through space last night. What would Freud say to that?"

John Fennel had stood up, and as Mike grabbed the check from his hand he smiled. "I can't see the good Herr Doktor playing with space ships, unless they suggested something womblike to him."

"What a movie his life would make—only the Breen Office bums would kill it," Mike said, and began to write out a wire to his New York agents on the back of the diet chart his doctor had given him, and which he ignored.

CHECK FROZEN COIN IN ENGLAND FRANCE ITALY NEED CASH FOR NEW PROJECT SEE IF YOU CAN CONVERT AT LEAST HALF A MILLION INTO USA NO MATTER AT WHAT LOSS SELL ALICES RENOIR.

Mike made the station introductions quickly and went off to send more wires.

"You're arriving during the last days of Pompeii," said the tall blond young man with the crew haircut—John Fennel remembered he had been introduced as Walter Chase.

"You can almost see the volcanic dust falling in the streets. The Cadillacs are already beginning to flee the doomed city, carrying the family silver and Picassos."

John Fennel grinned and stretched. After three days on the long silver train he blinked up at the white sunshine flooding in over the palm trees at the Pasadena railroad station. He wondered whether he looked just a little foolish carrying his rolled-up umbrella and a Homburg hat. He said, "I didn't expect to get off here. I thought Mr. Zelsmith and I were going directly to Los Angeles."

Walter Chase took two cigarettes from his beautifully tailored sports jacket and offered one to John Fennel. He brought out a battered brass lighter (with a Navy insignia on it), spun it alive, and lit their cigarettes.

"Mr. Zelsmith is always met at Pasadena. He hates Hollywood and avoids it as much as he can."

"Where does he make his pictures?" John Fennel asked as he watched the porters lead his two shabby pigskin cases with their scaling London stickers into the Lincoln's rear compartment.

"Hires space in Culver City. Would you mind acting up a bit for the press?"

Mike Zelsmith was back and he grinned at John. "Make it quotable."

"The press?" John Fennel lowered his umbrella point to the clean brick wall and saw three young men, hatless, tieless, and very cheerful and earnest waiting for him. Walter Chase said simply, "Boys, you know Mr. Zelsmith; this is John Fennel. Go easy on him. Just flew in from England and has been shaken to bits by the Super-Chief."

Mike said, "He's a real writer—books."

A tall thin man said to John as he held out his hand, "Somerset Maugham was here two years ago. Is it true, Mr. Fennel, you're a first cousin to Henry James?"

"No. My Aunt Martha was related to the Jameses. But I hope you will make clear I'm no real relation."

Someone asked, "You are his only disciple, aren't you, Mr. Fennel?"

John Fennel grinned and then laughed out loud and threw away the cigarette. It was mild Virginia Burley and he disliked it. "I'd hate to be caught out on that limb. Wouldn't you care to hear what I plan to do with my story for Mr. Zelsmith?"

"Walter has given us all that. Usual studio handout.

What about a few words from you and Mr. Zelsmith about the situation in Europe . . . as you two see it?"

"Sure," said Mike.

John didn't remember what he and Zelsmith said about the situation or modern art or the works of Kafka or the legs of American women. He was happy at last to be sitting in the big car driving off, between Mike and Walter Chase. He noticed it was neat and silver-fitted, not at all as gaudy as his English publisher's car that had a white goatskin foot rug. The driver was not in uniform and wore merely a battered cap with a patent leather peak.

"You're all right," said Mike in admiration. "Some of the trained seals we've brought in were really a headache with the press."

Yes, I'm all right, John Fennel felt. I'm a little tired and I'm not focusing my mind very well, but I'm all right. Deep down there wasn't much biting through. All the sunlight and all the new impressions of the place were jamming up, and he should really sort them out, put them in place. But he could only exist just now and walk about, or sit, and inside someplace the jolting of the now-gone train set up the shaking, like a jarring of bone ends and jiggling of marrow. He would have to forget the train and the land flashing by, so much of it and so little of it making any impression on him. Only Mike seemed real—and even he seemed different out here.

Maybe it was Europe being so crowded and being so small and this American world he had forgotten being bigger than bad dreams and larger than lifesize. Too much sun, too much loud tailoring and feeling; could this be America, the places and the faces he had known as a child? Was he coming back to something that no longer existed? A hell of a note, and everyone so kind to him and treating him as if he had anything of value to say. He had no answers, at least not any he cared to air, and they were all so eager to listen to him and jot it down.

Being a news item was all right if you felt you had anything to offer, but all his life had been an inner life; the lazy brooding life of a middle-class writer living mostly in a Europe that was beginning to smell of a tired old age, that senile cheesy smell of the very old. Just as well he was coming home; he was young, young as life went, and everyone had said *"California!"* as if they were repeating either a

11

dirty word or a magic omen. It was certainly more than he had expected, and just a little less real than he had imagined. Well, let it pass, let it be admitted to his pores and eyes just a little at a time. Oh, yes, he had been told he had been good with the press . . .

"I used to handle Army press relations in Egypt myself. Where are we now, Mike?"

"Moving out of Pasadena and heading for the Pacific Ocean. Anything of interest, you point at it and Walter will answer it."

Walter nodded. "M.Z. thinks I live a full social life out here."

They were passing palm-filled streets and pink stucco houses. On the right were lofting hills with carefully tended salads of overripe landscapes. Beyond them many black mountain shapes with yellow stubble where no water had been for months.

"Hollywood isn't what it was," said the blond young man lighting two more cigarettes. "Not that I knew it in its heyday. Got out of Berkeley in '41, got into a war, and came here five years ago on some fluke stories I wrote. But even I feel it running down, like a buck alarm clock getting tired, losing a few minutes every day."

Mike nodded, "Maybe now they'll make real pictures."

"Care if I smoke one of mine?" John asked.

"Sorry. Anyway, Mr. Zelsmith doesn't consider himself part of Hollywood and he's brought you out, Mr. Fennel, to goose the world into seeing he can still make great motion pictures. That's Glendale we're passing through—or maybe Eagle Rock. I read your book."

"Walter is my story editor," Mike said.

John Fennel waited politely. He did not like to talk about his writing. It was a part of him that was very unreal to himself and he was always amazed at the things people saw in it. The blond young man did not speak. John Fennel said, "You know, I write them because there isn't any Goddamn thing else I can think of doing at the time."

Mike laughed. "Get over being modest."

"You think it will make a good picture?" John asked.

Walter Chase rubbed his perfect nose and ran brown fingers through his short yellow hair. "We'll see. Say—how did you ever get yourself into this gold-plated trap?"

"I'm trying to find out myself."

"I've got you a suite at the Beverly Hills Hotel," Mike

said. "Anything else you want, just whistle for Walter."

Only John watched the traffic; so many shiny cars, so many suntanned people, following the long cement road toward the other roads ahead. The whole land seemed crisscrossed by these wonderful wide roads, and already they seemed overcrowded.

"America's a state of mind in Europe, but here it's so damn real, and so much of it."

Mike nodded. "It's a daffy place, California, and I was born here. Strangers come out here, sneer, fall in love with it, and begin to moan if they have to leave it. I like it."

"I like it too. I don't suppose I should have shot my mouth off to the press about it."

"Hell, yes," Walter said. "It's refreshing to have somebody from over there say a kind word to us Yahoos."

"I'm not from over there. I was born in Boston."

Mike laughed. "I read all that in the bio we sent out on you. I sent some booze over to your room. It's hard to get in London."

"You kept me supplied," John admitted.

"That's the boss," Walter agreed. "Booze and——" Walter used a four-letter sexual image out of Chaucer for women. "M.Z. thinks if you get plenty of those you can do anything. Maybe you're right, Chief, but it makes me wonder what the hell good an education is."

Mike said, "I like educated people."

The car purred on, eating up the white ribbon of highway as if swallowing it. They were coming now to a spreading city under black hills, and the air was scrubbed clean in a sunlight that hunted out every dark corner and exposed it. Mike Zelsmith seemed asleep—eyes closed—hands folded.

John thought back to Walter Chase's question: "How did you get yourself into this gold-plated trap?"

How? How indeed . . . ?

John Fennel had written ten novels before the public ever heard of him. The critics always reviewed him well. But his books never sold out their first small printings of three thousand copies. Frank Beaver of Beaver House, his American publishers, always said he published him "for prestige," and sent him a Dunhill pipe every Christmas.

As a young man John Fennel had gone to Paris, an amused, overeducated young man, to study art because he was bored with Harvard, and the family was dying slowly with great dignity and little money in Boston. His Aunt

Martha was an old lady, even then, and lived on a hilltop near Paris. She was once famous for a book, written in 1914: *The Gray Horde,* a study of France at bay; it was no longer read but had once had a huge sale. She controlled a little money and liked having John around because he laughed very loud. She hadn't cared for his painting, and when she died she left him some rather badly worn books and some original manuscripts given her by Henry James. John had gone to London and become a reader in a failing publishing house. There were wild rumors that Aunt Martha had been the mistress of George Moore.

John remembered her when she was young and he was only five years old on his first European trip. They were sitting in Henry James' garden watching the portly man peel an apple into a long, long string of skin (a feat he was very proud of), and then John sat on the lap of the man—he never for a minute stopped talking—and John slowly ate what was left of The Apple . . .

John had not meant to become a writer. But he had written *The Golden Moment* one summer after having a two-week affair with a shapely waitress at Blackpool. It had been a very satisfactory affair (at least from his side), for he was then a shy young man to whom the sexual functions had seemed rather exciting but vulgar. *The Golden Moment* had not done well at all as a book, but Galsworthy had written a most kindly introduction and John had been invited to tea by Virginia Woolf. The other books had come out from time to time, but they all sank without a bubble. He made a poor joke about them, saying, "their second editions are rarer than their firsts."

The war had jolted him out of too-set habits for three years. He had served at first in the Commandos with a lot of very brave young farmhands and titled homosexuals, and had been wounded twice and decorated. He never knew why, and he always dreaded to think what danger he had been in without feeling very much about it. He felt better at his job of handling the press for the high brass.

He had met Mary in Cairo, and she had been attracted to his six foot three, his broad shoulders, his head of thinning red-brown hair with the family curl in it. Later, after they slept together for two nights she liked his mind very much and they were married by a hissing little army chaplain. Two years later she had gone back to England—she commanded some kind of army staff of women who did secret

14

paper work. And a week after landing she was blown to bits in the most casual way by a V-bomb. He heard later she had said she was going up to the roof to wash her hair. To John, their two years together seemed a mockery of man's purpose on earth.

He had written then *The Sound of Bloody Laughter*, and the success of this novel had amazed him as much as everyone else. It was just like every other book he had written, a fictional section of his life; only he had written in detail of Mary and himself and how it had happened and how it was suddenly over. Like blowing on the head of a seeding dandelion in a windy field.

He knew now he had really been in love with Mary and she with him. They had been lonely and close in a far place and the days and nights had been filled in a warm, kindly way. That was the best he could remember of it. He never could, never, love again.

He had been sitting in his flat in London listening to a wireless concert of Bach from Albert Hall, when the phone call came from New York.

"New York calling. Mr. Frank Beaver calling Mr. John Fennel." The voice was crisp and impersonal.

"I'm here," John had said, and he was really amused how wonderful an invention he held in his hand. Across the Atlantic a voice.

"Hello, John old boy, how are you? It's Frank."

"Yes, I know. I'm fine, Frank."

"That ain't all, honey chile." Frank Beaver liked to talk like a hillbilly; it took the curse off the publishing of the few good writers, the "longhairs" he had on his list. "Mike Zelsmith wants to buy your new book. The Great Mike Zelsmith."

"Zelsmith? Who the devil has a name like that?"

"Don't you ever go to the movie? The cinema? Zelsmith next to Chaplin and D. W. Griffith is the greatest man of talent Hollywood has ever turned out. Even intellectuals respect Zelsmith."

"I'm sorry. Of course I know Chaplin's pictures."

"Well, Zelsmith's flying over to see you from the south of France. Be good to him, baby. The book business stinks. He's slipping badly and needs a prestige story. Let the Harry Wine office, our agents in London, talk business. You just be artistic and far away."

"Would I have to go to America?"

"Maybe. Why?"

"Hell, it's been almost twenty years, Frank. Maybe I don't think it wise to go back."

"Horseteeth," said Frank Beaver, or something like that, and began to tell him how to handle himself with Mike Zelsmith. "The solid red square of English masters against American cash. Play it big, sonny boy, but easy. Zelsmith is very smart . . ."

When John came in, Mike Zelsmith was seated in his white four-room suite at the Ritz opening packages of Rowlandson prints. He was as tall as John himself, and much wider, being given to some extra fat around the middle. His black hair was turning gray and it took a hard twisted curl that no amount of combing could get rid of. His big nose had been smashed flat at some time, and with his black-rimmed glasses he looked like a heroic Jewish copy of William Thackeray, or rather John felt, a Hebrew Victorian novelist of great vitality and strength. The mouth was powerful and sensual and had hard corners of character, and the rough and red hands carefully sorted out the prints with the skill of a man who respected good work.

"Nice of you to drop in, Mr. Fennel." The voice was heavy yet clear, with just an overtone of an American middle-class accent. "Do you like Rowlandson prints? Thomas Rowlandson."

"Very much. He got a lot of fun out of life."

"Jesu, the trouble I've had trying to get *The Dance of Life* in the proper first states. They try to ring in modern coloring on you. Well, how do you like working for me, Fennel?"

"Am I?"

Mike laughed, showing big teeth. "Sure. Papers being drawn up tomorrow. We'll get along all right. I'm a kind of an artist too. I know what life is and the lousy futility of it and the bite of it—as you guys say—but I can't say it the way you do. I can't write it or direct it . . . but I can make other people come through with stuff they don't know they ever had. Scotch or sherry?"

"Scotch."

"Good. Hate sherry drinkers, and bastards that smoke pipes and keep burning up matches."

"I smoke pipes," John said.

"Well, writers don't ever make much sense to me. But I like your story. Very much. I read your book. Walter Chase, my story editor, made me. Walter's overeducated, but very good for me. He comes from the best people in Sacramento and looks down on picture-making, and me, secretly. He's good for me. Gotta keep my damn ego down. Got one as big as a French army whore, you know. Scotch?"

"Sure."

John could see Zelsmith had belted a few before John came in. It was good scotch and hard to get in London, and John never had any trouble with his drinking. He swallowed the smooth scotch and let Mike talk. He rather liked Jews and this man was a fine craftsman and a real human being.

"I'm a great man they tell me; and there are people who don't like me. That news and a nickel will get me a cup of coffee. I've had a good ten years. I wanted to tell people the truth about life and I did it. With movies—imagine! I made classics. Stories about the good, full life. And stories about man's trouble with unfaithful women, and love, and the lousy agony of it all. I've had my share of it—glory and reward—and it's empty but nice. I've even given them real history . . . Ever see *The River Stays*? Won six Academy Awards for it."

"I'm sorry, I don't see many motion pictures."

"I'll run it for you this afternoon. I've got a 16-mm. print I always carry with me. We'll make—you and me—a great picture out of your story, *The Sound of Bloody Laughter*. Of course you're going to hate me before we're done. Have to change the title too. I'm a perfectionist. I know you can get things out of books—I read a lot—retain a little, but in me is a little tin whistle and when I've killed my writers, directors, set designers, and composers, I've got a great picture, because my tin whistle blew. Or maybe it's a bell that rings—I forget."

Mike Zelsmith got up and walked to the window and came back and poured himself some more scotch. He looked into the glass and flung its contents into the Adams fireplace, savagely.

"But I'm slipping, Fennel. Slipping. The critics said *A Case for a Goddess* was too slick and glib for all its merits. Hell, I lived with those two authors for months. They were only the pencils, I was the writer. It should have been great."

John laughed. "Maybe that was the trouble. Writers

aren't much use except for writing. Maybe I'm not the boy for you, Mr. Zelsmith. I'm the writer, not you."

The producer looked at his watch and began to undress. Calmly he climbed out of his pants. "Having dinner with Winnie and Tony."

"I better go then."

The producer slipped out of his shirt and tore at his socks, dropping chains and cuff links on a table. "No, stay. I want to talk to you. That's Churchill and Eden I'm having dinner with. The snob in me wants to be sure you know that."

"I thought it was they."

Zelsmith grinned and opened a trunk and took out some evening clothes and began to stick black pearl studs into a shirt front. "My valet became a cowboy star. I'm all alone —my wife is at Monte. Fennel, you're flying out of here tomorrow with me and going out to the West Coast. I want you to work with a new costume designer I'm trying out. Mollie Binning. She did a wonderful series of sets and costumes for a Shelley ballet in the Hollywood Bowl last year. Then slipped. But I think she still has it, someplace."

"My story doesn't need costumes and sets . . . it's modern. I should think a documentary feeling would be best."

"No. I need mood and feeling. All this talk about Hollywood and European documentary pictures being real is crap. It's just old-fashioned cops and robbers shot against a real street. Well, good-by. Call the Harry Wine Agency for details. Take the scotch with you."

"No, thank you."

They shook hands and the producer looped a white tie around his huge neck. "So long, Fennel, see you at the airport."

"It's all pretty fast, isn't it?"

"Yes," said Mike Zelsmith. He was naked and climbing into a clean pair of shorts. He turned and smiled at John. "You'll find out I'm a bastard, but a bastard who respects real talent. And if you're a genius someday I'll kiss your ass in Macy's window at high noon."

John grinned. "I'll bring my press clippings."

After he was dressed Mike felt lonely, but he left the scotch alone. He knew he was drunk and he had said a lot he shouldn't have said to John Fennel. But that's the way it was. Alice in Monte, and Mollie at Cortez Beach in California, and him between two worlds (just like a bad B picture at Columbia). A wife he was faithful to and a mistress he wasn't sleeping with, and never had. And in love with both. He kicked over the smoking stand. Why, if any sonof-abitch of an agent tried to sell him a no-good story like that he'd bar him from the lot for life!

It wouldn't have mattered in the old days when the damn tin whistle was always blowing—finished before you were forty wasn't any good. Hell, Goya hadn't painted a decent painting until he was forty, and there was old Tolstoi with his hot pants, and great stories near ninety. But he didn't think about Ludwig van Beethoven deaf and at the piano right up till the end, because he knew when he thought of *that* he was really drunk, and sorry for himself. He wasn't sorry, he was just angry because he was unhappy over his future and over women, and because he felt he could make better pictures now than he ever had. Only somebody had slipped in a phony world on him while he was sweating it out in cutting rooms and in story conferences. Yes, some bastards had blown up the world and invented popcorn and put up television towers. Box office, salary cuts, falling attendance, what did he care? He, Mike Zelsmith, didn't make pictures to make money, or for morons to clutch each other's parts in balconies. He made moving pictures because they were the most wonderful things the world had yet seen. Bigger than opera or composers or Renoir or Picasso, or Balzac or Shakespeare. Anyway, they could be. And they had to admit Mike Zelsmith had touched the hem, hell, he'd climbed into the laps of the best of the big boys with the whiskers from Plato to Bernard Shaw. Six times anyway. Six perfect pictures. He had been over every foot of them, every frame, every lap dissolve. Had listened to every note on the sound track, knew every pore of every leading star . . .

The phone dinged politely. It was the desk.

"Your cab is here, sir."

"Thanks, be right down."

"A Mr. Fennel left a package of books. Shall we send it up?"

"No, I'll pick it up later."

"As you wish, sir."

As I wish, he thought, and hung up and found his new overcoat. His Hollywood tailor would have sneered at it. Too narrow in the shoulders, too dull in the buttons, but *he* liked it, and when he put on his dark hat he decided to get a Homburg like Fennel's. Just before he turned out the light he stuck out his tongue and his image in the mirror cleverly repeated the gesture. This was one of the days he was not very fond of himself. He promised himself only one thing; he wasn't going to tell Churchill what a lousy painter he was.

Mike Zelsmith was hung over the next day in Harry Wine's office. John signed the contract for Zelsmith to take an option on his book for fifteen hundred dollars, and if John did a script in Hollywood that could be used as a motion picture, Zelsmith would buy the book. So it wasn't, John felt, as if he were getting rich on Hollywood money. He was to go out to California and get a drawing account against the final price of the book. Standing on the street after signing, his rolled umbrella in his hand, John wondered about all the wonderful talk among writers about rich success in Hollywood. But then perhaps Zelsmith didn't do business on a grand scale. But he was "a great craftsman" the agent had explained, and it would be worth doing a fine picture.

"See you on the plane," Mike said, and went into the best hatters he could find and tried on their Homburgs.

"Rather thin felt, that one, sir, for real winter," said the clerk with the twitch on the right cheek ("old Blitz wound you know, sir").

"I'm going to America," Mike said.

"Still very cold in Canada."

"Not that part. California."

The clerk put up no more fight against the sale. "Oh, you mean the United States. That is America too, isn't it?"

"Yes, the last time I was there. I'll wear the hat. Get rid of this one."

Back in his hotel there was a fat transatlantic air mail envelope labeled: FROM ZELSMITH PRODUCTIONS, and inside a batch of pencil costume drawings on onionskin paper. Also a short note.

Dear Mike:
Here are some sketches as to my idea of the characters of Mr. Fennel's book. I don't think they are any good.
                                        As always,
                                            Mollie.

Mike looked them over, agreed, and left to catch the plane to America—or rather the United States—with John Fennel.

It was a gray, grim day at the airport, the sort of grayness he had used in his first Scotland Yard picture. Only he had done it better. More black in it and deeper shadows suggesting menace. He grinned and decided that it wasn't his problem if the English didn't know how to dress a set properly.

John Fennel showed up with some shabby baggage and rolled umbrella.

"I've put my flat up to rent and stored the books. But I'm only subletting it for three months."

"Hell, I'll have you stuck on a mountaintop in a mink jock strap, and money you haven't had time to fold yet for the rest of your natural life."

John smiled. "Nice day for flying."

"You call this nice weather?"

"Well, Mr. Zelsmith, you get to calling it that after a while. How about a drink to warm us up?"

"Not unless you call me Mike. Zelsmith sounds like a low Dutch comic."

"This way, Mike . . ."

2

WHEN he could, Mike saw that his guests lived well. It was a cheerful two-room suite at the Beverly Hills Hotel with a small balcony overhanging Sunset Boulevard, and John looked out into Beverly Hills spread out before him, the running loops of tree-covered streets and good houses set down in embracing gardens, and beyond that the city itself falling away from the heights. On the far curving horizon he saw the oil wells on Signal Hill. Walter Chase pointed off to the right where a lead-colored haze sent out a spark of reflected sunlight from time to time.

"The ocean. When you're all set I'll give you a whirl down there. Like the rooms?"

"A little fancy for me. You live here?"

The blond young man shook his head. "Nope. I have a one-room slum under a fancy beach house near Malibu. I rent the space from Mollie Binning. This is just for visiting firemen."

"What do I do now?"

"Think for a week or two. We'll begin to talk story over in a few days so that when we see Zelsmith we'll be able to present him with a breakdown of the new story line. Something he can reject and we'll start over again."

John frowned. "New story line? He bought the one I wrote."

Walter Chase opened a mottled brown leather briefcase and took out some blue-covered shapes. "Here are some samples of screenplays M.Z. picked out for you. *Stage Coach, Citizen Kane, Gone with the Wind, The Informer*, and some others. Chew on these Mr. Fennel, and see how pictures look on paper."

"Not if you call me Fennel. John will do."

Walter grinned. "You sound like M.Z. being *just folk*."

"What makes him tick?" John asked.

Walter went serious. "That vulgarity and crudeness are all a big bluff. Its the coat of mail he wears to look like the real citizens of this town. A protective coloration."

"He doesn't respect the town?"

"But it's his town, see? And he wants to be part of it. Only . . ."

"Only what?"

Walter frowned. "I haven't figured him out yet. It's not easy, and the surface of him doesn't matter. What's he like inside? Sensitive, delicately tuned. He'll amaze you by that quality he has for taste and form and tone."

"I sensed something like that."

"They say when he was on top, really rolling, he was the greatest sonofabitch they ever had out here."

"What happened?"

Walter shrugged his shoulders. "What happens to people? Look, I'm still trying to find out what happened to me, and most likely you're trying to find out what happened to you . . ."

John nodded. "He seems to think it's the town, the industry as he calls it, that's against his way of working."

"Maybe. They hate real talent out here. Talent that wants to kick over the timetables and rules. Not much real stuff out here. Read those scripts and you'll see. And they're the best."

"I'll try."

"And leave word where you'll be. M.Z. will want you on call any hour, day and night."

"If that's the way he wants it," John said.

"Okay, you're in business." Walter held out his hand and they shook. Walter went to the door and opened it and stood there with his hand on the knob. He looked back at John and one corner of his tongue, just the tip, wet a corner of his mouth.

"What do you like? Women, trade, first editions, deep-sea fishing, or jam sessions?"

John grinned and scratched the back of one ear, a gesture of his when caught offguard. "That your department too?"

"I'm afraid so. It's just a Roman country town full of simple pleasures. It's not London or Paris. I was there in the war. Everything was real tired. It isn't tired here. You call me if you need anything."

"Thanks, Walter, but not just now. I'll just read screenplays and rest."

Walter nodded, deadpan, and went out. John sat down on a too-soft, too-low chair and looked over the neat smart interior of his suite. His shabby bags were open on the bed. There wasn't much to unpack. A volume of Gibbon; he always read a bit of Gibbon before turning in at night. A book of poems, three suits, and some well-laundered underwear. A few ties, the cheap blue paper he wrote on, some shaving kit, and that was about all. Walter had said something about a typewriter, but he didn't use one—he always wrote slowly with great effort on blue paper with a very sharp pencil that broke its point too often.

The pile of screenplays looked menacing and he picked one up and opened it and read:

SHOOTING SCRIPT—ZELSMITH PRODUCTIONS
FINAL

MAIN TITLES—
FADE IN:
EXT. CITY—NIGHT (STOCK AND PROCESS)
LONG SHOT—CAMERA ON DOLLY is on hilltop over big city. CAMERA MOVES IN on MEDIUM SHOT of parked car. Sound of *night noises* . . .

He closed the script. It was too much like math in school and he had never been very good at math. He got up, went

23

to the window, and looked down into the busy roadway where polite, panting cars all shiny with waxing and metal trim were waiting for the light to change. Then they were off like hounds at a dog race he had once seen in Liverpool. He took off his tie and jacket and poured himself four fingers of the rye that Walter had left and put in three ice cubes from the silver ice bucket. He tasted it and liked it cold and wondered why the English didn't ice their drinks. He smiled as he suddenly felt very American for the first time.

His stomach was still tossing from the train ride and he lay down on the bed, aching all over. The ceiling was new but already there were cracks in it and the very clean linen smelled of something they used to kill germs. He rolled over and saw between the cracks in the polished oak floor a line of tiny ants marching toward the wastebasket, coming and going. He had read as a boy of the tropics, and stories of great ants who marched, armies of millions of them who ate everything in their way, including full-grown adults. But these were only tiny ants, and he supposed there was no stopping them, even in California. They were part of this semitropical place, and no modern progress and fine building would keep them out all the time.

He was worried because the whole place was becoming no realer at all to him. He always liked to settle down in a place so that after a few days he wore it like an old coat and never thought much about it. He didn't like to get excited over old churches and fantastic landscapes, and he really disliked cloud effects—but was secretly a sucker for sunsets. They had good ones here and maybe after he saw a few more blood-red horrors painted on the sky it would be real and he could get that feeling of belonging. Belonging was what a man had to have in a place, even if he was only a visitor.

The big house that Mike and Alice Zelsmith had built overlooking the sea, "a leaping design for existing," the fancy builder had told them, was a landmark, and if there was such a thing as *too modern*, the Zelsmiths' place was it. Mike had never liked it and the things it was made of: the slabs, sheets, shapes, plate glass, redwood, poured stone, bent steel, and other functional trash that had been sold to Alice as the right thing *beyond* the last word. There were already termites in the foundation.

24

The servants were asleep, he hoped. The Great Dane, in front of the dead fireplace with the silly Jackson Pollack painting over it, lifted his big ugly head and growled. Mike suspected the dog was slightly anti-Semitic, and he said, "Hey, shut up." They had never named the dog. He was just called Hey. Mike put down his coat and hat and went into the small bar, unlocked it, and poured himself a stiff drink. The servants must have been at it somehow; it tasted watered down and warm as horse brine. Glass in hand, he dialed Mollie's beach house at Cortez Beach. He wondered why it was supposed to be better than Malibu. It had the same kelp beds, and dead sea lions from time to time drifting in with the breakers.

He heard the phone ring but there was no answer. He sipped his drink and refused to let his mind register any idea of where she might be. He hung up and called Mandy Rye's beach house. It was just next door to Mollie's. Mandy Rye, what a hell of a name, even for a young character actress playing witty parts. All the names were cockeyed out here. Mandy Rye; still it was her real name. He knew that because he had first found her in a small school play years ago . . . well, no use bringing all that up now for a dime phone call.

"Hello?"

"Mandy? Mike."

"Mike?"

"Speedy," he said, using a nickname almost ten years old.

"Mike, baby, how are you?"

"Fine, just got back from Europe. Mollie doesn't answer her phone."

Mandy's screen laugh brushed his ear. "She went to the movies with some of the beach bums. She really likes the cinema."

"How has she been? She doesn't write much."

"Pretty good. You really going to make a screen star out of her?"

"I only make actresses out of women, not stars."

"Well, save a part for old Mandy. Times are getting hard."

"I'll keep it in mind. Bye, Mandy."

"Sure. Night, Speedy."

He hung up and sat looking down at the empty glass. The pain was in him again, the mental knife of nerves all cutting deep and he sat bent over until the thing let up a little. He was a Goddamn fool about it—face it—he had always admitted it. This love business and this being in love. And always when a woman meant anything to him he had to be deeply in love with her. Now it was Mollie, and Alice. It hadn't meant a thing with Alice for a long time, yet he couldn't just tear it up because Alice loved him, and only him, and had nothing else unless it was her bastard of a father, and about him Mike wasn't going to think tonight. Mollie was something so fresh, so new to him, and still so much the mystery that almost in fear he decided to go right to bed before he got into a car and went down to the beach house to wait for her. Anyway, he didn't want to bring it to a climax yet. The night and sea and the long time apart might just about—he brushed the glass off the phone table and heard it break and went up to the bedroom. Just before he fell fully asleep he wanted to call John Fennel, but decided to let him alone for a few days to get him acclimated.

John Fennel picked up the Gibbon, broke the book open anywhere it would open, and began to read:

> The master of the Roman world, who aspired to erect an eternal monument of the glories of his reign, could employ in the prosecution of that work the wealth, the labour, and all that yet remained of the genius, of obedient millions . . .

Just like the motion picture industry, John thought, and decided to read the screenplays.

He tried to read them again in the morning. But the screenplay form was so confusing with its wordings of TIGHT TWO SHOTS and SLOW DISSOLVES and MONTAGES that he escaped with a small, bad-smelling Dunhill pipe in his teeth and walked up and down the winding streets for an hour.

The olive trees of Beverly Hills worried him. A great many lawns were shaded with the silver-leaved trees and now the fruit was ripe; the trees tended and fertile were covered with dark purple olives and the ground under the trees was carpeted with the fallen olives. No one picked them or processed them or ate them. The waste worried him. He had spent some time in Italy during the war and had seen the old Italian women grubbing for the last moldy olive on the rocky hillsides, and here the olive trees of Beverly Hills bore their fruit only for decoration. There was no table set in this tailored wilderness Mike Zelsmith called home, he felt.

He entered the hotel and nodded to the clerk and took the elevator (he must stop thinking of it as the lift). He walked slowly to his room, his mind on olives. The door was open and he went in and a beautifully put together very young woman was bent over his worktable. He saw first the curved lines of her slim hips, then the very fine legs in sheer silk, and when she turned and shook out her pale blond hair—almost white—and smiled at him—he noted the delicate intricate beauty of her. But it was the face that held him in the doorway fumbling his pipe. It was a beautiful face, out of a sweet period of Greek art the modern school was turning from. She stood there, small boned, really delicate, childlike. She was still smiling at him, and he smiled back, feeling the staring fool.

"Hello, I'm Mollie. Mollie Binning." Her voice had a Yankee ring to it—not at all Western.

"Of course. Walter said you would be up. John—John Fennel."

"I had them let me in." She pointed to a portfolio of fashion drawings open on the worktable. "I've heard about you, John Fennel."

"What have you heard?"

"You're a good writer. I haven't read anything but your last book."

"I've written ten."

She laughed; she had a small, ringing laugh that grew as it came up through her white neck, and then it exploded. It was a girl's-school laugh, very satisfying. What a charming child, John thought.

"I don't read much any more. Your book scared me. War books scare me. Not that yours is a war book. It's a bitter book full of fury. But your people were better in bed than in battle. What the hell are you so mad about?"

"You read the book." He took one of Walter's bottles and put some whisky into two glasses and pointed to the silver tray. "Water or soda?"

"Water."

"I'm angry about the girl dying, the brutal things that can happen to people."

She lifted ice cubes into her glass with long classic fin-

27

gers; he noticed her nail polish was colorless. "Walter says it all really happened to you."

"A great deal of it. I only write about what I know or have lived."

He lifted his glass to her and she grinned back and swallowed the drink slowly as if she hated the stuff.

Her hair close up he saw was pale lemon and old rose, not touched up with any beauty parlor red. Her small body and its wonderful curves, her striking beauty, amazed John. But what else did he expect in Hollywood?

He took the glass from her hand. He sniffed. A sharp odor filled his nostrils.

"Mike gave me this perfume. Awful, isn't it?"

"I don't care for perfume."

"All right, I'll stop wearing it as long as we're on the picture."

"Please wear it if you like it."

She stood up and the legs and hips were really magnificent under the thin silk. She asked, "How about lunch? Have you ever eaten a Caesar salad?"

"I'm game," he said. He felt clumsy and angry at himself and all thumbs as he took her arm and they walked down the hall toward lunch . . . Was he being disloyal to Mike Zelsmith? Anyway, she was too much the child to feel anything but—well not exactly fatherly—at least protective. It was a fine lunch . . .

The parking-lot man took Mike's car at the front door of the hotel and Mike went inside quickly; it was a very warm day with no sign of clouds except for some deep holes in the sky filled with cotton. The desk clerk said Mr. Fennel was in the Lanai dining room, and he found him there with Mollie, drinking iced coffee.

"So you two have met?" he said, very pleased, signaling the waiter. "Some cold salmon, some toast, and a big pot of real hot coffee," he ordered.

John Fennel tinkled the ice in his tall glass. "I've been introduced to California salads."

"You'll get to like them. Mollie, I tried to get you last night, and this morning again. Where the hell have you been?"

"To a movie, then boating, with some people from Pasadena. We had a real delightful time. I caught a sea robin, you should have heard it croaking on deck."

She was very excited and pleased with herself as she told it, and she sat there the beautiful little girl animated by her story, her graceful head arched to one side, and her clean-cut, amused mouth twisted as she tried to croak like the sea robin.

Mike laughed and kissed her cheek. "Mollie, you enjoy things. You really do."

She sipped her iced coffee and nodded. John decided her eyes were the bluest he had ever seen, touched with just a bit of ice-green and flecked with perhaps gold dust.

"I'm going to be fitted for new sandals. Golden ones, and I'm reframing my Degas drawing, the one you gave me for my birthday. Do you mind?"

"No, go ahead, reframe it. Listen, I want to give you a screen test in about a week. So don't get too much sun on that white skin."

"You really think I can act?"

"I can make you act," Mike said simply as his food came. "Acting is merely projecting some vital force into a creature, male or female. I mean real acting, not Hollywood acting. That's not acting, that exploiting the charm and personalities of shoe clerks and two-buck whores. Garbo was different, and Bette Davis before she ruined her style had just a touch, but the rest—bait for shark fishing."

Mollie smiled two rows of little white teeth, and she winked at John Fennel. "I'll smell up the theater as an actress. I'm a designer, Mike."

"If I had time I'd make you a great designer, but I haven't time. I can make you an actress. It's going to be hard work, but you ring the bell, Mollie, you've got it, own it, process it. I can't tell you what it is, but I know it when I see it. It isn't brains. You've got a good brain, but that doesn't ever make art. You've got a body, a tiny master-piece, the way you sway or walk, and you have the eyes for it. You really talk with your eyes and no great actor was ever as good with his mouth in talking as with the eyes. Waiter!"

"Yes, sir."

"The coffee isn't hot enough. John, how many people have ever really excited you in your life?"

"Three or four."

"Jesu, you've been lucky. I've met two. Chaplin and now Mollie. No, I guess Picasso did too. The others had

29

talent and a real flair, but people who stop you dead in your tracks, they're precious."

Mollie laughed the school-girl hoot and showed an inch of pink tongue. "Boy, will you be sorry when I turn out to be a dud."

Mike swallowed very hot coffee and looked at his wrist watch. "I'm due at the bank, John, and I want you to come along. You can look over the sketches later."

"Dinner?" Mollie said rubbing her wrists together as if trying to warm herself.

"I'll pick you up at seven. I'd bring John along, only I want him to work. I'll be cracking the whip soon."

"I've broken the story down into scenes," John said. "At least what I think scenes are."

"Work with Walter on them till I get the bank and the release set on the picture . . ." Mike grabbed the checks from the waiter and signed them quickly. He stood up and kissed Mollie on the cheek again. "Amuse yourself, baby, till I see you. Come on, John."

Mollie laughed. "You're the only man I ever met who acted important and really was."

"Clever?" said Mike to John as they started for the door.

"Thanks for the lunch and advice, Miss Binning," John said.

"Haven't you heard?" Mollie said. "We're cutting out the Mister and Miss stuff."

The headwaiter almost dislocated his neck in a bow as Mike slipped him five dollars.

"Meet me out front," Mike said to John. "I have to make a phone call . . ."

In the car on the way to the bank John sensed that Mike had had a few quick drinks during the "phone call." Drinking desperately to face the forces that would or would not give him the money to film this project.

Mike sat way back on his spine, with one fist gripping the velvet hand cord as the car went swirling through the sun-drenched traffic.

"Christ," he said, "the bums I have to flatter. The whole damn industry is afraid of me and yet laughs at me. An industry always forgetting essentials and turning out plausible trash. Vulgar, naïve, all their problems are surface textures and the primary emphasis is on moron bait. What's their lousy gimmick? Never give 'em life, the real emotions must be concealed. Don't they know you first have to have emotions, even to conceal them? I used to be able to stir them up, but now look at 'em, hopelessly rigid in stale chicken fat, full of tired clichés cleverly disguised, they haven't a pisspot full of true originality. They mask everything they say, make a burlesque of real emotions. If you don't they tell you you'll be kissing asses like Zelsmith for enough scratch to make a picture. Hide in banality, work the yaks into prattfall routines. Don't go near any real aspects of nature, give 'em the false nostalgia, and no baffling idiosyncrasies of life just this side of the truth. Crush reality down to the point of obscurity, and the old moral rigidity of the box office in West Hernia, Texas, is the only law. The result? The best remembered actor is still Rin-Tin-Tin!

"Only the lower simplicities for the children of all ages, no spiritual regions you can't express by a priest who plays baseball. Skip the autumnal desolation of civilization or any mature simplicity of style beyond cellophane pubic hair and rhinestone-filled navels. No new experiences, but the same old vaudeville bravura, and the least possible contact with life. No natural changes, just the weenie, the twisteroo. We can't have the spirit, let the flesh be found. And the lonely hunters, the exiled artists, never lose their isolation. I'm drunk, Johnny, I wanta puke."

"I never heard you talk like that, Mike," John said, "or as well."

"I know, but I have to keep reminding myself what I'm fighting when I face these frozen bastards with their icy little grocery stores that feed the industry."

The car had stopped before an imposing modern building of chipping granite and blood-red bronze lettering.

RANCHING AND CINEMA BANK
OF CALIFORNIA
Open a Tarzan Boys Club Bank
Account for Your Children.

A large colored cutout of the ape man stood in the bank lobby holding up a toy bank in the shape of a small plastic ape with a hole in his head for coins.

Mike turned back from the bronze-trimmed plate glass doors. He gripped John's arm hard and shook his head.

31

"How about it, pal? Want to buy old Mike one more drink before we go in?"

John nodded. "Sure, there's a bar two doors down."

Mike grinned. "Only one more drink. Then tell me what bank this is and how much I want, and push me in . . ."

The bank directors' room was paneled in colorful murals of chorus boys dressed as cowboys, and actresses in Adrian overalls as Barbary Coast Whores. All painted smartly, John noticed, in the latest designs from the School of Paris. The sweat and stink and danger of the wagon trains had become wallpaper.

It was not very frightening. They met some ex-football players in business suits—very healthy and tanned, two decent faces still full of Kansas features, and some brisk young men with retreating hairlines and very bland honest faces that peered from behind well-designed bifocals. The oldest of the young men shook hands with Mike and John and showed them to two waiting chairs of red leather, very comfortable. Each place had a clear crystal ashtray, two newly sharpened pencils, and a small scratch pad with the letters: ASSETS $4,000,000,000,000.

The old-young man smiled pleasantly and lit a thin cigarette. "Been playing any golf, Mr. Zelsmith?"

"No, I'm getting the script ready for my picture."

The old-young man slid the zipper off a square of fine leather in front of him and took out a folder full of thin typed sheets. "I've been playing the course at Bel Air, but it's chilly there in the morning." He flipped the sheets and looked up at Mike cheerfully. "This looks like a pretty wonderful motion picture."

Mike said, "You know the kind of pictures I make."

"Yes, we're pretty proud of the part we've had in the film industry. Too bad times have changed a little. Box office is down twenty-eight per cent, nationally."

A football player running to fat in his face said, "Thirty-two per cent as of this morning."

Mike looked up, his mouth held very thin in a razor-edge smile, and his brow was ridged as he opened his eyes very wide to look at the top of the head of the old-young man. "I have asked the bank for two million eight to make this picture. Four hundred thousand at signing, a million on day of start of principal photography, and the rest at stated periods, as in that paper before you."

"That's a lot of money these days for even an A picture."

"DeMille has just spent four million."

"Ah, deMille," said one of the board. "He's smart, he's still making silent old-fashioned movies that people like. Your picture is pretty modern."

Mike was very still. He spoke low. "If this bank doesn't want my business, we can all cut this short, and go and play golf."

The old-young man shook his head and grinned. "Now, Mr. Zelsmith, we've done lots of business together. It's just times are in flux. Suppose you arrange your release, sign your stars, and come back to us with it all, and we'll talk of a picture costing say, a million five . . . or six. A few hundred thousand one way or the other you won't find us tough tittie."

He looked around the board, rather proud of the last expression, and John could see they were really very nice people, just a little bored by banking morals.

Mike had stood up. "In other words, if my father-in-law gives me a release and name stars I can make half as good a picture as I intended?"

"Now, Mr. Zelsmith, you know good pictures have been made for low costs. We may even go to two million if you get a top director, but . . ."

Mike had swung around now and was waiting, poised on the balls of his feet, balanced gracefully for such a large man against the table by holding one hand flat on its shiny surface . . . the sting in the honey was about to be shown, John felt.

"But, you must understand, Mr. Zelsmith, that the board has full script approval before the final signing of the papers. Sorry those are the new bank rules. Full approval."

Mike was soft and polite. "The board?"

"The board," said the old-young man.

"This board?"

"This is the bank board."

"Doesn't my father-in-law and his group own controlling interest in the Ranching and Cinema Banks?"

"The bank stock," said a Kansas face, "is open to the public."

Mike locked and unlocked his fingers in an intricate pattern of digits. He said still softly, too softly, "It's no secret that my father-in-law can hardly read or write."

The old-young man smiled a careful smile now, and beads

of sweat were scarring his tanned brow. "He is a self-made man, but a very wise one. I've heard he reads Homer in the original Greek."

Mike turned and walked out and John got up and followed him. One of the football players stopped John. "Mr. Fennel, it's been good to meet you. I'm kind of a collector, own a few Keats and Shelley originals, some Kipling firsts, but I do have some modern authors in good states, most of yours. Palmer is the name. Like to have you over some night for dinner and get you to sign my copies. All mint conditions."

John said he would be pleased and went out after Mike. Mike was standing at the curb blinking up at the sunlight. "Jesu, what a country! No seasons, no colors of change, no storms or winds. Nothing but this Goddamn sun. And *then* one day a leaf falls high up in a canyon and they tell you it's winter!"

"I've never met bankers before, Mike."

Mike laughed. "Those pen pushers are all right, but they don't make the answers they give out. You met my father-in-law yet?"

"No, he seems to be important."

"Johnny, he's one of the few people in this town who is, and he *can* read and write. When you meet the sonofabitch, count your fingers after you shake hands with him. We don't get along, as you can guess."

"I can guess."

"He thinks I'm going to walk out on his daughter because of Mollie. Maybe I am, maybe I'm not. Want another drink?"

"No, I better go back to the hotel and get some work done."

"That's right. I haven't cracked the whip enough."

John called a cab. Mike sat a long time in his car and decided not to have another drink after all. He was not even discouraged. He'd beaten the banks down before.

John Fennel sat studying Mollie's sketches. The sketches certainly showed talent, but to what banal purpose the talent was turned. The girl had a real gift, something could be done with it. She could be in New York or Paris designing for the ballet or the modern theater.

A knock on the door made him lift his head as he said, "Come in."

34

Walter Chase came in, looking very fine in evening clothes and walking a little too gracefully.

"Hello, how's it going, John?" He shook his blond cropped head and sat down and took both his ankles in his hands. "Hadda go to Huntington to see a Metro sneak preview, then to a party to condole the director and producer. How you?"

"Pretty good, Walter. Been looking over Miss Binning's sketches."

"Mollie's work?"

"She was here this afternoon. We had lunch."

Walter grew suddenly serious. He made a small o with his mouth. "Great girl, Mollie. How do you like?"

"Seems very talented. Why hasn't she made more of a name for herself?"

"Conflicts. Everybody has big conflicts in this damn town. I got conflicts. You'll have 'em. Mollie—wonderful child—has man trouble. Can't find the right guy."

"She doesn't look it. She's charming, witty. I like her."

Walter opened his tie and sank back on the sofa with a sigh. "Mollie is still a school girl. Hasn't been anyplace or done anything, except marry two guys."

"You been married to her, Walter?"

Walter kicked a leg up in the air. "No. I rent space under her beach house. Believe me, nothing between us. Besides, there is Gene just now on her mind—now Mike is making up his mind."

"Gene?"

"He's her husband. Trying to be an actor. Out on the road in some turkey. They don't live together any more. Big problem, Mollie and Mike. Too big for me. I'm just a Sacramento society boy eating kosher down here. No time for problems. I'm tired."

Walter rolled over, his face in the cushion, and began to snore politely. John went up to him and shook him. "You can't sleep here. The sofa is too short."

Walter looked up, his eyes out of focus. "Can't move, too boiled to drive. Wreck myself before I reach the beach."

"Walter, about Mike and Mollie? They're people I'm getting fond of."

"Mollie is M.Z.'s latest prodigy. Don't look so smug. They haven't been to bed together. He really thinks he can make another Garbo of her. He likes playing Svengali, and he's done it before. M.Z. is a very great man, even I admit

35

it. He's set Mollie up in a very swank beach house, loaded it with art, and he can't make his mind up."

"What about?"

"That he wants to be in love with Mollie."

"I think he is, Walter."

Walter nodded. "I could see it coming. He's always in love. With something. It would be better if he had remained in love with himself. The ego is the best bed partner, they say. But M.Z. is funny. He's still an emotional little Jew boy in lots of ways. If he only had less talent and more *chutzpah* in emotional things he'd get by better in this town. He can't love 'em and leave, that's his trouble. That's *all* our troubles, isn't it, John?"

"What's Mrs. Zelsmith like?"

"Alice? She's due back soon. You'll meet her. A fireball. Nice gal. M.Z. likes her too, that's the rub. But Alice has two strikes against her. Her old man controls this town, more or less, and it isn't doing her any good to have Mike come asking Papa for favors. Mixed up, isn't it?"

"I feel sorry for Mollie."

"Why, John?"

"She's such a fine kid. She told me Mike reminds her of her father."

Walter whistled. "That ain't never happened before with her. This is very interesting. Love thy father image."

"I think they love each other very much."

"So make it love," said Walter. "After all, what is love? It's only a personal attitude toward what someone else has under their clothes. Gotta remember that. Good line."

Walter fell back on the sofa and went to sleep at once.

John didn't hear from Mike all morning, so he read the screenplays and brought his journal up to date. He liked working on his journals; it was interesting writing, not like the books he wrote, toward which he felt very impersonal. He tried to keep the cant down in the journal; in the books it often crept in.

The desk called. "There's a Miss Binning at the entrance with a car. Will you come down?"

"Miss Binning? Yes, I'll be down."

He looked in the mirror, scratched behind his ear, pressed his hair in place with the palm of his hand, and decided against taking a hat.

She was lovely—more childlike—in a smooth linen skirt and a curly sweater, and sat in a little English car.

These were a new kind of people out here and John couldn't label them and stick them into sections of his mind in which he filed all members of the human race. That sense of everything not being real was still with him. They were all a bit part of the landscape. Like those flat figures they painted on flat modern pictures and you looked at them and said, interesting, very nice use of pattern *and* line. Everyone out here was going to remain flat patterns and he wasn't going to get involved, not right away anyway, because he had come to a country, or a part of it, and it wasn't at all like the country he had left as a very young man who knew everything. Now he knew just a little about a few special things.

"Hello, Mollie," he said, and smiled.

"Hello," she said. "I thought we ought to go up in the hills and see some of the places Zelsmith wants to use for location. It looks like Italy up there, off the Pass."

"I've wanted to see the hills up close. Thanks."

He got in and she drove off skillfully but without much care, as if driving was something she did naturally without thinking.

She looked at him and made her little laugh bubble in her throat. He couldn't believe she had been married twice.

"It's an odd laugh for such a little girl," he said as he put two cigarettes into his mouth, lit them from one match, and handed her one. "I saw that in a movie."

She smoked and drove. "Mike doesn't let me see many movies. Spoil my style, he says."

A mountain road between golden weeds. The earth was dry and the grasses yellow, and here and there a pale waxy yucca shot up a stake.

He said, "It does look like Italy up here."

She turned off the climbing road onto a narrower one and backed the car around and they sat facing the world. Below them ran a busy road and across from them a hillside, and beyond that the city. They were high up.

"It's impressive," he said.

"Yes, it's like something I once read and forgot."

She was sprawled gracefully in the car seat. He saw her legs browned with the sun, and the small sandals with their crossed leather ties around her thin ankles. Her breasts were tight under the sweater. She looked out at the road. "There is a little bird there." She got out of the car and he saw a small dark bird, trying to flutter across the hot road, its mouth open, gasping, its pinfeathers still showing it was from some nearby nest. The heat was weakening it as the sun beat down. Mollie bent over the bird, cupping it in her hands, and turned to John, smiling.

"A car will come along and crush it."

She walked to the other side of the road and put the bird down in a clump of buffalo grass. She came back to the car smiling widely now, showing all her teeth. After the car was started and they were gliding down the hill, she turned to him, her blond hair swirling in beauty around her face, and gripped his arm with one of her little fists.

"We've done our good deed for the day."

John waited for Mike to call. He began to enjoy California; its weather, its food, and the continual line of mountains or sea that seemed to hem it in on all sides. He liked to hear the people talking, and he tried to remodel his own speech on the American pattern. He used slang and the special jargon of the motion picture industry. From Walter Chase he took over certain key words and special sentences. He put away his rolled umbrella and gave a Japanese busboy in the hotel his Homburg hat.

He bought loud low-collared shirts with tropical patterns, but wore them only in his room at first. He wanted blue soft suede shoes with heavy crepe rubber soles, but did not dare put them on after he shamefacedly bought them.

He set up a drink for a stray woman in the hotel bar and let an old unemployed motion picture director named Ed borrow money. He wondered if the bank would loan Mike the money for the picture.

"Hello, John Fennel?"
"Hello, yes."
"This is Miss Binning—Mollie."
"Hello, how are you?"
"Busy as a fiddler's elbow on the sketches."
"That's good."
"Mike asked me to call you. If you're not doing anything tonight, Walter will pick you up and bring you down to my place. No party—just an evening at the beach."
"Do I dress?"
"No, barefooted."

"Thanks."

"Bye . . ."

"Bye, Miss Binning."

"Mollie, you lug."

"Mollie."

FROM THE JOURNAL OF JOHN FENNEL

Mike was born here—Mollie was not, I gather, born in California, but this has been her world most of her life. It is world of much sun and loosely clad bodies and there is also a farness from the center of the earth. They read the new books and collect the most fashionable of art and play and drive the newest tools of the machine age, but someplace in them all there is a touch of buckskin and arrowheads. The hills look big and cruel and seem to mock the landscape gardeners.

It's good to find in Mollie no summary of the critical times, and she would reject as preposterous the anatomy of terror, personal and political, that lives in the cage of Europe. She is young enough to risk hope, and not yet old enough for the pivotal irony of existence. Mike is right about her—she is a personality—but as an actress, a great one, I wonder . . .

The expected sun is poised with skill and taste on my doorstep and beyond the palm trees wave and the sea is muscled in a light wind, and of course they all say, On a clear day you can see Catalina." As if that were a great treat.

I am learning new words and a new way of talking from Walter. It is the American speech, a blend of echoes that is frontier and underworld; the special jargon of bull ring and trout fishing; the smoke and noise of small bars and late nights smelling of native jasmine. Europe seems far away and I have almost, but not quite, forgotten my Yeats.

"Things fall apart; the centre cannot hold;
  Mere anarchy is loosed upon the world,
  The blood-dimmed tide is loosed, and everywhere . . ."

I notice that I have a bad habit of retreating to the poets and the worn-out classics when I am faced with a problem of living. I am old enough to know it will not do. It's all very well to remember Yeats as an excuse to avoid thinking of how beautiful Mollie is; and that's how we have all been living I think, refusing to come down to earth; and going what Mike calls "longhaired." We refuse to face the everyday healthy passions. Not that I know a damn thing about Mollie—and most likely she would be insulted to be called everyday and healthy; but we go into such a song and dance about spiritual rebirth after sinning and we try to dress up in the words of poets. I think we fool ourselves with good prose, hoping that way for some miracle, excitement, and sensation.

I must be honest enough to think of California and not drag in Yeats; to enjoy the sight of it without dipping into the spiritual sloth of most educated sensualists. There is too much nonsense in this journal already . . .

There is a big party going on next door. This is a land of parties and they all play the same records, drink the same booze, and scream in the same key. Someone is tickling a girl and soon she will begin to scream and then to weep and when it's quiet someone will knock on my door and ask for the use of my bathroom and I will be asked to come in for a drink. There is a true love of well-being and party-giving out here. Walter warns me against going to parties out of my bracket—I must ask him does he mean salary or social . . .

3

Now that he had sent the cable asking Alice to fly home, Mike Zelsmith had nothing to do but wait till it was time to go to Mollie's party. Mike sat in the modern living room under the too-modern paintings and he wondered if he should have sent for Alice. If he made the break now the bank would never be permitted to give him the money for the picture, and yet he had to have it out with Alice—had to settle one way or the other before he would be free to give his time and mind to the project. The armed truce between them was wearing thin, and the truce flag itself was no longer white, but frayed and gray. Damn, there he was thinking in picture terms, and that is where he knew he would never be able to understand fully his life away from images and into crowded female thinking processes.

He had felt for a long time a sense of being utterly alone out here. Mollie had been the one hope to cure it. Now he didn't know. The aloneness of being an artist out here; first the physical part of it, the smallness of man in these vast sun spaces of California and the lofting mountain ranges. Artists should work in great cities, not in arid deserts reclaimed by water as valuable as gold. Then the social misfit of being a creative artist in these factories of nonsense and popcorn sales charts. The psychological hollowness of living and working in a world where they did not really want inspired work and where what he did was misunderstood and condemned as art. Also being a citizen of this nation in this time of history was an ache. When the whole world envied America and hated it, when to be an American seemed to call for mistrust and blows. Yet he knew that the bite of effort, the ache to produce, was inspired by much of all this loneliness; if only he could get his personal problems in order, maybe he could have it again.

Whenever Mike came to trouble he liked to get a little away from it and look at it and think how happy he was going to be here, and everything he had always wanted was here someplace. The trouble made it even cozy because there was still work to do, and the sharpness was all there because he was seeing it in focus like a detailed camera shot. All he had to do was make it come alive. It was all like one of those wonderful Civil War photographs by Brady he had collected once: the sodiers, all posed and polished while any minute the whip would crack, the general would mount, the soldiers would march, the dust would rise, and the young boy with the big eyes and the dusty feet would be shot dead and the old man with the sword in his hand would scream. But nothing ever happened, it just remained a posed picture. So Mike always waited for his landscape to come alive, the people to be more than names and faces, and maybe this time this would be the place on earth where he could find the only things he wanted: a contentment, a fame, not wealth, nor too much of the passionate love of a woman (a little simple adoration and a fine understanding of close tenderness would be enough).

He could remember back where it had always seemed just right before it all became just wrong. And yet he had never regretted it. At least not most of it the way it had happened and the way he had suffered and laughed.

He never forgot the family in Asbury Park even when he was gone from them and only came back for a little while every few years. The old house was older and they no longer bothered to paste back the wallpaper that hung, with mice dung soiling it, from the corners of rooms in which tired voices spoke of the wealth they would have had if they had held onto that corner property until the drugstore chain had bought it. Uncle Ben was very old just before he died and he had an affair with a fat white-faced girl, a dreadful creature with wet eyes and wet teeth, and they wanted to shoot Uncle Ben, at least her brothers did, and there was talk of

41

twenty years in Trenton. But Uncle Ben made the last gesture and lay down and died just before the doctor was to take the stand and give medical details. The oldest aunt was the only one who had any money now, and she did things for slum children by bringing them to the sea in summers, where their skins looked fish-belly white on the churning surf and their scabby bodies were piled with sand. They dug desperately in the packed wet shore with many fingers as if they hoped in desperate agony to dig in for the winter before the time came for them to go back to the city slums.

Winter was the best those years, Mike felt. The crackle of sleet on the tin roof, the ice on the dogwood limbs and the deep snow sprinkled with crystals, and the chilled breath of running along the cold, cold seashore. Everything was gray and white and the sea was all black and just before dark the lost birds would fall against the house and he used to go out and bring them in and thaw them out by the stove.

The dog used to smell like a badly dried woolen mitten and the stored apples in the cellar like sweet mold, and the books were all soggy now and hateful to the touch. The night street lights were strung beads then, and he played pool in the Y and took factory girls out to the meadows and wooded lanes and fumbled and ached and made a damn fool of himself; and when he fell in love she was married and he grew to hate and admire her and he laughed when she sent him a Christmas present, a banjo he never learned to play.

But when he went away the family was nothing any more. Mike Zelsmith lived very deep, but not very wide, and he wondered if going deep was not wrong and that growing shallow and wide and covering a lot of ground wasn't better. But he couldn't change much, at least not until the war, when he wore an officer's uniform and made official films.

He didn't believe in the war at all, and he never saw any sense in fighting unless all the old men died off to let the young men make a mess of the world in their own way. He was letting Alice slip through his fingers now, he wanted to bury her decently, decently forget the things they had done, the laughter they had shared, because he wanted no cloud in his bedroom, no other image in his vision if he took unto himself something else that he hoped would last him for all the needs he had for that sort of thing. He knew he was a chilly romantic and that he kept himself in spiritual refrigeration, but it was better than offering up his throat to the knife of any casual woman's ego, at least until he knew better.

Meanwhile, since the war, the town remained the clearly focused photograph, and every day he hoped it would begin to move, to take on a progression of things that would seem to him of great value, even of passing interest. If there were only seasons here. If he could again walk in snow and feel a cold dismal wind and think how good a fire would be, and be wet and cold and head for home, when he could get dry and warm and have a good drink and stretch and look through the windows at the chill shock of a season moving toward its climax. Yet here there were even no germs, the swimming pools smelled of medical products, and he missed the pool bottoms of farm mud and frog slime and the green taste of brook water of those few years in the East. But in everything he was hopeful and in everything he was careful, because he wanted it to be right and he wanted it to be of value. The way the family had felt about real estate, that's how he felt about emotions . . .

Jesu, mooning again! Get that picture made! The creative surge and the final bringing of it to boil. Just to show the football players in the bank, just to show his sonofabitch of a father-in-law, and just to have something clean to lay at the feet of Mollie and let her laugh, that beautiful child, and let her kick him over, in play, with one of those beautiful legs as he knelt there. But enough of images.

He looked at his wrist watch and saw it was time to start. He didn't like to get there early. Gossip was bad enough already and he didn't want Mollie ever to feel that the way he felt about her was something like the hasty fumbling and casual bedding of the town. If it were that, hell, he'd call Madam Frank and have her send over a fifty-dollar whore. What the hell was it then? He didn't really know, but he could taste it deep inside him, the way it had been when he was young and had an idea how it would be to make a new kind of motion picture. The feeling was rare enough these days and he wasn't going to pick it apart now, like a snotty ape with an orchid in its paw.

He drove the big open car, and he drove it badly because he never loved machines the way most people did. He mastered them the way people used to master proud horses, only the machines didn't react like horses; they just died of no water in the battery or of stripped gears. They died all over without spirit and he hated things without fight and real spirit.

The sea road was crowded but the ca.. were moving with good speed, and as always at this spot and time he felt that no one knew the real California nights. And it was just as well. It was like a fine movie; the things you left unsaid were the things that mattered; a little obscurity was a good thing. But you could never sell that idea to a banker. He looked at his watch and slowed down as he neared the beach house. He'd give himself another five minutes.

"Everyone on the coast beach that matters knows the place as Mollie's Ark," Walter said to John Fennel. "It was built ten years ago by a Hungarian playwright with only one success at M.G.M. Studios."

It stood set off by lawns from the same kind of expensive cottages on either side. A six-foot stone wall topped by redwood palings separated it from the coastal road. "Cortez Beach is top drawer. It's a gold-plated section. Mollie thinks it much too grand."

Walter drove a Lincoln Continental, a long since discontinued model that had once been very impressive. But several head-on accidents, unrepaired, and its unwashed appearance were against it. Walter drove hard, bent over the wheel, and pointed to the low beautiful lines of the beach house as he slowed to make the turn to the other side of the road on which it stood. Its front garden looked neat and gave no suggestion of its sea struggle.

"Yep. Mollie's Ark. I live under it and have bad dreams."

John asked, "Doesn't the tide bother you?"

"No, it's like Bach—you ignore it."

They made a swift U-turn and pulled up before the gate and went into the garden. Two dogs barked. A mean-looking boxer and a mild, sad-eyed little cocker looked out at them. The sound of the score of "South Pacific" came from a turned-up record player.

"Don't try to meet everybody," Walter said. "Lots of beach bums, unemployed actors, second-rate producers, hungry screen writers, even a few artists."

Walter snarled at the boxer, "Down, Ed," and they crossed the formal garden path, seeded with a few dried dog turds, to the solid redwood door.

Mike Zelsmith stood there at the door looking at his wrist watch.

"Evening, M.Z.," Walter said.

"Hello," Mike said. "How do you like the lines of this beach house, John?"

"I think it fits the sea very well. Hugs the shore."

"It's a cozy place. Go ahead in. I'm taking a noseful of air."

They went in, and Mike stood there and decided he was a damn fool to wait much longer. Already there were at least six cars parked in front of the road wall. He grabbed the doorknob, the big polished brass shape, and turned and opened the door. He was at once pitched into a beamed-ceiling living room, everything of paneled pine with a huge whitewashed brick fireplace on one wall and a bank of windows on the other, letting out to a big open porch and sun deck and the wild tossing of the sea. The Hungarian had once collected an odd arrangement of furnishings. Big wooden farm tables, early American modern to sit on, flower prints, first-rate wood carvings of holy images from the Tyrol. There were also the good modern drawings Mike had given Mollie. Picasso, Graves, John, Miro, rather ironic in content. Books and magazines all over the place, and a big red cage of love birds. Among all this a dozen people drank, sang, sat, or danced. The record player was devouring a stack of records, and a very ugly bright-looking man was moving around with a tray of martinis. Walter grabbed his arm and took two drinks and turned to Mike.

"Steiner, meet Mr. Zelsmith. Harry Steiner, play writer."

"Hello," said Steiner, offering a gin-wet hand. "Have stills of all your movies. Sign 'em for me?"

The martinis were very strong. Mike grunted and nodded. "All right."

"Wanta talk to you about your method of character approach . . . Be seeing you."

He moved off and Mike finished his drink and someone gave him another one. He sat down on the wood box by the fireplace. A large, balding young man with boiled white hands made a place for him. Mike didn't remember him.

"Sontag is the name. Dr. Myron Sontag. I'm Mollie's doctor . . . How are you? I know who you are."

"Hello, Doc."

"All these Mollie's friends?" the doctor asked.

"Neighbors, mostly. It's a lousy artistic slum on the next beach. Everybody is either on his way up or his way down, here. Aging actors, ambitious stock girls, unemployed screen writers; people sitting in the sun with other people's wives or waiting out a divorce, or drinking their way out, or inventing a new sex. The tall guy is John Fennel. Very good. The rest don't look very healthy for beach dwellers, Doc."

"Too much drinking, too many sleeping pills, a little on the Benzedrine, and bitter about not getting rich. But they keep Mollie amused and busy cooking."

"Where is Mollie?" Mike asked.

"In the kitchen." The doctor pointed to a passageway and Mike excused himself. It divided into a paneled bedroom with a huge built-in wall bed, and beyond it a bathroom, and facing the other way a small kitchen with room only for a sink, an electric stove with evil red eyes, and a refrigerator. Mollie, beautiful and busy, was stirring a curry while Walter was beating up a sauce. There was no room in the kitchen, so Walter excused himself and went out. Mollie waved a spoon at Mike.

"I'm glad you got here." She offered him the spoon and he tasted the curry.

"Very good. The real Injan flavor, I suppose."

"Well, that's done. Come on in and help me make up."

Mike followed her into the bedroom. There was a drawing table and many paper-backed French and English books. Hung over the walled-in bed were some good marines and a large Matisse drawing of a nude colored oddly but powerfully. Mollie sat down at the drawing table and faced an old mirror.

"I hoped you'd make it, Mike." She wiped her face with a towel and pulled back her hair. She was wearing a tight gold cloth gown and golden flat-heeled slippers and discs of gold plugged to her ears. She held out her girlish hand to him and he took it and she smiled at him. He bent over her and the smell of warm wet flesh made his breathing hard.

"Kiss me, Mike," she said.

He kissed her and she came alive. She opened her mouth and he pressed against her and this was a real kiss. He stood up as the boxer came into the room and growled.

"Lie down, Ed," she said, doing up her living blond hair with pins. "That's a good dog. Ed hates all men who pay attention to me, but I think he likes you, Mike."

Ed swung his iron-hard tail against Mike's leg and Mike rubbed the dog behind his ears.

"You like this kind of evening, Mollie?"

"Sure—it's not a party. Wait until the fighting starts.

46

Harry Steiner is always picking fights; he takes either side."
She reached over to a highball glass and took a big pull and
stood up. She looked wonderful in the tight cloth of gold.
She had more than beauty, Mike decided, and she certainly was beautiful. The blue eyes and the way she carried
the perfect little head and the wonder of her small hips
made her very exciting to Mike. He backed her up against
the wall of the wardrobe and kissed her again, holding his
arms around her very tight, and as he kissed her, he pulled
her to him feeling her firm breasts strain against him, sensing everything alive and stirring in the rib basket.

"Hurt you?" he asked.

"No." She smiled. "I don't hurt. I'm hard."

"I'm sorry there are so many people."

"I like people . . . It's so alone here . . . People are
fun . . ."

"You have Walter."

"Walter is dear. Now Mike, you know there's nothing
between us."

"Walter explained that. Is your husband here tonight?"

"Gene?" She frowned, then gave her special laugh. "He's
on the road in Kansas City with an old Moss Hart show. He
can't live with me. He hates the dogs."

The boxer growled. She took Mike's arm. "Let's be gay."

"I'll watch you being gay."

The evening was going nicely. Someone was breaking
glasses in the fireplace and Lucky the cocker had retreated
under the sofa and showed only one worried brown eye.
Some of the party were out on the sun deck, locked in each
other's arms dancing, and Harry Steiner had a group
around him and he was talking very loud.

"The real movie is dead and you can forget it! Dead as
the dodo bird and great poems. It's folk dancing that will
be the mass entertainer that Dickens and Mark Twain and
Tolstoi were . . ."

"Oh, Harry, shut up," said a little girl.

Mollie went and changed the records and began to dance
with a tall, dark man who was from Pasadena and snapped
his fingers while he whirled her around. Dr. Sontag was still
seated on the wood box nursing the same drink.

Mike sat down by his side and offered him a cigarette,
but the doctor held up a thin black cigar in his white hand.

"I'll stick to the weed. I'm operating at nine." The doctor's expression was arch but not coy. "On Mollie."

"Is it polite to ask what the hell for?"

The doctor laughed and put his arm on Mike's. "Sure, why not? Let's both be sorry for her."

"Serious?"

"Oh, not that serious. Reshaping a nostril for a screen test."

"I'm going to make a great actress out of her. How's her health?"

"Mollie's built like a show horse. Heart and everything else in fine order. A little confused. She's very young. I served with the Army in their psychoanalysis department during the war, saw enough to send me back to just doctoring, but I wish Mollie would let me help her. Thinks she knows all the answers. Maybe she does."

"Mollie is pretty bright," Mike said.

Dr. Sontag shook cigar ash into the dead fireplace. It was used as a wastebasket: old newspapers, torn letters, paper napkins, dog bones.

"I think she wants you to dance with her."

Mollie was grinning at them, a full glass in her hand. She came over and said, "You two are stinking up my party."

"I don't like to dance," Mike admitted directly.

"All right then, let's get a noseful of air."

They went out on the sun deck and stood at the wooden rail facing the sea. A kelp bed floated a few feet offshore and a white dog ran up and down the beach trying to turn over a shuffling crab.

"That moon looks low enough to bite," Mollie said, pointing to the overdramatic shape in the sky.

Mike took her hand in his and she lifted his hand to her mouth and kissed it.

"Jesu—Mollie."

"I take these things big, Mike, and so far it hasn't ever happened for real."

"I've been through a bad one. I don't know, Mollie. I have got a terrible yen for you. It's like a stomach full of broken glass all the time I see you."

Steiner was shouting at someone, "You're a dirty fascist!" The little woman was pulling on his arm. "Oh, Harry, come home—you always pick fights."

"We need a drink," Mollie said.

John Fennel was changing the records as Mandy Rye

handed them to him. Mandy was a tall handsome woman (some even called her beautiful), with a calm, emotionless face, who played witty characters in movie comedies about the best people. She was not really humorous and rather silent most of the time, as she never knew what to say unless someone had written lines for her. People were disappointed with her off the screen because she never said any of the brilliant, witty things she did in the pictures.

"You have been to France?" she asked John, handing him a recording of "September Song."

"Yes, a great deal."

"I wish I could read the French poets better in French."

John Fennel looked over the tall, attractive woman in her rich blue evening gown, and her red hair worn in loops on the back of her neck. He said, "Do you know the one that goes:

> L'usage du cabinet
> Est inderdit pendant
> L'arret du train
> En gare . . ."

"It's one of my favorites," said Mandy Rye earnestly. "Is it?"

John excused himself to help Walter with the drinks. The little girl who had been taking care of Harry Steiner said to Mandy Rye, "Don't you know what that poem is?"

"Why?"

"You see it in French trains. It translates as 'Do not use the toilet while the train is in the station.' "

"Oh," said Mandy Rye, and decided she was in love with John Fennel. She nodded to Mike Zelsmith on his way past her to refill two glasses. She hoped he and Mollie made a go of it. They were both people she was fond of. She didn't like many people; her passion was collecting wormy English furniture, and reading detective novels about very tough private eyes who beat up women and bit their lips when they kissed them till they bled. It was a good evening at the beach. She looked over at John.

Walter and John were mixing a batch of drinks with long spoons. Dr. Sontag had taken down a book, *Los Angeles Murders*, and was reading. Lucky the cocker lay on his lap.

Mike filled two fairly clean glasses and went out on the sun deck. A wind was coming up and the kelp bed smelled bad. Mollie was staring out into the darkness. She took her drink and put her little pink tongue in it and then took a deep swallow. She looked small and delicate—intricately made.

Mike smiled. "I got most of the lipstick off the glasses."

Two people passed dragging Harry Steiner down the steps to the beach, and the little woman was behind him pushing. Steiner was still shouting, ". . . dirty reactionary! You'd let the world burn, let it blow up, a fat lot you care for anything but your fat placid indifference!"

"The evening is breaking up," Mollie said. "I'd better get some shuteye."

Mike leaned over and kissed her on the cheek. Then he brushed against her exposed ear and kissed that wetly too.

Mollie pressed her hand tight into his. "I think there must be a dead seal in that kelp bed."

Mike took John out to the Beachcomber's, a popular, rather exclusive eating place, and they ate in darkness the barbecued spareribs and the delicate flavors of well-cooked Chinese food. They drank big tumblers of rum called Test Pilots and dipped their fried shrimp in sweet and biting sauces, and chewed and drank.

Mike said, "I guess you know Mollie means a lot to me. She always marries the wrong guy."

"What kind of a guy is Gene?" John asked.

"Very nice guy. Clean-cut, handsome, not much of an actor, Mollie says. She mothered him. I guess now he's boring. She's cruel about his talents in the hay. Also, he hates the dogs. That's important with Mollie, you have to love the livestock."

"I'm worried about our screenplay, Mike. We haven't done anything, really."

"Give me a little time, John. How about another Test Pilot?"

"My kidneys are floating already."

"Lucky bastard—I need a real load."

FROM THE JOURNAL OF JOHN FENNEL

Long talk with Mike on California's car civilization. A novelist should trust his first impressions. I marveled at the splendor and the numbers of the automobiles here. It seemed to me that one was classified by the size and price of one's car. I felt this a foolish snap judgment, but now I'm not sure Mike isn't right.

This is a Cadillac town, first and last, Mike says. The fish-tailed jobs—as cars are called—are the normal means of transportation for everyone above a certain salary bracket, and for many who would like to be in that bracket. The Cadillac is not the real class car—that honor belongs to bigger, even more shiny cars, for imported models with leopardskin upholstery and silver- or gold-plated fittings. A man is too often judged by his car, not by his reputation or his abilities. One sees the cars at the hotel parking lots, at the country clubs, outside the night spots—the big expensive cars being wheeled by wild-driving boys to their parking spots. So the Romans must have admired the new chariots and their drivers.

No man dares buy only the car he can afford, he must impress the town and he must think of trade-in values and down payments and a quick place to get a fast loan on his salary when he needs it. This is a town that walks very little.

The roads are good. Many of the people are already skilled drivers at twelve years of age. They cheerfully bang and mash each other, they wreck and shake parts of themselves over the highways. The newspapers feature the big wrecks proudly. "Six-car Crash Blocks Parkway," "Ten Cars Snarl Traffic in Pass Half Hour." This is the brave world of the automobile, of the gasoline-smelling civilization. The white-walled tire is more impressive than a Phi Beta Kappa key to many people. Radios, built-in bars are everyday things; the people who have short-wave sets and a television in their job are the advanced ones these days. And on the horizon the oil wells signal all is dandy.

Not that the new cars are the whole life. Over four million people live here and they own small battered cars and rebuilt cars and cut-down cars. The kids smoke up the world with their hot-rod jobs and the Mexican gardeners drive vintage Model T's that groan and move.

Saturday and Sunday is car day. The restless American spirit to move on is most powerful and free then. The jalopies and the rebuilt crates are loaded with children in sunsuits, the family dog has his head wedged into a window, the baskets and the sun umbrellas and beer kegs attached to where they will hold, and in a stink of too-expensive gasoline, the whole town moves toward beach and mountain. Jowl by jowl the imported English car and the cut-down Hudson are standing on the hot road waiting for the light to change. The kids lick ice cream off a stick and the producer pulls his twelve-dollar necktie into place. A free swim at the shore, or gambling at Arrowhead is at the end of the run.

Mike says Mollie is not above this love of the automobile. She pines for a big, new job. If she had the money she would drive a fishtailed Cadillac with red leather seats and windows controlled by a press button. But when she has a little money

51

Mike says she spends it on clothes and liquor and fancy food. So Mike says she goes rattling along in a green car, the windshield dimmed with road dust, the back of the car full of dog hair and cartons of groceries—and a roll of toilet paper lurching free on the floorboards, to be used on the windshield when the fog comes in over the sea. Mollie is fully conditioned to the internal-combustion motor. All night the big produce-and-milk trucks come down the coast and past her beach house, howling and roaring in the night, shaking her bed and her body. Mike says when you see wrecks of heated iron standing in front of her door, you know Mollie is giving a party.

The relationship of Mike and Mollie is a puzzle because it is not sexual. He pays the rent but he doesn't buy her groceries or her clothes or get her a big car to drive. She is what the town calls a "protégée" . . . which doesn't have to mean anything personal. Agents, studios, and producers often put promising young actresses under contract and groom them, taking care of their expenses. Of course the town is cynical about such arrangements, no matter what they really are.

Walter says Mike is broke, and the rent on the fancy beach house hasn't been paid in three months. The moral values don't bother Walter. But I think they bother Mike. In his own unconventional way he is a man of rigid moral conventions. He may whore around and drive a hard bargain to get a film project started, but when it comes to someone as fine-grained as Mollie, the Laws of the Tribe, the family morality of the Jews, takes over and he is almost confused, numbed, and a little ashamed; not of his action or his emotions—he is an egotist—but of the fact he must hide his powerful interest in Mollie. Mike blames it all—after a few drinks anyway—on the fact, as he puts it— that a man has passions as well as needs. "You know, I really think mind and spirit are not realities, a guy's finest desires and his inspirations come in the end from his conscience."

Frank Beaver rang Jóhn up once a week, at least.

"Hello, old hoss, how goes it?"

"I really can't say, Frank. It's all what they call a hassel out here."

"You're catching on. Having fun?"

"No, just getting along doing my work."

"Getting *much*?"

"What? Oh, no, I'm not interested."

"I hear they do it in phone booths out there."

"I'll ask somebody I know, Frank."

"I knew you had a broad on a string."

"No—not really."

"It's better in the sunlight. Look, I'm calling from Toots

Shor's. They just got my table. Don't forget, you're a novelist, and we need a new book next season."

"Haven't even a glimmer of a book."

"Climb off that broad and git back to yer ole gal, literature . . . so long, John."

"Good-by, Frank, could you spare some cash?"

"Maybe. Christ, the only good authors are dead authors, or in public domain."

4

MOLLIE'S father—a much too solid gentleman—had been an Upstate New Yorker who manufactured iron products. He had led a stern, honest life—by his own standards—and it was only after he was fifty that he thought of marrying. It was in Chicago at a convention of iron dealers that he was introduced to a young singer, a beautiful woman— rather too good and shy—with a fine voice and large blue eyes. She took his fancy as a well-made product and he was not a man to shilly-shally or romanticize. He married her and brought her back to Whiteville, New York, a community that respected him, and to which he gave some of his respect. He was a proud man with a good tight mind that kept his prejudices from leaking out.

It was not a happy marriage, but as Upstate New Yorkers did not seek divorces, they remained married and Mollie was born. Her father was too old and set in his lifelong habits to change, but Mollie's childhood was a combination of happiness at the glory and pleasure of nature, a small town, and the excitement of hearing her mother sing at local social gatherings. Yet early in life she also knew the private family strife; the weeping mother. The stern male parent frightened her only a little, fascinated her much more. Her father was a man and to Mollie a powerful one, head of a family, respected, a solid citizen, and in his own business. As she grew up daughter and father were not always in conflict, for she had learned from her mother to respect and obey him in all things. Yet this vitality and strength drew from her a grudging admiration. He was bigger, louder, prouder than most men she had ever met.

She read a great deal, she dreamed of tall knights

53

in armor that smoked cigars like her father and sang with the same deep baritone he used in church.

Mollie was of course a beautiful child all gold and pink and blue-eyed. She painted in water colors and clipped fashion drawings from chummy housewife magazines, and she existed in a world of such fantasy that it was a shock to discover that Father's business had become very bad and that they were moving to California. Her father had found a respectable partner in Santa Barbara, among the best people, and there the art of real ironwork in the Yankee manner was to be given to the Native Sons. Mollie's father built them a mission bungalow in a neighborhood that was to go down year after year. Here Mollie watched the dreadful war of the sexes between her mother and father. She grew used to his stern commands, his hard, even voice, his dignified steps, and his habit of reaching for the bourbon bottle. Perhaps she even feared him at times.

The business failed and the money seemed to melt away and the proud man had to work for others, carrying iron samples in big rawhide cases and traveling to hardware stores up and down the coast and sitting waiting with patience until someone wanted to see him and order a keg of nails.

Mollie drew costumes out of her mind and the fashion magazines and hoped they would always be able to let her take horseback rides. They no longer had their own horses, but she rode at a livery stable down by the sea. It was Jack, the new groom who first scared her, talking in an amused, lewd way—and got her to thinking of boys' parts and becoming a woman and having warm dreams that somehow looked like Father. The stern father that one admired, but who drank too much now and said his heart was bad, ". . . but Goddamn it, a man could still get respect in his own house and vote the Republican ticket."

Jack, the grinning groom, used to lift her to her saddle and she would cling, pale and very worried, to the horse. It was like a lot of grown-up things and connected in some way with the things people did in bed. She didn't know just what but it certainly was a secret.

As a very, very little girl she seemed to remember Mother took her aside and told her what it was, and how beautiful it all was, like a flower in bud and the great plans of nature. But Mollie wondered what a flower had to do with the whole dirty business.

"Would you like a brother or a sister, Mollie?"

"It doesn't matter, Mother."

"We're a family, dear, just the four of us."

"It isn't here yet."

"I can feel it kicking."

Mollie would have liked to feel it kicking, but Mother wasn't the kind to ask that sort of thing, and Father frowned so when the talk got around to what he called "damn gutter stuff," so she just helped Mother wind wool for knitting baby things.

"Could I play with the baby?"

"No, dear, they are very delicate."

"I wouldn't drop it."

"I'm sure you wouldn't. Watch the wool, don't tangle it."

Her sister Belle was born one bright sunny morning, and Mother was very ill after that, and Father came home smelling of coffee beans and said, "Another mouth to feed. Well, it's long and it's perfect, a man can't do better than that, bring good healthy children into the world."

The groom worried her for years. She could never tell anyone of this lewd talk—not even her gentle mother, not certainly the big bear of a father smelling of the coffee beans he chewed to hide the whisky smell. A man must retain his dignity, come what may. It was a time of confusion and yet alertness to life. One day her father called her into the fern-hung den, the brass pots hung over the shelves of Dickens, Thackeray, and Teddy Roosevelt that her father read. He was over sixty now and aging fast. Large, handsome, the red-brown hair turning iron, and he sat in the big black leather rocker and looked at her, the whisky in a heavy kitchen glass in a strong brown fist.

"Mollie," he said, "I want to talk to you."

"Yes, Father."

"We're fine people, fine family. It's unfashionable to think of family these days. But you'll find out—stock counts. I'm not against the people out of the immigrant ships. We're refugees, ourselves, came here in 1743. But you've got to remember life is good only if you're good. Your mother's stock—French, Scottish, fine people. I'm going to die soon, Mollie."

"No, Father!"

"Bad heart. Getting worse. But I've sold out my rights in the rope factory back in Whiteville. You're going to a fine school—a good girl's school. Mrs. Baker's near La Juna. You're signed up."

"I don't want to leave you and Mother."

"There's a big world out there, girl, and you're going to be a very beautiful woman. You're smart too, Mollie. It's a man's world and a hard world and you'll have to be fit to live in it. I want you to study hard, get good marks. Then if trouble comes, well, you'll have the rules down pat. And don't think you'll ever fool me, Mollie. I'll know when you're bad and I'll know when you do wrong. Even after I'm dead. Yes, even then."

He patted her cheek with a hard hand and put down the kitchen tumbler and put his head down on his arms and she went away slowly . . . not daring to look back.

Mrs. Baker's was the best school on the coast. It cost a great deal of money. Mollie liked it, even when she was lonely and her small, pretty breasts ached. She was the school beauty. She worked on her costume drawings and acted in the school plays and late at night she talked of fantastic sexual passion with the other innocent girls and read some mildly dirty books that confused her more than ever. It was a clean, healthy, Protestant school with morning prayers and evening prayers and chapel and reading from the Bible (skipping the more interesting parts of the Song of Songs). The head mistress, who had a chin mole and bad breath—and hugged her a lot—liked her and forgave her the night the girls played games and someone dared Mollie to put the large brass doorknob to the bathroom in her mouth. Mollie did, but couldn't get her jaws open wide enough to get rid of the doorknob. It was a famous story about Mrs. Baker's school told for years afterward; how they had to wrap Mollie—so pretty and so scared—in blankets and bring in a plumber to unscrew the doorknob. Mollie had her mouth olive-oiled to get rid of the doorknob (Father screamed at the plumber's bill).

Mollie listened to the healthy lectures on clean living and shivered at the talk of insanity and evil. She kept a collection of actors' pictures and secretly took out art books hoping some day to find some without fig leaves.

The holidays at home were hard to take now. Father was paper-gray and no longer went out on the road to sell nails. And Mother looked sad and baked a lot of pies and Mollie helped. Cooking was an emotional release for the two women. Cooking made Mollie very happy.

"You mustn't get Father excited, Mollie."

"Oh no, Mother."

"Why don't you ride any more? Father is angry at the cost of the riding outfit and you not riding."

"But I don't want to ride. Not here."

"Please, Mollie—don't excite Father. He takes such pride in having you ride. You're a beautiful lady, and ladies ride, and you look so well on horseback, darling. You're going to have a small beautiful figure and my mother's legs."

She went riding. Jack leered at her as he saddled the horse, and when he helped her up he made grinning, lewd remarks. It was worse than it had ever been and it was a year till she rode again. His fingernails had dirty black moons on them. And Mollie wanted to see only beauty all around her.

Father was going very fast, and as the holidays ended he never got out of his big black chair much. Her beauty was dazzling that year; the little girl was growing up. He used to hold her hand and tell her of the hardships of his youth. "But we Binnings are a proud people. Never let us down, Mollie." Then he fell flat on the floor and whimpered like a little child, and his teeth clicked and Mother ran in. It was the first of the real big attacks.

Mollie went back to Mrs. Baker's school, but the flavor was gone out of it all and the girls on the basketball field looked dumpy and silly, the food was suddenly mean, and even God seemed vulgar in the strong chapel sunlight. Her prayers were mumbled and sterile. The wire that said Father was dead came as she was walking to her room late one afternoon from a tennis match, and everyone was so sorry for her that she wished she could show them how brave she was. But she cried a long time, ashamed the way her tiny body shook, and Betty, her best friend, slept in the same bed with her, their arms around each other all night, and they promised never to forget each other as long as they lived.

There was no money after that for Mrs. Baker's. Just enough for Mother and her and Belle. Mollie at fourteen took the morning bus at nine every week day and studied fashion designing with Mrs. Weatherbee who never admitted anything artistic had been done after Beardsley and

Whistler. Mollie had a natural talent but she was in very much of a hurry and the school seemed slow and dull.

Once a week Mr. Morton came and taught them anatomy. With stick figures and draped sedate photographs of lumpish females. Mr. Morton was over fifty and carried himself well in his corset and used to brush Mollie's soft blond hair back from her face and tell her she would "go to Paris some day and see a great city." Fridays she helped him carry the week's drawings back to his rooming house and they used to sit on the wide window sill and drink a poor California sherry and cheapen the sunsets.

"Ah, yes, my dear. You have the body of a goddess and the grace of a tiger. You'll always have grace. You're going to be an amazing beauty."

Mr. Morton was a lonely man who felt the sap of lonely misery rising in him again. He taught her how to walk and carry her shoulders, and he used to rub her legs and say "fine and delicately curved and very beautiful. Oh, the Greeks would have adorned temples with you." One warm afternoon her virginity irked Mr. Morton, so playing the gentleman of understanding, he took it away from her. It was nothing at all for her, nothing. It was the most disappointing thing that had yet happened to her. The shock of the nothingness of it amazed her. All the way home on the bus she looked at the people wondering if they knew that she had left her maindenhead with a fumbling old man. And what the hell was the shouting about in books and movies? Anyway that was over with. Father appeared to her in a dream that night and told her it was worse than anything she had done before. He looked so strong and handsome and was so angry. She gave up Mrs. Weatherbee's.

She lost interest in designing and when the local little theater group of artistic snobs gave Ibsen, she painted the sets wearing slacks and a man's dirty shirt. A stagehand gave her her first cigarette and she became a chain smoker. She loved the theater and the people in it and was sorry when it failed to make progress in the sterile soil of the town. Her life seemed over. She got out of the habit of riding and reading and sat at home and helped Mother cook. They tried out curries and chilies shamefully—as if sinning together.

A road company of a stale Broadway hit came to town

and Mollie went backstage and met a dark Irishman who had just failed as a planter in Cuba and was trying out as stage manager. Mollie married him one morning because he was going to live with his mother in Los Angeles. They had more theaters in Los Angeles, Allen said, and a girl with such a small Greek head belonged there. She was just fifteen.

The first time she saw Allen's mother, she didn't like her. A high and mighty old woman who hated "the Colonials" as she called Americans. She slept on the other side of the beaver-board wall in their dirty little flat near the Mexican section.

Every time Mollie and Allen took each other in their arms at night she would knock on the wall and say, "Can't you wait? I'm *still* up."

Naturally it didn't work out at all with the old lady on the other side. Mollie had no climaxes and she wondered if the books were lying about the big bang. Allen loved his mother and said he wished Mollie was more like her. Mollie washed the dirty wood floor, the stinking bathroom, and did all the cooking. Father would have called it "doing one's duty."

Allen soon lost interest in her and devoted himself to a small theater in the Mexican section that was supposed to attract the tourists and didn't. Mollie designed costumes and painted flats and took tickets. Allen began to come home late at night with lipstick on his lean dark face, and Mollie and a young comic actress, whose name was Mandy Rye, joined a group of actors in a bus and went out giving shows in the orange and grapefruit belt around Los Angeles. They gave historical dramas in high schools that smelled of chalk and ink, and gave gay comic things to ladies' clubs that fed them on chicken salad.

Mollie kept away from men who grew too amorous. When the bus broke down they all came back and rented a termite-shaken house in Hollywood and tried to get into motion pictures. Mandy played in cheap productions and when she worked they ate. Allen's mother died and he divorced Mollie and went into radio.

Mollie pulled out her paint box and when the Hollywood Bowl put on a dance pageant, she designed the costumes and the sets for a Shelley ballet. She worked hard on it and she was in love with Shelley anyway, and something of this came out in her costumes and sets. She became the talk of the town for two weeks.

It was only when she was invited to design the production of the Eugene O'Neill Festival at the California Theater Guild that she came alive again. It paid off in coast-to-coast glory anyway and everyone loved Mollie and she became one of the California Theater crowd—a very young, very beautiful child—drinking in studio courts and wearing cheap, tight clothing with a flair. She was nearly sixteen now and her pale golden hair worn in long waves behind her ears hung with hammered silver. Her breasts had grown just enough. She liked to parade around in shorts, with sandals on the feet of her beautiful tanned legs.

She frightened off a few bold males who tried to make love to her. Then Gene appeared at the playhouse one night in a one-acter and she saw his thin body and his sad eyes and his lonely look and she felt such pity that one day behind a production of *Riders to the Sea* he held her hand and said she was "the first decent woman I have met since leaving home." All she wanted to do was marry him and mother him.

She didn't expect any great sexual fire this time. They lived in a shabby, once very good house near the playhouse, in a tower room under a hot roof. After the first three nights she began to get up a fever, and fire ran all over her, and she thought now it was going to happen. But all the flashes and the fire in her belly turned out to be a bad fish she had eaten. It was no longer any fun with Gene. He developed a spot on his lung which made him just wonderful to nurse. She took his temperature and cooked for him all her mother's old dishes and she was very happy. This was all there was to life, she felt. She let her work go until Gene said there was no money to buy neckties. Gene was an actor, but the right kind of parts didn't come around often. To buy him ties, Mollie went back to Hollywood, lied about her age, and got a job at Warner Brothers. There she dressed aging actresses, but let the head designer get the credit. She met a refugee director there who liked to talk to her about Max Reinhardt. And he used to scold her when the costumes weren't ready on time.

The day after her sixteenth birthday her mother sent for her suddenly in a panic-worded wire, and Mollie was shocked to see how ill Mother looked. She was small and very pale in the big bed that she had shared with Father, the sheet under her loose chin.

"I want you to stay with me and Belle just a little while, Mollie."

"Of course, Mother."

"When the pain gets real bad I want you to learn to give me the needles with the drugs in them."

Mollie went out on the front steps and cried and when the doctor came (he was an old family friend), he said it was only a matter of a few weeks. Mollie learned how to give her mother the needles and when she wanted money for the drugs she sold the piano and the one real Chippendale chair. Mother was very good and would only cry out when the pain was too unbearable. Mostly she just lay and lost weight and it broke Mollie all up inside, for this was something much more terrible than Father falling on the floor. How quickly a family can disappear.

"How is it with you, Mollie?" Mother would ask.

"It's all right, Mother."

"Those men you married. I'm sorry it didn't work out."

"It will some day."

"Your Father was a fine man. We didn't get on, but in many ways it was a thing you could respect and accept. Maybe some day Mr. Right will come along, Mollie."

"It's time you had the soup."

After Mother died and the grim business, so chilling, of getting the remains underground and the house rented and Belle to live with an aunt, Mollie went back to Warner Brothers and the director for a month. He yelled at her more than ever when the costumes weren't just right. He took pleasure in making her cry. And she cried easily now. Maybe it was the little drinking she was doing . . . with Gene away on the road. She used to lie on the director's couch—a small, beautiful child—and cry because she liked to be shouted at, and yet it frightened her. The director used to take her to lunch and talk to her about European ways of making love, and Mollie used to listen and wonder. It sounded uncomfortable and rather ridiculous. The director never did anything about it. He was too frightened of his wife finding out.

Mollie was laid off during one of those economy waves that always hit a studio after a dozen bad pictures, and she went back to the stage and met a declining stage star who was tapering off by playing villains in Western pictures and directing plays at the Theater Guild. Lou was tall and very dark and looked like an Indian, and he had a deep voice like her father's. Lou was pleased to discover Mollie —he lusted for youth—and one night they went to a place called The Stuffed Shirt and they both got drunk and Lou rubbed her shoulder and grinned his dark Indian grin at her and asked her why she was such a shy one.

"Baby, you've come to the right man. It's going to be like lightning hitting you—the works—and how about another drink?"

"I don't need another drink for it, Lou."

"Oh, gotta feel good and gotta feel fine. Let's."

They had a lot more drinks and Mollie was pleased to see that Lou could talk very well about lovemaking. Even better than the director. They had to wait until it was very late, as Lou had a house on a very respectable street and his wife was away and "one didn't want to give the neighbors anything to talk about, did one in this lousy, snobbish town . . . no indeed."

They got to the house near morning and Lou fell over on his face and said with his mouth in the dusty rug, "Sorry, Mollie, little girl, gotta give you a rain check on it. Feel kinda drunkee just now." They both slept in their clothes on the living-room sofa and she cooked him some fine ham and eggs for breakfast and he made them both Bloody Marys for their hang-overs. He was pretty sheepish about it all, but being an actor, charming.

"I'm sorry, kid. We'll have to try it some other time. Too bad Helen is getting back this afternoon."

"That's all right, Lou. It wouldn't have been any good anyway."

"That's no way to talk about it. You're still a little girl. Gene may not be much but some day a good guy will come along and you'll climb the walls screaming with joy."

"Eat your breakfast."

"Don't want any breakfast. Got a real big head. You're a fine girl, Mollie, a sport."

Mollie had no money, only the small car with its slipping clutch. She put another mortgage on the Santa Barbara house that a cousin was living in. She was shocked the way she was growing old. Suddenly without warning she was nineteen.

One day she was sitting at The Players—the open section, with the sun on her face and hair. She was very well dressed that day. Her best flowered silk dress with the tight black belt, and her hair curled at the ends and rolled and worn tight on her head, and legs in almost unseen nylons, and little golden shoes. Two strangers stopped to talk to her, but she was used to that by now and she always drove them off with a smile, and by lying that she was only fifteen. Since jail bait was a police problem in the town, they always left in a hurry.

But that didn't stop Mike Zelsmith. He walked over to her from the bar inside The Players, his fist around a big drink, and he sat down and said, "I'm Mike Zelsmith."

"I know, I've seen your pictures."

"I'm not on the make. You're a very beautiful girl. How old are you?"

"Nineteen."

"Ever act?"

"Not very good. I design sets and costumes."

Mike frowned, as if trying to stir his memory. "Hell, yes. The Shelley Ballet, Mollie Binning."

Mollie said, "That's right."

"Drink?"

"No, thank you."

"Look, you might design for me. But I'm also giving you a screen test."

"I'm looking for a place to live. When I get set we might get together."

"I've got the place. A fatheaded actor I had under contract left me with a lease on a beach house. Move in and get to work. No strings to this."

"Sure, no strings . . . I like your pictures, Mr. Zelsmith."

"I like them myself. I'm going to try and make more like them."

"But don't think I can act. I smell on stage."

"Let's have some drinks."

They felt better—more at ease—when the drinks came. She really admired his work, and he was so ugly, well not ugly, but so square and solid with no finish or polish to his features. And he was bowled over by her face and voice and the way she sat.

He grinned. "Your the Goddamndest most beautiful thing I've ever seen."

"You don't have to say it as if I resent it. I've known a long time I looked pretty good. But it hasn't brought me any luck."

"It's going to. Don't ever be frightened of me, Mollie. There aren't going to be any passes. I'm facing a hell of a time making my next picture, but I'm building for the future too. You're going to be part of that."

"Sure?"

"We'll see. Just stay close. I believe in good-luck charms. You're the best I've seen for a long time."

She moved into the beach house. It was much too much for her and too fancy. But as Mike said, he was stuck with the lease. He sent her gifts, expensive gifts that she didn't know he couldn't pay for. And he kissed her when he left, but never went much beyond that. She didn't fall in love, but she admired him and grew very fond of him. When she was very fond of him she admitted maybe she was in love. After that they understood each other very well, but didn't do anything about it. A kind of suspended animation was between them, held them there frozen in space because they both knew when that ended the earth would wobble a little on its axis.

She had two dogs. A mean boxer called Ed, and a small golden cocker who was aging badly, a sad, nervous, little creature called Lucky. Also three love birds who needed lots of attention and messed up their cages and fought over the pecking order.

Money was a problem. It was hard to get Zelsmith to make any advance payments, but she did rent one of the rooms under her beach house to Walter Chase. A steep staircase led down to his part of the beach house, and Walter moved in his few books, his clothes, and rusty typewriter and he made himself casually at home.

He was wonderful company and had no sexual desires for her of any sort. They set up housekeeping. He ate her cooking, walked her dogs, and acted as her escort at previews, parties, and square dances when he didn't have personal business in town.

Mollie was a very good, graceful dancer and she was an ardent one. She liked to have all the beach bums from the surrounding beaches over. She wore out two record players that summer. She liked to get a little high on highballs or martinis and take off her shoes and dance wild sambas and tangos, and after everyone was all tired out she would dance alone and all the guests would cheer her on. The dogs barked and the liquor bills were too high, even on credit. As everyone thought she was Walter Chase's mistress or Mike Zelsmith's girl, she had a sort of social position in that part of the beach world that was on the wrong, or right, side of the palm trees.

She mothered and cooked for people and she never drank too much or went on crying jags. Everybody loved Mollie and liked to drink her whisky and eat her food and break her records.

Mollie met Dr. Sontag at an oil man's party somewhere on the fringe of Santa Monica's social groupings. He fell in love with her and she told him she was sorry, and he said it was all right if he could just take care of her. He had an office near the big shore hospital, St. John's, and collected old books and smoking tobaccos. Before the war he had been an important man in psychoanalytic technique and therapeutic procedure in New York City. He was viewed as an expert on its special hypotheses and doctrines. He lost his hair in the war, and from the various schools of psychoanalytic thought he put together an Army unit that worked out very well in Italy, until a general slapped a soldier in his hospital. He sat out the rest of the war after that and never went back to his old work. He was a good surgeon and he liked the full sunlight at the beach, and often dropped in at Mollie's for a drink and held the cocker Lucky on his lap and spoke to the little dog about "conscience is the inner perception of the rejection of certain wishes existing within us, eh boy?"

When Mollie had pains he had her X-rayed and then he put her on his special table with the stirrups for her slim legs and she lay back in an odd position and Dr. Sontag put on his rubber gloves—a red obscene color.

"I'm not afraid to die," Mollie said looking up at the ceiling, "but not the way Mother did. It was too cruel."

"No morbid thoughts," said Dr. Sontag. "The inner plumbing of women is a complicated thing."

After a minute he took off his gloves and wiped his glasses and let Mollie off the table and she sat wrapped in a sheet, her naked legs stretched before her. He wrote a long time on a card and then looked up and grinned and came over and gripped her shoulder through the sheet. "Everything is going to be all right. Nothing the matter with you. Nerves."

"If ever it isn't, just let something slip, will you, Myron?" and she came over and kissed him and he looked at her and kissed her cheek with a creeping, caressing motion.

"Mollie, you delight me."

So she decided to have Dr. Sontag do a plastic on one nostril for the screen test.

After the plastic was all over and her face was bandaged she just lay back and rested in the hospital bed. She didn't have a drink or a cigarette until the second day and she felt much better.

The second night she lay in bed—flat on her back—waiting for the two red sleeping pills to catch, and she wondered what being in love with Mike Zelsmith would be like. Maybe it was the tight bandages, but somehow she had never felt like this, and she hoped it was not like the time she thought Gene was going to be the real bell ringer, when it was only a bad fish.

"Well," said Walter, picking her up in a cab at the hospital gate, and continuing their talk, "you're both very nice people and I'm very fond of you two, and it should work. But you both seem scared of it. M.Z. is sorry he couldn't be here. The bank sent a fast wire."

"I don't think he's afraid to come and see me. I don't know," Mollie said. "Flat on my rump for a day thinking it out, maybe I'm not cut out for this love business. I've tried it on, but it always seems to come out two sizes too small."

"M.Z. is a very bright guy, but when it comes to love, I think he's a soaking romantic, and those kind of people never know the truth until it's too late."

"Well, I'll always have the dogs and the birds."

"Don't be funny, Mollie."

"Gene cried when he left me last time."

"He never made anybody cry on the stage."

"Gene's my fault. I kind of wiped his nose and patted his little behind and said, 'All right, go show Mother you're an actor; make Mother proud of you.'"

Mollie was a little puzzled by the attack of nerves that had sent her to Dr. Sontag. She didn't like nerves or the shakes and didn't know she had them. She thought she was a normal girl and under control. She would have to watch herself and take more exercise and make John Fennel take her out to play tennis. He was a good player and she looked very exciting and beautiful in white shorts, her hair in a wide headband, as she ran over the hard-packed clay. She got tanned and grew slimmer and John Fennel amused her and got her books to read. But that was all cut short when Mrs. Zelsmith got back from Europe and Mike buckled down to work on the motion picture. Mollie promised herself no more nerves.

5

FROM THE JOURNAL OF JOHN FENNEL

I keep thinking of Mandy Rye, much more than I want, and so to change the subject I have been doing something foolish, and Mike has caught me at it. I have been making a new version of Plato's *The Cave*. Mike saw it in my room on the dresser, and read it, and laughed. "I'm going to send this out as my Christmas card. Only they'd think I was trying to be funny."

He read it out loud. "Suppose a race of men who were born and brought up all their lives in a motion picture theater, who have never taken their eyes off the screen . . . That and only that is their world . . . Now suppose one of them is taken out, forcibly . . . out into the sunshine . . . What would he think when he was finally able to look at real things? Would he not be happy over what has happened to him, and sorry for them inside, even a little contemptuous?

"Suppose he went back into the motion picture theater and into the dark. His old friends would laugh at him . . . they would laugh at anyone who had been out and come back . . . And as for the person who had taken him out and might force another of them out, and set others free of their darkness, would they not want to kill him? Yes, they would . . ."

Mike threw the sheet of paper on the dresser, frowned, and looked at me. "Plato really write that?"

"Almost like that."

"Must read him. Here I always thought he was a phony like a Wilshire Boulevard rabbi. Pick up Mandy, and we'll all have dinner."

After he left I wondered if I wanted to see so much of Mandy. She had made a life for herself; cool, numbly cool, coolly correct, and I doubted if I could change it. People said she once had shown a great deal of promise as an actress. It had been expected she would become another Ina Clair, an Eve Arden, perhaps even a Gertrude Lawrence. But she had never gone to Broadway, avoided radio work, and continued to collect furniture and exist as a type easy to cast and popular in well-dressed pictures. What I wanted was to remain casual and not become involved. There was a sad lesson in the words of the Frenchman who has said, "There is not a woman in the world the possession of whom is as precious as the truth which she reveals to us by making us suffer." I didn't feel the need of any truths, not in such large heaping portions of suffering as seemed to be the habits of love life in the town. It was better to read Anatole France and agree that "hygiene is the only morality." But one becomes aware that choice is only the delusion of the emotionless, the living go in head-first knowing there is no choice in these things. We are trapped by a dissociated flood of images, ideas, perceptions, scratched on our hides by external stimuli, by various moltings from previous experiences. Only Mandy was protected by that coating of social ice, that deep freeze of the emotions. She was brought out only in front of the cameras; into her full charm and power. Mandy is full of the delicate isolation, inertia, and ennui of a proud woman, whose reluctance is the result of good taste, easy surroundings, and a fear of the town's cruel side. She exists as a kind of process of polarization, between experience and consciousness, sensibility and conduct, life and discipline. A balancing of a few impulses with control. She is held captive by some ancestral conscience, beating her old dogmas with no new sticks. An ego—for the actor is *ego* in its purest form—driven to suppress experiences. I say all this, and write it down, and I may be wrong. It's so much better in a novel where I can invent and twist and act very sure with a character. But in real life I can only touch something like body heat and feel it glow and from it try and guess the genes and glands and brain matter and chemical changes within the person. Yes, I can be wrong about Mandy. I wonder how much of this surface reading will be true a month, six months, a year from now, if I am still here.

There is no way of knowing the true diversity and intensity of experience, or how to peel it so it is not obscured as to value and meaning. Yet in the past I have often invented character and then found it all true in someone, and it has frightened me to see how close I am in drawing certain truths in some people.

Mollie and Mike seem more complex, but that may be because I do not want to study them up close, become involved in their problems. The town is shallow, even if they are not, and I do not want to judge them by its standards seeping into my thoughts. The instability and deceptiveness of the mere sexual act, compared to the tenacious rightness of being, of existing in another person, does not always hold true here. I must wait and perhaps it will come to me, not just come to me, invade me, roll for me on the floor, beg to be let into my understanding. It has happened, that which has been baffling becomes suddenly clear, too clean often, and then I regret having even thought about the matter and worried about not knowing it . . . Those spectral creations who repel and fascinate us in our inescapable personal realization of mortality.

Mike is the one I would like to understand the most, also his relationship with Mollie, the deep fullness he is perhaps himself hunting . . .

Under the crusts of surface Mike in his relationship with Mollie tries to avoid the modern evocation of sin in love, the agony of personal griefs, the calamitous sense of guilt that spoils so much of our lives.

To get some clue to Mike, inside himself, I have been running his old motion pictures, none of which I had ever seen (I was never very devoted to the film form). Sitting in the dusty, smelly projection room, alone most of the time, looking at Mike's work for the last ten years is an amazing revealing experience. Mike is, I feel, trying to say: "this is the contemporary artist looking for an identity, an art form in the maddening environments of today through which I can escape as a human being the sterile premature death of modern walking man." I know he'd laugh if I said that to him. But I think it's true.

Mike in his past has hunted for that calm, collected thing, a limited contentment; the river below the falls. His movies are free of any decadent aestheticism, and full of his earthy, even low, ability to show physical and psychological atmospheres with a deft indirection that makes the customer tell part of the story himself as he watches it.

Mike has learned a great deal. He seems to say in the film form that the pattern of living is a final enigma to be accepted with resignation. He avoids mostly in his work the trap of being balanced between the merely imaginable and the attainable, that ends usually in utter despair. As I sat, day after day, looking at his movies, too many of them at one time, I admit, and too close to his ideas collected in so many pictures, I got the feeling that he is one of the two or three men in the town here who have even been able to lift much of human experience up to a solid platform of lasting value. I understood suddenly why they want him to fail, why the industry is menaced by his abilities. His self-activated ego shakes their placid betrayal of life . . .

69

John Fennel had a date for lunch with Mandy Rye, but Mike had called a story conference that morning and John called her up and said he was sorry.

"Mike's in a hurry for this story," he said.

"I know, Johnny. I may play a part in it."

"He didn't tell me, Mandy."

"The British Embassy hostess."

"I'm sure you'll be very good in it. Witty lines. How about dinner if we break in time?"

"Love to, Johnny."

He had been out with Mandy twice. He had even gotten used to her odd name. She wouldn't change it, even for picture purposes. He liked being with her. Unlike Mollie, she wasn't quick and bright, and never got fussed or excited. He couldn't make Mandy out fully, but he decided she was kind and not very deep, and rather afraid of life. There was a conflict between her and her public character, the brassy witty woman of the world she played in pictures.

They danced together and had dinner and he liked holding her big body in his arms. He didn't know if he wanted to sleep with her, that is, he would have if she had offered, but he didn't want to make a fuss about it. He suspected she was frigid and perhaps a virgin; then he remembered that Mike Zelsmith had discovered her. Still, he didn't really know how Mike operated. Mike was a rare type—he decided—a person who looked crude and acted vulgar, but John already knew he was a kind of sensitive porous membrane reacting to external stimuli and inner vibrations beyond the emotional receiving apparatus of most people. He remembered Wordsworth's remark that poetry is emotion recollected in tranquility. That would explain Mike's brooding silent moods between periods of furious activity. John looked at his watch and saw that he would be late for the conference.

All of Mike Zelsmith's motion pictures opened with a fancy art shot of a great modern fieldstone house over which was imposed the letters A ZELSMITH PRODUCTION. The big house with its many windows was his own at Pacific Palisades, nosing in over a decomposing granite cliff that hung carelessly over the ocean. Zelsmith fought with poured concrete and reinforced steel forms to keep his gardens from falling away into the sea.

The cab tires were hissing over the blue stone drive to the big fieldstone, steel, and glass house. John Fennel paid the driver and pressed a golden button set in the middle of a great crimson door. A Chinese butler in a crumpled white coat let him in and pointed across some waxed stone flooring toward a room opening outlined in fumed oak trim.

The room, Mike's work room, was lined with books and cases to hold prints. A large, gloomy Picasso of blue suffering forms hung over a fireplace, and Miro and Munch paintings crowded the bookcases. Nothing was in order and only the long redwood table was cleared. It held some cheap glass ashtrays, yellow, blue-lined legal pads, and some very sharp yellow pencils.

Mike Zelsmith was lighting a cigar and glaring at Walter Chase cleaning his fingernails with a sharp pencil. There was a little bald man who sweated politely and rattled some production sheets, a very stylish girl in a tight yellow suit who held an open shorthand notebook, and a Great Dane dog that sat on the rug, mouth open and dripping. John nodded a greeting and sat down in the closest chair.

Mike Zelsmith looked up and rolled his cigar around in the ashtray in front of him. He stood and took a rough-cut blackwood cane up in his hand.

"A hell of a note, John. I leave you and Walter to give me a story line and I get an outline I wouldn't shoot as a Hopalong Cassidy." He banged dust from a sofa with the blackwood cane. "But it's my fault. The damn bank took up most of my time."

Walter winked at John and said in his clean, direct voice —yet a voice with a hurt, cold note in it, "I think you will find a great deal of the novel very well projected in our treatment."

"I don't like it!"

John Fennel folded his arms. "Then there is nothing more to say, Mike. I'm sure you can get better results with other writers . . . better than I have done. I don't really care much for this version myself. I feel we've stripped the story of character and made a chase out of it."

Mike laughed. "You don't get out that easy, John. There isn't another writer in town I'd trust with this story. All right, you put back the character. Take your time. I'm not making quickies, but I want the heart back in it. Where's Mollie?"

Walter raised his head from examining the ashtray. "Taking dancing lessons for the screen test."

The girl with the notebook said, "You sent her flowers this morning, Mr. Zelsmith."

"How are the costume sketches?"

John leaned back in his chair. "I thought they could be improved, here and there."

The bald man shook his head. "She hasn't got it any more. That Shelley ballet was a fluke."

Mike was deep in a study of the production figures. "All right," he growled, "let it go on for a while. Now I'm going down to Palm Springs for two weeks with Mrs. Zelsmith. I want John and you, Walter, with me, and we'll have story conferences every day. Prepare two cars and get the guest house open down there for them."

"Yes, Mr. Zelsmith," said the girl, making quick curly notes on her pad. Mike got up and dug a pointed shoe toe into the ribs of the Great Dane and walked around the table, puffed his cigar into life, and leaned back on the heavy cane.

"John, I picked up some fine Goyas. Etchings from the original plates. You must see them when you come in."

"Be very happy to. You very sure you want me to go on with the screenplay?"

"I'm not sure, but you're going on with it."

Mike turned away and whistled at the Great Dane. He walked out into the garden, the dog following slowly and with dignity. The girl stood up, stretched, pulled her jacket down, wriggled her girdle into place and grinned. "Who's staying for lunch? Hamburgers, chain-store pie, and High Life Beer."

Walter asked, "When will the cars be ready for Palm Springs?"

The production man wiped his face with great care. "At seven tonight. The Boss doesn't like to ride in the heat of the day."

Outside the sun was bright and high and John felt happy he hadn't walked out on the job. He was beginning to understand Zelsmith's methods, his search for perfection. He had never wanted perfection in anything himself.

Mike dropped in for an hour with Mollie. One of the beach bum's sunburned girls, in halter and shorts, was preparing lunch in the small kitchen of the Ark. Mollie sat on the sun deck in a blue dressing gown smoking a cigarette in a red holder someone had sent her. Mike smiled at her and took her hand in his and kissed her cheek, then fell back in the low porch chair facing her.

"Big day?"

Mollie waved the red holder and her dogs licked her hand; Lucky's little tail almost came off from joy.

"The animal farm is certainly glad to see me. Their eyes are popping out on stems."

"I have to go to Palm Springs tonight. Gét my personal life in order."

Mollie pointed to a blue bowl of assorted flowers dying in the sun on the porch rail. "That was a sweet note and all those flowers."

"Mollie." He picked up her hand again. It was a thin, long hand, beautiful. "Mollie, I'm worried about us."

"Don't be."

"I want to say something. Maybe I'll never get back in stride again. Maybe things will work out for us. When I come back I'll know something."

She pulled his hand up between her breasts, and he felt her flesh under the halter and she rolled his hand in the hollow.

Mike said, "Wish I didn't have to go to Palm Springs."

The beach bum's girl came out with a tray of food. "All right, Mollie, wrap yourself around this."

The Zelsmiths had left early for Palm Springs. Walter Chase liked it that way.

"There are many pioneer families on the coast," Walter said to John as they rode alone in the early night headed for the desert. "It isn't all gold and lumber and department stores and real estate. There is a small but clannish group of motion picture pioneers. M.Z. is practically the son of Dan'il Boone as far as movies go."

John Fennel had never seen the desert dusk. The low, leaping land and its odd spiky growths, the far-flung slopes where the yellow grasses grew and the lofting mountains cut from black iron and pasted against picture-blue skies. It had grown darker and the landscape had become more sinister and silent, now and then broken only by the wail of a train at an empty crossing, the neon blinking of some gas station and the pin-points of life—lonely houses at the end of deserted streets that led nowhere.

"It doesn't look like much of a land for human beings, Walter."

"It was meant, M.Z. always says, for desert toads, snakes, and low tribes of Indians that ate roots and each other. Man came and brought in water. Cut off the water here and this will all go back to the desert. The ocean will lap at the decaying shore cottages, and where Sam Goldwyn walks today the desert wolf will hunt gophers."

"Mike Zelsmith's folks settled all this?"

Walter put his crossed arms behind his head and yawned. "In a motion picture way. Around 1910 a lot of people came to California to escape Mr. Edison's habit of seizing their cameras for not paying royalties on them. Old man Zelsmith was real pioneer stuff. Hard, cunning, healthy, and had a way with a dollar. He floated the biggest of the early film companies and fought in the wars that saw them mergered and become huge. They done him in after a panic year. All his friends doublecrossed him and he killed himself in a messy way. Mike was fourteen at the time. He had six months of normal education, and a Dusenberg car as long as a tapeworm his father had bought him.

"He traded the car for a camera and some ends of film footage and made a short picture on race horses in slow motion. At sixteen Mike was the wonder boy of trashy quick-made pictures. At twenty-four he was running the old Triangle-Hart lot, and at thirty he looked like Thalberg, Selznick, and Zanuck combined. Nobody knows how he got it, but he had taste, ability, and nerve. Also he thought he could punch. John Barrymore broke his nose, and Tom Mix once threw him down two flights of stairs. Those were his woman-hunting days. He wanted to lay everything in skirts, beat up everything in pants, and drink up all the likker in sight."

The desert was very level now and the sky, the color of the inner skin of a plum, was sugared with stars. The car ran so smoothly that John had the sensation of floating over a landscape painted by Dali in one of his more kindly moments.

Walter was lying back on his spine, the car robe around his throat and his eyes closed, but he was still talking.

"Alice Garoyan tamed Mike, or at least housebroke him. Met him in the East when he was trying to do a play. A merger of dynasties, that's what it was. Old Edward Garoyan, always referred to in polite society as 'that Armenian sonofabitch,' wasn't a pioneer, but he got here early enough to see that the bigger pictures you made the better theaters you would have to build. He ran the industry up from a nickelodeon with the kitchen chairs and a bed sheet, to Garoyan's Royal Malayans . . . had a whole string of movie palaces built across the country."

"How did the marriage turn out?"

"Alice is a hellcat."

"He seems to respect and love her."

"You'll meet her, John, down at the Springs. Like her old man; hard, smart, kind of nice too. Knows the value of money and she wants to break into the Native Sons; that's real society. M.Z. is supporting the Republican party in the state to help. But things haven't been going so good for Mike and Alice. With Mike slipping, slipping so badly. Can't keep his hands off the pictures any more. Used to mastermind them, now wants to write 'em, direct 'em, and sleep with 'em. He's not easy to live with. Alice is thinking of going back to Papa. That means tighter bank money. Wait till she finds out about Mollie."

Somewhere on the horizon a spotlight was circling the sky writing silver circles, there were some palm trees bent toward each other, and the road was tinted pink on the edges.

"Odd-looking effect ahead, Walter."

"Palm Springs," said Walter, falling asleep.

The Zelsmith villa at Palm Springs was low, wide, and comfortable, Italian in style, a pale, fruit-looking green, all of it growing around a kidney-shaped pool and an over-heated garden.

In the morning John Fennel stood at his bedroom window watching an old Mexican gardener tenderly collect the snails off the flowers and put them into an empty Standard Oil can, and then stamp his foot in the can . . .

Walter came up from the pool, rubbing his lean brown body with a shrimp-pink towel lettered Z, the drops of water falling from his yellow crew-cut hair.

"Have your swim yet?"

"No, I was writing in my journal, Walter."

"Isn't that rather unfair on posterity? See you at breakfast in ten minutes. Get ready to charm Alice."

It was an ultramodern dining room, with a row of steaming silver buffet dishes on little oil lamps of burning alcohol.

Walter was already turning over the silver covers on the buffet and frowning, as John came in wearing a tropical shirt (seashell motif) and the baby blue suede shoes.

Walter shook his head, "Tepid Spam, Bird's Eye frozen French fries and cold eggs, and the bacon all fat. Wait till you taste the coffee. It's a crime against civilization."

"I've noticed Zelsmith's food," John said, spearing some sardines and sniffing at the cottonseed oil. "Why do they eat so badly?"

"Alice hates to spend money and Mike has a bad nose and can't taste anything, and the Chinese houseboys steal everything they can carry off except the red-hot stove lids."

Mike came in wrapped in a too-short terry-cloth robe around his heavy body, exposing tanned hairy legs. He growled a good morning and poured himself some cornflakes into a plate, poured cream over that, and spooned in three heaping orders of sugar. After two mouthfuls he felt equal to talking, and spoke with his mouth full, scattering flakes as he gestured.

"We start right after breakfast and keep on till dark. I must have a final story line for the banks. A hell of a note when the banks of the country decide what the art of the world will look like. Hello, Alice. Morning."

A tall, thin young woman had walked into the room, walked in with a shifting balance of her weight at every step, as if she were made of coiled springs and were testing them. Her long, pretty face had a fine nose and very big, dark eyes. Her thick, rich hair looked wet and was blue-black and coiled on top of her head, as if dropped on carelessly. She was still young and very sure of herself.

Mike made the introductions and a Chinese boy set a baked half of grapefruit before her. She grinned and looked around at the table and addressed them all, collectively, in an amused yet firm voice.

"The cars woke me last night. Tonight if anybody is going to town, coast down the drive, don't start the motor till you hit the road."

Walter stopped munching the French fries and reached for the coffee pot, a modern tower of gleaming metal with brown water bubbling in some intricate scientific system of its own. He poured an extra cup of coffee for John. It was the worst coffee John had ever tried to drink.

"Nice is fine," said Alice Zelsmith, smiling at John. "But I guess I'm just a sucker for California."

At three o'clock in the afternoon, Mike Zelsmith's polo shirt was wet on the shoulders. Walter had a pile of sixteen cigarette butts in the glass plate before him, and John had filled pages of doodles in the yellow legal notebook at his elbow. He slowly turned the sheets as Zelsmith paced back and forth at his end of the table and banged a blackwood cane on the tile floor.

"You've got to remember simple rules in telling a story on the screen. If the people don't move, the camera does. And don't make it talk too much. It's moving pictures, not *talking* pictures. Write a screenplay as if you were sending yourself ten-word telegrams. Keep it lean. Now let's take the second act again. Night in Cario, the hero is now sure the girl is married, but she will not admit it. How to do such an ordinary dramatic idea with new shock values? Now I'm not writing it for you boys, understand, just thinking in telephone numbers, out loud . . . Suppose we . . ."

Alice Zelsmith came in wearing smart harem pants of yellow velvet and a black turtleneck sweater. "Still at it? Well, knock off. I'm using the place for a swimming party."

Zelsmith sat down and wiped his face with his sleeves. "All right, type it up," he nodded to the girl with the shorthand notebook. "We'll start again right after dinner."

The desert nights are cold, a cold that chills the breath in the nostrils and makes the blood run a little faster, as if in fear of chilling. The maid had put the electric blankets on the big bed and connected them. Mike came in from his afterdinner walk and found Alice already in bed, wearing her sea-green nightgown, a smoking cigarette in her hand. She was reading.

"I'm reading John's novel," she said.

"Like it?"

Alice closed the book, putting in a bit of cigarette package as marking. "I don't see a picture in it. It's very well written."

Mike sat down facing her on a silly little modern chair. He was surprised how comfortable it was. "Alice, how about us having a talk?"

She looked at him and grinned, but he saw her hands were closed tight into dark fists. "You sleeping with somebody in town?"

Mike sighed. "Don't give me the Noel Coward dialogue. No, I'm not."

"Then you're thinking about it," said Alice. "You're too nice to me."

"Maybe I need that bank money. Your old man has got to pony up."

"Darling," said Alice, "you know I love you. Maybe we don't get along like people should, but you know how I feel."

"I know."

"Don't you care?"

"I care."

"I don't want to talk about Papa tonight."

"Jesu, do you think I do?" Mike shouted.

"He isn't going to let you down."

"The hell he isn't."

"Can't we make a go of it, Mike?"

Mike got up and reached for one of her cigarettes, thought better of it, and put one of his cigars in his mouth. He slowly puffed it alive and then inspected the glowing end. "Alice, I honestly don't see how it's going to work. I haven't fallen out of love with you. Not the way you think."

"In what way have you then?"

"What?"

"Fallen out of love with me?"

"I'm tight, I'm geared up. Even working on the picture hasn't gotten me over it. Maybe it isn't you. Maybe it's me. I'm not the guy I was five years ago."

"Stop kidding, Mike. You've got an ego as big as a horse. You still think you're the greatest mind ever to hit this town."

"They don't think so at the box office any more."

"Forget the box office." She got out of bed and put her arms around him. "Let's get away. Give up Hollywood, pictures. Just drift and have a life."

"We just tried that, didn't we? In Europe."

"I tried it. You ran around hunting stories."

"That should show you I can't give it up."

She folded her arms and her voice he thought sounded like her father's. "Going to wait till this town gives you up? Can't quit at the top?"

There was so much to say and he hadn't said it. He put his cigar out in a china tray. He was suddenly tired. "Let's go to bed. It's late."

"Tired?"

"Hell, yes. Bushed."

78

At breakfast Alice said to John Fennel, "I had no idea you were such a famous writer."

John didn't know what to say to that and he made some polite talk and moved off. She watched him go and decided she didn't like him. It used to be very important whom she didn't like in the Zelsmith group, but that time was a little past. Everything was a little past she would admit to herself (when she permitted self-pity).

Alice Zelsmith all her life felt she was somebody. Looks, brains, money. Not all just being Papa's daughter, but being Alice, and waiting for things and finding out after you got them you didn't want them. Looks and money hadn't helped. As a child things had been very bad because Mama wasn't good enough for Papa, or so he felt, and, well, things happened and there was no real family at all. Papa liked music and would have been best off in an orchestra playing Bach, but also he had wanted to be rich and so he gave it all up to become the most hated and powerful man in Hollywood.

But that wasn't important. Alice decided to go to Europe and study ballet, and without money or help from home. The hard way. There were a lot of long, dirty years and a lot of hard work, and she had a good, firm, beautiful body and danced well. Some of the other girls adored her, but after a while she decided she wasn't double gaited, or a great dancer, and gave it up. She came back to New York to be on her own.

There wasn't much demand for a half-trained classic ballet dancer, and she set up house in the Village ("it was something in those days, not Floyd Dell and Sherwood Anderson, and 'The Broom,' and Tony's real good speak any more—but something"). She rocked around that way, getting no real place as a dancer and then she met Mike. He and his brother were messing around with plays, and one night Mike and Alice noticed each other and he came to live with her, or she went to live with him (his relatives were real old-fashioned Jews, and so he didn't dare marry her at first). They were madly in love—whatever that meant, she wondered later on. It was very good and solid and she used to go out of her way to defend the Jews, even when no one was attacking them. She was extra loyal and extra angry when things didn't go well.

Mike's brother went back to Hollywood to write screenplays and he married an early screen star ("who never really learned to talk much," Alice always said). Mike followed and began to produce pictures. After that something happened that didn't make sense. Maybe she was too close to Mike and bothered him in his work, or she was just too crazy to sit home and forget all her hopes as a dancer. They had a huge Great Dane, and she went back to the stage dancing.

When a local ballet was produced, she cut her hair short and danced and everyone said she should go professional. She didn't. She liked to drink and talk on how dull life had been to her, but everything was going to be very good now. She was crazy about Mike and everyone knew it.

But they just couldn't make a go of it. She tried to be tender but she had a temper and a sharp tongue, and Mike took to going out on double dates with extra girls—with a fat slob who handicapped horses for Mike. But he wasn't really interested in it. His first success in films had come and he was working hard and trying to understand Alice. And why he had fallen out of love. He felt like a heel about it. Alice went back to New York. It was pretty wild, but she always said she had been true to Mike. Perhaps she had been. She had never been much of a sex ball anyway, except with Mike. They made it up and she came home and drank a lot, but everyone in their world did. She hired a dance coach, a crisp young man who wandered around the house, as much use as the Great Dane. But he was around when Mike was busy. And she was making her own friends now and giving them wonderful advice on how to be happy and grab hold of a real guy; and they nodded and wondered how it was Alice never seemed to take any of her own advice.

Alice saw it wasn't going to work out with Mike after all; she hated her sister-in-law, the silent-film star, for being happy with Mike's brother.

One night Alice decided to try attaching the vacuum cleaner tube to the exhaust of her new car, a present from Papa, and seeing if it could kill her. It almost did and they had a hard time saving her but they did, and somehow after that Mike was much nicer, with the hurt-dog look in his eyes, and they settled down to a kind of sterile domestic life, that was just satisfactory at meals and with company.

80

Every once in a while she decided to go to Paris or Mexico, and called a friend to come along, but they never went.

That was Alice, smart and clever, knowing now it wouldn't change or be better for a long time, and that about the only thing left to do was wait it out, and under it all love one man more than anything else in the world. It was a truly great love, a big, aching love and that's about all one could think about it. Lots of people in town said Alice was crazy and let it go at that, which was unfair, but Alice did nothing to change their minds. She spent a lot of time redecorating the big modern house.

The next time Alice saw John at Palm Springs she repeated the line about him being famous (she bought all the great books, but didn't read much).

"You are famous."

"I never think of it, Mrs. Zelsmith."

"Modest young man."

She gave him a thin smile that bent her mouth oddly. "I promised you at my party, John Fennel. Some college professors, and a woman who knows Einstein."

John said, "I'm no good at that sort of thing, but if you want me to come . . ."

"I do."

"Hello, Mollie."

"It's good to hear you, Mike. I've been sitting here combing burrs out of Lucky."

"Are you taking care of yourself, Mollie?"

"You mean am I drinking?"

"No, you're a born lush, a natural-born alcoholic."

"Thanks."

Somewhere in the house he heard another phone being lifted off its cradle.

"I'll call you again—soon."

"Sure. Bye, Mike."

Just before dawn Mike used to doze off and wake with the sun in his eyes and his mouth dry as pucker and he had a feeling that in ten minutes they were going to take him out to be shot.

At the end of the week they had a story Mike said was "fair." Walter thought M.Z. was processing an ulcer. The gardener's younger son, a dark tomcat, had seduced the girl

81

with the shorthand notebook, which made for gossip anyway. The last week seemed longer than it need be. Alice Zelsmith gave teas and John spoke at them for whatever cause she was collecting for. Mike managed to speak to Mollie almost every day. It was very unsatisfactory. Sometimes the beach bums were all around. Sometimes Mandy Rye answered the phone and said Mollie hadn't slept much last night and was catching up. Sometimes it was very near perfect and her bubbling little laugh and her ringing voice made him feel that he was still a very lucky man . . .

It was a hard job putting together a screenplay, for there was no reason for a screenplay, Mike felt. The old-time directors made it up as they went along, working perhaps from a short outline, but letting the full meat and marrow of the picture create itself before the cameras. That way was dead now because the screen talked and no director was able to tell his people what to say on the spur of the moment. The old form had been pure art very often; like abstract painting, it had created emotion without solid realism in what the characters said, but now a journalism of words, a kind of Dutch kitchen painting of little details that added nothing much to the whole was the motion picture.

Mike sweated out a script, bringing up from the deep sea of his writers the scenes and dialogue that were to be the framework of his finished project. Later he always wanted to pull away as much of this framework as he could, and leave, he hoped, the shape of something solid enough to be the virile, vital thing he imagined every time he started a film.

Alice found him by the pool staring into the pure filtered water. He looked up at her as she sat down by his side and leaned her chin on his shoulder from behind.

"How is it going, Mike?"

"It's going. John has it if I can dredge it up."

"We never finished our talk the other night."

"We never do. I don't know, Alice, talk never says anything. Not between us."

"I'm sticking, Mike. As close as I can. There is never going to be another guy for me. I know I spoil it and I don't make you happy. I don't know why it doesn't work, and why it can't, but that's it, I'm staying."

Mike frowned. "Maybe I can't work that way, much longer."

"Don't say 'can't.'"

Mike frowned. "I don't know . . . I don't know . . . And I'm a guy who always has to know."

Between Mike and Alice the truce went on. Nothing was settled when they left Palm Springs, the personal torment coming with them.

The night he got back from Palm Springs Mike called Mollie, but she had gone out. In the morning he called her again and she said he must come down. He found Mollie on the sun deck kicking the boxer dog in the ribs because he had made a mess on the sun deck, and she dropped the dust pan and the sand and the special little shovel and he kissed her.

"How is all the girl?"

"I'm fine."

He saw she was suddenly shy and that they were almost strangers again, and he took the dog shovel and pan from her hands and sat her down on the big beach chair and looked at her.

"Mollie, nothing has changed."

She laughed and her eyes wrinkled up and he wondered why he had wasted two weeks in Palm Springs. He even walked the dogs while she made a meal. He went up the beach after them, whistling Ed away from a dead sea gull and keeping Lucky from leaping down the sand dunes. He looked back and she was standing on the sun deck, arms up, and he waved to her and his heart filled with pity for her for some reason he couldn't explain. When he began to feel a little sorry for himself, he felt better. He always disliked self-pity and it made him seem foolish—and feeling foolish amused him.

After spending an afternoon with Mollie and when it was still too early to go have dinner and talk story with John, Mike used to go down to the hotel bar and nurse a couple of small drinks along. It was a dimly lit bar with comfortable leather chairs and a lot of people who didn't know each other very well. It was used as a meeting place, a spot to exchange local information, and of course to have a drink. Around six o'clock Mike would usually find Ed, the old-time unemployed director, standing at the bar, a glass of

Irish whisky in his hand. He looked a great deal like W. C. Fields, Mike thought, and he would talk to anybody who would listen. He hadn't made a picture in ten years, but seemed to have a small fixed income, and a desire for human companionship.

"Everybody is all excited about that actress running off with her director to Mexico, leaving a husband and two kids," said Ed. "Hell, what do you expect from actors, Zelsmith? I've handled thousands of 'em. They're not human, they're just exhibitionists that ape the human race."

"I've met a few fine people that were actors," Mike said. Secretly he agreed with Ed.

"I doubt it! Show me an actor and I'll show you a horse's ass. A beautiful piece of meat and a good dentist's job and I'll turn you out a great actor any time. But why does everybody get so excited when one of these zombies breaks up a marriage? You'd think there were no decent marriages out here. Hell, I've been married thirty-four years to the same woman, and been faithful to her. Must be five million people like me out here, Zelsmith. I was a young rip in the old days out here. There was plenty of tail, and I liked it, but once I got married my motto was, 'it's just as good at home.' I've seen them come and go; mating in Rolls Royces, or with a cactus plant under their hips in the hills, but I never get excited when the newspapers whip up a scandal. Every man I say is entitled to his private life and every woman has a right to her happiness as she sees it, if they have a decent personal code of conduct. They say it's the climate and they say it's the tropical sun, but people are people all over the world. It's just that we get our names in the papers a little more often. Mind you, I don't think it's wrong to look at the girls with the wonderful udders passing, it's a delight to an old man's heart to see the young things parading the flesh and standing in the good sun with little on. If God had meant us not to see anything, He'd have given us feathers. If you like duets in the hay, this town's a good place for it. Lots of wonderful-looking girls. Not as beautiful as in New York. Ah, Zelsmith, Fifth Avenue on a good afternoon; you meet a hundred Lillian Russells and Ellen Terrys. And when it comes to making sexual love, the girls out here don't know much about it, unless they've changed from my youth, which I hear isn't so. They're so busy being photogenic they don't really care about knowing their business as a female biped. And what's a woman's business? Well, now it's making man feel that what's happening is so special it's just been invented, and yes, I will have another drop of Irish whisky, Zelsmith. Not a small whisky, there isn't any such thing as a small whisky to a drinking man."

Mike was usually a little high when he left to have dinner with John.

The cameraman ran a tape line across six feet of space to Mollie's chin and the men in the background moved the spots to hit the back of her head and light up the fine spun gold of her hair. Mollie stood very still while a fat girl built up her mouth with a small sable brush loaded with color. The dress hadn't fit too well and some clips behind her spine, to make it smaller, were hurting her. But she didn't dare relax her smile. Mike sat astride a low kitchen chair, his arms across its back, smiling at her.

The lights were getting hotter. The cameraman put away a light meter and nodded to Mike. "I've cooled it off. You sure you want the shadow on the right of her face that deep?"

"That's right. Now I want you to dolly in slower, and when you have the frame for the close-up, don't sharpen the focus too much. But Jesu, don't go arty on me. No soft-ground stuff."

"Okay, Mr. Zelsmith, we're ready to roll."

"Ready, Mollie?"

"My mouth feels stiff."

"It looks fine." Mike turned his head toward the sound man seated at his piano of lights and dials—the ear phones at his head.

"Sound okay?"

"Okay for sound."

"You've cut out the echo?"

"The backcloth killed that."

Mike said, "All right, lights."

The work lights dimmed and the numbered spots on the catwalks overhead went on, the arcs making yellow areas of light across the small set.

"Gotta change the points in Nine in ten minutes, Mr. Zelsmith," said a voice from a catwalk.

A boy stepped up with a hand-lettered board, then walked away.

"It's a take," said Mike. "Action, Mollie, roll 'em."

Mollie walked slowly forward, then back and began to recite a line of dialogue that made no sense to her. Mike had explained it to her, but she didn't remember it now. But he had told her to remember the little Buddha statue in her bedroom and keep her mouth in that smile and the eyelids low, as if thinking beyond ordinary life.

Somehow it worked, because he said, "Cut. Print it. Change that carbon and we'll do the dance test next."

Walter came from the darkness where he had been sitting and bent over Mike. "I've got the tape recording on that Debussy arrangement. It's a little thin in the woodwinds."

Mike said, "The bastards said they would have a better tape. All right, play it back to me while Mollie changes."

"How's the test going, M.Z.?"

"Fair. Give me the sound tape on both mikes."

Walter signaled to someone and the Debussy music poured suddenly over the set. They played it twice and Mike had them add some wave sounds to the music. Meanwhile, Mollie had changed into ballet slippers and she nodded numbly to the dance director, a tall, thin young man with rubber limbs who was telling her to, "stretch it dearie—get the hips into it—dearie."

When John Fennel came in at noon they had taken the dance three times and Mollie was ready to weep. Mike was smiling and when her nerves were just about ready to come apart, he said:

"All right, Mollie, the hell with what we've told you. Do the dance just the way you feel it."

This time everyone was very much on edge, except Mike, who didn't even bother to watch it, but lit a cigar and studied the dirty floor. Walter noticed, however, that Mollie, for all her freedom to do it her way, had managed to take on some of the dance director's advice, and the cameraman's, and Mike's own orders of the day. John saw that the test, which would most likely run three minutes, employed at least twenty-two people. He wondered a little how much it cost, but Mike had said not to ever worry over costs. John felt, as he watched, there was no telling if it was going well or bad.

One of the men on the catwalks overhead was eating a sandwich with dainty care, catching the crumbs in his open hand held on his chin. John's head felt heavy from the smell of dust and greasepaint and heavy kind of burlap odor of the sound-proofing material with which the sound stage was lined. It all seemed vaguely foolish and dull, like children playing house on a rainy day . . .

Mollie firmly refused to see the screen test run off the next morning. She said she was g.d. tired and wanted to sleep, and besides, she didn't care to see herself "look foolish twelve feet tall."

It was a small projection room with a rain-stained ceiling and deep, well-padded chairs and chipped paint. The cameraman and the sound man and the dance man and the cutter sat in the first row of chairs and Mike and John and Walter sat in the second row. Mike was a little nervous. He said crisply to the cameraman, "What's the damn delay?"

"He's putting a new leader on it. We cut it together— used everything we took."

There was a buzz and Mike picked up the phone. "All set? All right, go ahead."

The lights went out and the screen went white and rolled some dots across its surface and then a big letter 4 leaped about and suddenly there was a blackboard with the words: —TEST: Binning, DIRECTOR: Zelsmith, CAMERA: Harkins— and lots of numbers and the date.

And then John knew suddenly what magic was. A huge head filled the screen, it did not look like Mollie, it showed none of the lighting and working crews, none of the dirty set and the dusty air. But a dream face carved and modeled in light and dark, and the whole thing was so unreal, so lovely, that the pit of his stomach turned and seemed to strain against his inner skin.

Now the camera moved back and Mollie spoke. The banal words of yesterday were gone. A kind of child spirit, a sort of powerful force and being, spoke of something vital and emotional—the voice was clear and singing, yet musical, and full of the throat and tongue. The face was part of real poetry; he didn't know why. But it was. As she turned and the whole range of her flesh tones, the carefully sure beauty of a body moving was like something no great painter had yet caught. The voice was part of the scene, of the girl there. Not just hasty dialogue he had labored over and only half believed.

John felt Walter clear his throat. He looked in the direction of Mike but it was too dark to see. When his eye went back to the screen Mollie was dancing to the sound of waves and music blended perfectly, and the grace of it and the clean firm sureness of it was something so real and yet so far off that he could not believe he had ever seen this thing shot only the day before in cluttered, broken-up confusion. It was no longer Mollie. It could never be Mollie, and yet it was. Whatever forces Mike had put into the test had turned a slim young girl, real, alive, and breathing, into a kind of goddess, still alive and breathing, but with something added that at the moment he could not put into just words. He thought of the aged liquid flow of battered Greek marbles, of tall trees bending in a misty wind, of the ache and the pattern of those rare moments when he had felt the rime and pace of life beyond its daily frustrations and the cloying limitations of reality. Mollie, the silver nitrate image on the cellulose film leaping before his eyes, was a sensual transfiguration, a thing of some soft and poetic passion far from the everyday Mollie they all knew.

She turned now and the great eye of the camera began to prowl toward her and the face filled the room, filled the throbbing atmosphere, filled John with a shape that in its nostrils, its huge eyes, the tilt of neck and head, the sway and rhythms of plane and surface was the very mystery of existence. The very substance of flesh and lust of love and the fleeing moments of life. The tragic awe of its own beauty, it said, is here—that too must pass away sooner than one could believe . . . Then a flood of bright nothing, a burning darkness that stabbed the eyeball, and the lights went up and only the mood remained in the common little room of stained beaver board and gray, chipping paint.

"The lab bitched up the printing," Mike's voice said. "Developed too dark. Get a new set of prints made. And how the hell, Hawkins, did we get those reflected headlights?"

"That new German lens you got, I guess."

"And for Christ sake, don't cut it so tight. The music still stinks."

John was rather shocked. Then he looked over at Mike and saw Mike was grinning, an inner satisfied grin, and John knew Mike was really pleased.

Walter lit a cigarette slowly. "You're right, M.Z., Mollie's the best since Garbo."

"Hell, she's going to be even better. I'm going to shoot color tests next. There has never been anything in Hollywood like Mollie when I get her just right. I don't like her

88

make-up. We'll try less pancake and a deeper shade of number two, Smithy."

A voice said, "Yes, Mr. Zelsmith. Less pancake."

Mike turned to John and grabbed his arm hard. "You see what I mean? What we can do if they let us? You and me?"

"I see, Mike. I don't know how you did it and yet I saw every move you made yesterday."

"You didn't see a thing. You just saw the crews and the lights and the cameramen and the sweet little girl in make-up. But I'll show you what to look for, what to put in, and what to leave out."

"You pleased, Mike?"

Mike picked up the phone. "All right, let's run it again and cut some of the wobble out."

John waited for Mike to answer his question, but he didn't. Mike was staring at the blank screen, the cigar clamped very tight in his jaw as the light went out again.

FROM THE JOURNAL OF JOHN FENNEL

I told Mandy Rye about Mollie's screen test tonight while we were driving back from the Bowl where we had listened to Mozart and gotten our behinds damp from the night dew. Bach and a cold, wet rump seem to be the highest form of cultural level available out here.

Mandy does not think Mollie is an actress, no matter how good the screen test. She admits Mike can make her look like one for one picture perhaps, but that Mollie lacks the true offensive ego of actors, their all-encompassing, loud public manners, and their undying desire to be noticed at all times. Pretty deep coming from Mandy, whom I'm getting to like more and more.

She thinks Mike is going downhill because he is too loyal to something she couldn't express. I said, "An inborn, instinctive moral sense beyond that of any of the nostalgia merchants out here?"

"Something like that. He doesn't give and sway with the punches."

"Most people I know have it, Mandy, that inborn moral sense. Not as strong as Mike—but how else can people live?"

"They have instincts here too, *other* kinds."

I looked at her and wondered if it were a line from one of her pictures. Her beach house is next to Mollie's, and she let me in and mixed me one drink, with a good gin base, and she lit the cannel coal fire in her Adams fireplace and we sat holding hands, congenitally happy about nothing. I kissed her goodnight, running my fingers up and down her fine back, and she remained as expressionless as a wooden Indian.

At the door (it came off a clipper ship, Mandy said, solid teak, with a Yale lock) she said simply, "I love you, Johnny." I wanted to come back, but she closed the door and I stood there a moment and said softly what Walter would have said: "No dice . . ."

Mike was excited by the success of the test. Later in his hotel cottage he was very tired. He shuffled through his mail, not opening it. There was a card from Saks Beverly Hills. He read it, feeling very sleepy:

Dear Sir, Mr. Henry Kamp Matts has given your name as reference to our credit department. Will you please fill in the following questions and return to us . . .

He didn't know anybody named Matts. He threw the card in the wastebasket and went to bed without even brushing his teeth. He slept badly, waking a lot and turning from side to side, and just before dawn decided he was just an animal with desires that were most likely not worth all the bother it took to fulfill them. He smiled and turned over and slept calmly for three hours . . .

BOOK TWO

" 'It's a poor kind of memory that only works backwards,' the Queen remarked."

—LEWIS CARROLL

6

MAY 2d. Mike lifted his pen and looked down at the date he had just written on the blank check the flower clerk had handed him. Three weeks already since he had returned from Palm Springs? Three big, fat weeks full of lots of talking to the bankers. So much talk. He filled in the amount of his weekly flower bill and pushed the check across to the sweating clerk, who was trying to look cool and happy. Mike didn't pay many bills these days, but he felt it a point of honor to pay for flowers.

The clerk smiled a professional smile. "Hottest day of the year so far. Isn't like California at all."

"I've noticed it. It never is."

"Everything been all right so far, Mr. Zelsmith?" the clerk asked.

"Just dandy . . . Fine and dandy." He left the flower shop and went into the hotel bar and had a brandy and stood leaning against the polished wood thinking. People sat around him and toyed with drinks. He was involved in an emotional thing over which he had no control. He had always rather prided himself on his control, and now it was gone. All he cared about was his picture and seeing Mollie. Each in respect of the other was sparring for time, almost, he felt, too decently. Decent people certainly make a mess out of love.

They lunched in small places in the Valley full of bad cooking and then drove up onto the cliffs to see the city together. It was a pleasant agony of mutual comfort and attraction—the few hours they spent away from the prying, leering beach eyes, away from the whole daffy organization that was ZELSMITH PICTURES. They were, Mollie said, like high-school students necking in a borrowed car on a hillside.

91

Only they were, he suspected, much more clumsy about it. It was certainly unsatisfactory. There were times when Mollie was the little girl, and there were times when, warm, close together, it all seemed foolish and crude and rather badly played. But then, when alone, they needed each other and when they met the next day there was renewed hope written all over them, in big gobs of emotion. This hand holding was becoming irksome, this stolen kissing on public roads and this smearing lipstick over paper napkins carried in Mollie's handbag.

And yesterday afternoon Mollie had said, "All right, Mike, we can't talk any more about it. You're so sure and I don't know."

"You're such a kid you scare me."

Mollie bubbled into her little laugh. She held his hand and lifted it to her mouth and kissed it. "I'll have champagne on ice next time you come."

It was certainly the hottest day Mike could remember in California. He drove down the hill to the sea and turned north at the soda-pop signs. The beach was full of people undressing casually, and children were being stripped down to baby fat in cars, and very brown girls were pushing back shoulder straps and rubbing their flesh with oils. Far off the great wall of mountains blocked in the summer heat like those Japanese prints he once collected. The clouds were much too dramatic to be really art.

Mollie's Ark baked in the heat. He leaned against the door and pushed. The heat had made it harder to shove and when he got it open he was damp with effort. Mollie, in a blue and yellow cotton dress, was standing at the love bird cage changing the drinking water and watching the little creatures fluff up their feathers for relief from the heat. The sea danced in reflected rays on the windows.

"Hello, baby," he said. "It's a hot day."

She grinned. "I'm glad no screen tests today."

He went up to her, opening his tie and shirt collar, and took her in his arms. He was brutal now, and very sure he was making a big mistake. The heat boiled under the low-pitched roof and banged on his skull. He kissed her and her beautiful head fought him and then relaxed. She kissed him back and kept saying: "Mike, Mike."

"It's all right, baby—it's all right."

He wondered, kissing her, where all the wonderful talk of

92

lovers was. They could only cling to each other and kiss and he marched his hands over her back and hips, held her to him, and ached all over. She pulled loose and said, "I've got Cooks. Two bottles of it—champagne! You go into my room. See you in a moment."

The dogs clawed at the glass sun-porch door, from the outside. Mike went down the passage to the bedroom and the shades were drawn and a big blue fly bumbled against them. Mollie came in, the pins out of her hair, and put down a tray of wide wine glasses and two big bottles of Cooks. She was suddenly frightened, he knew, and shy. She looked very young and brave.

"Mike, open the bottles. I'll be right back."

He twisted the wire and foil top off one bottle and worked the cork till it popped, not at all as loud as he had expected. He poured two boiling, yellow glasses full. He took off his shoes and his jacket and lay down on the wide wall bed without removing the cover with the silly modern stripes on it. He regretted it all, and felt pity for Mollie. The bathroom door opened and she came out, nothing on. Her eyes were round and very frightened, but she tried to stand so tall and proud. Her breasts were small and perfect, her legs and arms and face were deeply tanned and polished, but the rest of her was milk white and as delicate as rare china.

He handed her a glass of the golden, bubbling wine and leaned on his elbows and smiled courage into her.

They drank deeply and she still stood there and he put down the glass and smiled at her a smile of hope and comradeship. Her choked little voice suddenly popped out, "Aren't you going to take off your socks, darling . . . ?"

Later, fast friends, they smiled tiredly, tenderly, at each other through the heat that hammered down on them from the ceiling of the wall bed. Mollie drank more champagne and she turned on her side with a rolling gesture and fingered his neck.

"It was all right, Mike. I'll never forget it as long as I live, and if I ever do I'm a tramp and you can kick the ass off me!"

"That's romantic talk."

"It is to me."

"You're talking too much, Mollie."

"My life has been a lot of talking."

He lit two cigarettes and pulled back one drape and the

wet salt air from the sea ran over them. They lay and smoked, close, just touching like the feathers in an angel's wings touch. Just ghost touching, they watched the smoke rise. When one bottle was gone they opened the other. He leaned over and kissed the inside of her ear and blew on it and she giggled. He was no longer at all sorry, no longer unsure. She placed his hand on her mouth and kissed it a long time.

"I'm a deeply grateful little girl," she said, and went on:

> "Some say the world will end in fire,
>   Some say in ice.
> From what I've tasted of desire
> I hold with those who favor fire."

"Look, baby, we're doing all right without the poetry."

There was a lot more to May. Mike spent as much time as he had free at the Ark. They laughed like spoiled children and were very tender and loved each other very much. They talked till their eyeballs ached, and they did away with a lot of Cooks champagne.

"No crumbs," Mollie said.

It was an expression her mother had used when one gave everything to something—held nothing back.

"No crumbs," Mike said, holding her head in his hands and pulling on her hair and pressing her neck tight in his fingers at the base of the skull.

They bathed together in the sea and rubbed each other with big towels. They drank champagne all the time.

"Cooks," Mollie said proudly. It was the best she knew and she trembled with pleasure at everything.

He saw her now as no one had seen her—the true tenderness of her, the small girl in her, the frightened child expecting each time to be a failure and being so overjoyed when she wasn't. He saw her cry and held her to his heart, and he pitied her because she was human and would one day die.

He saw her secret side; the pride, the sureness of herself in many things. The freak habits of womanhood that no man can ever understand; the weeping moments when all women think they *give* and never *get*. Once they fought as to who loved whom the most. She began to shiver as if in high fever and her mouth twitched, and he could not stop her shaking. She was a stranger who stared numbly out at him. But it passed when he poured brandy into her, a full half glass.

They liked to lie together on a big beach chair on the sun deck, holding each other closely and talking nonsense and love and the future, speaking very low. There was about her something odd he could never get hold of. In the middle of the fullest moment she could say, "It will be real some day. Always you'll be here by me then."

"I'm here now."

She was very intense, as at some serious business, in her love making. He found her like nothing that had ever been before. All her faults he excused; there was so much of her that he took and enjoyed, and he made her over slowly. "Acres of little girl," he used to say, "and all mine."

She liked to cook for him. She had many cookbooks and mixed up odd, experimental messes and cooked up dishes that he could hardly swallow. He took digestive pills and praised her efforts. She used too much olive oil, and she liked Mexican food of corn meals and sticky mixtures. Her cheeses and stews were mysteries. He said they were fine and ate them gladly.

She dressed like a girl of twelve and looked very fine in frills and dirndls and childish blouses.

He loved her; without reserve, without a doubt, and when the last bit of Alice was gone from him he would marry her . . .

"Gene cried over the phone when I told him I had filed for divorce."

"I can't be sorry for him, Mollie. Nobody would be sorry for me if you went off with someone else. It's the sex war. We're enlisted for life."

She laughed very loud and stuck out her tongue.

Late in May, Mike moved out of the big modern house on the shoreline and took a small cottage behind the Beverly Hills Hotel. He liked to work at night. And John was busy writing. Alice had not protested. She had come in as the last bag was packed and Mike was wondering which shoes to take along.

"Moving out?"

"Yes, Alice. I can't stay here."

"You don't have to go, Mike."

"Maybe not. I've got a girl."

95

"I know that too."

He bent over and picked up two pairs of shoes he didn't need. When he stood up he said, "Oh?"

"It's all over town. I like Mollie. I mean, I don't hate her guts. I'm sorry for her."

"Why sorry?"

"Because you'll make her unhappy, and she isn't tough enough to take it, like me."

"I didn't make you unhappy, Alice. It's just that we haven't got it any more."

"You'll be back, Mike, and I'll always be around to prove that home is where you go and they let you in."

Mike sat down and snapped a suitcase shut. "You understand me, but you don't know me."

"Yes I do. You think if you stay and Papa gives you the money to make a picture you'll be a pimp living with a woman to get money out of her."

"Something like that." Mike nodded.

"So you're going away, and if Papa doesn't give you the money, you'll have saved your pride."

"I never said I wasn't a proud guy."

"Papa will cut off the bank loans right away if you go. Don't be a dope, Mike. Stay here with me. Have your girl. It can't last. In the end we're kind of doomed to have each other. Maybe we deserve each other."

"I don't get you, Alice. I'll be damned if I do."

Alice folded her arms. He was sorry for her. Hell, he was sorry for every sensual sonofabitch alive who got himself into a mess like this.

"I'll take you, Mike, on any terms, that's all."

He stood up and picked up a bag. "I don't know how it's going to turn out. I don't know."

Alice held a cheek toward him. "Kiss me good-by, Mike."

He kissed her cheek lightly. Her face was hot to the touch of his mouth and her long fingers ice cold as she gripped his hand. He went out feeling a heel, a lousy, no-good heel. If he could only get rid of that core of moral guilt that had been built into him at conception; if he could only bang around and not fall in love and not give a good Goddamn; but then his ego came to his defense; it whispered, "If you were like that and didn't have those values, you stupid bastard, you wouldn't feel and be and do as you have done.

You wouldn't be Mike Zelsmith, the great talent, the man who has showed them all."

"Damn you, ego," Mike answered back. "Maybe I'd be better off being a sixty-buck-a-week jerk in the prop department and living with Mollie in a cheap cottage in Tarzana."

"And," said the ego, "a hell of a chance you'd have to meet Mollie then. . . . She isn't a valley housewife feeling out cheap tomatoes in a Safeway Market."

"A fine mess you got me into!"

"Self-pity!" shouted the ego in joy. "That's right, feel sorry for yourself, when half the people in the world would sell their souls to be in your shoes."

"Where do I put them now? All right, don't tell me . . . you have a low sense of humor."

"Beg pardon?" said the Chinese houseboy, and Mike saw he was standing in the driveway and the Chinese boy was putting his bags into the open Buick.

"Nothing," Mike said. "I'll send for the rest of the stuff. And I counted the scotch, so don't give a ball."

"Yes, Mr. Zelsmith," said the Chinese boy, very deadpan, knowing Mike Zelsmith would never count the scotch.

The bank was very polite about it. They really liked him at the bank, Mike knew that, but they didn't run it, except as stooges in well-pressed tailoring using six per cent in as deadly a war as machine guns.

"You see," the old-young man said to Mike, "we must follow the SEC procedure on all loans. We must have approval of the finished script."

Mike grinned. "Well, and when I do hand you a script you keep finding something wrong with it until I get tired. No, thanks. I'll make a picture. I'll sell some old film to TV. I'm converting frozen funds in Europe into cash. I'll make some kind of a picture, somehow, and you can do me a favor?"

"Of course."

"Tell my father-in-law, when he dies I'll mate my dogs on his grave. He's got a death complex, hates to think of being buried."

"I doubt if I can deliver the message, Mr. Zelsmith."

"That's all right," Mike said rising. "He knows what I think about him."

He walked out of the bank like a man almost without a worry in the world. Except perhaps that Mollie would want to cook dinner for him.

7

MIKE swung his heavy black-rimmed glasses off his broken nose and shook his head. He was sitting on the bed in John Fennel's hotel room, a pad of paper on his lap, writing quickly many figures with a short pencil stub. He threw the pad aside.

"There isn't any real money in this town, John. It's all fairy money, phantom cash. Doesn't really exist. If you make five thousand a week you get a bit of colored paper and after agent, withholding tax, motion-picture relief, and a few other bites, your agent or business manager shows some low figures in a book. But you can't spend it. Real money, only bartenders see it. Wet silver on a polished bar."

Walter came in carrying some sheets of paper and handed them to Mike, and sat down by John's side and helped himself to a drink from the tray. Mike looked over the sheets of paper quickly, getting at a glance their complicated message.

"That's all, Walter?"

"That's it. You sure the bank can't change their minds?"

Mike waved a big fist at him. "No dice. I'll get the money somehow. I have six pictures to sell to TV. And I should get at least a half million on money frozen in England on pictures released there."

Walter said, "M.Z., you know what your bank balance is as of this morning?"

Mike turned to John and grinned. "You guess?"

John shook his head. "No idea."

Walter put down his glass. "One hundred and seven dollars and thirty-four cents."

Mike smiled. "So I'm not broke?"

Walter went on. "You owe the income tax people for back taxes one hundred thousand, seven hundred, and fifty-seven dollars. Rent on the beach house and hotel bills and bar bills all past due . . . and . . ."

Mike held up a hand. "Never mind the details. I need at least a million more than I can raise to make this picture."

He stood up and smiled at John. "You see why it takes me so long to make a picture? I've got to turn society boy and go out and raise the cash. I've got to get drunk with rich oil men and play gin rummy with the big bookies. I've got to charm, sexually, old ladies with inherited wealth. And rich fathers with daughters who think they can act are going to let me smoke their cigars."

Mike threw himself down on the bed, locked his arms behind his head, and looked up at the ceiling. When he spoke again his voice had lost its edge of humor. John thought the big man on the bed was going to weep. He didn't.

"They think they've got me now. The whole town, the industry, all saying, 'Mike Zelsmith, we got the bastard by the short hair now. Making that artistic crap of his, getting critic's awards, well you see where he is now, can't raise enough money to make a newsreel short.'" Mike sat up suddenly. "For Christ sake, you guys letting me wallow in self-pity! Give me a big drink and I'll figure things out! Walter, get the TV people on the phone and dump the pictures . . . whatever they'll give, but in cash. John, break down the screenplay into a short treatment cutting out the big sets and all that mob scene stuff. We'll just shoot it in master scenes with a narrator. That will save us a lot of expensive footage. A narrator covers a lot of ground you don't have to shoot. I'll see you all around ten tonight, I'm having dinner with Mollie. And go easy on charging drinks here. I've got to pay this hotel bill, some day."

Walter put back the extra ice cube he was going to put in the glass, and John took a very small gulp of his whisky. He wondered if he could get his flat in London back from the people who had sublet it. He hadn't heard from Mandy in two days . . .

There was one thing that really troubled Mike. Mollie wanted everybody to know she was in love and living at it. She wore his shirts, made love to him in public, and told the girls of the beach bums and certain special friends the exciting discoveries of their lovemaking. She walked around these days with a keyed-up look, like a hunting leopard; she had a vitality half inspired, half drugged about the whole thing. And yet Mike began to suspect she was dissatisfied about certain aspects of their life together. She remained lonely because he liked to work at night and lived at his hotel cottage.

She was fully possessive, he discovered, the way a mother is of an only child. She wanted every moment accounted for. They could not live as man and wife because of the town. His time belonged to his project, and, too, Mike was a man of brooding solitary moments when he wanted to sit alone in his hotel cottage and think things out. He did not want to be mothered or have his headaches patted away. He wanted this thing to be adult and deep and passionate. And free of the usual clinging, cloying sadness of his past love affairs.

"Thank God you don't brood over everything, Mollie," he used to say to her.

"Of course not, darling."

"Don't think about it so much."

"I never knew anything like it."

"Remember Proust saying . . . 'Nothing is important until you remember it.' Don't live too far forward, Mollie. You'll be all alone out there."

"You're right, Pappy. Let's go for a swim."

That was the day Mike discovered he couldn't make the picture based on John's book.

Mike came into the hotel bar looking for John Fennel.

"John, I can't pay you the next installment due you on the book."

"It doesn't matter, Mike."

"I've got to stop the production. I've got to make a cheap, fast picture for money."

John nodded, "Yes."

"John, can you write a thriller?"

"I suppose so."

"Knock me out an ouline of something I can shoot quick with documentary feeling, so I don't have to build sets."

"There's a story Walter told me of a big gambler who lost a hundred thousand in Nevada at cards. When they said they would kill him if he didn't pay up, he went back to his wife, seems she had money, and he planned to kill her to inherit her estate."

"What's the payoff?"

"He fell in love with her, desperately again, but he couldn't call off the hoodlums he hired to kill her."

"They knocked her off?"

"Yes, and he got half her estate under the California property law."

"It's downbeat." Zelsmith frowned, signaling the bar waiter. "Who you rooting for? A dame who gets killed? No. Work on it and keep the girl alive. Put in a nosey newspaperman who saves her in the end and loves her. Have the mob kill the gambler on his way to save his wife. Get it?"

"I guess so."

Zelsmith stood up and patted John on the back. "I know it stinks. Let's get this thriller made and I'll have enough to make your book."

"I suppose this means Walter and Mollie are off the payroll too?"

Zelsmith looked closely at John and sucked on his lips as the drink was set before him. He pulled off his glasses and looked at John with tired slits of eyes. "I've got to form a new company on the cash I got from TV. The old one is folded. John, I like you. You've done real things, not sat on your ass all your life making up things that never could happen. See me through this—we'll do big ones yet."

He nodded, seemed to think, almost said something more, thought better of it, and patted John's shoulder again.

"Get me a breakdown of *The Gambler's Wife* in a few days. Good title?"

"I'd rather call it *The Gambler*."

"We'll fight about it later. Bye."

John went up to his room, sat down and lit his pipe and looked over the desk loaded with its hundreds of pages of treatments and outlines and rough-draft screenplays he had done on his novel. It seemed such a waste. He thought of all the hundreds of writers in the town who sat night and day and ground out the words, and most of it was never used. The futility shocked him. He remembered Mike's remarks about the olive trees of Beverly Hills.

He picked up the phone and got Walter at the Club Galla, the place Walter usually spent a few hours a day drinking and talking.

"Hello, John, what's the uproar?"

"I suppose you know about Mike dropping the big picture."

"You should read the gossip columns more."

"He really in trouble?"

"Don't let it bother you, John. He's a clever dog even if he is a genius. Alice hasn't walked out on him yet. She still lives in the big house. He'll make it up with her." Walter

101

laughed far off. "He isn't like me, John. He's a genuine artist, which means he may crawl for a major picture release and first money. I'm betting Alice doesn't walk back to Papa."

"This puts Mollie in a spot."

"Mollie still has her witch doctor."

John hoped she had much more than that.

Mollie Binning had no formal religion any more— "Nothing beyond giving Christmas gifts"—Walter used to say. She believed in kindness and goodness and that everybody could get along with everyone else if they tried. She was no fool but she trusted people. Whenever life had clouted Mollie hard on the ear she had retreated into a kind of personal mystic outlook on life that had no pattern, that is until she met Mrs. Henry through the kindness of her friend Mandy Rye. Mandy swore by Mrs. Henry's control of the universe.

Mrs. Henry was a practicing mystic on a sound commercial basis. She kept a flat in Hollywood and here came many women to listen to Mrs. Henry explain it was all planned and all open to the inner mind of Mrs. Henry for direct help and cure. Mrs. Henry felt things. Things came to her. When trouble with Gene developed, Mrs. Henry talked to Mollie and explained to her that she could help her by her inner prayers and guidance. Mrs. Henry did not follow one school. She loved them all: the yogi, the Buddhist, the soul scientists of all faiths. All merged in Mrs. Henry's powerful mind and vision, she told Mollie, and while Mollie was under her protection all would be well; *if* Mollie obeyed the warnings and signs of Mrs. Henry.

"I can only help you if you believe I can help you," said Mrs. Henry. "I have helped others, for the life force is in me. I can help you, *but* . . ."

Some things worried Mollie and some of these she told to Mrs. Henry, who took the broad view. Sin and evil, illness and madness, all could be controlled by the powers of Mrs. Henry's life force—*if*."

At first the "ifs" bothered Mollie and she really didn't go for the screwy stuff, but as she felt herself lean more and more toward Mrs. Henry in her times of crisis, she began to put some spiritual and mental faith in Mrs. Henry. Mollie was amused, then puzzled, and then tried not to give a damn. If Walter talked badly to her, if she had no money, Mrs. Henry saw great shining success in the future. It was hard to really pin Mrs. Henry down, Mollie found out—she was an able and shrewd woman. Mollie laughed about it, but she used to come home from a trip to Mrs. Henry's Hollywood apartment shot full of some vague messages and a rather odd, taut optimism, and carrying three or four sheets of yellow, lined paper on which Mrs. Henry had written out, in pencil, a chart of events for the week. Mollie said they were whacky—but funny and for laughs.

MONDAY—*a good day. Full of electric elements. The afternoon will be very high and a good time to get things done.*

TUESDAY—*a gray beginning, but building up from noon on. Do not do any business on this day. Certain shapes trouble me. The life force is weak for you today.*

WEDNESDAY—*this is the peak of the week for you. You will be very happy and something will happen to widen this joy.*

At first Mollie would hide these form sheets for the soul from Mike, but of late she grinned and talked to him of Mrs. Henry and her system, and then showed him the weekly tout sheet. It certainly would be fun if it could work.

"I knew everything couldn't be right," she said, taking the yellow sheets from the worktable drawer. "Mrs. Henry said—listen—'A day for only quiet inner thinking. Nothing else. Any energy projected on anything will be wasted.' Sometimes she really comes close to something."

Mike shook his head. "Look, baby, I don't mind you keeping a tame soothsayer, and she can look in chicken entrails or make sacred circles in human bone dust, but hell —don't fool yourself—this is the twentieth century, a lousy era of enlightenment. You can't run your life on pencil markings!"

"Sometimes when I don't follow Mrs. Henry I get into trouble."

"Well, how do you explain all the trouble you get into when you follow her sacred scrolls? Like wrecking your car again."

"I only think I follow her advice. Maybe I only do part of what she says." She grinned, "I guess you're right. It's all hooey."

"Scientists have proved again and again this is all the bunk."

"I paid up for a month. I'll drop it after that."

"Mrs. Henry is a very clever bitch. Don't leave your brains on her doorstep and walk around with a rebuilt job she's made for you. What does she charge for this spirit-booster service?"

"Twenty dollars every time I see her."

"That's better than most professional psychoanalysts are paid."

"Mike, Mrs. Henry had a great feeling this morning about you!"

"I doubt it. I wasn't sending off any sparks."

"She felt something about Washington and you making a picture to cost three million dollars. A huge success. Something bigger than has ever happened to you before came to her out of the blue."

He looked at her and shook his head and went into the kitchen and dug up yesterday's newspaper. He brought it back to her and said, "Listen, Mollie, Walter invented a yarn about me and Washington and fed it to the columns. It's a build-up for the gambling story I'm going to make."

Mollie was shaken, but only for a moment. "But you've been thinking of getting Washington help?"

"No, it's all a brainstorm of Walter's."

Mike himself admitted he wasn't free of some little fetishes of luck and fortune. He would always fold his trousers a certain way and lay them on a chair with the belt hanging down. He always rolled up his socks and put them into his shoes after taking them off. He didn't really believe in these things but he never went against them. And when a black cat ran across his path he joked—but felt uncomfortable.

Mike spent a lot of time figuring costs of his quickie. When his head spun after a few hours of figuring, he had a few drinks.

The old-time director in the hotel bar was always happy to see Mike.

"I've become kind of an old bore around here, Zelsmith, but I know you don't mind sharing a little Irish whisky with me. And you don't let the town fool you like so many people who come here for a quick one with the industry. That novelist fellow who just went back failed to get a screenplay out of his book, never bothered to learn what a screenplay was. I hear he gave an interview in New York that really blasted the motion picture as literature. Well, sour grapes. This isn't a bad town. In fact I think it's a pretty good town. It's been good to me in my time. Suppose it doesn't want me any more, or any of us. That's its right. But I've been in a lot of places in my life and this town is all right. Climate? I like it. Scenery? What I see is very pretty and people who like scenery say it's the best. People? Well, everybody likes whom he likes and if you make your own friends into a group here you can find any kind of people you want.

"Mind you, Zelsmith, I don't say there aren't any phonies and that a lot of the big brass isn't worthless, but in the main everybody works too hard in the industry. And everything evens out. The big shot is broke next year and the has-been sometimes gets a break again. Do they ever learn anything? The out-of-work studio head pan-handling ten-dollar bills in Romanoff's is going to be just as big a bastard when he becomes a big shot again. And the busted star is going to throw it around like a grasshopper again when she has a surprise hit picture . . .

"But that's human nature and a man who tries to change human nature is put together wrong. You change human nature and what are you producers going to make pictures about? You leave human nature alone and keep giving us love tragedies and passion killings and warped minds and fat slices of the full, happy life. Without human nature you don't have the lovers suffering or the full, happy life. The world needs both to keep amused.

"That was a very fine little girl you brought in the other evening. What a beautiful girl. Yes, sir, a mighty fine girl. I could see it at once. I've known a lot of women in my youth, married though I am and faithful at it. She's a fine girl. A thinking face, though, but I guess you don't mind. Craftsmen, artists, and writers I notice pick 'em like that. Thinking faces. Those sad eyes now, they're wonderful. Yet they look as if she has seen the skull beneath the skin, as the poet says. But don't listen to me, Zelsmith. I bet it's just all right for you and just what the doctor ordered.

"Every man has his type, you know. He'll go once and
105

he'll go twice and he'll come right back and pick the same kind of girl that's going to make happiness and trouble for him again. And you know why? I went through it in the old days before I was married. Why? Because between the excitement and the loving that's where it's best.

"A mighty fine girl. True beauty you're after, I can see. Not made beauty. I've found made beauty is so full of itself and the mirror you can't find the human being. A good face, a full face with a truth to it. And a drinking woman. I always liked a girl who could punish the booze . . ."

That was the night the bar ran out of Irish whisky and they had to drink Kentucky Bourbon.

Mike still lacked two hundred thousand dollars to make *The Gambler's Wife*. He had gotten together most of three hundred thousand dollars from part of the frozen money in England, from the TV sales of his old pictures, from a senile oil man. He had never made a five-hundred-thousand-dollar picture, but he had to now. And raise the rest of the money. He had no theater release, but they would bid for it once he finished it. He would star a broken-down actor who had once been box office, and Mollie. He would shock the world into making a great new star, overnight, when they saw Mollie. A director was a problem. He couldn't work with a hack. Perhaps he would have to direct it himself. He had never directed a picture before, but hell, he knew more about directing than any of them. He had cut and edited many of their mistakes together. He felt cheerful and full of hope. A "sleeper" they called these little pictures that paid off. It wasn't really as bad as he thought. He must stop telling John Fennel it was going to be a stinker. Mike Zelsmith didn't make stinkers. He stood at the bar and dreamed of the finished picture. It was, of course, perfect. He got pie-eyed and it released his tension . . .

"You're drunk," Mollie said.

"Roaring, baby," said Mike sitting down on the sofa.

"You can't hold it any more, darling."

"Been drinking with Ed, the old-time director."

"Isn't he washed up?"

"They say I am too, Mollie."

"You're no broken-down Mack Sennet character, like Ed."

"Who knows?"

He pulled her down on the sofa and kissed her. "What do I see in you, Mollie? Just a dame I love, that's all."

She grinned. "Who writes your dialogue, mister?"

8

IN the beginning of their relationship Mollie was greatly interested in their ideas about morality, about codes of conduct. They went into a long series of crucial ethical decisions. Mike felt they believed in honor, in *noblesse oblige*, in certain chivalries, in self-sacrifice that made them almost "belong to the lousy eighteenth century."

In Mollie a great deal of this seemed to rule her life, except on a sexual moral level, where she was a little uneven. Mike had rigid moral standards; he could never be unfaithful to a woman during any period of an honest personal relationship. He disliked people who did not abide by this code. Modern amorality, anything unscrupulous and promiscuous, he could not long excuse. Deceit was only a step lower than humiliation with him. Mollie was for him a believable human, a fallible, sympathetic person, a complex but fascinating individual.

They met in a great emotional tension, but he felt he had a subtle understanding of her thinking. They often carried on intricate experimentation with each other's ideas and ideals. He did think her almost perfect, but even her small faults, at least most of them, he thought charming.

Mike grew to know her very well on a trip to Spanish Hill. The trip had comic results and rather deep overtones. Mandy Rye and her many projects were part of Spanish Hill, an old mountain town about fifty miles inland from the coast. Here yearly was held, in an outdoor theater, a series of plays and dances on themes of early California. Mandy Rye sponsored part of this, and that year she had enlisted Mollie to design a stage production of an early California story.

Three days before the playing of the show they were to go up. Mike and Mollie, and Mandy, with John Fennel as the companion and escort. They were to start very early in the day, but Mandy was delayed by the packing of the wicker hamper of lunch. She showed up at Mollie's Ark at ten. She was dressed in red, that being her color for the day. She was driving a gift from her agent, a Buick convertible covered with yellow wood paneling, polished and waxed like old furniture. Her horn sounded outside and the dogs barked. Rose Steiner had promised to feed and walk them and change the *Los Angeles Times* twice under the love birds. Mollie was running around collecting items for the trip: her little red overnight bag, the extra sandals, and bathing suits. Mike and John had each packed some shirts, slacks, and ties and shared a mutual bag. No one knew what Mandy had in the back of the timbered Buick.

Mike looked at his watch. "Let's shove off!"

They started twice, once they had to back around and find a gas station. Mike had four bottles of pinch-bottle Haig and Haig, and when they were sure they were headed properly for Spanish Hill John, seated alone in the back, opened a fifth and handed around stiff drinks in paper cups. It was all very jolly and sloppy. Mike seated in front between the two women, saw the dry landscape flashing by and remembered location trips. They got along very well, stopping twice to let the girls, as Mike said, "spend a dime." They didn't open the wicker lunch basket but stopped for lunch at a roadside place with a barbecue pit, and had some fine steaks and more drinks. The car was a little too hot to touch after lunch, and when they had gone ten miles they found out there was a short circuit someplace in the wiring, because the dashboard began to smoke.

They stopped to watch the car smoke. John passed out more hard drinks. Everyone was a little high.

"Goddamnest thing isn't it?"

"Don't just stare," said Mollie.

"Let it burn." Mandy finished her drink and turned and rubbed her cheek against John's.

"Going to be a great day, huh?"

"Great start for it."

"Men ought to know cars."

"Not any more."

"Can we blow up?"

"If it hits the lousy gasoline."

"Here, try some more Haig and Haig."

"Damn it, John, my new outfit!"

"Stop moving around. Let's just sit here and die together."

"Dry up in the sun?"

"Turn to mummies in a sick auto."

"Some day they'll find us, stick us all in museums."

"Petrified forms of animal life."

"Found near Los Angeles."

Mike tossed away a paper cup. "Goddamn it. Let's be practical."

"Listen to the guy."

"Mandy, put something in his mouth."

"We can't sit here."

"Plenty of scotch. Keep us alive for six days, anyway."

"Don't want to live beyond that, anyway."

Mike said, "Let's look the car over."

"Practical-type guy."

"Let's pull out some wires."

"Which wires?"

"The machine age," said John. "The more expensive it is, the worse it performs."

"Anybody know anything about cars?" Mike asked.

Nobody did.

They couldn't seem to find a garage in this part of the road and as the dashboard smoked worse, Mike tore out some wires, which seemed to stop the smoking but also put the horn out of order.

It was a very jolly journey with the pinch bottle passing from mouth to mouth when they ran out of paper cups. Mandy was relaxed and a great deal of fun. She told them about her youth in a small California town when she had wanted to be a comic dancer, and had studied very hard, only Papa felt it was a waste of time. She told some very funny stories about Mike during her early days of pictures, and it seemed she spent her life undecided between suicide, Benzedrine, and a projected trip to Europe to buy old furniture.

At dusk they discovered that Mike had also pulled out the light circuit, and they rolled blindly into Spanish Hill just as the sun set, and found the hotel serving dinner. They left the car at the garage to be inspected, and put down their baggage in the two little cottages they had reserved on the hotel grounds. Each cottage had a bedroom, a sitting room dominated by silk screen prints of parrots in brilliant color, and a sort of half-kitchen. John and Mike were down as sharing one cottage, but that was nonsense as they were going to re-exchange the baggage later. Mandy took the bedroom, and John would take the sofa, a pillow, and a blanket in the living room of their cottage.

There were a lot of people in the industry in town. This was the big week at Spanish Hill, and a good place to get away to; not too formal or stuffy. John noticed that the director from Warners that once had a crush on Mollie was also there.

They had a big dinner of roast beef and Yorkshire pudding, and met a lot of people they had left town to escape, ". . . and who, most likely," Mollie said, "had left town to avoid us." Nobody paid too much attention to introductions because it was hard to tell who was with whom. They seemed to John a privileged, weird, and threatened society.

After dinner they sat in the lobby and listened to a Spanish band kick it around, and Mollie and Mandy changed for the open-air theater. Mollie wore a very tight chalk-white evening dress with white kid sandals trimmed with gold, and Mandy was tall in pale blue, showing the arms and shoulders of a powerful tennis player. She claimed she was suntanned almost to a point of being barred by the racial-minded hotel.

They drove into the hills, making up a party with some actors Mollie had once met through Gene, and the Warner director and his party, which included his two screen writers, who laughed very loud at their own jokes. Mike called them "the dismal young men on the flying trapeze . . ."

The show wasn't really very much, but as the cast was full of Broadway and Hollywood figures tossing in their time for free, everyone applauded very loud and afterward went backstage and drank a very warm champagne out of Woolworth kitchen glasses.

Later there was dancing at the hotel, but Mollie and Mike walked over the ridge of the town and looked down on the silver pines and the great crags.

"It's pretty good, isn't it, Mike? Well, how do you like me so far as a traveling companion?"

"No demerits so far, baby."

"Why do you always call me baby? Darling, sweetheart, dear, honey aren't copyrighted by anybody else."

"I never had a girl I called baby before."

"You mean you had girls you called darling, et cetera, and so forth?"

He kissed her. "Don't wear white evening gowns in the moonlight."

They walked back to their cottage and found a party going full blast. Mandy was drinking a little brandy. She had her I'm-a-damn-sight-better-than-you-are air on, from her last picture. John was sitting on the floor pouring pinch bottle into teacups and handing it around while talking to a young English actor who was just out of the R.A.F. and not sure just how one handled himself with people from the industry.

The director was there with his screen writers. There were parties going on all along the row of cottages, and a lot of cheering came from time to time from the hotel itself.

The director tried to push Mollie into a corner at once, and the screen writers told what a witty show they were writing. John had to send out for more ice, their little icebox was fresh out. It got real rowdy after midnight and Mandy began to cry and John and Mollie took her out and put her to bed in her bedroom. They tucked her in and went out, leaving the door open. Back in their cottage Mike began to break up the party, and the English actor went on telling him how it is to fly a plane. He had been flying at Dunkirk on the real bad day when they took the men off the beaches in rowboats and speedcraft.

"How was it over Dunkirk during the worst of it?" Mike asked.

"Cloudy," the English actor said.

"Thanks," Mike said. "I didn't know."

The director and his writers didn't want to leave, but they did at last and Mike found three wet bathing suits on the pale green sofa and crackers broken all over the rug. The hotel pool was still lit up.

When everybody was gone, Mike smiled at Mollie who went in and had a shower and came out barefooted—hair down—and asked him for the heel of one of the pinch bottles. It was like the first time all over again.

John was feeling very good when he got back to his cottage. The bedroom door was closed so he put on just his pajama bottoms, unfolded the blanket, and rolled his head around until it made the proper kind of dent in the pillow, and he lay back and closed his eyes. He could hear the wind like surf in the pines and the hiss of tires on the driveway, and he could smell the fir needles as they had smelled outside Boston on his uncle's farm, and he felt young and American again. The sooner he got the hell out of California the better. Maybe he wouldn't go back to England but live on the family farm and write a book about California. Only he didn't know anything about California except that everything was a big party all the time and that Mike couldn't pay him, and Mandy showed no desire to let him make physical love to her. He had never met a woman like this before, a woman who said she was in love with him and who didn't seem to care what it did to him. Maybe he thought love in California is an illusion, it looks like love and inside there isn't anything.

He turned on his side and tried to sleep thinking of the pine trees and the smell of night odors. The bedroom door opened and Mandy came out wearing a low-cut dark blue nightgown and showing most of her large beautiful breasts.

"I can't sleep," she said, rubbing her eyes.

"I can," John said.

"I'm no good away from my own bed." She stood tall, expressionless, like a lost child.

"It's getting cold, Mandy. Better go back."

"Come in and talk to me."

"Oh, all right, but just for a little while."

She turned at the door and said with that expressionless face of hers, "And bring your pillow."

John picked up his pillow and followed her into the bedroom.

John got two cork-tip cigarettes later and they lay smoking and listening to the party noises all around, to a late radio and the last music from the hotel. Insects plunked against the screens and Mandy turned over and mashed out the last cigarette. She smelled of whisky and cigarette smoke and bath soap and Mandy.

"Huh?" she asked. "Am I your girl now?"

"Uh-huh," John said.

She turned over and went to sleep. The music stopped at last, and when John turned over it was morning, and Mike was talking very loud in the living room.

Mandy was still asleep, so John, Mike, and Mollie went into town looking for ham and eggs. It was not much of a town—a main street, steep sidewalks, and lots of green gardens. They found a popular local eating place smelling of fly spray and home baking, and ate ham and eggs and drank good strong coffee and read warm newspapers that had lain on the sidewalk since dawn.

They were all sun- and wind-burned and they felt gritty and very much at ease with each other. The three of them had always liked each other anyway, and Mike, free of the industry and his social habits, was very amusing.

"You can't prove it by me today," he said, "that man is the only congenitally unhappy animal."

Smoking after-breakfast cigarettes—the best of the day— they went back to the hotel and got a tray of orange juice, coffee, and rolls for Mandy. Mike and John went to the cottage to shave and change to bathing suits. The pool water was rather cold, so they just jumped in for a breath-taker, then lit cigarettes and waited for the girls. Mollie and Mandy came down in tight bathing suits. Mollie drew a few whistles, but they were used to that. A lot of cops down at the Plume Café, where they dropped in evenings for beers, used to wait just to see Mollie walk in.

The girls took a brisk swim and then came over and joined them. They all had drinks sent out from the bar, and the English actor and the director, and the actors who were friends of Gene's, came out. They all had lunch at poolside. It was very hot Spanish cooking and Mollie asked about the chili and wrote down how it was made on the back of a review of John's book from the *Kansas City Star*. He wondered what it was doing in his terrycloth robe.

They all had a nap after lunch in the cottages, Mandy and John making love, Mike and Mollie in the other room played Dixieland jazz for the English actor on the portable recorder. Then the actor had to leave to meet his wife who acted in the late afternoon show.

They all slept in the warm closeness of the day until a breeze at dusk came down from the hills to awaken them. They missed the afternoon pageant about monks and Indians, and dressed for dinner, which they had after a long trip to a private club that kept out oil millionaires and New Dealers. They had stuffed duck, wild rice, and special Southern breads and a lot of exotic drinks made with cherry flavor the barman insisted they try. Looking out of the great panes of glass, they could see the range of the far-off Rockies, or what Mollie said were the Rockies. It was blue and lonely outside, and warm and cozy inside. A band played later and Mollie danced with everyone. They almost missed the show on the outdoor stage that night, but they got into their seats just as it started. "It's pretty historic," Mollie said, "but not very interesting." And instead of going backstage for the drinks, they all went to the hotel cottages and had a real big party that ended in somebody being tossed in the hotel pool.

Mollie laughed a lot and John remembered going into the half-kitchen for soda and finding her backed into the ironing board by the director; she put out her arm and pulled John's ear as he passed and kissed him tenderly and said, "Tell Mike I love him."

Then she went back to talking to the director about Jack Warner.

This party didn't break up till dawn, and they smiled at each other and went to sleep at once. By the time they were ready to go home, it was all on a very solid basis between them and John was ready to take bets it was all going to work out all around. Mollie's stage designs, everyone said, were big and colorful. "Real big."

The yellow Buick had been repaired, at least they hoped so, and John collected from Mike and went to pay the bills. As they waited while he stood politely by, the English actor talked to the hotel clerk.

"But it couldn't have been six pitchers of beer. I remember ordering four and then one more. But six, really . . ."

"The waiter's slips show six."

"Well, I only make it five, but if he says six I'll pay for six, but there will be no tip for him."

"Just as you want it, sir," said the clerk politely.

Which made John wonder about the English actor and if he should look him up in town. The car drove very well on the way home, and they sat grouped around the car radio singing the popular songs. None of them had any real voice, but they felt tired and happy. It would have been perfect, but twenty miles out on a road where nothing lived, or cared to, the right rear tire suddenly blew. Mandy skillfully brought the speeding car to a stop and they got out and each one kicked at the flat tire in turn. There was nothing but dust on the horizon.

Mandy flagged a ride on a passing oil rig and said she'd send back a garage crew, or tow car, or somebody to change the tire. Mandy was wearing a big ruby ring and talked very flip to the truck drivers.

John and Mike saw the only thing to do was to change the tire themselves, and they hoped the spare had air in it. They changed the tire and tightened the wheel lugs, hoping they were doing it right. They washed up in a thermos of cold tea and finished the last of the pinch bottle. They drove on slowly and found Mandy in a tow car coming toward them. They gave the tow-car man five dollars who spit tobacco on the roadside out of a toothless mouth and said he bet they were "really kicking it around." Near town John found almost a whole bottle of Teacher's way down in the back seat and they all had a swig. They had just finished drinking when a police siren sounded and they pulled up as a red-faced village cop got off his motor bike and came over to them.

"Well," he said, stripping off his gloves.

No one answered because it was worse if they caught you smelling of liquor.

"This is a township and it's posted twenty-five miles an hour. You were doing thirty-eight."

Mandy nodded and Mollie tried to get the bottle of Teacher's covered with a car robe. The policeman wrote out his ticket and made Mandy get out onto the road and walk back ten feet and read the sign. Mandy nodded. "It says twenty-five." And the policeman said he hoped it was a lesson and they could mail it in, it would be twenty-five dollars. Fifty the next time.

"Dirty fascist," said Mandy very low.

They drove on, a little sad. They finished the rest of the Teacher's, and by the time they got to Mollie's Ark, Mollie was fast asleep on Mike's shoulder and Mandy had stomach pains.

9

The movie sets seemed very small to John as he followed Mike and Walter Chase through the cluttered sound stage, echoing hammers, hitting wooden forms. It wasn't much of a sound stage, an old one and a dusty independent lot that rented out space to corporations which rarely made pictures but had fancy names like Moonglow Productions, Sensational Films, Ltd., Grand-Glory Enterprises, Stallion-Condor Films, and one that just said: Swartz Films, T.V.

115

The sets were small and crowded and looked flimsy. They smelled of mice, mold, wallpaper paste, and machine oil.

Mike was talking to the cameraman, a short little Italian who smoked the smallest cigar stubs in the world. The little Italian kept nodding and rubbing his freshly shaved jug of a face that already was covered with a blue-black beard.

"Gotcha, Mr. Zelsmith, gotcha."

"Don't underlight, but don't give me the flat documentary either. And no more corny pull-backs from objects. No mirror shots either. No breaking glass."

"Gotcha."

"We'll be ready to roll in a week. This Miss Binning is something special. Figure out some startling angles and we'll talk it over."

"You bet, Mr. Zelsmith."

Mike turned to John. "A good cutter, a good cameraman, that's what you need. And a good story. Screw the banks. Mollie been studying her lines?"

"She doesn't seem happy with them," John said.

Mike said to Walter, "Stick to her the next few nights and make her give it a real reading. John and I have to make changes in the script. Mandy take the part?"

"She says it's written on a postage stamp, that dance-hall hostess, but for you and John, all right."

"Keep Mollie working, Walter. I'll polish the scenes with her alone before we roll a camera. Tell her not to worry."

Walter said he'd try. "Gotcha," the cameraman said to someone . . .

Mollie sat in a dressing gown, her golden hair up in a tight ribbon, the pot of black coffee at her elbow, listening to Walter read the dialogue. She only half heard it. Why was she here and why was she going to try and say those words in front of machines that photographed and recorded it? She had fallen in love with a guy she could at last respect, someone like her father, and now suddenly here she was being what she didn't feel she could ever be or do, and yet Mike, who had not been able to see her for three days, was so sure she could do it.

"My head whirls, Walter. Give it a rest."

Walter put his face into his coffee cup then and looked up frowning. "What's the matter with you, Mollie? Any dope from Central Casting could walk through this part."

"This means a lot to Mike, doesn't it?"

116

"M.Z. has built this whole thing around you. Look, don't even try to act when you read the lines, just remember they'll be shot in little bits, a few lines at a time, and they'll paste them together. You don't have to be Duse, or Helen Hayes, or Cornell for this."

"All right, where do I start?"

She read for two hours and at the end of that time she felt that perhaps she could do it. Walter, remembering the screen tests, nodded from time to time and got up to act a bit of business for her. He was sure Mike could make something out of all this. After another hour they began to snarl at each other and Walter wanted a drink and Mollie said she had locked up the liquor. He became very angry; his nerves were rubbed tender by these night readings. He made a long speech, none of which he remembered later, and Mollie told him to go to hell and locked herself with her script in her bedroom.

He tried to open the locked liquor cabinet with a knitting needle and left to find some drink in some of the bottle clubs on the Strip . . .

John had not found writing a screenplay easy work. It was a complicated medium and so patterned and ringed in by camera formula that he had difficulty getting any real feeling into it. But he worked hard. Zelsmith never started work on the script until late in the evenings, and so their nights were battles of scenes and characters and story line. John, like Mollie, could not change Zelsmith's night habits, so he worked along with him. He became very much interested in screenwriting and felt he was making some progress in it.

When alone or not out with Mandy Rye, he liked to work very late by the open window of his hotel on sheets of blue paper, hoping Zelsmith would not ring six or eight times before morning with an idea. He usually did.

It was a clear, soft, focused night and the traffic below hissed on the road, and John was making headway with the scene. He was remembering how to margin speeches, and to keep his camera action flowing, when there was a knock at the door. It was the night clerk who had been ordered to relay no more phone messages.

"There is a young man downstairs. Doesn't give his name. We can't let him up this late."

117

John broke his mood away from the screenplay and said, "I'll come down."

He tied his robe tighter and followed the clerk down to the desk. A tall, square, young man with short, cropped black hair and a big onion of a nose was standing by the desk chewing on a long fingernail.

"Yes?" said John.

"John Fennel? Walter . . ." He waited till the clerk was out of earshot. "Walter is in trouble. My name is Ironspinner."

"What happened?"

"Picked up for drunk driving and going through a signal. Wrecked the whole front of his car."

"Is he all right?"

"He's in the Lincoln Heights Jail. And he'll need bail in the morning."

"But he's all right?"

The man smiled. "Loaded. He's been on the town all night picking fights. Well, all his friends warned him moving in with Binning would get him."

"Thank you . . . I'll take care of it in the morning, Mr. —?"

"Ironspinner, Bertie Ironspinner. Good-by."

John shook hands with a well-cared-for set of fingers and the man walked slowly out of the hotel.

John turned to the desk clerk. "What time is it?"

"Twenty after three."

"Wake me at six, will you?"

The clerk made some neat marks on a bit of paper. "You can't get into the jail until nine-thirty, Mr. Fennel."

John gave him a cold look—he hoped as cold as he could make it—and went back upstairs. His work mood was over. He dozed till the desk buzzed him.

Walter grinned when he saw John and the lawyer that Mike had sent over. The fine was two hundred dollars and a stiff warning.

Once out in the sunlight, Walter blinked, yawned, and said, "Thanks, John. It was rather interesting in there. People are still people, even with fleas on them."

"That was pretty childish, getting drunk and cracking up your car because you and Mollie overstudied."

"Rather not talk about it. I guess she'll forgive me. Have you any money left?"

"Some."

"Let's buy Mollie something foolish."

They settled for a box of dog candy. The clerk assured them all the best dogs in California were eating it. "It's very new, this idea of candy for dogs. They say it has Hadacol in it."

Walter nodded. "That's just the thing for Mollie's dogs."

They ate lunch in the Scandia on the Strip. Walter said they could call it lunch, but it was really mostly drinks. They were saving their big meal until they got to Mollie's so that the three of them could eat together. Walter rolled the ice around in his drink and looked at John.

"I'm not going to talk too much about what just happened. But I'm going to tell you something that happened to me when I first hit this town. I had a promise of a job, but I had to wait till they were ready to see me. I rented a room with my last five bucks and I sat down to wait. I was hungry and I was excited. I walked around a lot, but I didn't know anybody, that is anybody who would talk to me. Two days later I was still waiting. Do you know what it is in this town to know nobody, to sit in a dusty rented room and wait?"

"I hear it's done a lot."

"I know a guy who waited three years. I didn't wait that long, but maybe it's worse when it's a short wait. I stole milk off steps early in the morning, and once I got a bag of rolls in a hallway. But I was hungry. A week passed and I felt the room closing in on me, getting smaller like that bed in the story by Wilkie Collins. Did you ever know the exact moment you were going insane?"

John signaled for two more drinks. "Once, in Cairo, but it didn't last, maybe twenty minutes."

"One morning at ten o'clock I felt a crack, a loud crack in my head, just a sound of something snapping, and I knew unless I did something, talked to somebody, I was ready for the nut hatch."

Walter waited till the waiter had put down the drinks. "Hit yourself on the head, breathe under water, and hate the world at the same time, that's the feeling. I didn't have enough money to even go to a movie. I hunted in an old raincoat and I found one dime. One tarnished dime. I walked over to the Farmers' Market; the tourists buying trash, and the movie stars buying the extra-thick English

119

lamb chops, and me, I bought three Mexican jumping beans for my dime. I took them home and put them in a plate and I named them Mac, Joe, and Montez. I figured one was a girl, maybe.

"I talked to them. I polished them, and they performed for me. Late at night when I was hungry and it was too early to go out and steal milk, I used to carry on long, long talks with my beans. They used to listen and once in a while pop up in the air politely. They were very good for me. I got to love Mac and Montez. Joe was kind of a lazy stinker, an intellectual; he couldn't lie still when I explained life to him. But they kept me sane. I had something, you see, somebody to talk to, somebody to watch move around. Three jumping beans."

He smiled and pushed down the blond hair, stiff as copper wire, on his handsome head. "Sounds funny, doesn't it; another bit of local whimsy, but it wasn't. It took nine days before I was called and got my job. I just about made it. Well, let's finish up here and go find Mollie."

John paid for the drinks. "What happened to the beans?"

Walter frowned. "I've got no idea what happened to them. No idea at all."

John went back to change and shower, before meeting Walter at the Cock and Bull to drive out to the beach and make it all up with Mollie. John was feeling a little gay and light in the head, and he couldn't find the shirt he wanted to wear and had to put on one with a very wide collar and two sizes too big. He had to admit he felt very comfortable and sloppy in it.

He left to pick up Walter. Walter was feeling no pain at the bar of the Cock and Bull, and said he hadn't even heard from M.Z., and in his condition never wanted to . . . Mike must be chasing a sucker with money.

The three of them, John, Walter, and Mollie, ate swordfish and drank highballs at Marino's up the road from the Ark that night, and then feeling very good and very fond of each other, went over to the Plume Café where Mollie fed coins to the juke box and danced with the biggest of the Greeks who ran the joint. It was one of their best nights and they got back to the Ark very late. Walter hadn't slept all night in the jail, and he went down to his room and Mollie and John talked about Mike and decided he was superior in kind, not degree.

Walter had to borrow a hundred and fifty dollars to have the Lincoln repaired just enough to run again. He never bothered getting the body work done. The Lincoln ran after that, with its mashed-in front to one side, like a crippled shark. Mike was angry when he heard about it. He was always angry these days; he was still two hundred thousand short to make his quickie.

"Where's Walter?" Mike asked the next night as John came into his cottage with some new scenes for *The Gambler's Wife*. "That Walter is riding for a fall. I like the punk, but he has no real feeling for motion pictures. He lives too wild."

"We all do, or wish we could," John said.

Mike scowled at him and took the new pages he held out. "Maybe I get loud sometimes, but remember this about me, John, I have self-discipline, not just self-control. How do you like these scenes?"

"They'll save us money in sets, but I don't like them."

Mike looked up from his reading and swung his heavy black-rimmed glasses off his face. "Leave it to me. This town is script-happy. Once you get a good story, never mind what it's like on paper. Film it and give it that touch that makes you forget the words on paper. How many pictures you know do that?"

"Very few. You think Mollie can do this?"

Mike looked up and put his glasses on again; his eyes looked huge and glazed, like a deep-sea fish. "Of course she can. I can make her a real actress, not one of the town phonies, a success that goes out like a candle after one big job. . . . I've asked Alice to file for divorce."

John didn't say anything. Mike looked up at him and smiled. "This can't fail. Everything here is negated and negated into a squirming mess of neurotic nerve cells, but not me and not Mollie."

That was the night they talked about love and its biological twists, but did not get very far except to become fascinated by nature in its more screwy forms.

John did not like the screenplay of *The Gambler's Wife*, but Mike reassured him it was going very well and they would start shooting "in a week, maybe two weeks, at least not before three weeks were up." If all else failed, he'd make it a three hundred thousand dollar picture.

"They can be art too."

Mike has been clipping out items on the mating of insects. He found one that can prove a male moth can find a female moth in the dark, seven miles away. This is a yen, he says, that holds the long-range record. There are no odorous particles; it's done by sending out infrared heat waves. The female shows a temperature twelve degrees above the surrounding air. She sends these heat rays out in a kind of irregular flashing code, a set of signals almost like love dialogue, and the male moth tunes in with his antennae. When his antennae are cut off the male can't find the female.

He says this very much impressed Mollie, and he said she certainly broadcast on a wave length that attracted the males, but he doubted if it could work at seven miles. She is going to try to reach Mike—just by thinking hard—from the beach at midnight to Zelsmith's cottage. That's about nineteen miles. Of course he lacks an antenna like the moth's, which is covered with short hair .00156 inches in length.

Mike does not get his science from *Reader's Digest*. Mollie when in school said she was measured and photographed and placed as a combination of the mesomorphs (square, hard, rugged), and the ectomorphs (tall, stringy). This in theory makes her aggressive, yet inhibited, and as a mesomorph, susceptible to acute appendicitis, as her scar tissue proves. Mike is very impressed.

As a writer, this all seems to me pretty much only for text books. It would be too bad if we had to write of people like a moth tuning in on a ray, or a girl who has to live up to her ectomorph's chart.

I have been quoting Stendahl so often to Mollie and Mandy that I have at last found a copy of his book *De L'amour* for them, but I doubt if they will do much reading in it. Mandy is not a reader of anything these days but popular murder, and I doubt if she has done any serious reading since her girlhood, unless it had to do with her work. Then she read a great deal, much of everything without real guidance. Mollie reads everything—and too fast.

I have been reading some of the book aloud to them: "Love is a costly flower, but one must have the desire to pluck it from the edge of the precipice . . . to love is to feel alive, to have strong sensations." Mollie perhaps has what the Freudians must call this erotization of fear, but she does not understand, as Stendahl did, that the first love of youth is not the strongest by any means. Later passion can be more desperate, more absolute than anything she has yet had with her husbands. Quoting Helvetius, that "Love is mere sensuality refined," or another who said, "Love is great friendship embellished by pleasure," amuses her.

Mollie has become interested in Stendahl's theory of the crystallization of love. I read it to her carefully after Mandy left. She sat frowning, making great effort to understand.

"Near the salt mines of Salzburg," I read, "a leafless branch falls into the depths of one of the mines; two or three months later it is found with its tiniest twigs, no bigger than a titmouse, entirely covered with an infinity of sparkling diamonds. One can no longer recognize the original branch.

"What I call *crystallization of Love* is the operation of the mind that draws from everything around it, the discovery that the beloved object has new perfection . . . In love one no longer sees things as they are."

Mollie was puzzled. "How does one know he's in love?"

"He divided the seven stages of love like this. One, admiration; two, the beginning of desire; three, hope; four, inception of love; five, the first *crystallization;* six, doubt and jealousy; seven the final *crystallization,* the confirmation of love. That's all there is to it, for the twig has turned to diamonds."

"He's a real Don Juan."

"No, he's against the Don Juans. Listen: 'The Don Juan type is based on strategy, tactics, as in military campaigns, the hunt or the gambling table . . . He takes and pays nothing . . . Woman is but a machine for joy . . . There are not over twenty different types of women, and when one has had two or three of each, the satiety begins . . . the misery of inconstancy is boredom . . . Great love is the fullest realization of the ego, the wonder of civilization . . . One must shake up one's life, else it corrodes us.' "

Mollie understands this. Not Mandy. There are times when I think Mandy is afraid of all mental processes except for food, work, routine love. She often makes it clear that she avoided men who had brains or had used them. She once said, "A thinking man is a novelty for me. Count up all my past and you find either male children or people who get by on charm or poise. I respect your mind, John, and that worries me, because suppose something happens and I lose faith in thinking?"

I have a feeling that if Mrs. Henry could be gotten rid of, Mandy Rye would be a different person. She must have been a nice school girl, and from what I hear of that period of her life, an alert child . . .

Mollie is still going to Mrs. Henry I found out—for real advice or amusement I don't know . . . I've certainly wandered far from the moth's love signals tonight.

Walter showed up for the next story conference and admitted Mollie was having trouble with her part. Mike refused to listen.

"The critics say the industry is too damn basic," Mike said to John and Walter, changing the subject.

"Well, isn't it?" asked Walter.

"It has to be. But as I tell Mollie, you're talking in pictures even if the words don't matter. You take the sound track off a great picture . . . it's still great."

"But you avoid real life," John said.

"You're wrong. We must make it simple."

"Too simple."

"We permit only two kinds of action."

"I bite . . . what two?"

"Fighting and f—," Walter said.

"You never really see the last on the screen," Mike said, almost sadly. "But we do plant it in the public mind. That's what they come for. As nude a woman as they can see twenty times life size. Clark Gable in heat. Maybe that's not art, but it's all we're permitted to sell. That and knock-out, drag-out fights.

"Why waste time on such a thing?" John asked.

"Because sometimes you can sneak in the truth. That's why they respect Zelsmith pictures. I give them the sex and the brawl, but also a little of the ache and the agony of life. The lousy beauty of it, the crummy pleasures of kids and family life, and art shots and a pain in the heart because life isn't as wonderful as it can be made."

"Let's get back to our story, M.Z.," Walter said.

"I'll do all the sneering around here."

"We're trying hard." .

"Not hard enough."

"We haven't got the twist yet, the wiennie."

"The twisteroo will come. Give me dialogue."

"You just said dialogue doesn't matter," John said.

"Sweat it out, you bastards. I'll throw out what I don't need." Mike grinned.

John closed his eyes and smiled, "I haven't got a brain cell working. Let's knock off."

"All right, but don't get too far away from the story."

"I dream about it," John said. "Badly written dreams. I used to dream in a much better prose."

"Prose I can't catch with a camera."

Zelsmith folded up his notes and threw them onto a desk and went to the table and poured himself a drink. He smiled at John.

"I told you I was a swine to work for."

"That's what people say all over town." He shook off the offer of a drink. "But I'm pretty fond of you, Mike. I don't mind if we get what you want."

"What the hell do I want? I used to know. First it was money, then it was women in love, then it was power. Then it was nothing at all. That scares a mug, having had everything."

"There's a school of thought that wishes are everything," Walter said.

"Balzac to them. I like things. I don't regret most of the loving I've done and some of it was pretty crummy. You regret any, John?"

"Sure. A lot of it. Maybe I don't know women. I'm usually in trouble with them."

"What the hell do you think love is, pleasure?"

"Some of it."

"Count me out," said Walter. "I'll play Boswell."

"Sure, love is pleasure when the dame is with another guy or dead or married to somebody else. When she's with you, it isn't always fun. Only later, and how much of that is in your head and how much in your groin? But since I found Mollie—it isn't like that."

"Maybe. Have that drink now?"

John said, "I'm taking Mandy out to dinner at a friend's house."

Zelsmith closed the bottle with the palm of his hand. "Nice to have a friend left in this fink town . . ."

10

AFTER John and Walter left, Mike felt low and rather foolish; he knew he often talked too much. When Mike was upset he liked a sort of active yet sterile social life. When he was contented and busy and his projects were going well, he was pleased to just sit around and hold a drink in his hand and talk with the few people he really liked. He had read a great deal, carelessly and only along special lines. He knew what he wanted to know very well. But on many subjects he was ignorant and admitted it. When under tension he could not read, his eyes blurred, and the strongest glasses did not help.

He found Mollie at the Ark—in silk pants and a Chinese

jacket—bathing the little cocker Lucky, who moaned in distaste at the soapy water.

"Let's not go out, Mike. I'll cook something and we'll play some recordings."

"I've accepted a dinner invitation for both of us tonight. We need a change. How's Lucky?"

"The vet says his heart isn't improving."

"He looks all right," Mike said, and patted the dog's head. "Hello, character, don't you want to live forever and get rich?"

"Who's giving us dinner?" Mollie pushed hair out of her eyes with a wet finger.

"Nevil Garrison, the popular writer. Is he really popular?"

"Real Literary Guild bait once a year."

"Maybe he'll be amusing. Baby, you look pretty good tonight."

She looked up and grinned and stuck out an inch of pink tongue. "Is it so hard for you to say nice things, Mike? To break down and say you adore me?"

Mike laughed. "I guess it is. I feel it, but I also feel so stupid, me loving anything as young and beautiful as you. Better get dressed."

"All right, Mr. Shut-mouth. Dry the dog, and be careful of his ears."

During the war, in London, making an Army film, Mike had met the American writer, Nevil Garrison. It had been the usual hasty meetings in smoky pubs and staff meetings over what kind of propaganda to write into films. The last he saw of Nevil in England, he was being helped into a transport plane on a foggy morning and Nevil was pounding his shoulder and shouting, "You ever get back to Beverly Hills, you look us up. Greatest little wife and greatest little cook in California. Greatest . . ."

Mike didn't know why he called Nevil up after all those years to renew their friendship; he didn't read his novels. Walter said they were loud historical things with a half-nude woman always on the jacket exposing her breasts, and a young man with a bowie knife in his hand or a battle ax or a horse pistol; but the girl was always the same, only sometimes her hair was blonde. Nevil was happy to hear from Mike, and Mike had to come out, and bring whomever he wanted, for dinner.

"Mollie Binning, would it be all right to bring her?"

Nevil shouted into the phone, "Hell, yes, Mike, boy, as long as she has two legs and isn't colored. Drag 'er along!"

"She isn't colored." Mike failed to see the point, if there was a point.

"Great to hear from you, ole boy. Talk over the late, lamented war. Them was the days! When we were men, not part-time geldings, eh?"

"Rather lousy days, I remember. Looking forward to seeing your wife. You were rather proud of her."

"Who? Oh . . . well, there have been a few changes made. Married again, Mikey. Pucky is fun, you'll love 'er. See you at seven-thirty."

"All right, Nevil."

"Good-by and hurray for French wines and American plumbing!"

Mike hung up the phone and promised never to look up anybody again. Walter was rather ironically impressed.

"Nevil Garrison, he sold his last book, *The Faithful Wench*, to MGM for two hundred thousand."

"That's a great deal of money, Walter. You read it?"

"I tried, M.Z., but it's pretty bad. I'd rather read Henry James if I have to suffer."

"Someday I'll make *The Turn of the Screw*."

The Garrisons lived on a street of trees that bore a fruit called St. John's Bread. Their house was a massive stone pile pasted over Elizabethan timbers, with a solid tower of bad design, in the nine hundred block, north ("Never go south of Wilshire, ole boy"). Colored servants with shiny, fat faces helped Mike and Mollie into the house and pointed them into a vast, raftered living room in which a huge fireplace was sending out sparks, even though it was summer. Battle flags, crusaders' swords, and rusting iron chains hung on the walls. A full suit of armor stood on duty near the French doors, and a collection of wheel-lock pistols hung between the windows in closed walnut cases lined with faded red velvet. There was an odor of cooking fat, damp bathrooms, and dusty rugs.

Three children, reading comic books, and several assorted dogs, were spread out on their chests and groins before the fire, Nevil himself, a little fatter, his ink-black hair bushy as ever, and wearing a blue smoking jacket, greeted them and offered them strong oversweet drinks in cut-glass goblets. He looked part Indian, his skin very dark, almost Moorish.

He introduced a very blonde young woman, heavily made up, who was examining her blood-red fingernails. "This is Pucky . . . and these are the kids. The oldest is mine, and the others are Pucky's from some past misdeeds. So you're working with John Fennel, Mikey boy. Overeducated swine, isn't he?"

"No, I rather like him. He's a very talented man."

"Arty, believe me. You in the industry, Miss Binning?"

"I'm a designer."

Pucky smiled, showing well-capped teeth much too white. "I can't get a Goddamn thing in town that's made for a real woman with hips."

"Great little town," said Nevil, putting his arm around Mike's shoulders. "Every artist should have five years of it at three grand a week. Every damn craftsman in the world! Where would this town be if there were no craftsmen, eh? They'd be growing mushrooms on their sound stages. Of course the pictures stink, but I always say it's the public's fault, what? If they didn't support bad pictures we wouldn't make 'em, eh?"

"You certainly have a big house, Nev," Mike said.

"Dreadful, isn't it? Built by Doug Fairbanks, I think. Looks like one of his fancy sets, doesn't it? But good enough for the kids and dogs, eh? Pucky, where the hell is the dinner?"

"Coming. I don't dare talk back to those educated dinges. They'd walk out in a minute and leave me holding the roast."

Nevil said to Mollie, "Pucky, she's from the South. Thinks we spoil our help."

"We don't take any sass from 'em where I come from. Here they go to college. Imagine a cook that can speak French and do math!"

A large colored man announced dinner and got out of the way. The children rushed in ahead of them, the dogs heeling and taking their places under the huge, round, split hickory table. Mollie, looking small and dainty, got into a huge mission oak chair.

"I don't believe in teaching children anything. Breaks their spirit, eh? The smallest one—ole dirty-face there—is in a progressive school. Got 'A' in sandpile the other day. Ha! ha! 'A' in sandpile, get it, eh? Remember the night,

Mikey, we got drunk in the Elephant and Castle and picked up the two tarts with no front teeth, and the air-raid alarm started?"

Mike said, "No, I don't remember."

"No? Say, must have been with Borey that night. Oh, don't mind Pucky. We lead a sane sex life. Nothing is such nonsense as not talking things out. Free souls, all of us here. The children aren't going to grow up warped. We walk around nude indoors, you know. The Indians had the right ideas."

"Nice of you to dress tonight," said Mollie, who hadn't said very much up to this point, but had been taking pulls of a strong drink.

"Eh? Oh! Ha-ha! We really believe the child that knows everything knows best. No use filling their little minds with the wrong ideas of things, is there?"

Pucky rang a bell and pointed out to the kids their right places at table. "Everybody set. The dinner is most likely spoiled, but the kids will eat anything. Don't mind me, I'm on a diet."

She put two rye crisps in her mouth and helped herself to a steaming plate of thick pea soup with frankfurters cut into it. Nevil poured out a good white wine and the children kicked at each other and slipped morsels to the dogs under the table. Mollie felt she was in a giant's castle out of a fairy tale.

"You're in a great town, Mikey. They need more men like us. Storytellers, that's us. A little out of fashion with all the fancy-pants boys, but we're solid. They'll always need story tellers. I'm sure glad you decided to film a best seller."

"Oh, it never really became that. We have a good story. It's an original—not a book."

"Wasting your time, you were, with that arty crap the critics liked. I never had a good review unless my publisher paid for it. They never read the books they review—the critics—anybody knows that. Mikey, you stick to solid stuff and get set as head of some major studio and you'll be somebody. No rattling around in those art houses in Europe, eh? Funny, thought it was you had the fight with the tart with the front tooth missing. More roast beef?"

The beef was well done and tasty. The children were gorging, juice running down their faces, pushing the meat onto their forks with their thumbs.

Pucky helped herself to the mashed potatoes and added some gravy and nibbled a rye crisp. "Where do you live, Miss Binning?"

"At the shore. Cortez Beach."

"We're thinking of taking a house there, but they're so strict there, no nude bathing, and Nevil and I both think the children should go in naked."

"Lots of people around."

Pucky wrinkled her nose. "Oh, dear, don't you find it dreadful, all those beach bums?"

"They're interesting people."

"Oh, I suppose so, lot of 'em rather shabby, no recent screen credits—seem to own only one pair of blue jeans and a bottle of suntan lotion."

"They have fun."

Nevil nodded and refilled the wine glasses with red wine. It was very fine Burgundy. "Strip the body, expose the soul, eh?"

"And the Jews," said Pucky. "Mind you, I believe in tolerance, but if you ask me why do the Jews and the Catholics get all the blame?"

Mike grinned and said nothing.

"More beef, anybody? Beef of Old England. Got three steers in my deep freeze right now. Those Reds in Congress can't lick me. Buy 'em alive, you know, and have the foreman butcher 'em and cut 'em up for us on our ranch. Nothing like slaughtering your own meat, real red blood spurting, eh?"

One of the children who was listening had thrown up and had been led away protesting at losing his share of the ice cream.

"Dirty little elf does it on purpose. Attention-getter."

Mike looked at Mollie and she was grinning and drinking wine. Nevil came around with a silver container of cigars and Pucky got out four little bottles of different colored brandies and poured little cups of the sweet, sticky stuff. Mollie lit a cigarette and asked Pucky if the paintings of dogs and horses on the walls were done by hand. Pucky showed her their fake Cézanne sailboats. Nevil and Mike took a walk around the house and Mike was introduced to the garbage grinder, the automatic washer and dryer, the dishwasher, the gas heating, the twenty-inch television set, the Capehart ("got the entire score of *Oklahoma,* in six languages!"). And to the writing room, a huge studio lined with bookcases filled with popular reprints of historical novels.

"I work here six hours a day, Mikey boy, and I mean work. Three hundred words to a page, ten pages to a chapter, two chapters a day . . . every day, skipping Sundays of course and the days I golf, and when my hay fever gets real bad. Last three all made book clubs. Knock it out right on the typewriter and I'm going to try recording it on tape soon. Easy to edit tape. Just cut out what you don't want with a razor blade and patch it together with Scotch tape. Could Balzac do that? Did my last book in eight weeks. John Fennel writing a book? Something juicy about Hollywood, eh?"

"He's thinking of a book. May write it in a few years."

"Public forget him in that time. Say, that Miss Binning is some dish. Getting *much* lately?"

"I'm going to marry Miss Binning after my divorce."

"The hell you say! Hey, Pucky! Get some of the real good wine out. What do you know! The kids are going to get married! How do you like them apples! They're goin' to make it for keeps!"

Pucky said, "Well, all right, if it's a habit!"

They watched a roller derby on the television set and Nevil brought out his collection of canes. "Phallic symbols, eh?" One of the dogs bit another dog, and Mike and Mollie left at eleven.

"See you again, Mikey boy! Must make a habit of it. Nothin' like old comrades, eh? Mustn't say comrades any more, don't want to get blacklisted by the studios, do we . . . ?"

Mike drove a long time before he burst out laughing. Mollie laughed so much it hurt. "So that's what I've been missing, Mike, the high and fancy life in Beverly Hills."

"Not every writer in California can be as stupid as Nevil."

"He's the most successful. Did a half-million dollars last year. Sold four originals."

Mike smoked a cigar and frowned. "He is successful, isn't he?"

"The biggest. He admits it frankly. I wish they'd invite me to watch sometimes. I bet Pucky eats rye crisp in bed."

"Old Southern custom, no doubt," Mike said.

"Well, the beach bums are going to look pretty good from now on."

It was a very still night and the shore road was bone white in the moonlight. Cars were parked along the shore and along the high cliffs overlooking the beach. Lovers locked together were dimly seen.

Mollie said, "Let's be vulgar. Let's park."

"Like high-school kids?"

"If I can find a spot."

The study of the script still bothered Mollie. She noticed that lately her moods had a way of changing. There was in her a great core of loneliness. She was a jolly person, given to great love of small and intimate things. The sea birds flying, or standing in long rows at dusk, their feet in mirroring water waiting for night; this could please her. The sight of a green, lofting cliff and climbing flowers, red faces to the sun, people that she liked around her, no matter who they were or what, these things were happiness to her. She loved her animal farm; her dogs, her seed-scattering birds.

The morning after the Garrison dinner, one of the love birds flew out of the window while she was cleaning the cage. She spent the day searching the cliffs before the house. She stood in the gold-flecked dusk watching the chicken hawks circle and dip as they hunted their night prey in the cliff grasses. She did not sleep that night, but heard the swooping cliff owls among the yucca weeds and umber night shadows. At morning she propped the door open and waited for Blue, the love bird, to come home. He never came back and she pictured to Mike the frightened, cage-born thing stunned by heat and dust, or already forming a pellet of feathers and bone in the maw of a hawk or owl. The agony of being torn alive by beak and claw appalled her.

There was no rest for her until Mike bought her another love bird and it was put into the cage, where it at once sank to the bottom of the pecking order. She couldn't stop shaking. Odd things, at least to Mike they were odd things, could make her sad. Mike spoke that Saturday at the Motion Picture Academy. It was for members only and he returned to the Ark to find Mollie crying because she had not heard him speak.

He lifted her small, perfect face. "But dopey, it was a dull talk on the History of Film Forms Based on Lens Devices. You could have come, I suppose, but it bored even me."

"I'm so proud of you, and I didn't hear it." She smiled. "Aren't you pleased I'm such a dope?"

A man from the British Consul's—a man who had known Alice in Europe, happened to meet them in an eating place and mentioned her.

Mollie was silent all the way to the Ark.

"Damn it, he's an old friend of Alice's."

She smiled wistfully. "I can't help it. Thinking of you once being tender to her."

He once mentioned to her that he had been to Atlantic City on a film convention.

"The year the beauty pageants got into trouble?" Mollie asked.

"Maybe. I was bored. I used to walk the beaches, all alone, and go to the pier with the big pickle over it and look at the bad paintings."

"Mike, we were there together. Father took us East for several years. We could have met."

"Mollie, we wouldn't have liked each other then."

"I know we would."

"The hell with the dream girl. You're here now."

And then there was Mrs. Henry with her feelings about Mollie. "Mike, Mrs. Henry just called. She said she had a feeling something was wrong with me. Something hovering. Crazy old bat."

"Stay away from her, baby."

Mollie laughed. "It's been fun. I think I'll send her a three-motored broom and call it quits."

That was the day Mike told John Fennel he was going to make the picture for three hundred thousand—he couldn't raise another penny.

Mike was rather tired when he got back to the hotel, and he poured himself a drink. There was a lot of mail he hadn't gone through. Book catalogues and some letters from somebody he had once done a favor and now wanted another, and a letter on the letterhead of the Mark Twain Hotel.

Dear Mr. Zelsmith,
I am in town on a matter that I am sure will be of value to you. I shall be in touch with you soon. I will be able

*to do you a service, a service I am happy to do for any-
one like yourself who has done so much for motion pictures and literature.*

> *Most Cordially,*
> *Henry Kamp Matt*

It took him a little while to remember that a Mr. Matt
had once tried to reverse the charges on a phone call from
San Francisco. And had used his name on a credit reference.
Still, there were no such named hotels in New York or London . . . Only a few people in the industry, like Zanuck,
liked writers.

BOOK THREE

"I returned and saw under the sun, that the race is not to the swift, nor the battle to the strong, neither yet bread to the wise, not yet riches to men of understanding, nor yet favor to men of skill; but time and change happeneth to them all . . ."

—ECCLESIASTES

11

MIKE took over the reading of the script with Mollie at the beach house. They worked late and hard, and often when John dropped in around eleven at night with some new lines of dialogue, they were worn out, sitting staring at each other; Mollie curled up in a deep armchair, legs tucked under her, looking more like a little school girl than ever, Mike staring at the crumpled pages of script covered with red crayon cues and bits of business.

Usually Mike and John drove back to the hotel together, and Mike would talk and John would listen, his head between the upturned collar of his topcoat wondering when this writing and rewriting would end, and why the nights were so chilled and dismal.

Mike turned the car up from the beach road and began to climb the twisting way between the loose, decomposed granite walls of the roadway.

"The town really thinks they have me now," he said cheerfully. "How the bastards love the idea of me making a fast one without real big money. You know why they hate me? Because I'm not a standard brand cynic like they are. The town knows a cynic will accept a situation, but a dopey idealist becomes a pest and a danger to them. They have a motto: 'In any critical situation principles are to be sacrificed to expediency.'"

"Aren't you doing that now, Mike?"

Mike fumbled inside his coat for a cigar. "You read biology much?"

"No, not since college."

Mike lit his cigar from the car lighter and puffed on it

with a sucking sound. "I never went to college. Biology is all I can read these days. Here's the way I figure it out, biology as a study of man is the sociology of a rat race. But it's a clue. I'm looking forward to something better. Laugh at me—I'm trying to find art. I feel art sometimes happens when you try to transform hard contemplation into direct action . . . How do you think Mollie's readings are coming?"

The more he worked with Mike Zelsmith, the more John saw what an artist the man was. Zelsmith was creative beyond anyone John had yet met; certainly he was a truer artist than John himself, for John felt that he wrote because he usually had nothing else to do but write. Zelsmith created with whatever material he had, and with a surge of power and cruelness that tossed everything in his way aside. He was an artist in a much cheapened medium, an artist fighting alone in a desert of minds and bodies that wanted nothing to do with true art.

Mike had come a long way and suffered and sweated at it without always understanding it, for he believed that he had no time to make it slick and beautiful. He could only carve out raw, ugly shapes and let those that came after him make them pretty and popular. His best work was behind him now, he knew that; but he also knew he could recover something of the early fineness if the town would let him be, in some quiet corner, and permit him the money and the time and space to do his best.

Zelsmith was the artist who did not paint or write or act himself; he collected odd things like words, or faces, films, and landscapes, emotions and little scenes, and cut and snipped them into an hour or so of something that was called entertainment by the town, and usually stank to high heaven in its most popular forms.

Mike was raw and heavy and badly educated, badly placed in time and space, John saw; but like the true artist he bruised the time-servers, the fat behinds in clover. Mike he knew was holding on grimly, and he would always hold until they took it away from him, or he made another big one that they would have to accept and bow to and say it was part of the town's best, even if they did not understand it.

"All the crap you hear," Mike used to say, "that it's vulgar to love one's country, archaic to love God, sentimental to love people . . ."

John decided that few people really knew Mike Zelsmith. A few longhaired critics (for the wrong reasons) and his wife Alice perhaps understood best the shaggy mind and its battling creative purposes. Maybe John knew a great deal about Mike, but it was all new to him, and still a method and a process perverted by business methods into little pictures of false emotions and unreal life.

Mike, John saw, was a sensitive traveler with elephant feet in a metaphysical jungle of steel-toothed rats, living in a solitude of Cadillacs and dollar-cigar minds, paying penance for every step forward he took, making a kind of despair of piety for his art form, keeping himself from ever selling out fully, and trying to stay in a sort of clinical detachment from the industry. He could not be merely urbanely skeptical of the town's product; he had to somehow blend his own work in with the miles of exposed film that was exploited and sent out into a dying market. Chaos was at the bottom of all the town's failures, a cheerful, repetitive pattern of chaos, a blind, exuberant belief that the suckers would take anything with their popcorn. No reason to foster in this precarious progress any need for the true artist. Just an opulent tolerance for action, the pretty body, fast riding, and sudden death in sterile melodrama.

Mike drank a lot and used to say to John, "Why kid ourselves that the town will ever change before they break it up into superfood markets? Conviction has deserted the mind out here. There are no good consciences out here, only option clauses. Deluded at five thousand dollars a week, how the hell can you expect any humanity when no one knows how to live the life of the world conscientiously?"

"Why fight it, Mike?"

"Because I need the protection of an outward, let's say specific, religion. In this case, art. I can't paint, I can't sing, and I can't write, so it has to be movies. My lousy theology is that there can be great motion pictures. But who cares? They just accelerate their own decomposition at ninety miles an hour, in Technicolor."

"You hate pictures?"

"No. The things we love most make all the trouble in the world for us. You think the town knows what it's doing? Only on the surface. Their own preoccupation is to be safe, to be popular, to be seen in the right places."

"Why not give it up, Mike? You could do something else,

do it better. Publishing, play production, even teaching."

Mike Zelsmith poured himself another drink and frowned; his big smashed nose, the graying curly hair, the whole head twisted into the frown. "John, my trouble is I've found it easy to give up the world. All of it but this daffy thing of making snapshots leap. The surface world doesn't interest me, because I know what it is and how bad it is. You can't ever get away from it too soon, John, if you can get something, well—eternal, to do. Like being an artist and thinking of bigger things than just living. I know most philosophy stinks, but the way I see it, an artist is a guy who doesn't fear dying if he has got a hunk of eternity in his fist. I don't want to be allegorical—maybe it's the drinks talking—but I've got to feel I'm something special in this town, or I'll end at Jerry Fairbanks', drawing talking mouths on dogs and horses for easy laughs like the others. No real artist can do that and not die."

John looked at Mike and grinned. "You know, Mike, your trouble is that in a time of crummy and rather prosaic utility, you're a pretty paradoxical contradiction."

"When you call me *that*, smile."

"The Greeks had it for art and life, they had a genius for wholeness. You have it—have it bad."

"Don't let it get out, John, or I'm a dead duck . . . I think we better get back to our script, after we kill the bottle."

That was Mike Zelsmith as John saw him, as the town avoided him. Several times Mike wanted to leave it all and take his aching head, and maybe Mollie, away somewhere and sit and think it all out. But what could he do? He had no talent for creating anything away from here, he had no easy talents at all, just the genius, a hell of a note and he knew it. He was a circle trying to live like a square, and he was a man who didn't have any answers as to why he couldn't live with his world and away from it.

He usually rose early from the short physical death of sleep and walked the hills.

He didn't drink too much during the day, and he liked to sit in the hotel garden and watch the dogs smell out earth odors. Or he went to his office and sat and looked at figures and listened to people struggle and juggle facts that he could have set in order in a minute; but they were paid to do these things for him and he let them stutter on, and later did it all over again.

He liked people at dinner, and as he had no taste in food, he ate a lot of whatever they set before him. He often felt tender and happy and went to Mollie's beach house. After two big drinks he would play a game that she was the most witty and most beautiful and most spiritual person he had ever known and that he was madly in love with her. They were, he felt, very good for each other, and then he knew they were the happiest people in the town at those moments. His ego was such that when he loved a woman, he built huge illusions into her.

There was in Mike, outside of all the things that made him a genuine artist, a direct contact with living that came out in understanding of people. He had failed with Alice because Alice did not belong to his stable understanding of what life was and how it was lived. Alice lived on no solid platforms, and so there was no ground under her feet. Mike knew this, and yet he knew that her love for him was large and wonderful; too bad it had no taste.

Mollie had taste for him. He could build turf under her feet, create out of his vitality and his knowledge, and she would accept it.

John Fennel studied him as he lived and worked, an artist going downhill quickly because he could not, John saw, retire like Bach or Van Gogh to one room and make his art true, alone and forgotten in a corner. He could not sit at a table and grind logic like Spinoza, or go beautifully mad like William Blake naked in his garden. Mike's life and his art was a public job, it needed the vast sound stages and the complicated camera details and a whole organization of hired forces alien to true art, and yet it was the only art form he could function in.

It was sometimes, John sensed, a kind of splintered pleasure, within Mike himself, to know that when he failed, when he was discarded he would join all those other artists before their time, forgotten, and covered with the dust of plethoric neglect while smaller minds and shallow talents reaped the rewards he never really cared for.

There were times when Mike felt Mollie could never surprise him again, and then she did. One day she calmly said to him, "My sister wants to meet you."

Mike was placing the large bottle of spring water on its

kitchen stand at the beach house—and he slowly turned the bottle over, pulled the cork, and put it tightly on the stand. "I thought you didn't have any family, baby."

"Belle is all the family I have, and she's heard so much about you from me."

"Where does she live?"

"In Eagle Rock, just this side of Pasadena. You don't mind meeting my family?"

"Hell, no, must be nice people."

Mollie went into the bedroom and came out with two faded photographs. "Mama was a singer. That's father before he began to fail. That's me and Belle as kids."

"Very fine-looking folks. Good heads, and, as my aunt used to say, solid features."

"You're not judging a horse show now, Mike. Don't you think father looks like you?"

"He's got about twenty pounds on me and a better set of features."

Mollie grinned. "Men were larger in those days. You don't mind having dinner at Belle's tonight?"

"No. What's your sister like?"

"She's like me, and married to a hardware man named Harley. They have a kid, real cute."

"You sound at home there, Mollie. How is it you've never told me about your sister?"

"I lived with her when I was first married to Gene. All of us in one small bungalow. We drove each other nuts. I had to get away from her, and from Gene."

Mollie was very gay all the way to her sister's house. She drove Mike's car skillfully at a maddening pace, moving in and out among snorting busses and taking short cuts.

"I used to come tooting home here nights from town a little high, four o'clock in the morning and never missing a curve. That's when the trouble started with Gene, and I didn't care much. He hated the dogs you know, and once tried to beat Ed."

"I can see he had to go," Mike said.

"Don't mock me, mister." She missed a truck skillfully.

They were passing low, cheap developments (like chains of pretty germ cultures), well-lit stores, and crossing railroad tracks level with the highway. As they passed an airfield, two small dark planes shot up like frightened birds from cover, their wing lights blinking red and green, and a little later a freight train held them up by crossing like an elephant parade in front of them. Mollie turned off on a side road, made a swift descent down a paved street, passed a huge flagpole, and turned off on a private street, crouching in darkness and lined with palms and elms. The houses were old-fashioned California bungalows of, Mike judged, the 1900 period, and of rather low real estate value. There was a night odor of jasmine mixed with road tar and just wet, still thirsty lawns.

Mollie tooled the car up a drive and they went along twenty feet under bearing fruit trees, a tall sycamore, and up to a low green painted bungalow. It was the kind of place that was considered old-fashioned by most people, but very comfortable, with a low overhung roof of green tarpaper, and an upstairs room in a sort of tower in the middle of the house. Sun, termites, and ants had worked on it a long time.

The car had no sooner stopped than two cats, three hound dogs, and a small boy came out quickly, banging a screen door, and Mike noticed that the child's hair was so blond it looked almost white. A darker version of Mollie came down the steps wiping her hands on an apron. She had the same wonderful body of delicate grace but carried herself with less care. A cigarette drooped from one corner of her mouth as she pushed the child back.

"Hello, Mollie," she said, "don't let him annoy you—just brush him aside."

"Belle, this is Mike, Mike Zelsmith. My sister, Belle."

Belle grinned and held out a strong hand. "You're the bastard I'm frying all the eggplant for."

"It's dangerous to tell Mollie you like anything. She floods you with it," Mike said.

"Well, come on in and sit down. Get away from your aunt, kid, or I'll put you in the dog house. I'll get Henry to lock up the hounds."

Inside, the bungalow was square, filled with shabby cheerfulness, furnished with things discarded by most people after 1929. There was a Whistler etching on the wall. A good modern print of a painting of a Rousseau waterfall. Lots of low furniture, a scarred piano, and a scarred radio and record player. Mike sat down as a tall, handsome man, very lean, came in carrying two cans of beer. He had the child's blond-white hair.

"Henry, meet Mike Zelsmith."

141

"Mollie's been talking of bringing you over. Drink beer?"

"Yes."

"Good." Henry slipped two knitted blue covers over the beer cans, popped off the caps and handed one to Mike. Then he sat down and took a long suck of the beer. Except for dinner and taking out the dogs, he sat most of the evening drinking beer. He was a bright alert man who worked hard all day and came home to rest.

"Like the dogs?" he asked Mike.

"They look like good hunters."

"I hope so. Don't pay any attention to the women, they'll be busy in the kitchen. Real fuss for you tonight. I had to buy strawberries and some fancy wine."

"Sorry to make so much trouble."

"Hell, no trouble. Good for the women to stir up something special. I like to eat well myself."

Belle came in and lit a fresh cigarette and told Henry to go out and "lock in the g.d. dogs." She sat down, faced Mike, and grinned.

"Well, how do you like us?"

"Very much. I once had an idea Mollie was found under oak leaves. Never believed she had a family."

"Mollie's the bright one in the family. I wanted to be a writer, still think of it, but then I met Henry and the kid came. We'll never stop, have a dozen most likely. What are you drinking?"

"I was drinking beer."

"How about some rye?"

They sat drinking rye, and Belle could belt it away. But there was no tautness about Belle. She was happy, settled, and very busy all day.

"I like you, Belle. Hell, I like you very much," Mike said and grinned. "In fact, maybe I should have met you first."

"That kind of talk will get you no place, even if I like it," she said refilling his glass.

Mollie came out of the kitchen with a huge yellow bowl. "Soup's on."

Everyone took his place around the table in a low, steamed oak room. The child sat between his parents and the two women served the salad, the soup, the roast, and the good red wine, cheap but powerful.

Henry ate slowly and a lot. The child had to be directed to watch his manners from time to time. Mollie was happy and excited and Mike saw she was trying very much to impress her sister. Mike winked at Belle and had more salad and then more wine.

"We're having some people over," Belle said, "after dinner. They haven't seen Mollie for a long time. Used to be great friends of hers."

Mollie asked, "Who?"

"Meadow. He's kind of a sweet guy," Belle said to Mike. "Advanced designer of modern houses and no customers. Hector. He's an Irishman, directs little theater groups, and the Felixes . . . he's in the lumber business or going out of the lumber business, and he's got a big yen for Mollie. His wife doesn't seem to mind."

"They're not *all* the cream of society," Mollie said. "Just friends."

Belle nodded. "You two go read our old magazines and I'll wash up."

Off the living room was a small room called The Nook. It was lined with bookcases and had a small, damp-smelling pine bar and a glass bowl full of slippery baby turtles. Mollie pointed to the books as she emptied an ice tray into a small bucket. "My father's books. He was a great reader of history. Also stuff Belle and I collected years ago, like *Trilby* and *Ben Hur*."

She put down the bucket and came close to him and he put his arm around her. Her eyes were large and staring. "What's the matter, baby? Everything is going off all right."

"They like you, Mike."

"I could have a real yen for Belle."

"Better not. Henry is one of those strong, silent men. Anyway, I'm the only Binning you're going to be in love with."

"I'm happy they're letting you keep me."

"Come up and see where I used to live."

They mounted the narrow little steep stairs and went up into the center of the house. It was still warm under the low ceiling from the heat of the day. It had windows on four sides and wooden shutters like casements on an old man of war, Mike thought. There was a huge, low studio bed and an open closet full of men's ties on special racks, some men's suits and slacks. On the chipping, gray, painted closet side wall were pinned autographed pictures of Bette Davis and Joan Crawford.

143

Mollie quickly pulled the ties off the racks and pushed them away out of sight in a drawer.

She sat down on the bed and looked around her. "I lived here with Gene for a couple of months. I almost went crazy. The heat bouncing down on us. Him sick a lot, me trying to get some money together to keep the house going; things weren't so good with Henry then."

"Well, it's all over now."

"It haunts me. I failed as a wife here, Mike. It's kind of bewitched for me, and I feel like I'm revisiting the scene of a personal crime. Night after night poor Gene trying, and me, with no more feeling than if someone were reading a newspaper to me. Afterward I used to go into the bathroom, turn on the water in the tub very fast, lie down in it and cry."

"It's a crummy kind of room," Mike said, leaning over and kissing her neck. "Things like that *could* happen here."

"They have. I used to have some kind of breakdown from weeping and lay here alone for days with Belle bathing my head with cold towels and feeding me a little whisky. Belle is a great girl. I'm not good enough to her. Things are hard for Henry and her. I ought to help them more. But I never seem to be able to pile up any savings."

"Let's get the hell out of here," Mike said.

Someone was hello-ing for them from the foot of the stairs. Mollie stood up and grinned and they went down to meet the company. Meadow, the modern builder and designer, was a tired-looking man with small regular features and an amused mouth. The Irish director was one of those scowling black Irishmen with a thinker's head.

The Felixes were really California society—connected with one of the big railroad fortunes. Fred Felix was large and wide and rather stupid looking, and appeared, Mike felt, to be in a state of rut every time he looked at Mollie. Janie, his wife, was round, red faced, and cheerful. Everyone seemed to know everyone else very well and the Irishman was soon behind the bar mixing drinks. The child in its sleeping clothes said its last "good-by and goodnight" and Mollie tumbled a whole stack of samba records on the record player and kicked off her sandals. She and Fred were soon in a wild dance. Belle and the Irishman danced and Mike sat talking modern art with Meadow.

"Madhouse, isn't it?"

Mike said, "It's cheerful."

"Great girls, the Binnings. The beloved for miles around. They used to have open house here and it was something out of Homer. I must have broken a hundred dance records myself."

Someone had turned the music up higher and Mollie was jiggling and bouncing until she suddenly sat down on the floor and grabbed her foot with a small, silly, happy expression on her face.

"I think I sprained something."

A new set of drinks came in and Belle put on a batch of Gilbert and Sullivan. There were more guests now. Tanned people of both sexes . . . and Mollie pointed out that one couple was Italian. He was her lawyer, she explained. "He handles all my divorces. Doesn't that sound terrible? He's started proceedings on my new one." She put her head down in Mike's lap, kicked her legs in the air, and managed a cigarette and a tall drink at the same time.

One of the guests was an expert on the American Civil War and he came over and said, "Zelsmith, I've seen your Civil War movie four times."

"I had to see it twenty-eight times rough-cut," Mike said.

The man nodded and put down a glass wetly (where it would do the varnish the most good). "But damn it, you're unfair to Lee. He was a greater general than Grant."

"We'll take it up sometime."

"Want you to meet the wife." The expert introduced a large, aging, fat woman with a bad complexion. "She played in the original film version of *Treasure Island*. Remember her, the slim little boy in pants?"

The fat lady giggled. "They made real pictures in those days. Of course, that was a long time ago . . ."

Mike imagined it was.

Belle sat down near him and Mike took her hand. "Interesting people, Belle."

"Sure, even the bores are fun."

"Mollie is dancing again."

Belle shook her head. "Ever hear about her trying to swallow the brass doorknob at school?"

"She told me about it."

Henry passed with two cans of beer, each can in a neat knitted holder. Belle grinned. "Henry holds a kind of world record for beer."

"One of the few worth-while records."

145

Mike went into The Nook for a refill, Meadow was behind the bar experimenting with layers of different colored drinks. He refilled Mike's glass and Mike took it and sipped it slowly; the bite was going out of the stuff.

"Tell me, Meadow, something been puzzling me for years. All these parties. Everyone is always giving them. Mollie gives them on a low plane and the big producers and millionaires on a fancy plane. I've known people to spend three weeks going to parties out here, and if they had their bags in the car they never went home in all that time."

"Hard to believe," said Meadow.

"What starts a party?"

"Don't know . . ."

Mike nodded. "You know, sometimes at the same hour I see all of California playing the same record on the same scarred record player and smoking the same lousy cigarette with the same-sized ice cube in every glass. Then it rains and they tell you it's summer coming."

Belle came in biting her lower lip and said, "Where is Mollie?"

"If there is music still on, she's dancing with Felix," Meadow said.

Belle looked worried. "There's going to be trouble. Gene's on the phone."

Meadow looked at Mike and made a small whistling noise, "Gene, isn't he on the road?"

Belle shook her head. "He came back to take a television test. He's screaming on the phone that he wants to talk to Mollie. He wants to come over and cry on her shoulder or do something. He sounds real worked up."

"Let him talk to her," Mike said slowly.

"In her condition? She's keyed up and he sounded as if something is cooking in him. Gene's going to make trouble. Big trouble."

Mollie came in and said, "Gene's going to make trouble for who?"

Belle shrugged her shoulders. "He's on the telephone and he wants to talk to you and he wants to come over."

The glass fell from Mollie's little hand and the dirty brown rug took on a new splashing stain. Mollie stiffened.

"Tell him to leave me alone! I gave him everything! I want to be left alone!"

"Talk to him, Mollie," Mike said gripping her arm.

"Let go of me! I'm not talking to anybody!"

146

"Do you want him to come here, baby?" Mike asked crisply. He was in no mood for nonsense.

"I want to be left alone! . . . I'm a human being."

"Stop acting like a kid."

"I am a kid!"

She sat down on the bench that ran under the bookcases and lowered her head, and her blonde silky hair fell over her face. She began to sob. She spread her legs wide apart and sat there in childish weeping. Mike looked up at Belle who went out to the telephone in the hall. Mike sat down and took Mollie's hand and rubbed it. Then he rubbed her neck, pressing in, under the skull, a gesture she liked. She did not respond. She made small gurgling sounds and had trouble clearing her breath.

Belle came back and said crisply, "He isn't coming. He only wanted his neckties and suits. He's coming tomorrow night for them."

Mollie looked up, eyes wide, a small child staring, and fell sideways on the bench. The guests had gathered, glass in hand and stood uncomfortable (but interested) in The Nook looking at Mollie, no one talking. From the living room the record player ground into *"Waiting for the Robert E. Lee!"*

Belle said calmly, "Let's get her to bed, she's dead beat."

Someone rattled his highball glass and the ice cubes made a hollow sound almost sinister in the silence. Mike picked up the light little body and walked toward the stairs . . .

Even the first cigarette of the morning tasted sour to Mike. He sat at the foot of the tower room bed looking down at Mollie coming awake. He had slept badly on The Nook bench on some blankets. Mollie looked drawn but beautiful. Her face had a white-green tinge—a touch of a Lautrec painting Mike thought—and the clear blue eyes opened in wondering amazement.

She stirred and said, "What fell on me?"

He went into the bathroom, upsetting the social plans of some roaches who were running about. He wet a towel, soaped a corner of it, and went back and washed her face tenderly. Then he held a glass of water while she brushed her teeth. She made feeble attempts to comb her golden hair. She looked at him and smiled.

"I must look like a pretty sad sack, Mike."

147

"I've seen hang-overs before. I've hung on some pretty good ones myself."

"What was I shouting about last night?"

"Gene wanted his neckties."

"Oh, sure . . . Why do you love me, Mike."

He began to laugh and went to the flawed mirror and knotted his open necktie. Mollie joined his laughter.

He went downstairs and while Belle fed the child, Mike read the morning newspaper still damp with the local dew. The world was still full of international troubles and things were getting no better, no quicker.

Mollie came down to breakfast crisp and fresh. No sign of anything that had bothered her the night before.

FROM THE JOURNAL OF JOHN FENNEL

I don't think anyone can write a novel about this town . . . In a novel Stevenson said, "You're always putting in the chairs and tables." In a journal you don't write prose, you just write.

Mike and Mollie and Mandy and Walter always called it "the town" and everyone else does. Even when they meant the fog over Catalina and the great trucks roaring past Topanga Beach while the people tossed around trying to sleep off a hang-over.

It was the town as far as Burbank across the river that wasn't there, and past Alhambra and Pasadena. Signal Hill's oil fields were the town, and the fancy gardens beyond Beverly Hills. At first I couldn't understand how it all was the town and then I knew because Mollie and Mandy taught me.

Mollie for so young a girl knows a lot. Riding around she would tell me of the houses in the Mexican section where she had lived in her theater days, where the sharp, dark lads stand in their wide-brimmed hats, twirling chains ending in cutting knives. And the smell of chili and raw whisky is everyplace. The whores come out at night and prowl around the Union Station, and you can get reefers and your pockets picked all at once. Mollie had seen it when she had tried to run a theater for tourists. It was a good night town with night faces and flares burning over popcorn wagons and a bad night town with drunks fumbling themselves in doorways. The rich nigger jazz and the high yellows gave it tone, and the full fat laughter of the town's servants on the tear for a day gave it body. But that I guess I learned with Walter.

I saw they played polo near the beach and clipped accents said "Well done, chap! Righto!" And the best people in the best cars looked at each other's wives and drank champagne from silver cups presented to them by beautiful horses. Mollie and Mandy knew the poverty of the extras up on Beachwood

148

Drive, and the broken-down cars that made the rounds of the studios with extra girls with pink-white hair and silver fingernails in bad taste and rayon over hungry little stomachs. Mandy Rye had been at Warner's, and served time at Metro, and had seen Paramount at its best. And everybody remembered her as "That big broad with the knockers." "Good-natured and married to that actor, or was it the radio guy, the year before?"

Mollie Binning had been to Pasadena and seen theater art under Gilmore Brown, the big, bright man with the great talent and the slightly dragging leg, who produced the only theater worth a damn in America. She knew all about Pasadena and the rich old bags who put up the money and the rich old bastards who said the refugees and the Greeks and the Goddamn Roosevelt lovers were ruining the world. Mollie knew the dude ranches for dogs, where Ed and Lucky used to go when she had money, and their pictures were taken with Stetson hats and kerchiefs and sent to her reading, "We're having a great time, Ma, at the Dog's Dude Ranch. Ed and Lucky."

Also the town was Walter's new Pompeii.

In the hills in chicken houses and garages and stucco termite traps, Mollie was getting to know "the better artists." Not the good artists, but the bitter young men, unwashed and out for a buck or a woman with money; from the slums and ghettos and the hobo jungles. People with no real talent but a desire to be called artists. They slept around in the canyons and hung out in lousy little bars smelling of urine, and gave parties and scratched each other's fleas and cooked up beans and dreadful messes out of Mollie's cookbooks, because she was "society" and "class." Yes, that was the town too, that and the nasty little fashionable art shows in Beverly Hills where all the big names sent their worst stuff, and rich mamas bought their son's paintings and gave them to the L.A. County Museum.

Believe it or not, Mollie knew all the joints the fags hung out in. The little clubs so gay and sinister and bitchy, and the places they dressed in drag and the bull dykes walked around like truck drivers. All the fags loved her. She went to their parties, all the parties that Bertie Ironspinner gave (when in the Army he was known as the most dangerous woman in Paris). Mollie went to his parties and all the boys would cry for her and she would put their heads in her lap and pat their shoulders and tell them it was all right; "you mustn't hate yourself in the morning." She was just the great big mother to all the world.

Mollie knew the best people in the big reactionary clubs in Pasadena. They liked to have her around. "Solid stock from Upstate New York, father big business. Nice Christian type, and those Greeks and Arabs in Hollywood touching it." She went to the society parties and knew people who were blood kin to the Huntingtons and the Stanfords. And one of her friends was mistress to a rich oil man who couldn't let her live in his guest house. ("How, honey, can I ever explain you to Hoover when he comes to dinner?")

Mollie knew the town along Vine and Hollywood. She used to sit in Musso's on the high bar stool in the favored back room with Walter Chase. And they knew her at the Gotham in the little bar where she sat in a corner and smoked cigarettes. All the joints knew Mollie. The Black Witch where the people were something special. And everybody watched everybody else and at about eleven people on the prowl would come in there to pick up some trade. Mollie sat grandly in the sun at The Players, her fine legs crossed and the drink cold in her little fist. Everybody knew her and came over and said, "How is it going?" and went away saying, "A fine girl, that Mollie."

It wasn't really such a sinister town when I got to know it better with Mandy Rye. A lot like other towns and other places, it had the good little eating places where you ran up bar bills and the beaches where you sat and got done up brown, and the shops where you ran up more bills. The liquor man liked you, and the grocery man liked you and the dry cleaners liked you. Everybody liked you and gave you credit.

There were harbors where some people had big boats and invited you aboard. And there was Emerald Bay down below the refugee belt and the Greek belt, where they hunted back three generations before they let you in. Mandy and I were there week ends and met popular Buick dealers and men who owned gambling places in Reno.

The town was also Eagle Rock and Inglewood and the homes of the Lockheed workers in the Valley. And the big open markets, and Forest Lawn where it was a pleasure to die . . .

John closed the journal and looked at the stains of fountain pen ink on his fingers. The old pen was leaking again. Maybe it was California. The pen disliked certain climates, and when it did it leaked. It was a gift Mary had bought in Cairo, and it had never leaked in Cairo. He went into the bathroom and washed his hands. Everything had been so simple in Cairo, and with Mary. His journals then were filled with local color for a travel book he never got to writing, and sketches of natives.

Now his life was mixed up with a screwball world that he liked more and more. He wondered how much trouble it would be if things worked out for him. Like some writers, he felt at times that the emotional life of an author was a little bit on the odd side and attracted life just a little bit off its trolley. He didn't know why. . . .

12

THE problem of the gambler and his wife in the new story had interested John Fennel. It was not just a thriller. He had written it quickly, getting down the main story line, developing his characters, feeling for the first time in his picture writing an interest in the everyday personal problems of his people. A man in love with a wife whom he had planned to kill made it not only good melodrama, but a side trip into the world of Dostoevski, the world of the inner mind sitting in darkness and sending forth emotions that colored the many facets of the human being; that inner mind that tricked and controlled us, John felt. He thought very little of most modern writers and avoided them; but Dostoevski and Proust he reread with relish. He had given Mollie many copies of their works, and he was amazed how well she understood what these men were driving at, but there was no discipline to her reading habits. She read everything with a sucking eagerness.

John found Mollie sitting on the sun deck of the Ark with Lucky on her lap. The little dog's nose was dry and his brown eyes sadder than ever. He made a feeble effort to wag his tail. Mollie looked the tragic muse, the full Greek work of art, her brown body escaping in classic order from a white bathing suit.

"Lucky has been very sick, John."

"He's a very old dog, Mollie." He patted the dog.

"He had a heart attack this morning on the sand."

"He runs around too much."

"Ed was chasing some bitch, and Lucky followed him, and then suddenly he went stiff and fell over and went into a trance—rigid. I carried him, screaming, all along the beach and up the stairs. The vet was very late." She patted the little dog's golden fur. "Lucky scaring Mother so. He's got to take a little whisky every day now, just like a little old man. And his mannitol-hexanitrate tablets. It's about time now for one. Will you hold him, John?"

He took the dog from her. She looked unbearably wonderful in a white bathing suit. He almost envied Mike. They had a little trouble with Lucky and the pill. He coughed it up twice, but they held his mouth shut tight and tickled his throat and he went away to hide under the sofa and cough.

"Don't worry, Mollie. Keep him from running around and he'll live till a ripe old age."

"You coming to my grunion run with Mandy?"

"I promised myself I had to see a grunion run."

"I've invited the Garrisons—Nev and Pucky—so there will be other writers."

"It's up to Mike. He may want to work tonight."

"Oh, I hate you all," she said grinning. "Lucky sick, and Walter hasn't been home for three days, and when he comes home he'll be so mean and say dreadful things to me. Mike promised he'd come. I'm mad at him."

"Well, if he promised . . ." John said, not asking why she was mad at Mike.

John went in to get the bourbon and water and came out to find that Harry Steiner had come up on the porch with a guest, a slick young man with a limp who wore a very expensive wrist watch full of dials that he was explaining to Mollie.

Harry made introductions, "This is John Fennel, writer chap. Want you to meet Max Reilly, he's looking for good writers for radio." .

Reilly sat down and rubbed his short leg. "Too many good writers staying away from radio and television. It's a mistake."

"I agree," said John, handing Mollie a glass and making an offer all around.

"Tell me about television, Max," Mollie asked. "You really think it's going to be something big?"

"Biggest thing you ever saw, Miss Binning." He moved to her side and sat down again. John finished his drink and listened to Harry Steiner attack Hemingway's last book. He patted Mollie on the shoulder and said good-by, he was having dinner with someone. Harry Steiner was trying to crowd into their conversation. "Television, it's just a damn repeat of bread and circuses for the mob. Nothing good will come from it. Pap for the moronic housewives, drool for the Main Street beer bellies . . ."

John, that evening, found himself having dinner with Alice Zelsmith at the modern house. It was served on Spode china with handmade Revere silver. But the soup was canned, the chicken packing house barreled, and the pineapple slices in syrup sickening. He wondered why Alice had invited him. Alice was wearing a tight white evening gown and large pearls hung on her ears. The biggest pearl he had ever seen was on a thin chain around her neck. She looked thinner than ever tonight, her shiny black hair pulled back from a big domed forehead, and her nose was longer and wider than ever in the nostrils. John found her very attractive, but somewhat frightening.

She leaned on her arm and looked at John closely, "You can tell Mike something for me." She gave a loud laugh.

John went on taking small bits of pineapple to his mouth. He watched the butler pour the red wine from an untouched glass back into a fine crystal bottle.

Alice Zelsmith said, "I'm not filing for divorce. Papa said no."

John pushed away the pineapple and took out his pipe. "Mike's in trouble, Alice."

The woman at the end of the table stood up and her face was sad and hurt. "Papa almost fixed Mike. Almost drummed him out of the industry. He says Mike will end up selling popcorn in a grind house playing old French pictures."

"He feels pretty sure he can do this picture alone."

"You will give him my message, John?"

"Yes, if you want me to."

"You'll see him tonight?"

"We're going out together tonight."

Alice nodded. "To Miss Binning's party? It's all right, I met Pucky Garrison at the hairdresser's. She said she was going and gave me all the details. Mike really want to marry Mollie?"

"He hasn't talked about it much to me."

"Don't be so Goddamn stuffy, John. You know that's what he plans."

John took his pipe apart and examined it carefully. "How are you doing, Alice?"

"I'm all right, John. I'm kind of like Papa I guess. I've been reading the Koran. I don't know why. It says, 'every man's destiny is fastened to his body.' I kind of believe that . . . that Mike and me, well . . ."

"I must read the Koran," John said.

"I can't give Mike up. I don't give things up with any ease, or grace. That's the Oriental in me."

John decided it was the woman in her, but he didn't say so.

Mike Zelsmith hadn't wanted to go to Mollie's grunion party. He was still undressed, sitting in his underwear on the bed when John knocked on his cottage door. He didn't seem surprised when John delivered his message, just hurt, like a little boy. His shoulders lifted a little and he grinned that hard-looking grin—an almost sad grin.

"This really makes it bad, John. I'm in trouble with Mollie, too."

John nodded. "She hinted at something."

"She doesn't want to act in the picture. She doesn't have any faith in her abilities. She doesn't want to hurt me, she says. What a lousy woman's trick . . . They all say *that*. They don't want to hurt you. Being human, they hurt you and themselves."

"Too bad," John said.

"And this thing isn't going to help. Not that Mollie gives a damn about marrying if we can't. But I want to get married. You'd think a moral New England character like Mollie would feel it's the proper thing to do, but, well . . ." He stopped and looked at his watch. "I better dress."

"Mollie is unhappy," John said.

"Is it my fault?" Mike asked earnestly.

"No, I think this Gene thing coming to a head, and her feeling about herself, that maybe she'll fail you in some way."

"So it is me." Mike stepped in his pants and began to open a freshly bought shirt. "Goddamn it, why do they put in all these pins and cardboard and plastic collar ribs! Maybe I've done her a big harm, John. Maybe I shouldn't have . . . oh hell, I've stuck myself. Look at the blood!"

He sucked his big thumb and looked at John. Then Mike laughed. "Give me a big fancy word to put me back on my trolley tonight. Alice's message kind of rocked me."

John thought and said, "You like *ataraxia?* That's Greek, means an indifference to the faults and troubles of humanity."

Mike sucked his thumb and then looked at it. "That's great. You can carve it on my tomb. But right now nuts to indifference."

Mike got, John suspected, a bitter pleasure out of everything he did. His ego would not let him avoid the bows and

154

not shout back and scream in rages and belittlings, but everything he took, everything, even when he didn't understand it, was part of what life was and what Mike expected from life. He could be as foolish as the rest—John knew that—could be in small things as petty and unreasonable, but on the full flavor of life, the bigness and greatness of it, he appeared (and was, John felt) a giant. Mike railed against the barbarians and the decadent technicians of the town, but really he brushed them aside and ignored them. He felt them merely crudely deluded, spiritually ill, "a commercial culture of sunlight and lousy chrome trimmings."

John would have liked to be like him, scarred but unhurt, battled but untouched inside, but he knew he lacked the genuine vulgarity, the bad taste, and loud ego of genius, real genius. All these things dropped away from Mike at his best, and his greatness remained. John knew that he had too much taste and tolerance, the curses of his times. He could never be the rational anarchist Mike was, and therefore could never be the fuller artist Mike was at his prime.

Mike would grin at him and say he was, "a thinking sonofabitch instead of a feeling sonofabitch," and John could only agree. And it was too late to do a damn thing about it.

"Anyway," Mike added, "maybe I stay here because I was born on this muckheap. And to a chemist a manure pile contains almost all the wonderful elements that scientifically make up the universe. Including grunion parties. Grunions are nice people I've found out."

Pucky Garrison caused a sensation at Mollie's Ark. And the Ark was full of sensation that night, John felt. Walter had returned, drunk, had had a fight with Mollie, and was sulking in a corner with his big-nosed friend, Bertie Ironspinner. Harry Steiner and his small wife, Rose, were making up an early-morning disagreement, and Harry was whispering to everyone as he passed the drinks that he had promised Rose that he wasn't "going to get into a verbal battle on art, literature, or world conditions." The beach bums and the unemployed actors and screenwriters were drinking Mollie's whisky and tearing into two chickens she had roasted. The dogs roamed around among the guests, Lucky wagging his tail in feeble salute. And Pucky, wearing a huge ruby ring, was cheering everybody up.

Dr. Sontag came over to Mike and shook his hand. The doctor looked tired—his bald head was peeling sunburn.

"That's quite a Christmas tree, that Mrs. Garrison."

"She's harmless. Where is Mollie?"

"Learning the television business on the sun deck."

"Oh," Mike said very politely, and Dr. Sontag did not lower his eyes. Harry Steiner put a drink in John's hand and one into Mandy Rye's hand and whispered, "First today? . . . Grunion due to run in ten minutes."

Mike sat down and took Lucky onto his lap. The little dog felt very light. He could feel the racing heart under his fingers. Everyone except Mike and Pucky Garrison were dressed in beach clothes much the worse for wear, and barefooted. A pile of fish-stinking buckets stood stacked in a corner. The record playing machine was on and Pucky was dancing with Harry Steiner, who was explaining why her husband's last three books were not art but money in the bank. Two more couples came in carrying hamburger rolls and a carton of beer, and someone slapped a woman who cried until someone asked her to dance. On the road just outside the door the great night trucks were passing, shaking the walls. Nevil Garrison watched his wife and drank.

The door from the porch opened and Mollie came in with Max Reilly. Max's arm was around her hips. Mollie was wearing one of her men's shirts and blue jeans with a very tight black leather belt about six inches high buckled to the last brass eyelet, as tight as it could be pulled.

"First call for grunion! Coming on the tide . . . Everybody out!" She seemed keyed up.

Mike went over to her and greeted her and Reilly. "You don't mind if I don't grunion tonight?"

"Why should I mind? Max, get our buckets."

Mike watched Max limp off, then turned to Mollie. "Let's not be foolish, baby. I had to go off the last few nights to work. You're just upset."

"I'm upset about a lot of things. And a little drunk, too, see. It's not going to work out, you and me."

"What a lousy romantic speech, Mollie."

"I've been studying your screenplay."

Reilly came up to them waving the buckets. Mike wanted to say something, something cruel, and hit somebody. But there was no time, everyone was piling out into the porch and down the winding stairs to the moon-coated beach.

Mike turned slowly back to the bar and poured himself a stiff brandy. Dr. Sontag came up and raised a glass to his lips and smiled.

"Bad, Zelsmith?"

"Pretty bad. You love her too, don't you, Doc?"

"Yes, but I can't be hurt. I just stand and adore on the sidelines. The perfect love affair. When she dies I may even get her body and stuff it. It's a wonderful body. I've seen it as much as you have, only professionally."

Mike sat down and listened to the shouting from the beach. "Don't be cynical, Doc."

The overwhite hands of the doctor took Mike's glass and refilled it.

"You don't grunion?" Dr. Sontag asked.

"No." Mike pulled some magazine clippings out of a pocket. "But I've been reading about them this afternoon. It's pretty fascinating."

"Is it?"

"Listen." Mike began to read. " 'The grunion is a fish about as long as a man's hand. The grunion has come to recognize the rhythm of the tides, the monthly cycle during which tides are higher. It has so adapted its spawning habits to the tidal cycle that the existence of the species depends on this adjustment. After each full moon from March to August, the grunion appear in the surf on the beaches of California as the tide reaches flood stage, and begins to ebb.' "

Dr. Sontag nodded. "No more free agents than the tourists in season."

"You're getting it," Mike said. He read on. " 'On the. waves of the ebbing tide, the fish begin to come inshore. Their bodies shimmer in the light of the moon as they are borne up the beach on the crest of a wave; they lie on the wet sand, then fling themselves into the next wave and are carried back to sea. For an hour after the turn of the tide, thousands upon thousands of grunion come up on the beach, then return to the sea. This is the spawning act of the species. During the brief interval between waves, the female and male have come together in the wet sand, the former to shed her eggs, the latter to fertilize them. When the parent fish return to the water, they leave behind a mass of eggs buried in the sand.' "

Dr. Sontag lit a cigar and gave one to Mike. "I suppose they get fun out of it. They must think *our* sexual patterns pretty dull."

Mike read, " 'With the new-moon tides the waves wash over the places where the masses of grunion eggs were buried, the surf stirring the sand. As the sand is washed away and the eggs feel the touch of the cool sea water, the membranes rupture, the fishlets hatch, and the waves bear them away to sea.'"

"Don't draw a picture too close to the human animal," Dr. Sontag said. "His behavior is a little more varied."

"Not much," Mike said, 'if you strip away the fancy-nancy trimming. Only we think we're the grunion hunters. Our ego. And we're really the grunion."

"God's creatures all," said Dr. Sontag, lifting a fresh glass. "You believe in God, Zelsmith?"

"I'm polite to him."

"An attitude of wonder toward the daffy abstraction of the Absolute?"

"—" said Mike, tossing his clippings in the fireplace. "I'm tired of fancy words."

Nevil Garrison came running up from the beach, his pants legs wet. He said curtly to Mike, "Where is Pucky?"

"Down on the beach with the rest of you," Mike said.

"You think so, eh?" Nevil said.

He looked around, scowled, cursed very low, and went out and down to the beach again. Mike said softly, "Wife trouble."

"That too is part of the grunion world, the two-footed, Cadillac, best-seller grunion world," Dr. Sontag said.

Mike turned to face the doctor squarely. "What do you think about Mollie?"

"As Mollie, or in relationship to yourself?"

"Don't get so snotty professional. We're just two guys at a party."

"Talking about our hostess."

"That's right. Drink?"

"A short one . . . fine."

"Something I've done, or haven't done, has upset her," Mike said.

"Mollie is a child about a lot of things, Zelsmith. You're the first mature man that has ever come into her life, emotionally. All her husbands were little children she took care of. I could talk to you a lot about the scientific texts, the fundamental factors underlying her personality, but I'm not going to. I'll keep it on floor level."

"Thanks. I've got no head for the big words tonight."

Harry Steiner came in and grabbed a first-aid kit and a

bottle of bourbon. "Somebody stepped on some broken glass!
Boy, are they running! Come on!"

Harry ran out and Dr. Sontag went on slowly, as if remembering old classroom lectures. "She said you reminded
her of her father. You did more than that. Mollie's early
childhood was dominated by her father. He was the big
male, the large, stern figure of her girlhood. They were in
conflict. But he was also the normal expression of her sexual
imaging of what a real man was. Her inner mind, the secret
mind that the outer mind can't control, merged her romantic
yearning with the father image. When she got out in the
world she fooled herself. She turned as far from the father
image as she could. She married weaklings, mothered them.
But the real woman inside Mollie was never touched. Nothing ever set fire to her until you came along."

"You simplify too much, Doc."

"Maybe. Unknown to Mollie, she got what she wanted in
you, her father image. It was normally transferred to you.
It worked. For the first time Mollie wasn't a child any more.
She was a grown-up, passionate woman."

"Then what's the trouble now?"

"Mollie has tendencies—throwbacks—to return to her
childhood state. It's a protective thing, fully automatic at
times. When say, her work goes bad, when she's broke,
when she's alone too much, she becomes the child again."

Mike said, "I know you're being very scientific, but I
think there's a lot of Mollie you don't understand. I do."

"Ego, ego, Zelsmith. You've got more than a bump of it.
Everybody thinks he's a little Freud and knows everything."

"Reilly is so repulsive," Mike said suddenly. "That dragging leg of his."

"It isn't repulsive to her. He's like a hurt child needing
pity, to Mollie. Like Lucky taking his pills, or the birds
needing attention. Gene, remember, had weak lungs. The
first husband had a mother to fight over for his attention.
Mollie likes, in certain moods, hurt and feeble objects.
Don't underestimate Reilly's leg. It's his best bet tonight."

"You've got a dirty mind, Doc."

"I'm on your side, Zelsmith. Don't insult me."

"Sorry."

"A child often does mean, spiteful things. It likes to
shock the adult world. Walter was cruel to her tonight. He
hates the whole world when he's on a bender. Lucky had a

heart attack. She adores him as a child of her own. You have personal problems. It all adds up."

"I don't want to hear any more, Doc."

"All right, I'll stop talking."

"Let's go fishing."

"I hate wet feet."

Mike took off his shoes and socks and rolled up his pants legs. He went out onto the sun deck. The sea was coming in fast breaking white and sounding very strong. The scribble of night on the horizon was not very clear and he saw millions of little leaping fish left on the shore line by the retreating waves. All along the curving beach people were scooping up the little fish and shouting at each other. He walked down the stairs and his feet sank into the wet sand with a cold shock along his spine. He could not find any of Mollie's party. He went up the beach among the busy fish catchers. At a pile of driftwood one party had built a big fire and were frying the little fish. Beer bottles were being opened, and the feasting and drinking faces in the firelight were masks of people seen at night and excited by the hunt. Everyone, it seemed, was having a good time.

Farther up the bone-gray beach where it made a wide curve and ended in a long line of rusting iron shapes stuck in the ground, there were fewer people. He walked along, stepping on the bubble pods of sea weeds that cracked under his feet with a pop. He saw Harry and Rose Steiner pulling a sopping Pucky Garrison from the sea. Water was running from her as from some foolish garden fountain. John and Mandy were pushing her from behind.

"I've lost my ring!" Pucky was shouting. "My big ruby ring. I can't go home without it!"

"Easy does it," Mandy was screaming. "We'll find your Goddamn ring! But stay out of the waves with that dress. You'll drown!"

Pucky appealed to John. "Help me find my ring! Please, John. I don't dare go home with Nev without it!"

A big, snarling, dog-headed wave came in and knocked her down and tiny fish wriggled against and over her wet body, and the Steiners and John and Mandy pulled on her arms till she screamed in pain.

Mike went slowly up the beach. It was lonely. The Steiners had a little cottage here on the sand level with a bit of covered patio and a big swing. He and Mollie used to walk up to here a lot, holding hands, their faces held high in the salt wind. And they often stopped here in the patio to wipe off fuel oil spots with nail polish remover from the bottoms of their naked feet. They usually walked back on the dry sand higher up, reciting limericks, of which Mollie was very fond.

Mike crossed to the loose, drier sand where a high tide had left wonderful coral forms and kelp patterns, old tin cans and discarded contraceptives, small, washed tree branches and old-rose clam shells. There was no light in the Steiner place. Mike crossed the feeble weeds and dying flowers they tried to grow in front of the cottage. A *creak* from the big patio swing came to his ears. He stood very still and listened. Mollie was giggling her choking laugh and he could hear Reilly's whispered sallies. He remained there just a little while more and the whole of his chest was so tight he could not swallow air. He had never been so sick before in his life. It was as if someone held his flopping heart in his hand and were closing his fingers tighter. An ache filled the back of his throat and a pressure pushed at the roof of his mouth. He moved away slowly and when he could no longer hold it back he vomited into the sand.

He remembered walking down the beach and suddenly seeing the red angry face of Nevil Garrison shouting at him. It took him some time to focus on his words.

"You can't trust any of 'em, Mikey boy. Fishing she tells me! She gave that ruby ring to some tramp for a quick one! I know her!"

Behind the angry man appeared the face of Pucky also talking fast. "You've got to make him believe me, Mike! I was fishing! I lost the ring on the beach . . ." She grabbed the big man and swung him around. She shouted, "I've been fishing and that's all." She pushed her hands up to the man's face. "Here, smell my fingers! Smell them! Grunion!"

Mike walked slowly away and left them there, waving and gesturing at each other. He had suddenly a poignant disregard of his life—like a casual suicide . . .

"What do you think Mike will do?" Mandy asked John. They were wrapped in blankets and lying by a dying fire, the heavy chocolate surf churning a few feet away from

161

their toes. The beach was getting lonely, and the far-off hoot of a sea lion, that deep drum cough, and the hiss of scud and wind drift on the sand were about the only noises. Once in a while they heard the scratching of a crab passing them, as he carried his green stone armor on some secret expedition.

John said, "I don't know. I don't know Mike that well."

"Mollie doesn't mean anything by it. What would you do to me, John, if I acted that way?"

"I'd black your eye maybe."

"Darling!"

"What would you do, Mandy?"

"Oh, I'm old-fashioned. I've got a gun. I'd shoot you."

"It's killers like you that gave the West a bad name."

"I'm worried, Johnnie, about Mollie."

"I know . . ."

"Want to go up to the house?"

He didn't want to; he was thinking about that gun. Mandy had no reason to shoot him, as yet, but the California newspapers were always full of women shooting their men. The men didn't shoot much; they usually bashed in heads or tried to make it look like an accident, by auto or a drop over a cliff. And thinking all this, the blankets slung on his back as they walked arm in arm up to Mandy's house, he realized that love had come to John Fennel . . .

Mike couldn't sleep. No matter how he tried, no matter what else he tried to think of, he could hear the *creak creak* of the Steiner swing. He could see the dangling leg, the warped limb stiffly pressed against Mollie, and Mike rolled over in bed and groaned.

It was no good; he punched the pillow and turned it over and tried again to sleep, but the *creak creak* sounds came again.

He sat up and turned on the light and went into the bathroom (they had forgotten to fill his water pitcher again) and had two glasses of tepid water. He lay a long time staring, then turned out the light and almost put his thumb in his mouth, and fell asleep. When he was six he had had a bad summer and the thumb had helped him go to sleep. Things were better for a while after that summer; Mother and Father made it up, and he stopped sucking his thumb. He remembered he was very proud of giving up the habit, and when he was seven he was given—for his good habits—

a red cloth cat with a clockwork stomach that one wound up, and it ran across the living-room rug . . . *creak creak* . . .

13

It was one of the times that Mike did not want to wake up. He usually bounced up, vital and full of plans. He was moored now like a deep-rooted tree in some troubled sleep, and he tore himself free and came half awake and stirred in his bed, his mouth tasting bile and early sorrow. Through his half-lifted eyelids he saw the white sun of noon bleaching the cottage room, and he lay there tasting the stale bitterness in himself. It was some minutes before he moved at all, and then he rolled over with a groan and shut his eyes tight and tried to drown out all thinking and feeling. He failed and sat up trying to fight off his demon so urgent and insistent.

He was sitting there too miserable even to reach for the whisky bottle on the dresser when there was a knock on the door and Walter Chase came in looking like the romantic wreck of a human being. His eyes were bloodshot, his unshaven face had a yellow stubble on it, and he seemed to have difficulty focusing his mouth to form words. He looked like a big, soiled infant.

"Hello, M.Z."

" 'lo."

"I don't know which of us looks worse, Chief."

"I'd hate to think I look like you this morning, Walter."

"Got a little of the hair of the dog?"

Mike motioned limply to the dresser and buttoned his pajama top.

Walter poured two and they drank quickly, shivering for a moment as it bit and then spread out to soothe them. Walter sat down facing John and twirled his glass in his fingers.

"Things are in a mess. What a hassel last night."

"No post-mortem."

"Gotta have a post-mortem, M.Z. My fault. All of it."

"Your fault Mollie fell for Reilly last night?"

"That can't be true."

"Never mind."

163

Walter rubbed his head with his fists till his short hair almost sparked. "Look, M.Z., you and Mollie can't break up like this. Everything went wrong. She upsets very easy. The beach hasn't been such a good idea for her. All the bums drinking and eating there and her living alone with her dogs and bird life."

Mike stripped and went into the bathroom. He showered, first very hot, then very cold, and combed his hair carefully, being sure none of the ducktails in the back stood up. In his dressing gown and smoking the first cigarette of the day, he was comfortably miserable.

Walter had ordered over coffee and rolls and was making an effort to eat. Mike sat down and took the scalding coffee cup but couldn't eat. Walter carefully buttered a bit of roll and set it experimentally between his teeth.

"What are you going to do, M.Z.?"

"I don't know."

"Did you hear about Pucky Garrison asking Nevil to smell her hands to prove she was fishing?"

"They find the ring?"

"Hell, no. They have a lot of Pacific Ocean to hunt in. Want me to stay?"

"No thanks, Walter."

After breakfast Mike took a long walk, climbing into the hills behind the hotel. Tractors were plowing up the dried-out hillsides as a fire-prevention method and as the dry, dark soil rattled off the polished steel plows he wondered why man had ever come here. Perhaps it would be better if all of southern California went back to the desert, the olive, and St. John's Bread trees. The water would fail soon —the far-off rivers that fed it would dry up and then like a ghost town, like one of those Nevada villages eaten by pack rats and sun, this foolish civilization would dry up and blow away. In Asia it had happened, many times, long ago. He remembered the detailed pictures in the copies of *The London Illustrated News* that he preferred to *Life's* sleek cant. Those foundations of forgotten cities and civilizations whose water had failed, and the winds had pushed on them, and the sand had plucked out their eyes.

Smiling at his dark trend of thought Mike went slowly back to the hotel and ordered a lunch he couldn't eat. The elderly waiter was worried.

"But is anything wrong, Mr. Zelsmith?"

"No, Greg, just some iced tea, please."

"Shall I toss you another salad myself?"

"It isn't the salad."

"Perhaps the dressing was too tart. Less lemon."

"*Just* the iced tea."

The afterlunch cigar tasted dreadful and he threw it away in the Chinese vase full of clean white sand in the lobby. He went to his cottage and was trying to pick out a book to read when Mollie suddenly came out of the bedroom. She was wearing slacks and a faded nylon blouse. Small and delicate, she looked sensationally beautiful—a new kind of beauty. Her hair was in disorder and looked like thin golden wire.

She stood there, expressionless. "Hello, Mike."

"What do you want, Mollie?"

"I want you, Mike," she said frankly, the large very blue eyes unblinking.

"I doubt that."

"My cables are tight again."

"You didn't think so last night with Max Reilly."

"Nothing happened."

"You lie, Mollie."

He went up to her and gripped her by the shoulders. "You couldn't ever tell a good lie."

"Don't stand there, Mike, do anything you want. Hit me, break my jaw."

A quick heat burned in him. He closed his fist slowly and lifted it, flexing his muscles; to his horror he felt his lips pull back from his teeth. He measured skillfully for a punch (one good one, you bastard, no prolonged brutality).

"Go ahead, let me have it."

"Jesu—what a dame."

His arm dropped to his side (he knew this kindness was a mistake). "Sit down, you look tired."

She sat looking up at him, the way Lucky stared at people. He looked down at her feet. He knelt down and took off her white leather sandals, carefully opening the carelessly knotted ties. Then he went into the bathroom and came out with the bottle of nail polish remover and some swabs of cotton.

"Your feet are full of beach tar."

"I never said I was neat, darling."

Carefully he wet the dabs of cotton and slowly removed the beach tar stains, one by one. She watched him, blue eyes flecked with gold, biting down hard on her lower lip with her teeth.

"All last night, Mike, it was like Anna Karenina, the parts I read where the more she loves her man the more she keeps tearing it up, and she knows she's tearing it up and yet she can't stop herself."

He carefully cleaned his hands and leaned over and kissed her long thin toes. "We're not going to talk about it any more."

It was the best it had ever been.

FROM THE JOURNAL OF JOHN FENNEL

Mike and Mollie have made it up . . . I try and think how life would be with Mandy in some not-too-distant future. I do not talk to her about it because she becomes so emotional that I wonder if she has ever been even for a moment or a day happy with any man in domestic closeness. Being in love with Mandy is an escape not from truth but from despair. A kind of narrow escape into a new faith that had no known boundaries, into a country she had never fully explored. Love, Mike claims, is a cause for delight, a universal cause, even if the knowledge of this delight is often pulled away from under us and we are left facing each other puzzled, but aroused.

In love I find that every moment seems an eternity, and in passion all of eternity is only a moment, a moment keyed to a mortal understanding of the shortness of life. We can un-mortify ourselves in those rare moments of passion and I hope that in the future we can affirm our love, and assimilate all of life together, and perhaps that comradeship we both need. It would be easy, but most women preserve some kind of little death in themselves which their lonely selves fear. They have a vulnerable pleasure in things but there is lacking any hard-won faith in the permanence of anything. They can never fully redeem their joy and understand it.

All this beach life makes me feel like those characters in Proust's pages who do the oddest things, unexplained at first, half mad, while keeping up the veneer of the society they move in, and then suddenly everything is explained as play-acting, being nothing but a hood for their vices. So the beach and town often impress me. Like the people in Proust's novels, their oddness and madness are only things they use to cover their one big vice: to get a firm place in a studio. At first this seemed so true that it was like a difficult problem solved, and then I saw that while most of their lives had been an affair with the studios, there was something else, deeper and closer to them, that also colored their lives.

I shall take Mandy away as soon as I can, and living with

her elsewhere I think her problems will seem smaller. The beach woman has a problem. Life is not real to her, but that is not too bad, for she is beginning to understand that realistic love is not realistic at all. We just slice the top off a passion and meet as human beings for the first time in a kind of frenzied dream world of half darkness and throbbing shadows. Realistically it is only two bodies, but the mysterious creatures that we become, the metaphors that we are at such moments, reveal to each other some new character of human nature. We become a lesser preposterousness. We do not temporize at all at such moments, and even the final indignities of physical loving leave us with an austere feeling of that which is *only* deep as love, is *very* deep indeed. Mollie understands this—Mandy refuses to think of it.

Love to many people is often new ways of feeling old trivialities. But not for Mike. He says it must never become the final inconsequential decomposition of all the feeling and pain and effort that goes into it. He scowled when he said it . . .

Lucky lay stretched out on the sun-deck floor coughing, his little brown body shaking, his brown eyes turning to watch Mollie setting the small, blue-tiled table in the open air.

"I think he'd better have a pill," Mike said from the big beach chair where he was ruffling through his account sheets and studio costs.

Mollie nodded, put down the bottle of grocery store wine. Then she gave Lucky his pill and held his mouth closed until he swallowed it, and then they forced some whisky down his throat. He choked, gagged, coughed, and retreated under the sofa with a hurt expression. Ed the boxer tapped his hard tail against a chair.

Mollie grinned and said, "He's become a drunken old man, hasn't he?"

"A happy old age in a bourbon fog isn't bad."

"Nothing is going to happen to Lucky?" She was suddenly taut with a small fear.

"Nothing."

"I've had him a long, long time, since I was a small kid. He's all I have left. Twelve years. Except for you, Mike, nobody means as much to me."

"I'm in a tight private group, baby."

She lit the two big blue candles in the rusting iron holders and went in to bring out the dinner. Mike looked out over the dimpling sea and the black ugly cormorants riding the waves and the far-off lurch of a public fishing boat hurrying for home. Sandpipers—speckled birds with thin wet feet—ran along the fringe of the scudding sea and put long tubes down into the sand hunting for sand fleas. All along the curve of the beach, shore houses were lighting up and one could almost smell the cooking pork chops, fried shrimp, and even the garlic bread of beach life. He put aside the studio cost sheets.

There was the ring of the phone inside the house and he heard Mollie talking to someone for some time. She came out carrying a large plate of salami and smoked salmon, little Italian peppers and some kind of pallid calf's-foot jelly.

"That was Reilly," Mollie said, putting down the tray. "I cut him off short."

He helped himself to the salami. It was gritty and tasted of goat and candle wax.

"I got your favorite salami. A little Italian place where they hang those obscene-looking cheeses, like genitalia, in the windows."

"Thanks. I don't deserve it."

"You do."

He tried the smoked salmon on soggy crackers. Mollie came back with the soup tureen and spooned out a pale gray stew. "Chicken okra with everything cooked together a long time. Real New Orleans style. And wait till you taste the main course."

Mike ate slowly and forked up a sticky Mexican dish of corn meal mush and smoky, gluey cheese and sliced black olives and, as usual, too much olive oil. More cheese followed in reeking sections, all local products, "as good as anything they made in Europe." The wine was a native thing, weak and bitter, and he was thankful he didn't know good coffee from bad. They sat smoking their afterdinner cigarettes, holding hands, and Mike wondered how he could excuse himself to go in and have a few digestive pills. He had a lot of work planned for the next few days.

It was very dark now and the brisk wind was stirring the candles and Mollie was making puddles of warm candle wax on the cloth with a long finger. A seal barked far out at sea, and on the road above the house the big night trucks were already beginning to pound by, with that shattering roar, and the faint smell of diesel oil. Mike liked it and felt at home.

"It's fine here, us alone," Mollie said.

"But you don't like it alone," said Mike, lighting two fresh cigarettes and handing her one. "You can't sleep, you have nightmares when you're really alone here."

"All girls cry."

The front doorbell rang. The dogs began to bark, rasping throaty sounds that tore at the eardrums.

"Let it ring," Mollie said. "They'll go away."

They sat and listened to the ringing and the dogs barking. After a while Mike said, "Better answer it. The barking isn't good for Lucky."

Mollie went into the house and came back with a small, round, little man with loose pink features, pencils stuck in his vest pockets. The candles had blown out by now so Mike switched on the sun-deck lights.

Mollie said, "This is Mr. Crawford. He's from the insurance company."

The little man nodded and put a briefcase on his lap but didn't open it. "That was a ten-thousand-dollar ruby Mrs. Garrison lost. I don't suppose there is anything we can do but investigate your guests, Mrs. Reegan."

"Mrs. Reegan?" asked Mike puzzled.

Mollie nodded. "That's Gene's last name."

Mr. Crawford slowly looked from Mike to Mollie then back to Mike. "You're Mr. Chase, I gather."

Mike growled, "I would be if I weren't Mike Zelsmith. Mr. Chase lives downstairs under the sun deck. He isn't home tonight."

"You don't live here, Mr. Zelsmith?" The little man seemed fascinated by the secret lives he was probing.

"No. Get on with your business."

He saw that Mollie was beginning to shake. Mike said to Crawford, "Don't you think all this crap is nonsense? The ring was lost in the sea. I was there when she lost it. There is nothing to be gained but ill will for your company by investigating the people on this beach. They're just people like other people. I don't think they'd steal a ring."

"They're all my friends!" Mollie suddenly shouted. "They wouldn't have anything to do with your damn ring! You can't insult my friends!"

Mollie was screaming now and she stood up and held her arms to her side and looked at the little man.

"I'll see you tomorrow at my cottage, Mr. Crawford," Mike said, "back of the Beverly Hills Hotel at eleven. I'll give you all the details. Goodnight."

When Mr. Crawford had slipped out, his eyes wide, his briefcase under a well-worn coat jacket, Mike took Mollie in his arms. He helped her with a big handkerchief.

"Sorry I get so high-strung."

"We'll spend a quiet evening at home, darling."

She sniffed, smiled, and used the handkerchief again. "I just remembered Oscar is waiting for me in his law office."

"Who the hell is Oscar?"

"Oscar Pagano, you met him at my sister's. He's my lawyer. He handles all my divorces. He's got a property release from Gene and the divorce papers. I must sign tonight before Gene changes his mind."

"At this hour?"

"It's only in Santa Monica. Oscar is waiting, he called while I was cooking. It slipped my mind."

"This is no time to think of divorce agreements. You're upset."

"I'll be worse with Gene on my mind all night."

For some reason Mollie insisted they take her car. The little green car wouldn't start for a long time. When it did, its clutch kept slipping. They sat close together, Mike's arm around her neck. She was shaking badly now and he wondered if they should turn back.

"Mollie, you're in no condition to sign legal papers."

"I can't have Gene hanging on my mind. I'm always like this when the final papers come through. It all starts so well and ends so sordidly in a lawyer's office, dividing the community rags."

She stopped the car and let her head sink down on the steering wheel. He could hear her teeth chattering now.

"Buck up, baby."

"It was so brave and warm with Gene at first, I thought. We'll never get together, you and I. It can't really last."

"Come on home and lie down . . ."

She had not stopped shaking, but she insisted they drive on. The lawyer's office was on the tenth floor of a sun-weathered building. It was full of overdone dark furniture and many old historical legal documents on walnut paneling rotted on the walls.

The lawyer was a young Italian American with a broad dark face. He remembered Mike at Belle's and smiled. "I'll have the papers in a moment. I must go down the hall and get a seal on it."

Mollie sat in a chair and shook. She had no control now and no matter how much he wiped her face it remained wet. She stood up. "I'm going to the little girl's room."

"Shall I get someone to go with you?"

"No . . ."

She went down the hall and Mike sat watching the sea wind fluttering the faded apple-green curtains. He felt a moment of premonition come to him. What was Mollie doing? Was she standing—a little girl—at another window staring out, looking down ten stories?

"Jesu," Mike said to himself. "She can't jump!"

It was one of the darkest moments of his life: he felt pushed back into a pit, and his hands were tied. He remembered something he had once read and been impressed with, that the true, tragic element of life begins only at the moment when so-called adventures, sorrow, and dangers have disappeared. All significance after that is inward. We are then, he suddenly knew, the heirs to our ancestors who conceived life as something primitive, arid, and brutal. But this was no help. Nothing could reach Mollie now. He saw it in camera angles. She was alone, she was on the window ledge, she was launching herself into space, and gravity had her in its arms and was pulling her down to the last shattering of the vital spark. An angle shot, over-dramatized, with a wide-angle lens . . . the tiny body falling.

Footsteps, and he opened his eyes to see the lawyer looking oddly at him. "Where's Mollie?"

"She'll be back in a minute."

They spoke too calmly of the hopes of the theater in California, and the trouble in the citrus groves, and the size of fish one could catch six miles out.

Mollie appeared, looking almost composed, and sat down and signed where she was told. Mike said he hoped the lawyer would excuse them, hoped he would pardon the rush, but they were in a dreadful hurry. He walked Mollie to the elevator and she sank against him and he could feel her shaking. He did not bother with the car, but took a taxi back to the Ark. All the way home in his arms, she kept shivering and making odd little noises.

He stripped her and dried her and wrapped her in a robe and got her into bed. She was staring now, ahead of her, never stopping her shaking, and she did not know or see him.

He poured a little brandy into her and she opened her mouth but did not focus her eyes, and some of the brandy came up.

"I want Mother," she said, in a little girl's voice. "Please tell Mother I want to talk to her."

"Mollie." He rubbed her hands and cheeks. "Mollie."

"What's keeping Mother? She always comes in after I turn the light out."

Mike called Dr. Sontag's office and sat very still while the answering service tried to find him. At last a crisp voice said, "Dr. Sontag is in emergency surgery. He'll call us soon as he's free."

"Be sure of that. It's vital! See that he calls!"

"Yes, sir," crisp, impersonal, bored.

He went back to the bedroom and his heart broke. He had never believed in that expression, that "hearts ache." But he could feel his in his chest, the pain and the hurt . . . the tightness. He looked at the wet face and blew her nose and sopped her lips. He sat and rubbed her hands.

"Mother! What's happened to Mother?"

Mike leaned his head down on the bed and sobbed as he had not sobbed since an uncle beat him at the age of nine. He had not ever cried over his hopes or early troubles. This time, in abject pity for the tortured creature on the bed, he cried. Sonofabitch, he felt, poor sonofabitch, how did it all come to this?

He cried because he was sorry for her, because she was hurt and so strange, and because he could not see anything this alive and beautiful suffer.

All the stored-up, crystallized pity he had withheld all his life he now gave to her. And he knew that his lousy pity could not help her at all.

Was he too kind to her? He wondered. Too-long periods of living in a world of little kindness, with men who were casual and almost indifferent had kept Mollie from being emotional, and now his kindness had driven her into some complex mood. If only he had not been so kind to her! She would have remained easy and amused perhaps, interested but not too deeply involved.

Mike knew his own nature well enough to see that he had never accepted Mollie on her own valuation. He had to make of it an intense, almost unbearably sentimental love, and he could see that too much sentiment reacted on Mollie like a virus, making her toxic and in fever. It would make

172

her whip her senses beyond satiety and she would end up moaning in childhood.

"Never get to know the woman." That was what an uncle had once told Mike. "Let 'em stand for just sex, that's enough, boy. Don't go mucking about in their souls. Perversion, that's what I call this sentimental stuff, handholding and staring in their eyes."

Of course Uncle Ralph hadn't had a happy end. Like almost everyone else, he had died the hard way, whining with a heavy ache and holding his housekeeper's hand and asking her to kiss him before he died. (What was keeping the Goddamn doctor?)

14

DR. SONTAG, blandly professional and silent after cleaning his needle in the bathroom, came out buttoning up the little leather case that held his hypodermic set. He looked over at the wall bed. Mollie was sleeping now, her mouth open, snoring slightly. A picture of innocent calmness.

The doctor came to the bed, felt her head, brushed back the damp hair, and nodded to Mike.

"She's all right now, Zelsmith. I'll keep her calm for a day or so. Can I have something to eat? I came here right from the emergency room."

Mike nodded numbly and went into the kitchen. He heated up the remains of the chicken okra and cut two slices of French bread, came out and laid out a knife and spoon on the living-room table. Dr. Sontag came in, sat down, and began to spoon up the thick soup quickly. He ate with keen relish. He broke off big bits of bread and chewed hard, looking at Mike cleaning the ashtrays by throwing their contents into the well-filled fireplace. He ate, chewing carefully, enjoying his food.

"Well, how do you like seeing a patient in a state of shock?"

"She's not a patient, she's Mollie," Mike said.

The doctor waved his spoon in the air. "She's back again in her childhood, a little kid calling for her mother."

"She didn't know me. It was Goddamn frightening."

"It happens."

"What did it?"

"Everything she's been bravely fighting all her life, added to the shocks of late. The lost ring, the man from the insurance company. The nasty bit with Reilly; she wasn't very happy about it this morning when I talked to her."

"Skip Reilly."

"The world is full of people who want to make love to Mollie. In a way it's a compliment to our mutual taste, Zelsmith."

"Coffee, brandy?"

"Some brandy." He took the brandy from Mike and sipped it. "Then on top of everything, that trip to sign the divorce papers. You see, she comes from a fine family with decent feeling."

"She's not a tramp."

"Anyway, it was too much for her nervous system."

The doctor finished the soup, swallowed the last bit of bread, and took a long suck on the brandy.

"How is she really, Doc?"

The doctor laughed and rubbed his white hands dry on a paper napkin. "There is hope for everybody. But you must want to be saved. Does Mollie?"

"Sure she does."

"Her preparation for a return to childhood is so complete. She has an instinct for its rituals and ceremonials. We've just seen her own long rite of confession and a form of extreme unction. Let me draw it for you in simple terms. Mollie is ashamed of her past. She messed it up. She hunted for a childhood instead of a mate. She meets her father image, the man she can respect, who can make her a woman. She takes it all and is happy, but other things still bother her. She isn't sure of you yet. Something from your own past rides on you, rides lightly, but rides on your back, Zelsmith."

"Cut the lousy poetry. Will she know what happened?"

"A great deal of it. But the stuff of the inner mind will not be clear to her. She's in love, but good. You're not much more of a bastard than most men in such a situation."

"Go to hell, Doc."

"To be scientific, she's suffering from hysterical absence. She yields to her suggestions and reproduces psychic creation or *psychi traumata,* as we call it. Pathogenic memories in certain chronological sequences. The fixation of many of us is conditioned by using the past to hide in."

"Now you're scaring me," Mike said.

"Cheer up. Most of the time there is nothing so abnormal in these fixations. Mollie has a double personality, or a double conscience. She can be fearing the modern world on one level and be a child at her mother's side in the other. The unconscious we used to call it. Mollie's ashamed of herself, in her unconscious."

"Will she wake up tonight?"

"Not with what I loaded her with. You staying alone here?"

"I'll get Mandy Rye from next door."

"Good. Take my advice. Take two sleeping pills yourself when you get back to the hotel."

"I'm sleeping out here on the couch."

"I'll give her a last look-over."

Mollie was sleeping peacefully now, squarely and solidly on her back. The doctor held her pulse, nodded. "Pulse a little fast, but good. Heart action like an army tank. You can't kill her through the heart, anyway."

He stood back and looked down at the sleeping girl. His face relaxed its usually ironic expression.

"Look at her. At this moment she is most likely the happiest five-year-old on the block."

The phone was ringing, a long, long alley of biting sound, and it was like sticking pins into Mike's eyeballs. The dogs were barking. He came awake feeling the ache in his back —the whole spine—from the uneven surface of the sofa. He rubbed his eyes, kicked out at Ed, the boxer, and stumbled to the phone. He was having just a little trouble remembering just where he was. He had a feeling he was back at the hotel, in his cottage, and on the big patio of his modern house. By the time he had lifted the phone off its cradle, his mind was clearing of its deep, drugged sleep.

"Hello, Mike?" It was John Fennel.

"Yes, John." His mouth tasted like spoiled leather.

"Why don't you go home sometimes? You didn't show up for last night's story conference."

Mike looked at his watch. 10:17. He said into the phone, "Had a little trouble. Mollie isn't feeling well. I'll see you later."

Mike hung up and looked down at his wrinkled underwear. He climbed into his pants feeling clammy and soiled, and put on the shirt that was far from clean. He set the glass bubble of water boiling for coffee and went and knocked on the bedroom door, knocking very lightly. Mandy Rye, her eyes puffy with uncomfortable sleep, opened the door and nodded to him.

"Hello, Mike."

"Still sleeping?"

"Still out. I'm worried over her."

"The doctor said she'd be like that. He loaded her."

He went over to the bed and looked down at Mollie. She had pushed her face deep into the pillow and all he saw was one warm cheek. He bent down and rubbed it and noticed that Mandy had combed her hair and tied it up neatly with a thin blue ribbon. Except for her breathing, she did not stir.

"She looks better, Mandy."

"She doesn't move at all."

"I'll get back as soon as I can. Rose Steiner will take over when you want to leave."

"Doesn't she eat?"

"Give her some tea or broth."

"Anything to drink?"

"If she insists, a little brandy."

Mandy nodded and began to open the blinds. The wild sunlight hunted out at once the dark corners of the bedroom and filled with color the wall paintings and the book jackets. Mike went out to see if the water was boiling for the coffee.

Jesu, he'd become a regular Florence Nightingale . . .

"You're hiring the camera crew by the day," the little cameraman said, sucking his cigar stub into fire. "You're payin' them if they work or not."

"I can't start shooting this week," Mike said. "Mollie isn't up to it. Next Tuesday."

They were seated in Mike's cottage, the production man, the assistant director, the cutter and editor, Walter and John, and the usual girl with her notebook taking everything down; although, to John, it all seemed of no value, at least not to record.

Mike got up and picked up his blackwood cane and whacked a few sofa pillows very hard. "That's it, next Tuesday." He grinned. "Always started my big ones on a Tuesday."

"Yep," said the cameraman, not a man to commit himself.

"This means," Walter said, "we'll be two weeks late on

the shooting, and will have to pay to keep the sets standing."

"I know, Walter. But I want Mollie to feel right when we start. How is she this morning?"

"Cheerful. I just stopped her from running the dogs up and down the beach."

"Get an item out to the columns that we're rewriting her part, she looked so good in the tests . . ."

Everyone had one more drink and left except John. Mike looked at him and shook his head, pulling off his heavy framed glasses. "I could shoot around Mollie, you know, but that money I was getting from England has been held up by banking red tape a few days."

"I'm rewriting the big scene at the end." John wanted to say more, but he saw that Mike was in one of his nonlistening moods when you could talk at him, and none of it got past his ears.

Mike patted his arm casually, absent-mindedly. "That's the boy. I'll run out and see how Mollie is doing."

Mollie's beach house was silent when Mike got there, but at once the dogs greeted him with barks and leaps. He pushed open the front door and found Mandy Rye in the kitchen cleaning up.

Mandy grinned and did a comic take in one of her voices. "Madame's up and has been asking for you."

"Thanks, Mandy."

"The doctor was here and told her she was too tough to die."

Mike walked softly into the bedroom. Mollie was sitting up in bed, wearing a pretty blue bed jacket, and her hair was neat in two braids held by little ribbons. She was examining her neck and throat carefully in a hand mirror.

"Hello, baby," he said, stopping short of the bed.

"Been a pretty bad girl, haven't I?"

He sat down on the bed and took her hand in his. "Feeling any pain?"

"Feeling no pain." She grinned.

"Think you can start Tuesday?"

Mollie sighed. "As ready as I'll ever be to be an actress. . . . Do you remember me asking for my mother?"

"Don't you?"

"I don't remember any of it."

She held out her arms to him.

There was about her an earnest yet calm urgency, and

he held her and her very blue eyes grew wider and calmer. "I'm all right again," she whispered.

The night-coughing trucks were running in the early-morning hours when they woke up. No need for talking, just making a touching contact with the sea wind ruffling the drapes and the salt smell of the high tide knocking wetly against the pilings of the house. Near dawn they heard Walter's old car drive up and heard the slamming of the front door, and his fumbling steps as he crossed the living room and whispered the dogs into silence. They heard him cross the sun deck on unsteady feet, and then go down the stairs to his room. Then two shoes falling and a big rattle of bed springs as he fell. Then again the trucks and the waves and the dogs moving about.

They heard the love birds begin their predawn gossip in the cage. Then they slept—tight little personal deaths of warm relaxation—and did not wake till noon.

FROM THE JOURNAL OF JOHN FENNEL

Mike is going through a period of re-examining his moral values. Ethics and morals are a thing he has long struggled with. Good and bad, right and wrong are as clear to him, he explained, as sweet and sour, or black and white. "But the trouble is no moral question, it is either sweet or sour or just black or white. It's often bland and tepid, or gray and tan." Evil on certain levels he can understand, but degrees of wickedness and punishment puzzle him. Theft and adultery are supposed to be on the same evil level. To him a state of love is beyond that moral fence. "A man and woman in love commit no sin if their codes are decent and they are honest only to two people: each other." The Biblical word *fornication* has been shortened by Anglo-Saxon usage; of it, Lord Chesterfield is said to have remarked that the cost is dreadful, the position ridiculous, and the pleasure too fleeting; but Mike doubts if he made that remark at his peak. Ants are about the only perfect moral citizens he knows; he says he knows so little about them that he is sure he is wrong. "They never appear in divorce courts, go on strike, write best sellers or find one particular ant more attractive than any other ant."

I had felt that it is this device of romantic personal love (a late invention, by the way, of the early Renaissance) that is causing all the trouble. One particular woman. Or, as Mike defines it, "Love is one particular attitude to a section of a particular woman." It has certainly played the devil with mankind.

I agree with Mike that people who can avoid this emotional trap seem to be no happier, however. The town's moral values are rather odd. Emotions almost always follow salary brackets, Mike admits. A woman star can go through four husbands and a dozen affairs in no time and still retain that earnest hunt for a romantic perfection that she knows will bore her. There is no secret about anything here and the pairings-off and the hasty matings are items every day in the world press. It may be the climate or it may be a certain connection with the simple, trashy stories they film, but few of them really become cynical or defeated in their hunts for romantic perfection. Few see that they are incapable of honest emotional thinking.

There are of course the noted males of the town, the stallions at stud, who are the escorts of the lonely ladies; but these are problem children who cannot find, or lack the ability to find, real emotional stability. They become show horses, exhibit their muscles, their tennis playing, their handsome coats of tan, around town, but rarely find any joy in their work except at that moment when the camera bulbs go off in some popular night club. "Only orgasms in public," Mike says, "would satisfy them."

Mollie is of course sure that there is the perfect mate for everyone *if* such a thing, can be found; this explains a great deal about her. I may be wrong about Mollie's social grouping. She may be more part of the town than I am willing to admit. This may be the reason for her returns to her childhood state, so cruel and painful. A journey between the pain of her childhood and the problems of her adult life. The unreconcilable, sound moral values of her father, and the slippery ice of the make-believe world of the motion-picture industry. There is certainly a conflict. Mollie settled in Santa Barbara or in Pasadena, married to a successful manufacturing plumber or a doughnut promoter, might be normally happy . . .

Mandy Rye is a different kind of woman. She is a little hung over this morning. The whole town seems hung over; the hotel waiters were rushing the Bloody Marys of tomato juice and raw egg into discreet bedrooms, the moist-eyed drunks were standing at the counter of Schwab's drinking bromos with loose mouths. The town is amused about its drinking. It speaks of lapping up the booze, tying one on, pub crawling, bending the elbow. One could collect a nearly complete anthology of alcoholics out here, and the mental disorders that either bring it on, or, I suppose, result from it.

Mandy doesn't like to talk about it or its devastating prospects. Her thirst is the result, Dr. Sontag thinks, of a once-unquenchable ambition to become famous and rich in her youth.

"A future without drinking," says Ed, the unemployed director, "is unbearable, dull, dry, barren. I couldn't face it. There is no fun or enjoyment without alcohol for anybody who's lived in this town as long as I have. I'd feel deprived of my manhood. It's cozy in the bars, it's warm and close here and my friends live here. They like me in the bars. I'm a great guy here; any place else where they don't drink they look at me as if I were a pathological liar, a cheat, a mug incapable of any real affection for anybody but myself."

They drink a lot in the industry. From the fancy Romanée St. Vivant 1936, Meursault Perrières 1942, to the rum drinks and the scotch of studio parties, to the derelicts on Skid Row who beg for a half dollar for a bottle of cooking sherry 40-proof, or grocery store port fortified with grain alcohol.

I've had them all here: Piesporter Goldtropfchen, Auslese, Dom Perignon Champagne, or a corn whisky that could run jet fighters, all in the same house.

Mandy drinks to keep her ego walking the tightrope that is her waking life, and Walter drinks, and I help them drink; but I'm not part of the town's drinking scene. Sometimes I think they drink because the industry has made of their lives a landscape haunted by an unsettled past and an unknown future. The just-lived past survives in bad debts, or an English car, or a lost wife; and the moral strain is the ever-present fear of being left out of the industry. The industry is always on their backs—and no matter if it promises to make their work impersonal, mechanized, and depthless, even the artists want the comfort, the rewards, it can offer.

Mollie is as yet merely on the fringe of this world. The real aristocrats of the town, the top directors, the fattest producers, the box-office stars, lose themselves in a false gentility, in alcohol, shop talk, rhetoric, and greed. Sometimes their degeneration hits bottom by buying faked modern art or acquiring a phoney Oxford accent. Sometimes they dabble in homosexuality, the Freudian couch, the country life in expensive outdoor leather and Stetson hats—ranching at a loss of only a hundred thousand dollars a year. There is, Mike says, none of the real Faulknerian fury in them, the earthly harshness of common rape or Latin castration or the incestuous horror of small-town Americana. They are bored or amused or clownish with the sexual act and perform it with no instinctive sympathies. They endure their humiliation with patience and a certain drunken dignity, while the floors beneath them are rotting away; the termites eat up their great houses; the ants and sunlight destroy the beach shack, the hill hovel. Perhaps Mike is right.

"The images of our lousy social and moral disease," Mike says, "are fashioned by the best tailors, the best bootmakers, and the best car bodies. Our dimensions of reality, Johnny, are distorted so that anything normal frightens us. Imagine living all your life with one wife, or never getting five hundred dollars a week. Most of us have made more for a few years. The bait is always there for us. The town has its complacent provincialism, so we accept the second best of everything. Our art, music, and literature is always what's been tossed away by the genuine cultural centers. There is a true Dostoevskian flavor—to quote Walter—about us, but it tastes of suntan oil and Max Factor make-up and everything is sunkissed a Goddamn Van Dyke brown.

"There is so much yapping in the big houses late at night . . . The drinks are poured and everybody wants to tell how badly they have been treated; how love has let them down, how much their income taxes are, what their doctor told them about their glands, the cost of servants, the trade-in allowance on their last car, the trouble with their water-head director, producer, writer, star, or agent . . . so we drink."

Mandy crosses her long legs up to her pelvic section, sinks back into a too-low modern chair and smiles and sips. Tall glasses, the ice cubes rattling; showing more leg and thigh every time she has a refill. She looks comfortable, but there appears an icy urgency about her drinking; she wants to get it down to forget everything that will make her moody, that will worry her about money, about the fact that the big studios aren't even asking her out for interviews any more, that her agent isn't really in the top class with the Morris Office and MCA, that no first-class agent invites her out now for lunch at Romanoff's. And also I sense—as I smile at her—something secret that feeds on her, that I know nothing of, but I can feel it almost like a doctor a lump on a suspected breast. I know her, I don't know her, and my kidneys ache and I've had too much to drink myself. And Mandy goes to the little girl's room and comes back and crosses her legs like a lady and takes a refill in a brown fist.

The phone rang and Mike Zelsmith looked up from the cost sheets and put down his pen and went over and picked it up.

"Zemmich?"

"Zelsmith."

"That's right, Zelsmith. Well, Mr. Zelsmith, I'm an old fan of your pictures, see everything you ever do. Matts' the name. Henry Kamp—with a K—Matts."

"Yes, Mr. Matts."

"I've just organized the Matts Comic Adventure Group. Adventure stories in comic-strip form."

"I don't read them."

"Look, you can clean up. I want you to write one for me."

"What the hell!"

181

"Look at Al Capp, at Milt Caniff. Look at Milt Gross, retired a millionaire."

"I'm not interested in lousy comic strips."

"It's big time now. Real money for producers, creators."

"No, thank you."

"Mr. Zelsmith, listen."

"I think you got the wrong man."

"Look, big shot, don't kick a chance like this in the ass, it's . . ."

"Good-by."

He hung up and went back to the cost sheets and picked up the pen and cleaned its point on the desk blotter. He had to take two drinks before he could get his mind back to the cost sheets.

They started shooting the picture on Tuesday after all. A little weak in the pins, Mollie didn't make it, but they shot the gambling-house scenes around her. By Saturday Mollie had done a scene and it had looked very good the next day in the dailies. John had always thought the snips of film that were shown the morning after they were taken were called rushes. But nobody in Hollywood called them that—they were called dailies. The story was never called a scenario either, but always the script. And there was little excitement or fun to making a movie. It was a slow process of shooting a few seconds, or a minute or two, of moving lights, of tearing out a wild wall of a room, of lifting a table or a chair or wooden blocks to fit into the camera setup, of actors standing round while make-up people wiped the sweat off grease-painted brows.

Mike sat in a sawed-off kitchen chair without a back, twirling his cane, and directed with a crisp, snarling voice, impatient at the usual delays of props and lights and dolly tracks. Walter shook his head over the slow thud of carpenters' hammers.

"That's why M.Z. never directed before, only produced. He likes fast action; he likes a thing done with a flow and a rush—and great pictures are made like that. It's the grind of taking two lines over and over again. Wyler does forty takes on some of his scenes."

"Quiet!" shouted the assistant director, who was picked for his voice and not his brains.

"Jesu!" said Mike, "give me one good one and let's get on to the next lousy scene! Stop goosing those broads!"

By that time John knew broads were lights, not women. It took three more takes before they had one they could print. Mollie appeared small and beautiful before the camera, like something that looked like her, but not in any real way. They made progress too slowly. And they could not go slowly, Mike howled, for they were on a limited budget and had to be in the cans before their money ran out.

At the end of the day Mike would wrap a towel around his wet neck and sit in the wheelless trailer that was his office on the set, and drink beer out of cans.

"We'll never get done at this rate," he said. "And all that location stuff to do yet."

Walter looked up from his notebook. "We've found a grape farm near Fresno that is just right."

"Good roads for the cameras and light crews?"

"Fair, M.Z."

"We'll cheat on the location stuff, Walter. Shoot a lot of background plates for process, and instead of taking the cast up on salary after they're finished, we'll use doubles, filming them from the back."

Walter frowned. "It's a good location. Why not really work in our stuff and cast up there?"

Mike shook his head and wiped his face with the towel around his neck. "Can't afford it. By the time this picture is finished, I'll be scraping the bottom of the barrel. I want enough left over for a big première."

John asked, "You think we can get a major studio release on this picture?"

Mike grinned and threw the empty beer can out of the open trailer door. "I better, or we're all up Stink Creek and no paddle."

Mollie came in still in make-up. She grinned. "You killing actors these days?"

"Sorry, baby," he said. "You were good today. Really looked good in there, didn't she, John?"

John nodded but said nothing, and Mollie pressed his arm.

"He's learning, Johnny is. Never commit yourself, just nod, and if you have to talk, say 'interesting.' "

Mike pulled off the towel and began to take off his wet shirt. "Let's forget the picture for tonight and go and eat at the Plume Café. Walter, get me fifty dollars from the cashier."

183

BOOK FOUR

"For all that happens began in the past and presses hard upon the future . . ."

—T. S. ELIOT

15

THAT season there was little rain, hardly any real rain at all. As the summer advanced, Mike, driving to the beach house from Beverly Hills, could see the garden hoses and sprinkler heads and the wet, whirling, metal arms fighting to keep the green little hearts of front lawns and gardens from burning up. The sharp-edged hills turned from yellow to orange and from orange to brown. Later the fires came in the hillside brush and left evil-looking black patches, like some sinister skin disease.

Passing the big polo field, Mike saw that the blue gum trees were getting frayed and tired. The yuccas had long since become dried-out sticks and only when the sea appeared was there a pure color on the good days; if the smog and the mist did not roll in over the treetops, and everything was gray and really sad.

On the coastal highway there hung a continual curtain of dust. The cars and trucks swept it up from the road bed and moved it around in clouds until everything, signs, poles, and beach buildings, were covered with a gritty layer made up of decomposed granite from the sea cliffs and blown beach sand full of old newsprint and the ground debris of gardens and fields.

The tides were very high and savage and ate away the beach front all along the curve of sea where Mollie's beach house stood. It seemed that the very foundation would be dug up and the pilings under the houses were exposed for five feet or more. The old-timers said not to worry, it happened every year. When it was at its worst Mike had to put down a small ladder to get them on to the beach. One night the wind shifted and the tide worked and the sand was all back and Mollie had a beach again.

Work on the picture went on slowly. After work they were

tired and they spent a lot of time at the beach house. The wind tore and battered the canvas sides of the sun deck, but when the wind stopped they were sorry; the heat baked the beach house and the pitch pole pine rafters began to sweat resin through many knotholes.

The people on the beach got friendlier. Mike grew to know the beach bums, and even to like some of them. At first they had been only a collection of sun-browned faces and hairy legs with sand in their pores. Faded beachwear and oiled flesh smelling of suntan lotion and cold cream. But soon the regulars became familiar to Mike. Rose and Harry Steiner were a cut above the rest. Rose took care of Harry and anyone else on the beach who needed help. There was also a screen writer with a red beard whose last motion-picture credit was in 1935, who fished for a living and always had a new girl. There were assorted forgotten people who came and went. A man, a schoolteacher, who came down only on Sundays, who had lost a buttock in the Pacific during the war, and said, "Why, you're Lana Turner, only better looking," or "I mistook you for Shelley Winters, honest I did," or "Beg pardon, you aren't Katie Hepburn, are you?" And there was Meadow, the mad, charming builder of modern houses, who was so far advanced in the craft that he couldn't make a living. And on week ends they were usually children. Once Belle's child with the white-blond hair teased the dogs and threw up on the sun deck and had to be pulled from the surf to have water pumped out of him. Also arty ceramic makers of signed plates, once-popular magazine writers between success periods, painters of fast-selling clowns and popular desert landscapes who cursed Picasso and said Michaelangelo was a nance bum. And John and Mandy. Sometimes Walter.

All drank and all ate Mollie's food and those who were still able made love and fought and made up, or were catty and bitchy to each other. Feuds went on and somebody usually got a black eye, but mostly they sat on the sun deck with a glass in front of them or a chicken bone in their hands. Or they danced and talked bitterly about successful people. Mollie, however, was never bitter about other people's success. She admired success.

The group attracted many strange people that summer, but none more strange than Beppo Kubelik. He was the product of a Pennsylvania coalmining slum—a transplanted

Mittel Europa peasant—without education or breeding, but with a veneer of polite manners when he had to use them. He was a sculptor of little torsos carved out of driftwood. He had a real talent, but there was money in popular little female torsos. So he carved them mostly because they sold. He was a born sponger and lived in any beach house that had a spare pillow. He had grown up in a dreadful Polack mining poverty and was a glutton who could outeat anyone. He ate and lived, and made "love."

Beppo was very amusing when he wanted to be. He was blond, lean, and handsome—like a Polish aristocrat, for some reason. Women were attracted to his lean blondness and his vitality. But his affairs were casual and did not interest him. He was very young, nearly twenty-five, and Walter said, "The sonofabitch is looking for some woman with money, or a good job, to take care of him." Walter, the Sacramento aristocrat, and Beppo, the slum horror with the face of a refined Warsaw baron, did not hit it off very well. "It's nonsense to think," Walter used to say, "that all poor people are fine and honest. They have just as many stinkers and heels as any other class. Beppo should be mopped up and squeezed out in the drain."

Beppo and the Steiners got on very well. He sponged on them and once in a while gave them a little torso that was cracked and couldn't be sold.

In the late afternoon when Mike was free, and before he had to go and have dinner with John and work at night on the script change, he used to sit with Mollie on the sun deck, the dogs pattering around them asking for affection. He often read to her. They didn't talk about the picture after working hours.

"I like stories about people," Mollie used to say.

Mike looked up from his book, *Ellen Terry and Bernard Shaw, a Correspondence*. "Do you like Shaw?"

"Very much."

He discovered she knew a lot about Shaw. She had seen *St. Joan* and other plays of his done by students at the Pasadena Playhouse.

"Listen to this, Mollie. 'I do not know whether women ever love. I rather doubt it; they pity a man, mother him, delight in making him love them, but I always suspect that their tenderness is deepened by their remorse for being unable to love him. Man's one gift is that at his best he can love . . .'"

"You picked that out on purpose! He's just full of apple juice and carrots."

"All right, I'll open the book anyplace and read. Here. 'It must be curious to be a mother. First the child is part of yourself, then it is your child; then it is the father's child, then it is the child of some remote ancestors . . .'"

She gripped his arm very hard. "I would like to have your child, Mike."

Mike said, "The little punk might look like me."

Mollie shook her head. "I like your looks. What else does old smarty pants say?"

"The old boy could really make love, on paper, anyway. Listen to this bit of passion to Ellen: 'Nothing for nothing. I must be *used*, built into the solid fabric of your life as far as there is any usable brick in me, and thrown aside when I am used up. It is only when I am being used that I can feel my own existence, enjoy my own life. All my love affairs end tragically because the women can't use me.'"

"What are you frowning at, Mike?"

He closed the book and put it down on the battered canvas of the sun deck. "He's such a Goddamn woman, that Shaw. He says and feels things like a real woman."

"He likes to talk about it."

"I don't think he likes to do it. Maybe he sees things so clearly because he only watches."

The rest of the afternoon he read from Boswell's *Johnson*. She said it was fine, and very dull: a real classic.

One week end when the house was really jumping, Mike got two rods and took Belle, Mollie's sister, surf casting. They went a long way down the coast away from the home grounds and he baited their hooks with sand fleas, big fellows in shiny shells. They cast out on the leaden sea and reeled in. A rough surf ran between their naked toes.

Belle laughed a lot; she had a deep laugh, not Mollie's throaty tinkling. They stopped casting after a while and ate cold food and drank beer.

"What do you think, Belle?"

"On what subject?"

"Mollie and me."

"That's not a subject, that's a book. Don't expect me to have any answers."

187

"You know it's going to work out."

"Sure, I read it in the stars." She laughed. "Don't think I'm as goofy as Mollie and her Goddamn Mrs. Henry. A fullgrown woman playing around with a fake mystic."

"I've weaned her of Mrs. Henry's mumbo-jumbo."

"How's the picture going?"

"Bad. Short of cash. May have to shut down."

"Let's fish."

They fished till it was dark and wet and cold. They had a bucket of small, flat fish and two crabs and they felt it was time to pack up. It grew foggy and wetter. They covered themselves with a rubber cloth and walked slowly back, the rods sticking into the air like the feelers of some odd ants, and the fish swishing in the bucket of sea water. It was a gray dusk and the *geek* of seabirds died away at last. They stood under the beach house looking up. The windows were orange squares of light. The record player was on and someone tumbled down the back stairs into the sand. It was Harry Steiner. Glass broke someplace above and someone said he "could die laughing!"

Belle grinned. "Just another great little week end."

They stood Harry on his feet and mounted the stairs to the sun deck. Two strangers were on the sofa very close together and holding each other tightly. Ed, the boxer, was watching them, his mad, pale eyes very white and large.

Mollie was taking Italian food from the stove. Mike kissed her cheek and got out the scaler and the old rose shears and began to clean the fish.

At first the shooting of the picture had gone very well. Then Mike had gotten angry at the cameraman and the art director and there had been a long hassel until the unions stepped in and said things had to change. Mollie had begun to blow her lines a lot and Mike had broken up the takes so that every time she blew a speech he did not re-take the scene, but moved the camera in and took up from where she had muffed. He hoped by cutting the scenes together to make them play, cutting out the blown lines with overlapping dialogue-scenes from another angle. Mollie felt very bad about it. She was becoming tense and she didn't sleep well and she was brooding over the fact that she was letting Mike down.

Mike didn't want to be cruel to Mollie, but he was, and she recoiled a bit from his harshness and his curt, biting

188

orders. They were all taut and snarled a little at each other, even Walter at John. The picture didn't look well in the dailies and in the scenes cut together, so it seemed to John anyway; very dull. But Walter and the cameraman said they were the best things they had seen in a long time.

Then they ran out of money, cash, credit, everything. Mike's English funds had run into red tape. He came to John and Walter and shook his head.

"Close down shooting for a week or so. Keep the sets standing and give the crews we have to stand-by pay."

"We've got over half the picture in the can, M.Z."

"The location stuff is going to be a bastard. John, let's rewrite that ranch scene, tighter . . . play it off Mollie, not with her."

John knew that Mike was still sure Mollie was a new Garbo, but he was playing scenes around her now, as much as he could, rather than trying to get the full drama from her. It was a clever procedure. A few popular stars had been made that way.

Several days later the studio threatened to pull down the standing sets. Then Mike lost the cameraman (he went to Warners on a Western).

Several times there were messages that Mr. Matt had called Mr. Zelsmith. There were even two letters explaining how many a famous person was turning to writing a comic strip. All Mike had to do was write out the text and an artist would put it in pictures and he would be rich and famous.

Mike gave orders that Mr. Matt was not to be put through, but every phone call now became an expected call from Mr. Matt. One night at Mollie's he got through to Mike on the phone.

"Sorry to barge in like this, Mr. Zelsmith. It's Matt."

"At least you have my name right now."

"Sure, never forget a name. Well, what about it?"

"What about what?"

"The adventure strip. Something juicy, in your best style."

"I'm not interested. Don't call me again, bud."

"I can't let a good guy toss away his chance."

Mike hung up on Mr. Matt. The next day there was a letter explaining the whole idea again. He asked people about Mr. Matt. But no one had ever heard of him. Mike wondered if he existed. Perhaps, he would feel better after a few drinks. Mr. Matt was a character from an unpublished story by Kafka—a character who had escaped and was living like a bubble in the air. He could use a phone and could write a letter but no one ever saw him. But that was nonsense; yet the idea of an imagined Mr. Matt bothered him. Nobody read Kafka in the town, but they had his books around and one night Mike looked through a collection of stories expecting any minute to run across the story of a Mr. Matt and his comic strips. But he didn't.

Mr. Matt stopped calling and writing for a while and Mike wondered, even worried, if anything had happened to him, and then one morning he called again. After that Mike was more than ever convinced Mr. Matt was an escaped spirit from an unwritten story.

16

JOHN FENNEL was busy writing in his journals when Mike came in and looked at him with that grin of his that usually said he wasn't feeling very happy, and what the hell was he grinning about. He pushed his heavy rimmed glasses over his eyes, tried to read some of the journal exposed to him on the hotel desk, and then suddenly seeing it was a personal journal, turned and said to John, "I need you boy, need you bad tonight."

"What for?"

Mike swung the glasses off his battered nose. "The royal summons, the Goddamn official order. My father-in-law, that sonofabitch Garoyan, wants to see me. Tonight."

"Scared, Mike?"

Mike shrugged his shoulder. "I don't scare easy. I told him I was bringing you along. He didn't seem to mind."

"That's nice of him."

Mike said, "You've heard a lot about him in this town. And you've wanted to meet him . . . well, here's your chance."

"I was just wondering, Mike, maybe he wants a personal talk with you."

"He does, and he'll get it, but with you there, I may not

strangle him to death with my own hands. I don't promise."

"I'll go."

"Alice will most likely be there. She hasn't filed for divorce, you know."

"I know."

"Don't let me get stinking. I have to stay sober. Stone sober, remember that."

John said he would.

Edward Garoyan lived in Bel Air, on a private mountain behind big stone gates that were opened and closed by remote radio control. He had not built the place himself, but bought it during a depression from a broken-down banker. It was kept, as he often said, "green as grass." John had never believed such a place existed except in old-fashioned motion pictures. It was vast, of Tudor and mock Spanish, creeping stucco, stone, and timbers over a hill. It was well staffed, and a general plundering of all the good and bad taste of Europe had furnished it. Ed Garoyan did not make motion pictures. He financed them, distributed them, built theaters to show them in, and (with his holding companies of holding companies) saw to it that the stockholders did not get unduly rich. He had the best brain in town and hired the rest. He believed that one day soon he would fail to say good morning to his mirror.

John, Mike, and the old man ate alone in the dining room. The interior of the house had been redone recently in white and gold. Flowers and ferns stood against the walls. Braziers of charcoal glowed to warm the guests. A chef in white linen was standing behind a table full of rare game, hams, sea life in aspic, a whole suckling pig in some yellow varnish. Strange little forms of sea life, turtle soup with sherry, and smoking turkeys nude and indecently being invaded by silver spoons hunting dressing in their interiors (like a surgeon, John thought, probing a womb).

The old man said, "In my country food is prepared in the room you eat it."

John looked at a large Rosenthal plate and moved with a fork some white meat and salad around its gilt surface. At his elbow stood a tall drink, and a colored man dressed in a white jacket carried a silver case hung from his shoulders from which he took out piping hot rolls with a great fork and seemed hurt when John refused him. Mike sat scowling, not talking.

191

A slim young man with a silver bracelet played on a white piano in the next room. Bad Chopin.

John found himself staring at Ed Garoyan. He was a stocky, solid man in his graying sixties, with an unhealthy-looking skin, a face like a mask of flesh cut open here and there to admit wise little eyes, a hawk nose twice as large as his daughter's, and a mouth like a surgeon's slit twisted into a smile. He smelled of shaving lotions and expensive male perfumes.

"You like good food, Mr. Fennel?"

"Not on such a large scale."

The old man looked wise and sure of himself, but he did not look at Mike. "I want to talk to you, Mr. Fennel, about Alice's idea of opening a big modern art gallery out here."

"It's a worthy project, Mr. Garoyan."

"I don't support worthy projects. I run a business. Oh, I know you think of motion pictures as art, but to me and millions it's entertainment. I've never watched a picture being made and I never will. That's Mike's job."

Mike looked up and reached for the brandy.

The butler came over, a little too fat and pale to be a proper movie butler, John thought. The butler said to Garoyan, "It's the Columbia Broadcasting System again, sir."

"Let it keep for business hours, Kaplin."

The butler shrugged his shoulders in a very unprofessional manner. "It's about our radio-controlled gates, sir."

"What about it?"

"You remember, sir, we control it by a wave length from the front door. It seems, in some way, our wave length is on the Columbia Broadcasting System."

"We're not broadcasting."

"No, sir, but every time we signal for the gates to open, it cuts into their broadcastings with a dreadful sound. They're going to take it up with Washington. We're infringing, they say, sir."

"Get the wave length changed then."

"Yes, sir, but that will take a few days. Shall I disconnect the gate signals, sir?"

"You do, Kaplin, and you're back as casting director for Eddie Small."

"Yes, sir," the butler said and walked off with an un-British sag in his shoulders. Garoyan smiled at John. "Well,

192

how do you like this crazy town? My gates and the network on the same wave length."

"It's rather odd."

"And tomorrow the newspaper will carry a story I did it, instead of a bad workman, and everybody in this town will say I'm getting a bigger ego."

"Why not just leave the gates open?"

"And knuckle down to Paley of Columbia? After all, my income is twice his."

Mike said suddenly, "Why don't you make pictures?"

"I've never bought a story or hired a writer or director personally, but I've sold the pictures, good or bad, and Alice is like me. So if she wants an art gallery, why not? She isn't going into anything to be laughed at. Nobody ever laughed at me," he grinned, "not to my face. They call me that Armenian sonofabitch. More wine?"

John said, "It's very good."

The old man took the glass from John's hand and had it refilled. "You may be amused at the idea that I like to be respected. But when you've been a goat herder and lived on an onion and a slice of cheese a day, you feel respect is coming to you if you pay for it. How much can Alice lose the first year in an art gallery out here? Showing only top-rank men?" He pulled a list from his pocket and began to read: "Picasso, Soutine, Renoir, Cézanne, Matisse. I want to buy them all up outright. Of course, the list is not complete. I have people working on it."

Mike stirred and said, "A lot of those people are dead and their work is pretty well bought up by museums."

"Well, we'll make other painters great. I made the star system in this town. When I came out the actors had no names. They were known as The Cowboy, The Blonde, or Fatty. I made names mean something. You get the paintings, Mr. Fennel, and I'll see the publicity department builds 'em up."

"Painting isn't like stars," Mike said. His face was red.

The old man laughed and his shaving lotion smelled very pleasant. "You think I don't know what I'm talking about? I've been to Paris and seen how the big dealers and the bought art critics make painting reputations."

John nodded. "You're right, of course, Mr. Garoyan. It's just never been done in this country."

"We'll have to get together again . . ."

A thin, gawky little girl of about ten with a very high

193

forehead had come into the room up to the old man and stood there holding a bunch of roses in her hand. The little girl stepped forward and made a bow. Her voice was shrill.

"Happy birthday, Mr. Garoyan, happy birthday to you from the staff of the studio, who wish you a long life and a merry one . . ."

"And a *happy* one," corrected the old man.

"And a *happy* one."

The old man smiled and kissed the little girl on the cheek and ran a heavy, veined hand over the top of her head.

"Our biggest star, Mr. Fennel, my house guest, Maggie White. This is Mr. Fennel, Maggie, a famous writer."

"Pleased to meet you, Mr. Fennel, I'm sure." She looked wise beyond her age, and her big dark eyes filled with tears. "I've got to go now. It's past my bedtime. Thank you for letting me come, Mr. Garoyan. Goodnight."

She walked off. The old man shook his head and smiled. "The little ham. She turns those tears off and on like a fountain. And my birthday was last week. Well, we'll talk some more some time, Mr. Fennel—have lunch. I'll call you."

A solid old man sure of himself, sure of his brain power; evil perhaps, John thought, but evil in a strong way; he liked to be hated. You respect things like that.

"If you'll excuse me," the old man said, "I'd like to talk to Mike. Cigar?"

"No, thank you," John said. "I'd like to see the view from the terrace."

He left the two of them and went out on to the long marble terrace, and the world below seemed far away and unreal. The rows of lights on the streets, and the pinpoints of house lights and so much dark green landscaping of the hills. What the hell was the old man in there really like? Owner of the weird sisters of credit and cash.

And he wondered how Mike was doing. He could see them through the drapes on the great dining-room windows, the shapes of the two men bent toward each other talking, like silent films, the glass cutting off their voices.

John wondered what they wanted of each other, and how any of it could merge into any common effort. In their own way both were a powerful force for what they wanted to do. Was it worth all this conflict, John wondered? Mike was shouting. He could hear him now . . .

"I don't need your Goddamn money to start the picture

again," Mike was shouting across the table. "I'm getting frozen funds from England."

"Good," said the old man. "Your pictures are very good ones. We've made lots of money from them."

"Damn right," said Mike.

"But what can you make on peanuts? Let us take over the picture and give you a real release and good studio labs and men."

Mike looked around the room. "Is Alice here?"

"No. I decided it would be better without her. Look, Mike, I know what you think of me, and you know what I think you are. But I respect you as a man who makes fine pictures. There isn't more than a hatful of brains in this industry, and most of them are in my pocket. No, we're not modest, you and me, we know what we have and what we can do. But you forget one thing, Mike, you didn't fall in love with money."

"No, I didn't."

"I did. Remember the man in Shaw's play who, when asked what his religion was, said, 'I'm a millionaire'? That was a true answer. I love money not because I'm vulgar but because I have to love something. I tried art and literature and they were empty, small egos shouting in the dark. I tried women, lots of women, spiritually and in bed, but I guess I have ice water in my groin. The women I might have liked locked themselves away from me with a glassy stare. So it had to be money. Just think if you had money, Mike."

"I'm thinking what God could do if he had money." Mike sat well back in his chair, his face flushed, looking at the little old man across the table from him. He could hear John's heels walking the terrace outside. "But *just* money, no."

"You want God, too?" The old man grinned. "I build churches and feed fat priests, but there is a God, Mike. There has to be or I wouldn't be so scared of dying."

Mike leaned forward; he knew he was already drunk. "In the twentieth century, God became a mathematician, and in algebra he recreated the world and all the lousy planetary laws."

The old man grinned. "You're drunk, Mike."

"I don't dare come here and stay sober. You're the people who don't let me make pictures, don't let me make wonderful things. And you think because you treat God like a classmate he's going to forgive you. Nuts he is! Come on, what do you really want?"

"Go back to Alice, be a husband to her."

Mike stood up, it was not easy, but he did it. "No, old man, no. I love Alice, I guess, in my own way. But it's not a happy love. You gotta be happy in love. No, old man."

"A fool would make you an offer now. Alice and picture money and a release. I promise nothing. Just try it again."

Mike shook his head. "It's no good for her either, only she'll never admit it. Best this way."

The old man said, very low, "Goodnight, Mike."

Mike grinned. "Goodnight, Pop."

The old man sat a long time after his guests had gone. He wondered why he had talked so much to Mike about himself. Why did he want Mike to like him, respect him? He had no love or pity for Mike. He was going to let him ruin himself. It wasn't all because of Alice. Alice was too much the woman to understand. Sons would have been much nicer, but there had been no sons. For all his women he hadn't been very fertile, and now he was all alone really, and very old.

John Fennel sat on the sun deck and listened to the door-bell ring and Mandy talk to a bill collector. It did not bother her; she promised to "put something on account as soon as she could." John could not understand this sort of life. He lived out of two suitcases and owed no one anything if he could help it. Mandy collected rare furniture.

Mandy came out with some letters in her hand.

"Here's a letter for you, care of me."

"That's odd." He took the letter and opened it. There was a check for five hundred dollars in it and a note reading: "For services as an art expert. With much thanks. Edward G."

Mandy read over his shoulder. "They pay you to go to dinner?"

"Give me an envelope. I want to return this."

"You talked art to him. Keep it. He only respects what he pays for."

"I went only as a guest."

"It doesn't mean anything to him."

But John tore the check into small bits and put it into an envelope and addressed it to Edward Garoyan in care of his studio, and marked it *personal*.

After that John felt better and fell asleep in the sun while Mandy lay on his feet and read an old furniture catalogue and planned dismal victories among the worm holes . . .

FROM THE JOURNAL OF JOHN FENNEL

The trouble with Mike is he wants a picture of everything. Even emotional things, things like physical love. Most writers have tried, and failed to express the agonies and exaltations of physical love. It either descends on one side to mere pornographic picturing, or on the other becomes an erotic experience told in a symbolic evocation, nothing named or identified, but drawn with images of good taste from the facts, and projected in words worn too smooth and stale by older poets. The physical passion is not too analyzable, this intense sensation that is an overpowering of reason. The precise understanding of physical experiences calls for the closest study of the nerves and emotions, perhaps beyond the mere art of making marks on paper. But Mike will not accept this as an answer.

The efforts of Mandy to drain the last quiver of physical desire is of course the outcome of her sterile life. Clumsy, almost ignorant of theme and variation, there is in her, for me, the sweet savor of something new, and something expected and often lacking.

Her hands are long, thin, the body is milk-white and tautly smooth like a child's where the sun has not worked on it. Suntanned, it is smooth as an egg—shaved and shiny, the muscles glide from sockets and round out the forms into lines of artful purpose. The legs are longer than life size and the feet and toes beautiful in their overlong use of line. What else is needed?

> "Ah, love, let us be true
> To one another! For the world, which seems
> To lie before us like a land of dreams,
> So various, so beautiful, so new,
> Hath really neither joy, nor love, nor light,
> Nor certitude, nor peace, nor help for pain;
> And we are here, as on a darkling plain
> Swept with confused alarms of struggle and flight,
> Where ignorant armies clash by night."

Mandy believes that she alone gives and never takes. Still, her possessive moods are material and worldly; she counts her blessings in the real things that she can touch and understand. For all her musing, there is under it a desire in her to do well in this world, to be taken care of, to be important in the things she values. Her good sense is so drearily appalling in the smallness of her desires. Yet from her I reach this rare moment of love and oblivion that most men hunt and few

197

get. I have failed to get down here in this journal any of the great gout of passion love can sometimes produce.

I wonder if this journal is the fit place for this sort of writing? The calm of Montaigne is what I wanted to put down, the inner thinking of one man in a rather strange tropical place meeting his fellow man, and woman too, I suppose; all members of the same club, the human race . . .

Mike says the California women are often all alike. He sees in them a continual performance of sexual crucifixion, a bedded martyrdom that begins at the climax, the moment of release of tension. She is cursed, he thinks, with some original sin; the inability to really love physically. The natural at times must appear with her to be a series of grotesque obscenities, she is devoured at all times by her environment, for the setting is of great value to her, and the taste of what she thinks is vice and venality often excites her, overwhelms her. A certain atmospheric evil must stain her bright sunshine. She makes an effort to be predatory, but she is encased and hooded in her efforts like talon-bearing giant birds—tepidly narcissistic. But no mere matter of gynecological facts can explain her little dramas that begin so well and end as naked inquisitions with torture for herself. Her world is only fitfully recognizable as she flagellates herself. So Mike on women. Not Mollie he says—but all the others.

I think it's deeper; the local woman here in an odd tropics does not understand, with D. H. Lawrence, whom she will not really read, that love and sex and excitement are mutual and meant as a kind of freedom, a truth, and a joy between two people. For her it is too often a kind of death, a gasping, expiring, to be flogged with one last effort into some catalogue of effects that misses for her, I think, the genuinely poetic sensing at the gates of true desire.

John wanted to write more, but Walter called from downstairs saying he was bringing a friend up. John put away the journal and Walter came in with his friend, the one with the huge hawk nose, the close-cropped, black kinky hair—Bertie Ironspinner.

They were both high, and Walter said Bertie had been very low, he had just lost a job. Bertie looked up from the sofa, his large cow eyes very glossy.

"Walter says you can help me. It's my damn dead father."

John laughed. "He's wrong. I can't help you."

Walter said, as he sat down beside Bertie, "He had a pip of a writing job at Fox. But he found out suddenly he couldn't write a line."

"Usually it just pours out of me."

"Not a line, week after week."

John asked, "How does your father enter into it?"

Bertie wiped his wide lips with a crisp linen hankie. "My father killed himself. I was in school in Europe. He was in trouble and I knew it, but I didn't come back."

"What's that got to do with writing at Fox?"

"This morning I went in for a story conference. I suddenly saw why I hadn't written a line. It was Zanuck."

"Zanuck?"

"I knew suddenly he reminded me of my father. A perfect father."

John sat down facing the two on the sofa. "Zanuck?"

Bertie wrung his hands. "Don't you see, if I had written a bad script, I would have been letting my father down again. I didn't write a line, couldn't write a line, because if I had I would have been killing my father all over again."

John stood up. Bertie asked earnestly, "Don't you see?"

Walter grinned. "He's not kidding."

John smiled and then began to laugh. "Get the hell out of here, both of you."

Walter turned at the door. "M.Z. called. We start shooting again Monday."

John asked, "He make a deal with the old man, his father-in-law?"

"No dice. He got some more dough out of England."

John frowned. "You think the picture can be any good?"

"If Mollie doesn't fall apart. She's too sensitive to really be made into an actress this fast. Something has got to give."

Bertie Ironspinner looked at the delicate Swiss watch strapped to his heavy wrist. Walter nodded, and they went out. John went back to his journal, but he didn't feel like writing any more.

The picture started again on the dusty and already disintegrating sets and Mike hurried to catch up on lost time. Mollie had become a problem. She did not know why, but her part in the picture seemed to be running down like an unwound clock. Mike tried to explain to her that a professional actress would try and sustain the mood of her part, no matter how she felt about it. She said she would try and she did, but she was no professional and she could not, bright as she was, seem able to see the finished project made up of the little parts of the picture that was sweated out, shouted out, moaned out, every day. She wondered how even bad pictures ever managed to be made.

Walter had been right about Mike, he was no director; his thinking was so large, his capture of an idea so swift, that the piddling little things that must go into a fine director's job were not only boring him, but made him angry. He had tried to control his temper, but he failed. He lashed out at everyone. He shouted and groaned and the sets became a hell for himself, for the people he worked with. Time and money—he began to hate them both.

Yes, he made progress, and the wise ones, the cutters, editors, cameramen, said he was getting a remarkable picture onto film. Mike wished there were time for taking scenes over again, for refining the ideas before he cut them together into reels, but there was no time, and less money. They had to finish on the sets soon, and then Mike would go north for the location stuff. The last of his money was running out. He still had to get some company to show the picture. But he would wait until it was finished.

Another thing that bothered Mike was that he felt he had hurt Mollie. He never admitted, even to himself, he had pushed her too far and too suddenly. But he did know he had been brutal to her on the sets, and had driven her almost into a breakdown by his demands of what her performance should be. The reward, he explained to her, would be on the screen. It would be worth it, baby . . .

John found Zelsmith sitting in the hotel garden under a blue and white lawn umbrella marking up a copy of the script with a big blue pencil, always the changer, the perfectionist. It was almost twilight but Mike didn't seem to notice.

"John, we're leaving soon for location. Walter's found an island off the coast and a house that will be just the thing for the wife's house."

"The script is in worse shape than ever. You've made so many changes, Mike, that it doesn't make sense to me."

"I can't teach you what it took me a lifetime to learn. I never taught the town anything."

John sat down and nodded. It was cool in the fast-dropping dusk.

"It's a dying town," said Zelsmith, digging his blackwood cane deeply into the rich turf. "You almost smell death in it when the wind is blowing the right way. All cutting costs, cutting productions, remaking old stories. No courage here, John. Nothing but rich living between their ears, and a habit of seeing their names in print in puff sheets."

"I've seen some interesting things they've done this year." Mike smiled. "Been getting the movie habit?"

"I go at least once a week."

"It isn't what it used to be. You would have liked this part of the country twenty or thirty years ago. Doug Fairbanks, Chaplin were active . . . there was lots of hell-for-leather drinking and talent then. Real moving pictures, and what a place it was. You wouldn't believe it. Sunshine all the time, none of this lousy smog, and the weather, you know the winters *have* been getting colder. Nothing is the same. Later I'm going to shoot your big story in Egypt, John. I'll have some more frozen coin in England and France. I'll make all my pictures there. Mollie, she's never seen Europe. I guess a man renews himself, seeing life through a young girl's excitement. You ought to pick 'em younger, John. Not so ripe on the vine."

Mike sat looking at the well-cut grass. He was, changed somehow. John could sense the difference in his talk since their first meeting in that London hotel room. He had slowed up, perhaps mellowed a bit.

Mike said, "I wish I had your education, John. I wouldn't get so excited over things. Hell, maybe I'm getting soft. We'll give the script one more long polish; that means work every night, John, and we'll go on location. I want you up there."

"Mollie coming?"

"That's always a problem; the dogs to take care of, who will feed the love birds. We've shot all her scenes."

Mollie was not happy to hear about the coming location trip or the added night work on the script. A maddening possessiveness urged her to keep him in her sight every minute. She admitted it was almost pathological, but she couldn't help it.

She said, "Mike, when you're away I could go crazy here. Do you think I like the beach bums or the crazy parties and all the talking and dancing?"

"Yes, Mollie. Don't ever fool yourself that you'd like nothing better than to curl up with a good book for a bit of sewing evenings and watch me smoke a pipe. You'd go daffy in a week. You're a social creature."

201

"Mandy's giving a party tomorrow night. Her Indian curry and chicken."

"I'm taking night shots downtown."

"Beppo Kubelik has sold a torso to Ronald Colman, and we're celebrating."

"Jesu, how can you stand Beppo? He sits and follows you with his eyes, his tongue hanging out. He and that guy with a beard—and the Greeks."

"The Steiners are bringing a New York art dealer."

"I'm going to have to work."

"Damn it, you said it twice!"

She looked at him and began to shake. But she recovered and grinned. She kissed him tenderly and said, "I'm all right now. All squared around. Solid."

17

In the night the dream came. Mollie could sense it was only a dream, yet how was she going to break the membrane of sleep and come away from it gasping awake? She was walking, head down, in a field of blue and yellow flowers and she was sad and heavy, and she knew that everything in the last weeks was again piling up on her. This was a field she used to walk in as a child. Father appeared on the path and he stood very tall and stern. "Now, Mollie, you're not fooling me. You have been doing things and feeling things that aren't at all the kind of things I taught you. We Binnings are a proud people, and . . ."

"Father," she said, timidly and with respect, "you must understand that it's all too much for me!"

"Jesu," said Father, "you're old enough to know you can't play the lousy innocent, not knowing what it's all about." And somehow Father had become Mike, she didn't know how, but Father was still Father and he was Mike, too, and she was afraid he would ask questions she didn't want to answer. She hated him, the nosey-parker, and she pushed hard against the glossy thin skin of dreams. Somehow the scene changed and she was walking along the wet shore line, a dead seal bumbling obscenely in the hissing surf, and Mike was talking: "We can't hide the truth from the inner conscious, no more than we can hide the eye placode of a tadpole by removing it from the head of the

202

tadpole and grafting it under the surface of the creature's belly. The surface skin becomes transparent. And the abdominal eye develops a lens and a cornea!"

"Must you read those kind of books, Mike? I'm frightened."

Mike went on speaking with a clear Upper New York state accent so like Father's. She looked up to see if he was mocking her.

"Now in a frog's egg of two cells, which normally would make one frog, you cut off one cell."

"But I don't want to. I hate frogs, wet and phallic, cold and green. Please, no frogs."

"Cut off one cell and do you get half a frog? No, you get a perfect frog, but of a smaller size. It's like love, Mollie, when you share it around, you don't get half a love, you get a runt, a warped replica . . ."

"But you understand, Mike, when you're not around it's just . . ."

She was suddenly fully awake, sitting up in the wall bed, and from the road came the roar and grind of the night trucks passing, and from under the drawing table the dogs stirred and opened their eyes and she could hear their tails thumping the floor. She was wet, her hair damp, and she was tired, but the dream had fallen away. How hateful her father had been, how stern and foolish from a stone age of American pasts, and she shivered as the sea wind stirred the curtains.

She got up, her legs full of shakes, and had a tepid glass of water from the bathroom tap. Then she turned on the desk light and lit a cigarette and sat hunched over in misery, smoking too fast. Lucky came over to her, wheezing, and she took him on to her lap and rubbed his head and he looked at her, his big eyes balls of gold in the half dark.

Oh, dreadful dog, so unreal in the night. The dog of god (and dog was god spelled backwards). Was she in the presence of evil and the absence of good? Alone in the night anything could be, for sin is the normal climate of night, and everything else is at a physical standstill. Now come all the obsessions of a jealous appetite, the tiresome inconveniences of an unsleeping mind. I have caught love like a new disease, I have taken love as I took life and now it is frightening in the night. Oh, to have an unselfish sense of pity, for love is a terrible thing, and in the night, alone, love is the worst passion of all. It's a mad blasphemy, intense, obsessed, and yet I have no curiosity about fellow sinners, one becomes primarily and passionately concerned with self.

She sat as the night unwound, she sat and nothing came out right. All the answers were loaded. It had all seemed so good, and she was perversely tearing it up, to bits.

The bright blood-colored flowers in the blue vase caught her eye. They were dying. She would throw them away in the morning. She slept until just before dawn. There was no work for her that day on the picture. Mike was shooting local exteriors.

That night she went to Mandy's party and danced very late with the beach bums. She didn't want to go home, and slept in Mandy's guest room, with the old-fashioned thunder mugs under the Colonial bed, pots filled with growing ivy to take the curse off the vulgar texts printed in gold on the bottoms of the big-handled shapes.

The mornings that Mike wanted to jump up from bed were getting fewer. The night work with the cameras was tough. This morning it was like waking from the dead. Before his eyes opened he heard the phone ringing. He groped for it, sleep binding him, and shouted, "Hello."

The top of his head ached. His fingers seemed stiffened with starch instead of blood, and he knew his breath could not be pleasant. The warm, sleep-smelling bed revolted him. He needed lots of coffee—hot.

"We've been trying to wake you, Mr. Zelsmith."

"The hotel on fire?"

"No, sir, but Miss Binning has been calling."

"Any message?"

"Will you please call her right back?"

"All right, give me the switchboard."

He sat waiting for the call, hoping Mollie was over her depressive mood about her acting. He couldn't take that this morning, not with the hammer banging on the back and top of his skull—two places at once. He wondered if she had been in an auto accident. Every morning now he looked at the accident news first, almost expecting to see her name listed. She drove with a great and furious skill, and drove best with a few drinks in her.

"Your Cortez Beach number, sir."

The hysterical voice of Mollie broke in, "I've been cleaned out, stripped!"

"Easy does it, baby. Take it slowly."

"I've been robbed . . . while I was at Mandy's last night!"

"Robbed?"

"And it's Walter's fault. Everything taken . . . all my new clothes, the little iron Buddha, and the necklace and my earrings. My wonderful necklace and earrings!"

"Have you called the police?"

"I can't . . . I'll tell you why . . . Come down here, darling."

"All right. I'll be right over. Now sit down and smoke a slow cigarette."

He hung up and stood puzzled at why she hadn't called the police. Damn, he had a half hour of cut-together scenes waiting for him in the projection room.

The locked door of Mollie's bedroom closet had been forced open and empty hangers filled the racks. The rows on rows of sandals were untouched. A few sports outfits, blue jeans, and an old coat were left in a heap on the floor.

Mike turned from the closet door and patted Mollie's shoulder.

"The robber showed good taste."

"My good jewels—what little I had—all gone!" She flung a tin case on the worktable. Nothing was left but glass, paste, and some rather overlong earrings. "The good stuff, *all* gone! Oh, Mike, *our* necklace!"

"Sit down and tell it from the beginning."

"I spent the night at Mandy's. This morning I came home and I saw first thing it's all gone. I ran down to Walter. He was out, out cold. Cold drunk. I got him half out of it. He said he brought somebody home with him last night. They got tight in town and got tighter here. The drunken sots! Then Walter remembers passing out. His partner came up here and cleaned me out!"

"Walter remember anything?"

"Just being picked up at the Tail o' the Cock, and passing out. Doesn't know by whom, never saw the person before, never will again, I'm sure."

Mike frowned. "I see why you can't go to the police."

Mollie wept and he comforted her. He said, "Walter is our friend, isn't he? It's human to have failings. Look, kid, I'll get some money and replace the necklace and the earrings."

"Walter has promised to replace everything at so much a week. But I wish I had our little Buddha back, and the earrings you spent all your good money on."

"I'll go down and talk to Walter, and you whip up one of your tasty lunches for us."

"I don't want him in the house."

"You know we all love Walter. You don't want him to leave."

She stood up and reached for a cigarette and kicked at Ed the boxer. "I'll fry some eggplant. You like that so." Mike seemed much nicer than in the dream.

Walter's littered, damp-smelling room—it was almost below sea level—was in darkness. Walter was sitting naked, except for his shorts, bent over, staring at a bottle of whisky. But he was not drinking. Mike snapped on the lights and sat down on the bunk bed, kicking over a pile of *Art News*. Walter bought and read all kinds of magazines and never threw anything away.

"I'm sixteen kinds of heel, M.Z." He was feeling very bad. "She's so angry at me."

"She's got a big heart. She forgives you."

Walter looked up, his eyes were bloodshot and his lower lip trembled. "I'll make it up to her, week by week. I'm dickering for an advertising agency job when you don't need me any more."

"Let's not talk about it. How about getting dressed and coming up for lunch? I'll mix some Dubinque cocktails."

"Not too sweet," said Walter, smiling. He rubbed his face with his long brown fingers. "Christ, the things that can happen to a guy in this world."

Mike gave him a friendly punch across the back and quoted Walter's favorite own line to him, "If you don't like it, don't knock it."

The eggplant was badly fried, too much fat and not enough flour. They sat in a close group, Mollie, Mike, Walter, and smiled at each other, and drank a whole quart water pitcher of Dubinque cocktails between them. When the ice had watered down the heel, they added more gin and went on drinking.

They had no secrets from each other. They knew each other's weaknesses, and took each other as they were.

Mollie was beginning to sweat and there was a tic in Walter's cheek. Mike didn't feel too good himself. The nerves in his stomach bothered him (like an expanding rubber ball in the guts). He pushed aside the plate of fried eggplant and finished off his last cocktail.

After lunch he helped Mollie wash up and Walter shaved and went into town to see if he could find his last night's companion. He had no hope of finding anybody, and Mike and Mollie knew he wouldn't, but it was good he was out of the house.

As Mike brushed the dog hair off his clothes with the special brush he had bought for the purpose (no matter how the house was cleaned it was always afloat in dog hair and dog dandruff) he looked at Mollie, so beautiful, and he pitied her.

Lucky was coughing again and looking miserable. Mike gave him a mannitol-hexanitrate pill and patted his head till the tail began to wag again.

Mike was not in a happy mood about all he saw in the projection room. He sat in his trailer talking to John Fennel.

"What do you know about women, John?"

"When I was twenty I knew every Goddamn thing. Now I know very little and that little is out of date."

"I came to women early. My father was an old lecher and I came by it honestly. I was in love with our half-Indian cook at sixteen and would have married her if my mother hadn't shipped her back to the reservation. I only had two feelings about women; there were those I wanted to go to bed with and those I didn't. But when I get the love bug I'm in trouble. Don't ask me why it makes any difference with a bed partner if you think she's the most wonderful thing ever created, or just something between you and a damp sheet. I never figured it out. How many times were you ever really in love, John?"

"Two or three times only. My wife was the best of all."

"Pretty old-fashioned."

" 'It's better at home' was my motto then. I guess Mary had everything any man could ask. Beauty, culture, brains, a body, a mind, and a something you couldn't name, but it floated in the air like a wonderful net of gold. When it was lost, I guess something left me forever. I never expected to fall in love again, but I did. With Mandy."

"She's pretty dumb, in a very nice way, I admit, but dumb."

"No," said John, "I don't see her like that at all. I like

207

the idea she's been everything and still came up seeing the world like a child. She's almost innocent, not dumb, Mike. She's good company, not stupid, even if she doesn't know much and hasn't been anyplace other than the coast."

"Better than the wife?"

"Those moments when the magic is working there is nothing alive on earth can touch it. She's that way too."

"Maybe you're going queer," Mike said, grinning. He was a practical man. ("In emotional exchanges," Walter said, "M.Z. always asked for his change.")

"No," said John, "it's only women for me. Something out of D. H. Lawrence, but not twisted like his girls, not so high on the tree. She's American and that's why maybe she's for me. I've never read about anybody or seen anybody like her before. A writer knows when words give out. Mandy can't be explained."

Mike shook his head. "Let's get that screenplay out and whack at it again."

They worked very late at Mike's cottage. Around one they knocked off and had some food and some drinks, and walked in the hotel garden. It was very cold and the air had a vitality that the day never had. It was an odd country, with the day bright and numb. It was not alive, John felt, it was not alert at all. One passed the time, one sat and waited for the sun to set. Then one dressed and took on more drinks and went out. Always the recording machines and the wail of popular music and the parties going on all along the street. The road and the very coast seemed to shake.

They walked among the rose beds, past the trees pumped alive by tree doctors, by beds where the manure was rich as gold plating, on grass that died every day in the sun and sucked damply in the night never getting enough of the dew. The whole garden crouched like a whipped dog, resting, knowing tomorrow the sun would flog it again. Mike and John went twice around the hotel pool, where two toads were silently drowning, and then went in and worked on the script till almost dawn.

18

THE afternoon they finished shooting the picture at the studio everyone was very tired. Mike decided to make a rough cut of the picture before going on location for atmosphere shots. It had been a hard day, very hot, one of those days when the desert air, heated a blinding white, comes down to the coast and all the talk about the wonderful climate is forgotten. The stages Mike was shooting on were old and tattered and had no air conditioning. Mike said to Mollie, "I liked it. Let's go have a drink in the trailer."

Mollie said, "Aren't we going to have the usual party for the cast and crew?"

"It's too hot here. We'll have it tonight at the beach house. Invite anybody you want. I'll get Chasens' to cater the food."

"Not all of it, Mike."

Mike wiped the perspiration from his face with a towel and patted her arm with it. He didn't try to understand her fully any more. He just wanted her to be happy, to be in love. Let her cook if it gave her a bang.

Mike's trailer had a big, noisy fan in the wall, but it didn't help much. Walter went for ice cubes, and John and Mandy opened the bottles and everyone held a glass in a damp hand and said the picture looked fine, it was going to be great. Mike smiled and said not to forget the party tonight at Cortez Beach. You can't finish major photography without a real party—a Zelsmith party.

At four everybody went home, if they had one, limp and tired, and Walter took down the sign ZELSMITH COMPANY from the stage door. Mandy went off to help Mollie get ready for the party and John and Mike went to the hotel and showered in the cottage bathroom and put on silk robes and rang for ice cubes. Mike got out the good cigars and lay down on the sofa, his hairy legs crossed on the Chinese pillow. They smoked and sucked up whisky.

"Jesu, the picture is in the can anyway. Now for the real hard part, the cutting."

"You pleased, Mike?"

"Pleased? How the hell can I be? Crumby sets, no retakes, and I still don't know where I'm going to show it.

But it's a picture. A real honest-to-God-cross-my-heart picture. It's real, under the skin, John, not the glossy crap they turn out."

"I'm no judge, Mike, you know that."

"You don't have to yes me. I know what I try to do. If I fail it's because I like to swallow a lot. It's a new world all around us, John." He took a big swig of his drink. "The lousy physicist plays with three-dimensional atoms the way Picasso plays with a three-sided primitive fetish. We have to show that in movies, just a little, to keep up with the world."

John said, "These studio parties fun?"

Mike shrugged his shoulders. "It's the custom of the natives. A party when you finish shooting the major photography. The cast and crews expect it. They all worked hard."

John went off to shake out his white summer suit and Mike slept deeply, his broken nose pressed into the sofa, his naked legs showing large and hairy under his robe. He did not dream but he awoke tired and damp and saw he had overslept. His sweaty fingers broke a shoelace in dressing; he always had considered that a bad omen. He smiled; he was as bad as Mollie and Mrs. Henry's fortunetelling.

The heat continued after dark, hovering and melting his shirt collar as soon as he buttoned it. The hot desert wind banged down on the roofs of the beach houses.

Mollie had cooked vast pots of food till five; then, when Walter came in with long loaves of French bread and extra scotch, she had taken a shower, and put on a flaring magenta Mexican skirt of wide yardage with flannel inserts of yellow Mexican themes. She wore her best golden sandals and a checked linen shirt, cut very mannish, with a brown belt, wide and worn so tight she had trouble breathing. Her cheeks were flushed; two red spots on brown skin. Slim, delicate, she looked more beautiful than usual, as if in a fever that heightened everything. Lucky the cocker was lying on his side on the bed groaning, and Mollie stopped to pat his head. He drank the cold water she gave him eagerly.

The first guests arrived. Mollie buttered the sliced garlic bread and popped it into the oven. Meanwhile, Walter, quiet as a lamb, began to mix the first martinis. John and Mandy came in with liquors. There was supper music: Victor Herbert and Irving Berlin on the radio, and light classics. The Steiners came over with their house guests, a pansy art dealer from New York, and Beppo Kubelik, who looked like a starved aristocrat in his ill-cut city clothes. Walter found him more objectionable than ever. But Beppo was very polite to Mollie. He had manners when he needed them. Everyone had the first round, letting it sink in easily and slowly. The level of the drinks dropped in the glasses and Walter repeated the mixture as before. People began to come in from the beach side. A group of screenwriters herded together as if for protection.

Mike came in with a huge ham. Several married couples from Pasadena (one of which had just failed again in the lumber business) were there. There were soon too many people in the living room and on the sun deck, which did duty for the overflow. The sun had set and the night insects avoided the last seagulls. The prop and studio crew people formed little groups of their own.

Mollie let Rose Steiner light the candles, both indoors and out, and the love birds began their peeping until someone put a crayon-blue cloth over their cage. At seven, Ed the boxer got into a rage and tore a sofa pillow open, and when Mollie beat him with it he tried to bite her and gummed her hand very painfully without breaking the skin. Harry Steiner got into his first fight of the evening, claiming that everyone hated him because he was a Yale man. Walter and John smoothed out the little war and turned the bar duties over to Harry Steiner. Some blueberry pies were a great success.

Mike was not dancing. Beppo was dancing with Mollie, holding her very boldly, when Lucky had his first heart attack. The little dog had suddenly stiffened out on the rug, feathered paws held rigid as paper-ended lamb chops, and he was passing water with no control. Mollie picked him up and put him in the passage leading to the bathroom, and tried to get him to take a pill. But she could get nothing down. Everyone gathered around with advice and sad looks. It was plain now that the little dog was dying in fearful agony. Mike held his head up.

Mollie went down on her knees and began to weep, her face damp with fear. The studio crews felt out of it and stood back against the walls.

Harry Steiner said, "It's the best way to go, the heart, no prolonged suffering."

"Lucky! Lucky!" Mollie looked down at the little dog and brushed his head, but he strained away from her and began to yelp in great pain. He suffered for an hour, and Mike tried to get him to take another pill. It was useless. The little dog wanted to drag himself along on his front feet, but his cough grew so bad he fell into another stiffening trance. All the people present were in awe of this fearful, prolonged death, and the party became sticky.

Mollie was weeping in the living room. She couldn't see "her baby dying." But every ten minutes she would shudder and go in and shiver as she looked at the small body wracked by pain, its mad, rolling eyes past any recognition. Mike tried to get a vet and cursed and said good-by to his camera crew; everyone else stayed.

At ten the little dog was still alive and Walter went out in his car to find a vet to put it away. He came back in half an hour saying, "No dice."

Harry Steiner suggested to Mike that they *help* the dog, but no one had any idea how to kill it without driving Mollie mad. Mollie was half insane now, and her wet face, her drooling mouth, twisted; she was as frightening as the little dog. At eleven fifteen Harry Steiner announced that the little dog's heart had burst and "the blood was running into his lungs and he was drowning." Mollie screamed and fell into a faint, her body hitting the floor with a clatter, exposing her naked thighs. She looked more than ever like a little girl being naughty at a party.

They carried her into the bedroom, undressed her, and put a nylon nightgown on her and covered her up. She was shivering, staring at the knotty pine ceiling, and making little sounds in her throat. Every few moments she would turn her head and watch the little dog strangling. He did not die for a long time; blood and foam blew through his nose and mouth, and he snapped at anyone who passed like a dying fish on land. Mike covered him with copies of the *Los Angeles Times* and when everybody thought it was all over, the little dog was discovered crawling toward the bed, trying to reach Mollie. It died horribly, Mollie's eyes fascinated by the ghastliness of it. It lay, dead fur on end —already a corrupting object to all.

When it was all over, Mollie began to breathe very hard, and after that she knew no one. Mike tried to get Dr. Sontag on the phone, and John Fennel took the little body into the living room and covered it with a rug. Mollie was lying in a trance, her throat twitching. Somewhere down the row of beach houses another party was on in high. Mollie began to call for her mother near midnight and they made her drink some brandy and swallow three sleeping pills. Beppo Kubelik had been roaming around, his eyes beady and black, very excited. When Mike went in to tell Mollie that they had located Dr. Sontag, he found Beppo with his hands under her nightgown fondling the unconscious girl's breasts. Mike back-handed Beppo a hard slap to the chops and Beppo went out of the room quickly without a word. Mike wondered how long Beppo had been there. He was sure, as he told John later, that if Beppo had had the opportunity he would have raped Mollie that night. Some death thrill had excited him beyond control, Mike felt—and he was sorry he hadn't broken Beppo's jaw.

The party had broken up into silent drinking groups on the sun deck. They whispered sometimes, and some couples went home thinking of man and animal brevity on earth. The party was gloomily running out of scotch and finally drank what was left in the bottles. When they had no more ice, Mandy went next door and got her ice trays. It was two in the morning when Dr. Sontag got there. He looked tired and ill.

"I've been at Balboa treating an expanding gall bladder."

He and Mike went into the bedroom smelling of fear and death and Mollie. She was lying on her back, breathing hard, her stomach muscles twitching. Dr. Sontag took her pulse and listened to the heartbeat. He turned to Mike. "There isn't anything to do. She's in a state of shock again."

"Bad?"

"Not too good. Get me some hot water and brew me some tea. I'm tired. Get someone to remove the dog. Have it cremated."

"It isn't just the dog . . . a lot else has happened," Mike said. "I don't know just what."

The doctor shook his head. "Lucky was the only tie with Mollie's childhood. This can have serious results for her."

Mike wondered why the doctor scowled so. He got someone from the Plume Café to remove the body of the little dog and he helped wash out the spots on the rugs in the hallway and the living room. Ed the boxer wanted to howl, but Mike took his steel chain lead and beat him with it, a pleasure he had looked forward to for some time anyway. Just before dawn, when the few remaining guests had curled

into corners to sleep, the love birds began their brisk, metal-
lic chatter. Mike felt as if there was sand under his eyelids.

Mollie awoke screaming and asking for her mother and
begging that her father should stay out of the room. Dr.
Sontag looked up from his fifth cup of tea and went in and
prepared a needle. When she was sleeping again, he went
into the living room, pushed some people off the sofa, and
went quickly to sleep. He slept silently and deeply and only
awakened to Mike phoning Bertie Ironspinner, who owned
a French poodle, for the name of a good dog cemetery.

Mollie did not even look up at Mike and the doctor. She
sat in bed and said, "My little dog's dead. Lucky, he's dead.
I'll never have him any more."

"What the hell, Mollie? We've been expecting it for a
long time."

She looked at him, expressionless. "It was horrible.
Everybody says a heart attack is the way to go. But it was
horrible. Papa died of a heart attack," she stared hard at
Mike, "but I wasn't there when he died. What have they
done with my little dog?"

Mike said, "It's all been taken care of."

"Ten years. You grow fond of something in that time.
I've never been able to keep anything else for ten years.
Myron, oh, you'd better have them put me away. Have
them lock me up where I'll be safe and no bother to anybody. You sign the papers, Myron. They'll believe you."

"Oh shut up, Mollie," said the doctor, handing her two
pills. "Swallow this and calm down. You can be a real ham
when you want to. Your dog's dead. He had a full, fat life,
full of more than I ever had. Ten, twenty, thirty years we'll
all be dead, unless the atomic scientists work real fast and
rush it. It doesn't really matter what's dead, or when. Too
much talk about something that doesn't matter, to the dead
least of all. Now pipe down."

"It does mean something to the living," Mollie said.

Mike put his arm around her slim, naked shoulders. She
shivered to his touch. "It's bad, Mollie, I know, but things
are often bad."

"I think I need a drink."

Mollie slept until noon. She had stopped weeping, and
while she shivered from time to time, she had made a much
better recovery than Mike expected. She looked away from

the damp spot on the rug to a bowl of large assorted flowers in all shades of red.

"Who sent the flowers?"

Mandy, who was washing up, answered, "Beppo. He went to town just to get them for you, honey."

"That was sweet of him."

Walter snorted. "Red appling you already. Have any idea what happened here last night?" He looked out to the sun deck where Mike and John and the doctor were talking earnestly together. "He tried to get in bed with you, and you lying there out to the world. That Polack ape has the sex habits of the jungle."

"It wasn't that bad. I remember, my breasts. He likes my breasts, he always tells me any artist would." She sat down suddenly on a chair. "It's hard to believe Lucky is dead."

She began to weep and Walter gave her his handkerchief. He flipped his cigarette butt into the bowl of water holding Beppo's flowers and thought them vulgar and already smelling of death.

Dr. Sontag was rubbing his white hands together and flexing his fingers as if getting ready to operate. "I'm worried about Mollie, Mike. She's had a dreadful shock and it may be more permanent than we think. There's hope for her as long as her father's image holds, and you're in control."

Mike frowned. "I don't think this beach life is good for her. She belongs in a better setting."

Dr. Sontag bowed. "Away from this beach slum and us bitter misfits?"

Mike laughed. "You can't get me wound up—you know what I mean. As soon as I'm finished with the picture we're getting married, if we can. I own some property near Paris. Big, well-worked farm, and an old white brick house and maples. In the fall they turn gold and red."

"Very pretty, Mike. It sounds like a Van Gogh."

Mike shrugged his shoulders. "Maybe it does."

"Spare me," said the doctor. "The two of you should be very happy there. Well, I've got to go and take a tumor out of a maker of very bad cheese crackers."

Mollie promised to be very good and take it easy, and Mike spent the day with her.

"Wasn't it nice of Beppo to send flowers? You never send flowers."

"Flowers are a form of emotional blackmail."

"To hell with it. Blackmail me, Mike."

"I will when I release the picture. You're very good."

"I plug at it. But I haven't got a big talent, Mike. I'm not Jane Austen or Katie Hepburn. I used to be able to make a living, that's all. But no self-pity. It will be all right and you can tell me so, Mike. A girl likes to be told things she knows. It doesn't matter what, keep telling me nice things. Say all the wonderful things you can say. You don't talk as much as I would like. I'm a little mixed up today, but you know what I mean. A girl likes to be reassured. All women are like that. I'm not so different from most women."

"I lack lots of the easy graces, Mollie."

She suddenly said, "If only I had a bad heart like Lucky."

Mike grinned. "Now you sound really corny."

FROM THE JOURNAL OF JOHN FENNEL

The party and Lucky's death have depressed me about the town. The town for all its charm, as I get to know it better, is part of a disintegrating society. Walter's Roman pleasure city under phantom volcanic ash; Mike Zelsmith's "fink town." There is however absolutely no use talking to Mandy in allegory, or expressing anything in abstract meanings. For a romantic and mystic she desires a little too much the concrete material forms of society. The psychological and social must be entertainingly mixed for her, and she brushes over their extraordinary complexity and their usually absolute final results. Life to her is a prolonged and disastrous conflict of personalities. Her protagonists are always real, to her anyway, and never allegorical.

Mollie is a different type. She is very convinced all her choices are free, and thinks she decides them by ethical principles as taught to her by her father. This is not always true with her.

In a novel it's so easy to be sure of things. The character develops the way you want it to. In real life I remain confused. I must get to know real woman better. I often find in a woman a certain endless provocative phrase that appears and disappears, but must always have existed in their imagination and fears. I don't like to call them fears, for a great deal of their charm is due to their oddness. Their practical preoccupation with happiness is always implicit in them. All of this seems right now, today, to be so explicit and logical that the whole texture and color of all adult relationship is often luxuriant and eccentric in a very low, comic vein.

The women out here cannot long remain austere; the true, important simplicities of the natural world baffle them. They remain charming though somewhat theatrical; I doubt if there is any other town that gives its citizens such a quality. Their emotions appear to be transfixed rather than released by love, and projected by extraordinary, busy minds into what are, at times, overflowing and spontaneous qualities that make them good company and interesting lovers. But the borderline between the full, wonderful moment and certain awkwardness and naïveté (that would, I suppose, to outsiders make them look silly) are always present; when they are keyed too high, have laughed too much, and reached for the bottle once too often.

I notice I write of *women*, not of a woman. No generalization like this can be true, at least in all cases . . . If one could only have one's doubts thrown out with bell, book, and candle.

19

IT WAS hardly ever known for Edward Garoyan to call any-one on the phone. Even when people called him they got someone else. He called John Fennel one afternoon.

"Look, I've been thinking of our last talk. You make sense."

"I try, Mr. Garoyan."

"Come over and see me. Tonight."

Garoyan, shaved and neat in a smart white suit, sat on the terrace.

He said to John after helping him light a cigar, "I'm a mountain man, and like all mountain men, I can't get used to the sea. That's why I bought this place. Off there it's like the place I was born in, rough, hilly, goats, and vineyards. I own a lot of it."

"It must make you feel important, owning."

"That's where you're wrong, Fennel. It makes me feel mortal. That I'm going to die and leave it . . . to whom? Alice? The church? Planning does a man no good. Here I am, no sons and enough to leave for ten families. I pulled up roots too soon. I could have been a big man in the old country . . . maybe a dictator. You don't like that, but I've learned it takes someone to get things done."

" 'Power corrupts, absolute power corrupts absolutely,' " John quoted.

"That's pretty good."

"It isn't mine. An English writer first said it."

217

"Look at Alice. What has power done to her? Made a half-crazy wreck out of her. Married her to a man who doesn't think of money, only of making great, arty pictures. Hell, what's as dead as a movie three months after you release it? Why waste time making it art? If you could hang it on a gallery wall for a hundred years, yes, but not for a lot of stuff the public takes like candy."

"Mike can't help himself. He's a great craftsman. Anyway, he's going to make one for money."

"He'll fall flat on his face. Then Alice will get him back maybe."

They went inside as it grew cooler. Edward Garoyan sat by a fireplace made of coral rock, the roaring fire of drift logs taking the chill off him. He was holding a half inch of brandy ("Napoleon never made all the brandy they charge you for") in a big glass ball, and looking out from under the two slits that were his eyes.

He smelled the brandy and watched John sip it. "I've only got a hundred bottles of this stuff left. I wonder if I'll ever live to see it finished?"

"You could take it slowly. It could last a long time."

"Nobody has that much to take anything slowly. I'm backing Alice in that art gallery. I figure with her trust fund and her income from stock in my companies, a loss of about a hundred thousand a year would be just what she needs for income tax purposes."

"It seems a sound business procedure, if you're looking for losses."

"That's the trick in business. Not to make the most, but to keep the most. Fennel, you can do me a favor."

"If I can be of help to the gallery."

"No. How would you like to write my life?"

"I write novels."

"Where do you get your material?"

"From people. I've never made up anything in a book yet. I just arrange it . . . but . . ."

"Then just write a book about me Only use the right names."

"You may not like the book. I don't know, because I don't know anything about you."

"This is nothing. I can get you facts. Listen, I'm an old man who has everything and feels he has nothing. I don't like people. People en masse are stupid, and alone they are stupid and greedy and easy to exploit. I've got a hundred million, who knows how much I have? I could have a hundred billion, it's that easy once you find out how to pile it up, but I'm getting bored. Now I want to know, am I right or am I wrong?"

"I like people. That is, I like them as people. I don't like crowds," John said.

Garoyan laughed. "The democrat, and the man who uses the people. Will you do it, will you write the book?"

"I'll think it over."

"Either fifty thousand for the book or two thousand a week while working on it."

"I have no use for that kind of money, believe me. I've never held on to any and when I have a lot of it, it depresses me. I have to think up ways to spend it."

"I ought to write *your* life." The old man grinned and poured a drop of brandy on his tongue. "We'll talk about it again. Give my love to Mike." Garoyan drew a finger in a knife gesture across his thin neck. Then he laughed, and John drank his brandy quickly.

Everything was normal at the beach house. Ed the boxer limped from a bad bite from a dog fight with a chow on the beach. The pecking order in the bird cage had been changed. A mild gray bird had suddenly taken over and sat on the top rung, swinging himself back and forth, while chattering like mad. The other birds nibbled at the red paint on the bars and paid him no mind . . .

FROM THE JOURNAL OF JOHN FENNEL

There is a power and a vitality in old Garoyan that shocks me. The town and the industry have a grip on the people here that does not appear as yet to be breakable. They are part of the town's primitive social values, full of its superstitious fetishes and beset by most of its anxieties. Their frustrations in the studios are many, and like all frustrated people, they like to talk about it, always ready to "talk things out" without really reaching the core of any problem. There is a constant worry in the town about being discarded, about being used, being fired.

The town is loaded with elaborate taboos closer to the primitive tribal laws than civilized procedure. "Here the biological nature of man," Mike says, "is a mink coat of many moral views worn in any weather." And he is right; but Mandy, who has been trapped so often by the mere instinctive biological act, that has no value for her, has been able to rise above it a great many times in the past without understanding the tearing inner harm it has done her. She does not willingly, I think, join in the town's condescension, contempt, and hostility of those outside the industry and its morals, but she can repeat the latest gossip without understanding the warping of honest social pattern it represents. She sees nothing wrong in the studio contempt of people as property, and would welcome a seven-year contract with all its slave class clauses. Her life has been manipulated, humiliated, and her talent destroyed by the industry, but she has been able to live on in an atmosphere of continuous anxiety and crises upon crises; an amorality of power for power's sake.

None of them will see, or cannot, for their thinking is in the hands of their agent and soothsayer, so that they are victims of mental inefficiency and deep frustration. Good work cannot remain second rate, but will become third rate unless they lift themselves from the rut into which their lack of strength has put them.

As Ed, the unemployed director, has said so often, "You come out here young and able and you enter a studio and you look around you one day, and you're suddenly overnight sixty years old." The jobs became fewer, the interest less. I see them in front of Schwab's drugstore, picking unfed teeth with free toothpicks while reading the film trade papers; they appear at the Academy showings of old pictures to see their work done years ago; they are arrested driving an old car without brakes; sometimes they appear in court for an hour and some reporter remembers them. They are living on their own tails, like wrecked monkeys, all along the beaches at Santa Monica and Topanga and Malibu; aging, wrinkling, souring, and lamenting, and *waiting*. They never give up waiting for the industry and the town to make that one phone call, for the agent to say, "hang on, you're hot at Paramount . . ." I've heard it a dozen times. "I spoke to Dore Schary about you at lunch today. He asked how you were, kid, remembers when you were at Metro with him ten years ago." Or, "Steve Trilling at Warners said hello too. He did say he might dream up something for you, baby . . ."

In this way they become conditioned to hysteria. "They think with adrenalin glands, not a brain," Dr. Sontag says. "Everybody is a gambler here. All gamblers are really scared people, and all regression to early infancy of childhood is a desire to recapture something from the past."

Mollie still said Mrs. Henry was only amusing, but at any moment of the day or night Mollie would pick up the phone and call Mrs. Henry, dress carelessly, and dash over there for a "little talk." Mike felt that Mrs. Henry cleverly seemed to sense that she could not share Mollie's mind with him; here was a rival that would in the end do away with the need of a Mrs. Henry. But it upset Mollie to have Mrs. Henry talked about, unless she, Mollie, did the talking herself. Mike decided to wait out the matter of the charlatan soothsayer.

They had lost something, Mollie knew. Just what she didn't try to put into words. But she felt now that the walls of the beach house were growing smaller. It had been such a big place once, in the happy hurry of its first moments. It had been filled with sunshine and the world was a crayon blue outside its windows with the yellow sands and the umbers of the tall dry hills behind. Now the place under a heated roof was small, and she felt its walls pressing in on her as if peering over her shoulder to read her mind. She was always in panic now, always feeling that somehow, so young, she had been trapped. Trapped in what? Trapped how?

It had perhaps begun with the acting, acting which she had never cared for, but that, she had to admit, Mike had done fine things with. So it wasn't all the acting. The death of the dog, the little dog with the big golden eyes; that too, was it enough to make her feel the universe growing smaller? Maybe it was all inside her, something hidden away, buried and covered over, emotional turf that hid whatever the grave inside her held. But that was romantic nonsense, images out of half-digested poems. In the morning when the sun was very strong and she sat on the beach, the house crouched behind her back, and she looked out across the ocean—toward China she supposed—the day seemed alive and alerted and painted in harmless colors like children's toys. In the afternoon things were not so good and the beach boys came to cheer her up. There was also Beppo, who was so Goddamn possessive now and tried to kiss her on the wooden stairs going down to the beach. Who leaned against the bathroom door and talked to her while she dressed. Who ate her food and drank her whisky and told her what a great man he was and what bars of pleasure the cage of his arms could be.

The walls of the beach house more and more leaned inward and she came awake one night and saw the shining eyes of the dog burning in the night, staring at her. There was something in the beach house—perhaps a message (in the night she did not laugh at Mrs. Henry)—she sensed it and she picked up the flashlight, the big heavy one she owned, and she called Ed, the dog, to follow her. She went into the big living room. The fireplace was dead and the room smelled of the flowers Beppo had sent her, the spilled beer, the cloying stuff they pumped into the cesspool and the wet salt wood on the sun deck. The big windows facing the sea were open. She looked out into the pearly gray sky with a clot of racing moon behind inky nets of clouds. Far out a fishing tug hooted a wailing cough. She stood there looking out, and all space was a desolation to her and all time was eternity, clicking, clicking like a big clock in her chest, just as she had believed in childhood. A clock in the tummy. She knew she hated the nights, all nights, because they left her so alone. And that in heaven it must always be sunshine, always high noon.

She kept from Mike all her moods, but he must have suspected, because when she turned away and he thought she couldn't catch him at it he would follow her with worried eyes. And often she would turn and look back into his staring face. It was all becoming a kind of agony for them, but neither would admit it because they wanted it to be as it had been in those days in the beginning when, like everything fresh, it had seemed as if it would last a thousand years in the warm surprise and the wonderful ache of the beginning of all things.

The sun made her head ache. Beppo's flowers made her sneeze. Ed, the mad dog, tried to bite her, and she woke up from heavy dreams panting, as if she had been swimming in the oily ocean of sailors torpedoed at sea. Yet when she sat on the beach chair in a white bathing suit, out on the sun deck, her legs crossed and her feet in golden sandals, a drink in her hand, she was the little girl all golden and pink and smiling with very blue eyes. The delicate, intricate daintiness of her was to everyone who passed, or stopped, a work of art and no one bothered to ask or believe that there was anything the matter . . . anything the matter at all in the beach house . . .

FROM THE JOURNAL OF JOHN FENNEL

Mike has infected me with his depression. Something is bothering him. It would be foolish to think of love as a triumph of the will alone, and I am not the man to do an intuitive study of it at this time. This town to Mike as he expresses it, and the whole Southwest, is becoming a sort of cocoon of sentimentality, in which he appears to himself as a grub smothered in silk smelling of a woman's body, thrashing around trying to tear himself out. The immediate sense of life is lost in this place. He claims the intense conviction of actuality has almost left him. The sun shines, the people grow bigger and more full of health. He moves among them and wonders where is their sense of doomsday, the true dark of modern existence. Don't they know the present era, the perpetual war it is? He seems to them, I'm sure, strangely alien, and they, to him, take on a hostile gayness . . . I wonder sometimes if California is not an ironic dirty trick, something someone is laughing at and not much concerned about. The black mountains, the blue beating shore line, the palm and olive trees that serve no purpose, spell out at times an anonymous panic that no one here seems equipped to comprehend.

Can there ever be, Mike asks, an age of anxiety in such white sunlight; what use are the stoic virtues in this dreamboat of a place when *courage* and *fortitude* seem like dirty words no one dares mention? The curse of this place is that one must run and pant and sweat, and play a good game of tennis, drink everything in sight, and fornicate the tanned, smooth, dry flesh, and never be granted stoic resignation. Perhaps like the poet, they are all intoxicated by the idea of damnation and are too drunk by pleasureless pleasure to care. They seem to believe in the urge to move quickly and act violently . . . they chase out of their way the years that leap up when they reach them, for there are no seasons, no snows, no chill of April springs. Everything eludes them, but they do not care, for the jobs will be bigger tomorrow, the pay more, the girls more beautiful, the sunlight blinding, their skins tanned like leather, and every orgasm will be publicly posted against the record. They look well as they reach for life, but somehow they are always empty-handed.

I know what Mike means. Everyone laughs at what he does and yet none of us here can stop creating the nonsense we laugh at. It is more than a Bohemian notoriety, more than the peculiarly empty pleasures of joyless gay days in well-tailored slacks. Some spark is lacking, that leaping electric thing that can translate faith in something into any real medium of art, even shoemaking or an honestly cooked dish. It is not only the preoccupation with the mortal nature of men that is avoided, but the fact that we are all well aware of the complete aloneness. The feeling that catches us at the big party, in the din of the record player, over the breaking of glasses and the pouring of whisky, at that moment of great doubt when the thing close to us is a true monster, for we dread the moment when even the monster will be lost to us, for a monster is better than facing this country of gay sunshine, the bright colors, alone . . .

John noticed that Mike had stepped up his drinking. There were times now when Mike spoke through a film of liquor, his brain functioning almost in a fever brought on by the alcohol. The big man was hurt inside, puzzled by something he did not fully understand.

They were seated in his cottage drinking, John and Mike. Mike was taking it fast and swallowing with cheek and neck muscles tense and bunched up with power. John was just sipping and drinking, letting it flow, feeling nothing much, not unhappy or happy, merely contented.

Mike looked into his empty glass and reached for the bottle.

"You know, Johnny, half swacked like this I can admit Mollie worries me. I can't say why yet. I don't know how. But it's like cutting out a vein from the body . . . you know the blood will find another passage to flow back to the heart. Something happens to our love sometimes: we cut a big vein, and the blood finds its way back to the heart, but it's not the same. I don't know the answers and I haven't the time. Hell, the only people who have time to think are the sick, the ill on their backs, knowing nothing matters but staying alive. I keep thinking I know a few answers and I don't. I used to think, Mike you old dope, stay in the stream, live the life of the perfect Spinozan universe in which each single part of it is a little mirror that reflects the whole. You're not laughing, Johnny. Maybe it's not funny. Like the time my father grew a beard and instead of people not knowing him, *he* refused to recognize any of his friends. Sometimes I think Mollie and I put on mental beards and pass each other by. Then we get together and the cables hold and it's all right.

"Sure, I'm not drunk. Just floating and it's not bad. In the morning I'll be fine. Everything will be a ball, as Walter says, just a ball. Just one more, Johnny, and—all gone? What a ball!"

There was a kind of rhyme and pacing about picture-making that John was beginning to understand. As the picture came closer to what they hoped was the last shot to be cut into it, the taking of the pills grew faster. They were almost all taking pills now. At first, in an amused sort of way, then with the regular gesture of habit, as if drinking water.

First the big, fancy vitamin pills to keep one fit and keep away colds and brush off allergies, "new kinds of allergies for each picture," Walter said. Then the sleeping pills, the powerful red ones, for a good night's sleep, and of course in the morning Benzedrine, or the newer Dexedrine to put the punch and pep into one. Doctors had grown rich and famous in Beverly Hills by just writing prescriptions for pills.

When the pains started there was Empirin, and if that didn't help after a while there was codeine. A swallow, a half glass of water, and one went on working. John had a picture in his mind of the town, well dressed, smart at its parties, rich (on paper anyway), at its banking hours, with the pills rattling around in their taut stomachs. Soup and brandy often floated these drugs in solution until a picture was finished.

But John was mostly interested in the actual putting together of film footage. Mike had exposed and developed fifteen thousand feet of thirty-five-millimeter film. Not in one big length, but in bits of a few hundred feet each, that now ran day and night through the little clicking machines called movieolas. In the big projectors when they viewed a section cut together, it ran along at the rate of ninety feet a minute. Mike knew that it was too long and that his footage would run two and a half hours. He would have to cut out almost an hour. *What* hour to cut was the problem.

20

THE cutting together of the picture continued—a long and painstaking task. To John Fennel it remained amazing technical magic, this clipping together of short lengths of exposed film, of matching sound, of adding noise effects, of developing dark or light, of marking checks and crosses on the film strips that would become dissolves and fade-outs. It was all so mechanical and yet so much part of a finished picture.

Mike, wearing white cotton gloves, ran lengths of developed film through a movieola, and through a viewing lens big as a teacup saw the action of the film length. Then he cut and trimmed, and helpers spliced. They talked of lighting and sound and projection, and cursed the lighting or the clouds or wrong kind of effect. Slowly there began to emerge a rough-cut version of a scarred, scratched movie, the working print. The sound was not on this film, but on another film, a blank film; John discovered the sound and the film would not be combined until the final version of the picture was decided on.

So, without music, without actual dissolves and fades, but only symbols of them, John sat through a dozen versions of the picture. He no longer knew or cared much if it were good or bad, if Mollie were a great actress or not. John did not see how *anyone* could know at this stage. After all the numbing effort of watching it so often, no one, he felt, could know if it were good or bad. There were dark, blank sections with a sign reading SCENE TO BE SHOT ON LOCATION. Mike would sit very still after the lights went on, then banging his cane into the dusty seat in front of him, he would frown. Then he would lift his head, again expressionless, pull his glasses off his face, and wet his lips carefully.

"We've got to cut tighter. Take out the long walk from the door, and cut the opening of the dolly shots in the hotel scene."

Mollie refused to come and look at the rough-cut versions.

FROM THE JOURNAL OF JOHN FENNEL

I am beginning to see what Walter means about Mike's outlook on his work changing. That he is no longer the pure raw ego trampling on all to get his way, but beginning to mellow, even doubt himself in many ways. This does not make less an artist, for many fine artists doubted themselves and did great work. Baudelaire's clock, I remember, had no hands, but he managed to understand the fearful pace of time. Mike knows now, he says, the belly-world of greed and fear that surrounds him, that element of guilt and expiation that is the town's favorite subject.

When Mike drinks he likes to talk, to talk in images that are almost film scenes, for he sees everything in pictures, even his vast cluttered reading when he talks about it, takes on a composition you could almost film. He is a little letdown, Mollie worries him, he is not sure he is doing his best on a picture so limited by budget and time.

He said today after a few drinks, "Art has an indecent power to reproduce itself—as if love were always attacking its body. Hell, we think we tell art what to do, and suddenly, it's a

226

monster, Frankenstein's bogey-wogie man pushing you aside and taking over. It makes me think maybe old Doc Freud had something. He said, quote—'art is a substitute gratification, an illusion in contrast to reality. Unlike most illusions, art is almost always harmless, it does not seek to be anything but an illusion. It shares the characteristics of the dream element to become a distortion, a sort of inner dishonesty'—unquote." He refilled the glasses and looked at me and laughed. "A sort of inner dishonesty—that's art? If I believed that—but I don't, I can't . . . The hell with it. Let's have some dinner."

There were days when Mike Zelsmith found himself involved in small accidents and in the perverse habits of inanimate objects. This morning he cut his upper lip shaving, and when he put on his shoes, a frayed shoelace broke off in his fingers. His laces were a mass of knots. He discovered a seam had opened in the back of his jacket (the hound's-tooth sport jacket that was almost the uniform of the industry in Hollywood). Going down to get his car, he got a cinder in his eye. He decided to visit the beach house. He had learned to take such bad periods calmly and avoid working; he supposed in the old days he would have been considered mildly bewitched at such times.

He drove up to the beach house and the front door of the place opened and Beppo Kubelik came out. It was rather early in the morning, near eight. The men greeted each other and Mike noticed something about Beppo that puzzled him; he was fully dressed, yet he acted like a man caught naked in some sordid situation. Mike frowned and pushed in the front door of the beach house that was never locked. In the fuzzy outer frontier of his mind something mean and nasty was forming, certain heavy, fusty notions, but he drove them off and looked over the living room and the sun deck beyond it.

"Hello," he said out loud to the house.

He heard Mollie stirring in the bedroom, and he went down the passage and found her in bed sitting up in a nightgown, lighting a cigarette. He noticed some mashed-out cigarettes already in the willow pattern plate she used as a bedside ashtray. She stared up at him, her mind and eyes not yet in focus at his sudden appearance. She looked a beautiful child still unaware of reality.

"Early today?" she asked slowly.

"I guess so."

He had a wild sense, some keen bit of impulsive instinct, that the room had a beast-pit odor, the tight acid bite of a room in which love had just been made and he also suddenly got that band across his chest, tight and bitter.

"What's Beppo doing here so early in the morning?"

"Ali Baba and his forty weeds," Mollie said, pointing to a huge vase of fresh flowers. Now Mollie was not a witty person at waking, and he wondered at her sudden flippancy. Jesu, could it happen to him?

"Walter hinted he's been making passes." Mike sniffed at the flowers, broke off a loose leaf.

"Just the usual beach tries."

"I'll kick his lousy tail off."

He felt reassured by her voice. She was not a good liar, and he felt he would have known from her tone of voice if anything were wrong. The tightness did not leave his chest and he felt sad and sorry for everybody, in dread of something he could not box in and examine.

"You don't look so good, baby."

She mashed out her cigarette and slid her small buttocks under the blanket and yawned, stretching, her joints cracking.

"What's it like outside?"

"Mist, no sun, and lots of dust."

They talked in almost aimless boredom about little things, and Mike felt in them something too casual, and yet on guard. He wanted suddenly very much to make love, to reweave in passion a soothing cover to his fears, to coat his doubts in intimate remembered pleasures and warm details . . .

They lay side by side smoking, looking at the pine knots on the ceiling. He said, "Am I beginning to bore you, Mollie?"

"That's nonsense."

"Anything the matter, baby? Something you want to tell me? Something seriously the matter?"

"Nothing is the matter."

"You can talk to me."

"Talking isn't real good, anyway."

"All right, kid."

He left her in an hour, her face pink and sweet, yet her sleep uncomfortable, her fists clenched. He kissed her cheek tenderly and again felt that beast odor; but it might have only been the smell of Ed, the boxer. The dog slept, since the death of Lucky, on a canvas beach pad under the work-table in the bedroom. He would watch them, his mad gray eyes sparking in the semi-dark of the shade-drawn room, and often he would growl until Mollie ordered him silent or beat him with his leash. He resented men around her and it had taken time for him to half-accept Mike. He loved to be fondled and petted by Mollie, and when excited and locked out on the sun deck he would scratch furiously at the window screens. Bringing him indoors had not pleased Mike. He never got completely used to the staring dog on the beach pad under the worktable.

The few days before they left for the location trip to the island were bad for Mike at the beach house. Their few times together were unsatisfactory. He did not meet Beppo again at the place, but he noticed that the flowers were now fresh every day. Mike's pride would not let him comment on them. Mollie was not being unfaithful to him. She seemed lazy and indifferent to anything he said to her.

The night before he left for location, she said suddenly, "Walter is leaving me."

"Walter moving?"

"Since the robbery he hasn't been happy here. Besides, it's a long trip into town for him."

"So what?"

"Walter doesn't approve of me, I think."

"What the hell, Mollie."

"Anyway, I'll be here alone with just Ed 'til you get back. I'm going to get another boxer, a girl for Ed. I know one I can get. She has one blue eye, one brown eye."

"You're too fond of animals, baby."

He went into the kitchen to get a drink of spring water. As he stood there, glass in hand, he heard Walter moving around in his room below. Mike went down the staircase and found Walter packing his few belongings into two battered straw cases. He looked at Mike and went on packing.

"Really going, Walter?"

"Yes. I've got to get the sets torn down while you're gone."

"You sore at anything?"

Walter stopped packing and began to run through some old copies of the *Saturday Review of Literature* he was leaving behind.

Walter turned around. "Going to be gone long?"

"Two weeks."

"I'll be seeing you, M.Z."

Mike went back upstairs.

Mike said good-by to Mollie in the morning. Walter was already gone. She looked sleepy and grinned as she yawned. He held her in his arms and kissed her.

"Easy does it, baby," he said.

"Sure, Mike."

She kissed him hard on the mouth. Outside a car horn sounded. It was the company car. He was riding with John and Mandy Rye.

She did not walk him to the door. She stood in the wan morning light, Ed at her feet, and she watched him cross to the door. He felt all warm inside and not at all confused. He *knew* Mollie was deeply in love with him.

They went up the coast two hundred miles and then took a boat to the island twenty miles offshore.

The trouble with most location trips is the weather. It rained a lot, the sun was never right for the cameras. Then the clouds were the wrong shape. They sat a week in the flea-proud hotel and read old magazines. The rain streaked across the windows, and at night the camera crews went into the little island port and got tight. They had trouble with the woman who had rented them the location ranch. She suddenly doubled her price. The head cameraman had disappeared on the mainland, and when they found him again he was drunk. The first day's shooting was discarded because of streaks on the negatives. They shot for four days in mixed weather.

John found the making of a motion picture a dull affair. But the island was wonderful. He and Mandy explored it.

FROM THE JOURNAL OF JOHN FENNEL

The island had been carelessly placed twenty miles off the coast of California. A misshapen island, as if some great hand had set it down, and gone on after trying to pull it back into shape with clumsy fingers. About ten miles wide and twenty miles long, with the long end pointed north like a Moorish lance. Great seas beat on its rocks. There was a huge stone pimple rising very high that showed the scars of old volcanic flames. But no smoke ever came from it. There was a big green beard, a lonely immensity of forest across one range of broken hills, where black teeth of rock appeared from time to time to show that in some places the soil had never been formed. There was only one place where a boat could land without being crushed and eaten by the rocks. At the southeastern tip a skillful skipper with a small yacht of shallow beam *could* aim between the mouth of rocks and hit the bay.

Here there was a dock and the beginning of Tonto Road . . . a heavy white surf ran on, and cut into a beach where little pink and white houses ranged in disorder across the lip of the bay. I joked to Mandy that this island is all of Eden we shall ever see—but she was not amused.

The southern part had boats being repaired and some goats fenced in across a cliff, where they ate salt grass and gave birth to little kids that roasted very well and tasted fine with a local wine. The friction of silken limbs was no stranger there either, by the way, but when guests were there, the island girls were deeply polite and fully clad in serving aprons. The local women have a peculiar intensity of very dark eyes and a sultry, modest, bedroom unobtrusiveness.

The cliffs were pocketed with bird nests and small animal life. There was a tower of stone, and wild grass, with weak wooden pegs inside that had once held a ladder or staircase, a tower the shape a soft candle takes. No one knew why it had been built. It was not Spanish or Mexican. It was just a piling of stones, some rough-cut or hacked with dull tools. Some day someone would dig wonderful trash from its base and make it a history.

And that was the whole island. A great rock formation and two openings, one for bathing and one for boats to come in. A scribble of sea all around, the geek-geek of gulls all day, and the full fury of wind-sea at night.

Mandy and I worked on a natural history of the island, with the aid of a sea-stained old book, and the remains of my formal education. By nature the island could be treated like one of the Galapagos . . . its resident birds were colorful, foolish, and given to overbreeding and too much loud mating in the limestone and granite cliffs. Its giant tortoises wandered on the bars off its coast and laid many leather eggs. Few, if any, little turtles ever got alive into the sea, for the fishes and the birds feasted on them. Once in a while the islanders, not for sport but for soup, caught some old turtle king or horny cow, and with a local sherry and the right kind of dry toast, the soup was very good. They made combs of the shell, pre-eminently classical in design, of lucidity, precision, and balance.

There were mockingbirds, a rare kind of finch that loved to steal toilet tissue, and thirty-eight kinds of plants rare in the rest of the world, ten of which, we thought, were found no place else. Some of these made fine salads, if one was daring, with olive oil and red pepper.

Snail evolution was very advanced—the island priest told us they had recorded three hundred species of land snail alone. They kept out of the way, but sometimes spoiled one's tennis shoes during the damp morning hours on the concrete courts . . .

Bird lovers could point out the long-tailed tit and the red bullfinch . . . most of the other people just said "damn birds" and let it go at that.

Fishermen liked the lake in the volcanic crater. Not that it was stocked with trout or land-locked salmon. It was a bottomless lake about two miles wide, fed and drained by some underground source. The fish were odd creatures. Charr of various kind, bendace, gwynaid, and pollan. All had too many bones and were hard to spell—or clean.

Offshore there was a shallow-water octopus—*O. App. Appollyon*—no great menace but the ladies did not like to find one embracing them with a gleam in its jello eye.

There were many red and yellow poppies in the wild grass. In these flowers, chromosomes came in sets of seven. A native who knew this, however, failed in his main purpose of flower study, which was to produce a smokable opium.

Tides, sea drift, bird litter, winds, and wrecks had played hell with the vegetable and animal life of the island. The crabs on the shore had too many claws and the males were bright red and given to climbing trees. The females spun blobs of jelly all day and had paws with blue ends, which they kept just under the surface of the water, and with which they nipped at anything passing; in revenge most likely against the males high up in their exclusive Union League Club trees. The males were cocoanut eaters and would twist the nuts loose during the night, dropping them on the rocks below to break them open. No one ever saw this animal-thinking in action. The natives were not bright enough to figure it out . . . but *there were* the open cocoanuts and *there were* the fat crabs.

There were no night insects smaller than beetles. The wind was said to sweep gnats and other such things back to the mainland. Each beetle was of pure, heavy gold-and-green-bronze finish, and after drying them out a few days some of the native women wore them pinned to their dresses.

The wine was very good. It was pressed in the wooden press at the Rancho de Verano . . . pressed, aided by the bare feet of the young girls . . . who had been bathed and their virgin feet tended to, and then the wine vat blessed and the bath water poured out under the mimosa trees.

There were two wines made on the island—something like Romanee Condi, and a Château Lafite (somewhat like the 1893), which were the best the natives made. These were kept in cold, dry caves and bottled and cared for and casked just right. There was also a substantial red wine . . . some Burgundy and some chianti which everyone who could get it drank every day.

There was even a little experimental vineyard that gave some sort of a Nuits-Saint-George type of wine.

The priest on the island was worried about his wine drinkers, for they all had little hidden patches, half-wild yards that grew grapes, which they fermented for their own use (or when they could steal from the priest's own cellars, they drank his wine). But when Garoyan's doctor told him that wines contained practically no carbohydrates, and yet had plenty of vitamins of the B complex group, riboflavin, thiamin, and B-1, the priest felt it was all right. It was the pantothenic acid in the vats that convinced him there was no harm in wine, for that acid is an anti-gray-hair vitamin, and the priest was beginning to brood over the few silver threads in his own very red hair, he confessed to us.

There were low dogs who made a foul white lightning from the juice of certain cardones, columnar cactus, and the drinkers of that could only lie around and stink and moan and hardly stir a limb for days. They could not work in the Father's fields, or fish, or carry stone. These the priest cursed out and told them they would fry in the very front grill in Hell.

Mandy is very different here—she has almost forgotten her rare old collection of furniture.

They went on making the picture, having troubles. The hours of standing and waiting, the measuring and moving, the posing and chalk-marking. Mike Zelsmith was an angry director, he shouted, the propmen shot crap, and the cameramen talked about lens sizes.

Mike wrote to Mollie every night. She had only answered twice. Dull little letters, typed on her rusty Underwood, with careless spelling and not even the typing mistakes corrected. She had ended her letters in pencil, merely, Moll.

He was writing her a long letter when there was a knock on the door and the script girl came in. She held a fistful of letters in a wet hand, and her oilskin coat was dripping wet. She blew a damp strand of hair out of her face and said, "Just went down to the harbor and got the mail. Two for you, Mr. Zelsmith."

One was from Mollie. It was on the stationery of the Mark Hopkins Hotel. He picked up the envelope. The postmark was San Francisco. The letter was very short:

Dear Mike,
  Things got very dull at the beach house. Rose came over to take care of Ed and feed the birds. Beppo was

*having a show of his little figures up here and he asked
me to come along. I've been here two days now and he's
dragged my tail through every museum and gallery in
town. Never knew there was so much art in the world.
How's the island? Still raining?*

Cordially,
Mollie

Mike stared down at it in a state of shock. He felt it the
cruelest letter ever written. Yet, wasn't it the message he
had been expecting for days? She had been unfaithful to
him for some time. With that filthy bastard. She was living
right now in San Francisco with him, bedding with him at a
good hotel. And she had written this letter in her own way
to let him know just how things stood.

He felt no self-pity, just a shocking feeling that things
could not really be like this. Even now that he knew, and he
admitted now he had known for some time, he still could
not believe the fine, sensitive body of Mollie in contact with
Beppo. Jesu—hell, no! And yet he knew that's the way it
was. It could all end here, finished like a cheap movie. If
his ego would let it . . .

John Fennel was sitting on a sofa reading Mandy Rye her
lines for the next day's shooting. She would nod, and when
he wasn't looking, she yawned. Someone knocked on the
door, the door opened, and Mike came in smelling of brandy
and stumbling against the furniture.

"You're drunk," said Mandy kindly.

"Stinking," said Mike holding his shaking fingers before
his face, "and I don't wanta hear any more about that. John,
I gotta have a speedboat and driver to the mainland."

"What for, in this weather?"

"Gotta get up to Frisco tonight."

"What's so important?" John asked.

"My whole life, Johnny. My whole life. I've been f——
off! Pardon me, Mandy. I've been f—— off!"

"What you talking about?"

"Do I get a company car? Get the f—— boat!"

John came over to him and put his arm around the shaking man.

"Sure, Mike, I'll get the boat."

"Thanks." He sat down quickly as if his feet had just
been pulled from under him. "I like you, Johnny. Every-

body told you I'm a sonofabitch, but you didn't care. You're an artist like me. We haven't got many real artists in the world. Just little old stupid people in power, little s——minds in clover. You're a man, Johnny, and they'll break you, too. They're laying for you—everybody is laying for somebody! You find that out."

"It's pretty bad, Mike?"

"More than my belly can hold. More than my mind can stand. You knew about Mollie?"

"In the end it can't hurt you, Mike."

"I know. They said a heart attack is the easy way to go. And the little dog died of drowning in his own blood. Sure, I'll hear it a long time now . . . . *in the end it can't hurt me.* Well, hell, it isn't hurting me in the end, it's hurting me in the marrow and the blood and in all the little places you store up sweetness for your old age. Christ, all the secret corners of a man can fall in on him like a wall of bad bricks."

"I saw it coming, Mike," Mandy said, very low.

Mike stared, his drunken eyes not pin-pointing properly. "You know too? Everybody knows but the lover. The old lousy French comedy. Well, I sit here and feel the pain. Feel it bubble and burn, and everybody knows about it. Jesu, it's terrible to be so naked and bare-assed in public. To collect pity in a basket like a beggar taking up bits of bad meat. Where the f—— is that speedboat!"

"I'll send for it. You're not fit to travel, Mike."

"Fit, ready, and able. I've seen everything and done everything. You ever been in a war? Seen the dirt of it, the ignorant mess of it? Ever look at a dead face and curse whatever made you and is going to take you away? Ever wonder in the mystery of the bed why you had to have an attitude toward only one woman's body, one set of genitalia, one way of doing it with some special . . . ? What's the reason for it and what's the why or wherefor?"

John covered him with a blanket from the bed and said kindly, "You've really got a load on. Get some rest and I'll have the boat made ready."

John stood for a long time listening to Mike mumble, his eyes closed, his damp hair over his eyes. Then he turned back to the sofa and saw Mandy staring at him. John felt the futility of all human endeavor in one small room. He picked up the phone.

It was the rainy season on the mainland too. John got Mike's car out of the garage, but Mike didn't want him along. Mike never was to remember much of it. He remembered the hot black coffee burning the lining of his stomach, and the big car on the wet roads roaring to the coast. He remembered the borrowed hat and the borrowed raincoat and three whiskies in a row as soon as he got to Frisco. ("They prefer to call it San Francisco.") It was raining. He got very wet—to the skin, under the skin, his shoes were wet, his toes swam. He got no satisfaction at the hotel. There was no Miss Mollie Binning, and no Mr. Kubelik, and no, it was "not permitted to see the cards the guests registered on." Mike sat damply in the lobby until the house detective moved near him and he went back to the desk, dripping, hatless, almost blind with rage and bitterness.

He remembered something. "Is there a Mrs. Reegan here?"

"No, there isn't."

"Small, very beautiful girl—good legs—kind of."

The clerk was shaking his head, not listening.

Mike went out into the rain and bought two bottles of brandy and found a little hotel full of worn red rugging and took a room and ran up a big phone bill calling art galleries and art dealers and museums. No; perhaps; well; Kubelik? Mike was too drunk to make much sense of what he heard. He drank brandy raw from a toothbrush glass and tried to read the "Song of Songs" out loud in the sticky hotel Bible. He added certain verses of his own. He only remembered later the one ending, "Take you the power of the bitch goddess, let the sons of Zion strip her, and may the wolves of the desert lick out with their tiny tongues the eye sockets of a whore . . ." He was ashamed later—it was such early deMille.

The air in the room, the color of his sleep, the dampness of the bed, were real.

Mike awoke late the next day, the hotel radio still playing and his face lying in his own spilled digestive juices.

He felt nothing. Neither pain nor remorse, regret nor fear. His heart had not burst. He could think calmly with a head he did not dare touch. It was a head made of some newly discovered plastic, he suspected. He took an ice-cold shower and shivered and dried himself. He got the phone girl to look up the beach house number for him.

It took a half hour for the call to come through.

"Hello?" He was crafty now. "Is Miss Binning there?"

"This is Miss Binning."

"Mollie?"

"Yes?"

"It's Mike. I'm in Frisco."

"Oh." There was no fear, only a slight tremor of her voice.

"I can't talk over the phone, Mollie. Want to see you."

"It's no good, Mike."

"I'm taking the Lark back tonight. Meet you tomorrow someplace. Where?"

"Anywhere."

"The Players—at twelve?"

"Yes. I want to say . . ."

"No, Mollie, say it to my lousy face. Remember the good, clean teachings of your mother and father. Your code of honor. Mrs. Baker's school, the Republican party, the decent white Protestants . . ."

"You're drunk, Mike. I'll see you at The Players tomorrow at noon."

He was very sober. How wrong she was. He took one more big suck on the brandy bottle and went down to get his railroad ticket. The rain had stopped pattering on the street, but the day was gray and the boat whistles moaned and brayed from the Golden Gate. "Greatest city in America—greatest state in the union," he said to the ticket agent. "Great little country. The dames are all fair and young and keep their legs crossed with strange guys."

"I *beg* your pardon!"

"You got a right to. Me, I'm the last fighter in the lost cause. Don't remember the Goddamn cause."

Mike sat in his underwear in a booth while they pressed his suit up front and sponged the smell of vomit and brandy and sweat from it. He sat in his soiled shirt and his shorts looking over the dreary respectability of picture magazines while a large colored man shined his soggy shoes.

"In the third round I was holding 'im up and I said to Max, 'I can't carry 'im no longer.' And he said, 'You just

hold 'im up, we gotta let him kayo you in the sixth . . .
that's the way the money is laid out'. . . Well, you know he
was almost asleep by the sixth . . . he sure looked bad
. . . Other shoe, please."

"Didn't you do that one yet?"

"No, sir. You said I should start on the right foot and
put in new shoelaces. These sure knotted . . . Coming out
in the sixth frame this bum he trips over himself and falls
flat on his kisser and the jerk counts him out. I didn't get
no part of the gate, and I can't get no fight no more. Wax
finish?"

"What? Any finish you want."

"So I'm riding the leather polishing shoes, but I've got
my eye on something. No more leather, no more canvas-
diving. A bottle club for people out for a little fun. Coupla
high yellow gals and some Dixieland music and a fat
singer . . ."

The seedy-looking presser came in with Mike's suit on a
wire hanger. "You lost a button someplace."

"That's all right," Mike said.

"Imagine that sonofabitch tripping on himself."

The presser held out the pants. "Them ain't American
buttons, or I'd give you one free . . ."

"Bought the suit in London."

"Sure, they don't know how to pad a shoulder."

"I gotta put in the other shoelace, just a minute."

Mike sat down and decided to think of chess. He used to
play a lot of chess as a boy. It was a good game, all brains
and skill. Not an art, thank God. He began to slowly play
in his mind Alekhine's thirty-fourth game against the great
Capablanca. When he finished that, he played the Peters-
burg game of Steinitz and Lasker. Then he played just a
game for himself against the world. He tried the Queen
Pawn opening, then he decided to shoot the works . . . the
demonic move of 2I Q-Q 2. It was a hell of a game, the
Goddamnedest game you ever saw . . .

"We gotta close up soon."

He was looking into the wide primitive mask of a broken
Negro's face, the eyeballs very white with just a tinge of
egg yolk on the corners. "What?"

"You just been sitting there, staring."

Mike said, "Been playing Capablanca. Chess, you know
it?"

"No, sir . . ."

He handed the man a dollar. "Beat the pants off him . . ."

Mike left some bills in the front of the shop and went out. The rain had let up and everybody was walking on the still-wet pavement with a twin version of them walking upside down on the sidewalk under them. Mike was very pleased with himself for not thinking of death, and he repeated a favorite line of his Uncle Ben, that didn't mean anything when he first heard it long ago: *While I exist death is not and when death comes I am not.* Somehow the longhair line made him feel better. You just stepped across a line if you wanted to, and there it was, no pain, no feeling, no nothing. He wasn't going to use *it,* but it was cozy knowing *it* was there, on order. His feet felt good, the new shoelaces were neat and tight.

21

HE knew now one did not fall quickly into the full horror of anything; there is a slow, descending spiral.

Mike had a good night's sleep on the train, and a big hot breakfast. He drove to his hotel cottage, showered, shaved, and put on his best suit. The agony was all gone out of him now. He had never been calmer in his life, he decided, and he needed a haircut. He had his hair trimmed and took a cab to The Players, where he sat down at one of the small tables, his back against the sun-heated wall. He ordered a whisky sour and drank three inches. An agent who knew him casually waved to him, and some hostess he had once met over warm cocktails said "hello" and offered him half an invitation to her house. Several groups of picture people were huddled under the terrace umbrellas talking business. He felt free of craving and aversion, pleasure and pain, growth and decay.

He saw Mollie come up the narrow steps from the streetfront parking lot. She smiled and came toward him, the small jewel-like girl.

"Hello, Mike."

He stood up and motioned to her to sit down at his side. "Hello, Mollie."

She was neatly dressed—her very blue eyes very large.

"Buy you a drink?" he asked.

239

"Only one. Beppo has me on a quota. One a day."

"Her master's voice," Mike said, and motioned to the waiter. "What will it be?"

"Gin ricky."

"A gin ricky for the lady, and I'll have another whisky sour."

Mike looked at her closely, feeling nothing, and smiled. "You're really involved, aren't you, Mollie?"

"Yes, I guess I am." She almost whispered it.

"You happy?"

She shrugged her shoulders. "I guess I am. Yes, I'm happy."

"You fooled me, baby. I should have known the day I met Beppo at your door, and you couldn't make it over the big hill with me. Me in the afternoon—him at night."

"He's so forceful and simple."

"You're back where you were with your husbands. Playing house."

"I didn't want to make any change but . . ."

"Let's stick to your story."

"I fought it, Lord knows I fought it. I love you, Mike, as I'll never love anyone else in my whole life. You've been the one big love of my life." She stopped talking and began to weep. She took out sun glasses and put them on.

"I'm all right. I'm not alone any more."

"No, you're not," Mike said.

She sipped her drink, teasing it with her tongue. She was dying for a few good belts of liquor, Mike could see that.

"Beppo has chased out all the beach crowd and closed the bar. Nights we sit around the fire and he works and I read. He's only a kid and he wants me to marry him. I think I will some day."

"Don't you find him stupid?"

"He never had much education—a terrible coal mine town. Poverty. Hates his family. Lives from hand to mouth. But he's very sure of himself."

"Don't you find him stupid?" Mike repeated.

"He's young and doesn't know much. He hasn't, well, lived."

"Want another drink?"

"I told you . . ."

"I know, the toast of Cortez Beach having one mild ricky. Funny, Mollie, I didn't know what we'd talk about today, but I didn't think we'd talk like this. So banal, such

B-picture dialogue. I kind of expected to do the big Hemingway or Bogart thing. Slap you down in front of everybody. Or be real tragic and full of crummy poetry."

"You'd never hit me." Mollie turned him the delicate beautiful face, almost shocked.

"No, but Beppo will . . . So, it's over, Mollie?"

"I told you I'd never love anybody as I loved you, Mike. But I've got to be a realist. I need a real home. You're tied up with your picture-making, you're not part of the beach world. Beppo is real, he's something I understand right now without trying."

"Hungry?"

"Not very. Beppo isn't getting much. I'm pretty second-hand."

"That's childhood talk, Mollie, girls' school talk."

"What Myron calls my return to Mother, huh?" She smiled, bending her mouth with effort.

"Tell me, Mollie, how does this fit in with all the mystic corn Mrs. Henry told you?"

"It fits in perfectly."

"Didn't she say everything would work out for us by midsummer?"

"She did . . . and it did. It has worked out for me, and for you. The trouble, she said, is I always expect it to work out the way I thought it would, not the way destiny meant it to."

"Destiny?" Mike did a small comic take. His head ached —a delayed hang-over most likely.

"She knew something would happen this summer, and it did. I must say I was a little surprised the way it worked out. But Mrs. Henry was right."

"Her inner voices said it was going to be Beppo?"

"No, just that something would work out."

"Did she warn you against me?"

"She said you'd try and break it up now, make small of Beppo."

"Clever Mrs. Henry, so very clever Mrs. Henry. How does Beppo feel about you keeping a private crystal ball?"

"Don't mock me, Mike, I'm very tired."

"Not me. Just my head. It went soft for a baby-faced broad. Feel, you can push your finger in it like into a pumpkin. Ever make grinning heads out of pumpkins when you were a kid, Mollie, and carry them through the street with a bit of candle in them?"

"Of course." She sat there, the little girl listening to childish chatter.

"Well, that's one thing you and I still have in common. I'm sure Beppo never did."

She wiped her eyes under the sun glasses.

"That's about it, isn't it, Mike? I'll get out of the beach house soon. We're going to Mexico to paint."

"Yes." He stood up. "Pretty anticlimactic. No tomb of Juliet. No poison or dagger. No lousy Trojan Wars. Drive me back to the hotel?"

"I'm passing right by."

They drove toward the hotel. Mike said suddenly, "Let's go see the city from that cliff in the hills."

"You really want to?"

"Yes . . . I'm neat. We used to go there to talk, the first few times. I tie up my little bundles tightly."

"Beppo never talks like this."

"Lucky Beppo—acres of girl and no thinking."

They drove up the road and Mollie backed the car around and it was as it always had once been. He put his arm around her neck and pulled her toward him and she came willingly. Mollie did not fight him.

Mike kissed her and she kissed him, but the ache and the rhythm were gone. Only the desire remained. He remembered a line from Kant, "You ought to, therefore you can." The hell with it!

"Going to tell Beppo you're cheating on him, necking in the Hollywood hills like high-school kids?"

"We'll still be friends; we'll still see each other, Mike. I need so much of you to round out my life."

"What will Beppo say?"

"I don't think he'll mind when he gets used to it. He respects you very much. Thinks you're a fine man."

"I think he's just a slimy rat getting into another man's bed when he's away."

"You'll spoil it, Mike."

"Yes, I mustn't spoil it, must I? I'm the gentleman, the old-fashioned gent who suffers. Nuts, Mollie!"

He kissed her and she clung to him and held his hand very hard. He knew if he took her now—. He did nothing.

She dropped him at his hotel and drove off, grinding gears, almost tearing a curb guide out of its steel holder. Mike went slowly into the hotel feeling nothing. He had never been so empty of worry. He didn't have a problem in the world. They could take all time and eternity and shove it . . .

When Mike woke up the headache was only a ghostly far-off thumping. He remembered his Aunt Ann and how when she had died he had also felt that empty feeling. But he was a boy then on the Jersey shore and not very sad because she was older and his own old age was very far away. She had been buried in the country cemetery among the pines and they had all come back, the family, he remembered, the modern little rabbi passing the wine bottles around the well-filled table and reciting:

> "First our pleasures die—and then
> Our hopes, and then our fears—and when
> These are dead, the debt is due
> Dust claims dust—and we die too . . ."

Only Mollie wasn't dead, which was too bad. What a sad, graceful wearing of mourning it would have been; all their friends would have remembered her in her best moments. But she was alive. People, Mike felt, did not make a proper climax to their lives any more. He had tried often to explain to Mollie that one must live with a style to one's life. She had never understood that. Her romantic need was everything; but he smiled to himself and stopped such thoughts. One must not think evil of the dead or those who to him were as good as buried. And he knew his big problem was how to pass the time, without thinking at all.

He was still lying on his bed relaxed, nothing at all on his mind, having nothing he wanted to do. The weight of minutes and hours hung over him. He was neither hungry nor in need of entertainment. He had tried to read, but all the prose stuff seemed dumb nonsense. Books were really a waste of time. People needed them to put on their shelves in good bindings, and men made money printing them. But it was all nonsense. Like motion pictures? No book could ever explain what had happened to him. He didn't care if it could be explained. The pain was far off, like an old toothache under a sore tongue.

In a few hours he would get off the bed, have a drink, order some light dinner, maybe take a walk or see the motion picture. No—that was too much to expect of him. Tomorrow? Well, tomorrow would be like today. Weeks, months, years, what a hell of a lot of them. He would take them in his stride. Figuring twenty years more, maybe thirty, if he stayed off the booze and fat food and whores. He sat up suddenly and rubbed the back of his neck. Let time take care of itself: Sonofabitch, he was Mike Zelsmith, not a puking college boy. He read the headlines in the newspaper. It seemed odd that so many things should be happening and so many international troubles brewing when he had been going through that climax with Mollie all these days.

He looked neat and fit in the mirror and decided the barber had done a good job. Not a very handsome face, but solid as a brick outhouse. Character in it. Mollie had that kind of character, but Mollie wasn't a subject to think about any more.

He counted his shirts and shoes and decided to replace all his shoelaces. He looked at his wrist watch. Three-ten. He couldn't eat for at least four hours yet. He didn't feel like a drink, and anyway, Ed, the unemployed director, would nail him at the bar and tell him about the good old days. "We made pictures, not words." He could write a letter, but there wasn't anybody to write to that mattered. Somehow he felt as if he had resigned from the human race.

The phone rang and Mike picked it up. His heart actually skipped a beat. He had always suspected that the line "heart skipped a beat" was written by popular trashy writers for effect, but no, his heart had really skipped a beat. His diaphragm had pushed up, his breath had stopped for a split second, and he had had the brief feeling of ecstasy. But it wasn't Mollie. It was Dr. Sontag.

"Hello, old horse, feeling any pain?"

"No, I'm all right, Doc, really I am," Mike said.

"Well, watch out for a reaction. If you feel anything, get off your feet, take a physic, nothing like an empty bowel to make an empty mind. And read Proust. I always read Proust, and look at me, nothing wrong with me a dozen wise old duffers with axes couldn't cure."

"I had lunch with Mollie."

"Boy, you can take it!"

"She doesn't look happy," Mike said.

"Why should she? She's pulling herself apart. How about having dinner with me, Zelsmith? I'm cooking a big chili and I usually eat it alone with a native girl. Come on over, we'll kick it around. I don't think you know what's happened to you. When you do, you won't be so happy. At seven, the Sontag Clinic, Santa Monica, around the back, the wormy-looking little house where the dogs come to squat."

He felt a little tired when he hung up, but the bed no longer looked inviting. He went down to the hotel lobby and bought a fifty-cent cigar, set fire to it, and watched the women pass. He tried to remember a few cynical dirty stories John Barrymore used to tell him. When the cigar was half finished he threw it away and bought three daily newspapers. He looked at his wrist watch; it was only four-twenty and he hadn't thought of Mollie more than a thousand times in the last hour. He felt he was pretty well along the road to recovery.

There were several messages at the hotel desk that John Fennel and Walter Chase had called him. He ignored them.

The Sontag Clinic was in the shaggy palm tree, rat-infested district of Santa Monica, where a sort of lower-class slum had grown, made up of gardners, fishermen, injured Mexicans and Negroes who could no longer work a full day, poor whites who had come to the sunlight to die of old age and failed, young people on a GI monthly bill of rights, starving on beans and culled oranges rejected by the packing plants, and a lot of people who had no energy to turn their backs on the sea and head for high ground.

"Every morning," as he said, "before cutting into million-aires, society beauties, and decaying railroad presidents," Dr. Sontag went through half a hundred patients in his free clinic. He saw no difference in these people and the rich. "The same badly designed inner plumbing, the same clap and whooping cough, and the same blood pressure and mixosophia."

He lived in a decaying little house of peeling stucco under a broken red tile roof. It was a house built in 1898 of varnished golden oak, dark with age inside, and big leaded windows, and mice under his canvas ceiling. A Negro woman came three times a week to stir the dust, change his bed linen, and move the rope-tied copies of medical journals from one spot to another. His library of medical books were all over the house with bits of paper, old gloves, and match sticks stuck into them to keep his place. Rare parts

245

of favorite patients swam in sealed glass jars over his fire-place. He also collected odd bits of driftwood and asked if you didn't see "a horse, or a mermaid, or a shark" in the twisted bits of weathered wood.

Mike found him in the kitchen, apron on, cigar in mouth, shaking a big spoon at a pretty young Mexican girl grinding up black pepper under his direction.

"This is Mike Zelsmith, Lana. He has had much sadness in the heart, but he's feeling no pain. This is Lana, Zelsmith. She renamed herself after a movie star last year. She keeps house for me and makes me sweet, fragrant, and clean."

Lana said with a giggle, "The chili is about ready."

"Don't tell me when chili is ready. *Santissima Virgine,* you Mexicans think you know how to make this, hell . . ." He tasted with a big spoon and nodded. "Not bad. Pull up a chair and bring it with you."

They ate on a patio looking down to the sea gleaming like fish scales about half a mile away. They had chocolate with the chili and crisp, warm garlic bread and a white wine. Afterward they sat, their feet on clay pots of pinks and small desert flowers, and smoked thin black cigars. Lana washed the dishes and sang in Spanish.

"Well, Zelsmith, I've seen this coming for some time." Dr. Sontag inspected the end of his cigar. "I have an uncle, Dr. Edward Sontag, in New York. Most likely the greatest man in psychology in the world, and he's afraid of his wife. So I'm only going to give you the facts about Mollie. You put them together yourself, any old way you want. Psychoanalysis, rationalization, senses of reality, pedaniysis, and psychopathology, and dream symbolism, and social mechanisms . . ."

"I've had enough," said Mike.

"If we hadn't been so blind we could have seen it—the big break coming. It all started the night the little dog died. Something else got in trouble with Mollie that night; *you,* the father image. With the death of the dog, Mollie went into a state of shock and went back into her childhood. She hated the world that night for killing her little doggie. She spoke to her mother and father. Remember, Mollie is a mystic; she's been going to a Mrs. Henry to get her future told and polished up, even if she laughed at it. Anyway, the

246

shock brought her in contact with her father again. You were the father image, you had to go too. She hated him and admired him. He was her first great sexual image. To escape it she married misfits. You were real and big and it was all right until she worked too hard, doubted herself, and the dog died. Then her world fell apart again."

"She came out of the child trance."

"But how? Being groped back to life by Beppo? Sure, here suddenly was the solution to her problem. She could punish her father; she could punish you: she could have another man child to mother—Beppo."

Mike stood up and threw his cigar as far as he could into the ivy bed below the patio. "He tried to rape her."

"Maybe that's Mollie's big number now. She degrades what you and her father think of her by becoming the tramp. She has an affair with a man she can't ever show in her Pasadena and Santa Barbara society. She gives herself a swift kick in the behind and loves it, for the moment anyway."

Mike said, "What the hell does all this talk do?"

Lana came out with a bowl of fruit and set it down on a low table. The doctor kissed her and she called him a wine-soaked *viejito*, and he watched her go back into the kitchen. Then he turned to face Mike.

"This Beppo is a smart operator. Walter couldn't stand it. He saw Beppo working on her fears night after night, talking to her, explaining how wonderful she was and how you were neglecting her. How she'd fail as an actress. He was always around. Walter was there the night it first happened between them. Worn out, she gave in to him. That was the morning you caught him leaving. Walter was sure Mollie was an insane kid that night, as nuts as any case of paralogy. He was so disgusted he didn't even talk to her. He just moved."

"They're going to Mexico to paint."

"You think it can satisfy her?"

"She's a very wonderful child."

"Too bad you got caught in the middle, Zelsmith."

"This is nonsense, Doc. She has perfectly good reasons for leaving me. I wasn't around enough. I was tied to a picture, to a wife who will never free me."

"Those reasons are of no value to a doctor. Without her complexities she'd have waited for you for years. Don't forget, Mollie is a romantic. Has a real code of honor. This you don't tear up and forget. It's going to eat out her vitals like that fox that ate the Greek boy's stomach. She'll hug her decencies to herself, secretly, where the muck of Beppo can't enter. When she wakes up, what's going to prevent her from screaming her way into a madhouse? Only you, Zelsmith. Mollie lives now on the razor edge of sanity."

"If she hadn't met me, I suppose this throwback to her childhood wouldn't have happened?" Mike asked.

"Nonsense. It could have happened a dozen different ways."

"And the father image?"

"If it was fighting in her, it would have come out in some form."

"You're very encouraging, Doc."

Mike wondered what Mollie was doing, then decided he didn't want to know. He must remember she no longer meant anything to him.

22

FROM THE JOURNAL OF JOHN FENNEL

Mike isn't the kind to bleed in public, but he is hard hit and tries to cover it by a forced stoppage of the sensibility. He reads and he drinks, not too much of either. He is fascinated by my copy of Pascal. He has marked a passage in it: "Imagine a number of men in chains, condemned to death, some having their throats cut every day in sight of the others, those remaining wait their turn, staring at each with anguish and without hope. Such is the picture of the condition of man . . ."

This is a new kind of thinking for Mike; he always saw the mediocrity and frivolity out here but he never knew the deeper darkness of many moments in life, not as fully as he knows it now. He talks of the disintegration of mere satiety, a decay he calls "inherent in the Goddamn flesh." Art is about all he has left, he feels; and he chases it into corners and tries to examine it closely. What has he come out with as the result? That, true art, beyond the art of today's motion picture, painting, or music "is the capacity of getting way outside of the human being, the mugs as we are, of extending human consciousness to take in all that damn wonderful mystic perception of nonhuman phenomena—you follow me, chum? It could still be alive, an attitude of fertility, making a sensuality of distinction possible, instead of Calvert drinkers.

"There are a lot of wars going on here all the time, not just the sex war, but the race war, the class war, the age war, the war against the fat cats that sell out the real stuff. The town is full of that anal type when it comes to a real art. You've seen them, full of tidiness, parsimoniousness, and obstinacy, no matter how much they gamble at Las Vegas and get untidy in a whore's bedroom . . ."

It was as if he had been very ill, or had just recovered from a rare disease, or he had been found in the wild mountains after all hope had been abandoned, or he had drifted at sea after a shipwreck and been picked up, that was the way they treated Mike now. He didn't like it, but it was not something he cared to talk about. John would go over footage lengths with him, or Walter would bring in cost sheets and they would sit and talk about anything but Mollie.

They had finished the picture. At least as much of it as would ever be finished. The island footage had been developed and the cutter and editor were putting it into place. Mike hadn't seen it and didn't want to. There was still footage missing, but they would fix it up somehow. It all lay there on the dirty cutting room floor near the old mouse-traps, eight cans of film, rough-cut, with its dirty white label: *Gambler's Wife*—Zelsmith Prods.

Mike knew he would soon have to run it and score it with music, and plan exploitation and sneakview it someplace, and find a theater and work up the heat of a première. But that was like a deadly needed medical operation; in the future, and like the patient, he didn't let himself think too deeply about it.

He sat in his trailer on the lot, he sat in his cottage, he sat at the Cock and Bull, or Chasen's, drinking and smoking and he didn't care that most people didn't stop and say hello and stir up the latest gossip with him. He kept himself carefully neat and shaved every morning. He was not a beachcomber. He had no money at all but he could still charge almost everything. He owed months of rent on the beach house and the real estate people were very nice about it and offered to sublet when it was empty, but he said, "No, don't bother, you'll get your money when everyone else does."

It was not such a bad existence. Not bad at all. Alice was in New York preparing to buy pictures for her art gallery, and now there was no need for her to get a divorce. Walter was going into television production, and of course, Mike would pay him his back wages when he could. John Fennel was going to leave for Boston after the opening of the picture. He was planning a novel. Mike wondered if Mandy Rye was going along. He couldn't see her in Boston, but still she could play a part skillfully—the witty hostess of polite society. She had done it often in films and she was a quick study.

No, life was not bad at all. Mike rose late, ate a little, had a few drinks, walked under the unpicked olive trees of Beverly Hills, talked in the bars until they closed. He came home to the cottage slopped, crocked, and read till two or three in the morning, thick books he had always wanted to read and had no time for before.

There was, he discovered, not much in books, even real good books. Life had a way of trickling out of books as time passed, even from the lousy classics. John had lent him a copy of Pascal's *Pensées* and that he enjoyed. It rubbed him hard the wrong way. "We are not satisfied with the life we have in ourselves, and our own being; we want to live an imaginary life in other people's idea of us."

The old sonofabitch was all right. He put it right on the nose for you, he didn't horse around with facts like the other wise waterheads.

The next morning Mike phoned the lot to have the picture ready to run off for him at ten o'clock.

It wasn't so painful to watch. It was just a job, and a picture, and it needed cutting and trimming. It wasn't Mollie up there. It was an actress. Sometimes a very good one. Once he saw Mollie herself in a big close-up real and alive and full of juices, and he went out and tossed up his breakfast. They made two very good cuts before noon . . .

Mike wasn't eating much. Walter came in to the cottage and switched on the lights. Mike was sitting on the bed. He looked up. Walter was wearing his hair long now, not in the crew cut with which he had come out of the navy. Walter knew where the bottle was, but Mike waved off the drink.

"You were sitting in the dark, M.Z."

"Walter, tell me something?"

"Within reason."

"Why did you let it happen?"

"Mollie?"

"You didn't even warn me."

Walter tilted his head and swallowed the drink. He sat down on a chair and played with a cigarette without lighting it.

"What could I do? I could have beaten hell out of her, I could have told, and you could have beat the bejesus out of them both. But it was on before I could do anything. He used to spend evenings with her when you were working on the night shots. I could hear them talking over my head. Mollie was putting up a good fight, and I thought she would win. But he talked, talked. Your working nights was the final straw; she just couldn't face being alone with only the dogs. I guess it's mental with her, but the night the talking stopped I didn't go to sleep. I just walked around all night hearing them in the hay. Mollie cried a lot. I guess it was like the old joke: rape, rape all night. Do you mind me talking, M.Z.?"

"No, I'm pretty much over it. Only Mollie worries me. I want to see her just once more."

FROM THE JOURNAL OF JOHN FENNEL

Mike has begun to talk about it. The horror of the thing to him is that there is no visible horror. He says he never felt so much the hollowness of the arts of pleasure as at this moment. Mike thinks Mollie was always a little more aware than him that she was working on the destruction of the human spirit, not only in herself, but in him. One part of the human psyche must be set against another, her demon said—loyalties divided, consciences stilled; not that she knew all of this or could figure it out. It was in the end an automatic process with her. Terror of thought, her own loneliness she found a superb instrument of annihilation of feeling, first in herself, then in Mike. So Mike thinks anyway.

Reading back in this journal, I am only a little shocked to see how Mollie has changed in my eyes; beginning when she was still "Miss Binning" to me, the image of her has become less confused, but never simpler; clearer, but not more understandable. I remember reading once, I told Mike, about a sect in old Russia called the *Raskolnikas* who resorted in despair to self-holocausts, self-burial, and strangulation by request. Mollie may be like them at times, and like them an apostle of violence, a violence directed inwardly.

Mollie, as Mike says he sees her now, is a survival of moral nihilism, that old-fashioned and deadly romantic vice, for nihilism on a personal plane appeals to neurotic complex minds weighted down with the fearful pressures of modern existence. It offers simple solutions and astonishing half cures. The important solution is invalid in human terms, but to a person controlled by a fortune teller there grows up unknown an appetite for inhumanity; "It's all in the stars anyway, honey." Mollie can travel her road to the very tragic end stepping over such obstacles like faith and love. She has no patience with the practical details of life, except to make enough to exist and find a partner. Not content to destroy small things, she is pleasant most of the time, but she knows inwardly she must destroy the whole. Like all nihilist minds, and Mike uses the old-fashioned word nihilist because he doesn't know a more fashionable one, she has subtleties not always immediately apparent to an adoring eye. She does not fully destroy herself, yet, and all about her, only because destruction, destroying, is a too easy escape from her obsessional neuroses. This gives her a strength with which she destroys. She is confused, perplexed, many heavy strains are on her; her problems are complex and no solution seems in sight, so she piles up all her strength, perhaps even without being aware of it, in one final vindictive act of self-abasement . . . Poor Mike, is he right?

Mike, if he thinks this all out, can understand something of what happened, can go on to something else. At first there was no pain, then there was the dull ache, and now there is only a sterile, puzzled numbness. The deeper, darker secrets he will, perhaps, never find. And soon there will be no pity in Mike at all for Mollie. And then will come forgetfullness, I suppose. She will be just a dim name, a remembered series of moments, a few words whispered in moments once sincere, and then, nothing, nothing, nothing. Even this journal will be lost, or forgotten. Perhaps that's not a bad idea.

No one expected Edward Garoyan to really die. His heart attacks were old stories. He usually had them at the proper time, before mergers, to impress stockholders' meetings, or to scare off a lawsuit.

But during the night he sighed and took down the jeweled Greek cross from over his bed and said slowly a little prayer his mother had taught him. He saw again the wild mountain lands of the Old Country where he had grown up and the tender green of trees and vineyards. The barefooted women driving the goats. He tasted the good sour bread and the fig brandy, and his hands wanted to reach for something high up in the bed . . . (the tears on his mother's face that he had never brushed away when they arrested him for stealing those cheeses). He knew he had lived an evil life and he expected to be fully punished. He tried to call out, to shout a call for human contact, but by the time the nurse came running in, he was dead in Queen Elizabeth's second-best bed, in the big house, on the expensively tailored hill.

Mike came into John's room dressed in neat, dark clothes with a dark tie. He said to John, "Come with me to help bury Edward Garoyan."
"Can we?"
"He'd have done the same for me, gladly."

Edward Garoyan had left fully written orders to be buried in the open. He did not want any of the interior decorating of the inside marble vaults. He was buried on a slight rise in a handsome bronze coffin with no markings on it; he had picked it out himself, testing its ring with his thumbs. Bronze was solid and lasted: look at all the recovered Roman bronze.
· It was much more impressive than the trooping of the colors at Buckingham Palace. There was a Greek priest in a beard and a tall black hat, and a great many people, almost all of whom had hated the dead man. They took their revenge staring up into the beautiful day, their smooth faces almost shouting, "You're dead and we're alive!" Alice (who had flown back from the East), deeply veiled, stood with the boards of directors of the studio and the theater chains. To one side were the lesser people, the servants, the few poor relatives, and then Mike and John. Police kept everyone else off the grounds.

The Greek priest finished waving his cross in the four directions, the choir boys threw spices into the grave. Maggie White, the studio's gawky child star, stepped forward. She was dressed as a small nun except that the headdress was left off. Her straw-colored hair was braided stiffly down her back. She held a sheet of paper in her hand, her mouth open. As someone signaled her from a newsreel sound truck beyond the grave, she unfolded the paper and began to read. The shrill voice filled the hillside. She read slowly and her dramatic feeling was just a little off key.

> "O Captain! My Captain! Our fearful trip is done,
>   The ship has weathered every rack, the prize we
>   sought is won,
>   The port is near, the bells I hear, the people all
>   exulting."

Whitman's lines to a dead Lincoln mocked the bright day. Mike shifted to his other foot and stood waiting for the thing to end.

> "But O heart! Heart! Heart!
>   O the bleeding drops of red,
>   Where on the deck my Captain lies,
>   Fallen, cold and dead."

The soundman on the newsreel truck signaled little Maggie White to move in closer to the microphone hidden in the blanket of tuberoses.

> "My Captain does not answer, his lips are pale and still,
>   My father does not feel my arm, he has no pulse or will,
>   The ship is anchored safe and sound, its voyage closed
>   and done,
>   From fearful trip the victor ship comes in with object won,

> Exult O shores, and ring O bells!
>   But I with mournful tread,
>   Walk the deck my Captain lies,
>   Fallen, cold and dead."

Someone started to applaud, and stopped suddenly.

The big radio-controlled gates no longer worked and had been propped open. Mike drove into the winding driveway and as he got out of the car, he saw Alice sitting on the marble terrace. She had not overdone the wearing of black, and looked pert; only her eyes were a little swollen. Her voice was as crisp as ever; he had noticed that on the phone when she had called him to come over.

She looked up at him as he walked across the terrace toward her. She sat back in the wide bamboo chair and peered up at him.

"Thanks for coming, Mike."

"What the hell—it's little enough."

"Do you think the burial was silly?"

Mike sat down and shrugged his shoulder. "In a way it fit the old man. He would have liked the corn."

"The studio took care of it." She looked at him closely. "I was kind of crazy about the old man, even when I disliked him. I used to think when I was a kid you had to love your father, so I hated him. Then I found out the modern doctors said you don't have to love anybody, so I got very fond of him."

Mike nodded. She went on talking. "I didn't mean to come back, Mike, not until you sent for me. But this happened. How are you?"

"You can see, big and ugly, as usual."

"The girl walked out on you. It's all over town."

"Let's talk just about what you wanted me here for, Alice."

"That's it. About Mollie taking a powder."

Mike stood up. "No, Alice. No. You wouldn't want me on a bounce. I wouldn't be good company. No."

"Were you surprised?"

"Right now the only thing in the world that would surprise me would be a pregnant man."

"You're bitter, Mike."

"Jesu, hasn't a mug got a right to feel things!"

She shook his hand and patted it. "All right, we'll not talk about that. How's the picture going?"

"We're doing the final cutting. I think it's very good. It didn't cost a lot, but it's good."

"You're not letting anybody buy in on it?"

Mike grinned and patted Alice's hand in turn. "No, not my wife, anyway."

"I didn't think you would."

They didn't talk much after that. They sat relaxed, almost comfortable, and looked at the landscape and the life below them. Alice rang for tea and Mike had two big doubles of scotch. They patted—on the surface—cheerfully, both still a little numb without knowing why, but also perhaps without knowledge of it; feeling perhaps there was at least one other human being in the world who had sorrows.

"Let's have dinner some night," Alice said as they parted.

"If I can get away from the cutting, I'll call you."

They let it go at that. All the way driving down the hills toward the town, Mike kept wondering why he had felt nothing, but nothing at all. After all he had been pretty fond of Alice. Well, a guy reached a certain point in his life and all that stuff kind of dried up, or became walled up, or the cat had eaten it, or something—anyway, nothing.

BOOK FIVE

'And hearts that we broke long ago
Have long been breaking others . . .'
—W. H. AUDEN

23

REMEMBERING back, Mike had always been told by people (whose opinions he only vaguely respected) that one should, at times like this, throw oneself into hard work. But Mike could get no real comfort or pleasure from any work. It seemed savorless and foolish to be putting together a motion picture, or even building a bridge or frying an egg.

He could, at one time, have done a lot more drinking; instead of which he used to sit in his hotel cottage, read all the newspapers, open a few magazines, and then go to the studio and work on the picture being cut together. John was always with him. It bored John. He found the music score interesting enough and the way the score was fitted to the dialogue and the action, but as he had never been really musical, it palled on him.

"Don't look so sad," Mike would say. "All pictures look bad when you're snipping and fitting them together."

"I want to leave for Boston, Mike. Let's finish it."

Mike looked closely at him and nodded. "Sure, I know. You want to go some place and let the wet wind hit your face, and you want the feel of this town behind you . . ."

"Now you're talking like a romantic, Mike. I've resigned from the romantics' club. No silent ache, no Goddamn self-pity. I just want to get away from the wholesome sunshine, and the industry, the good food, and people passing me in cars with kids in the back going to the beach. Maybe I've had too much of a good thing."

"Look, if we don't get a good picture for a preview, I'm not going to be able to pay you off. I owe you a lot of money."

"I don't want to take anything out of this town." John smiled and rubbed his eyes. He needed sleep.

"Write me some wild lines, John—where the gambler walks up the hill in the long shot."

"You don't need any more wild lines."

Mike frowned and bent over some lengths of film footage.

John Fennel and Walter Chase, when Mike was busy, ate together in a small French place where the food was very good and the murals very bad, and old Caruso records filled the place with sound.

Walter swallowed the last of his oysters on the half shell and said, "You look pretty good, John."

"I know. I eat well, I take walks and I sit in the sun a lot. I'm sorry I don't look like a man worrying over Mike and Mollie."

"Mollie's pretty desperate. Money. Been borrowing all over town. But can't get much. Beppo has really moved in. Likes his three big meals a day. I hear she washes and irons his shirts."

"It sounds ideal," John said. "Thought they were going to Mexico?"

"As soon as Mollie raises the money." Walter put some liver paste on thin rye toast. "How's the picture coming? I've been away from it arranging some damn television."

"I don't know, Walter. Mike talks very big."

"You know, John, I wonder if it's any good."

"It may be a really great one."

"With M.Z. it's happened before."

The potted hare came and they ate very well and had the red wine and the white wine, and for a French place, the coffee was very good. They sat smoking cigars, twirling brandy in big glasses. The people at the next table put on paper hats and talked very fast in French.

Walter asked, "What are they celebrating?"

"The big guy with the white hair has just retired from the medical rubber business and his daughter, the pregnant lady, thinks she is going to have a son after four daughters. The priest is the fat lady's brother, and he's just come back from Indo-China, where he was knifed by natives and is going to be operated on tomorrow. It's a very delicate job —a brain probe—and they're drinking to the surgeon's success. A Dr. Tracy Putnam."

"You're lying."

John grinned. "Yes, I am. The pregnant girl is getting married to the little man with the rubber band mustache tomorrow, and they're all celebrating. Sordid, isn't it?"

Walter shook his head. "That's the trouble with writers. You never use the real, ordinary stuff. You invent knife wounds and Indo-China and a medical rubber business."

"Think how dull life would be, Walter, if you accepted it as it's dealt to you. Look how Mollie reshuffled her cards."

"I see your point."

They didn't talk very much after that, just listened to Caruso in "Faust." They knew they had a friendship, a real friendship, even if it would end in a few days and they would never write to each other, and die separately (years from now, they hoped) on opposite sides of the world. Caruso's ghost walked in the grooves of a resin disk, a steel silver grated against it, electric trickery made a voice of a long-dead man rattle the dishes on the table.

The Palmers were very nice people and John Fennel went there often with Mike for dinner. Mike went along to avoid sitting in his cottage alone. They had some fine pictures and their Degas and Turner drawings were very good. One evening Mike sat there. It was a very neat library and he sat at a small kidney desk reading a book on the ocean tides. In the big living room more people were still coming in, and spread below the bow windows the whole city was a pattern of winking colored lights. Mike didn't feel equal to an afterdinner group.

A very handsome young man, well dressed and carrying himself proudly, came into the library, holding a highball glass in his hand. He saw Mike at the desk and said in a well-modulated voice, "Oh, pardon me." He turned as if to go out, then looked again at Mike, smiled and came over and held out his hand.

"Zelsmith, Mike Zelsmith?"

"Yes." Mike pulled off his heavy glasses.

The handsome young man nodded and grinned. "Reegan, Gene Reegan."

Mike stood up, looked at the regular features, and decided to grin in return. "Hello, Reegan. You know if I were directing this scene in a picture of mine I wouldn't know how to do it."

"No, I suppose not." The young man sat skillfully balanced on the edge of the desk. "Funny, meeting you, and the whole town gossiping over Mollie and her affair with this Polack."

"You still bitter?" Mike asked.

The handsome young man laughed. "Hell, no."

Mike began to laugh. "I've been sorry for *you* for a long time."

"Mostly we should be sorry for Mollie. She's a fine woman, you know, but always a little nuts. Like this thing with this bum artist. She really doesn't want to do it, you know, but she gets panicky and she's alone. She grabs anything that's around; the worse the better, it's her way of punishing herself."

"Reegan, you amaze me."

"You always want to give her a good kick in the ass and straighten her out for her own good . . . but you never do, you never can, can you?"

Mike closed the books on the desk. Reegan opened a cigarette case (as only a good actor can) and Mike took a cigarette. Reegan held a small silver lighter to it and they inhaled and blew smoke toward the paneled ceiling.

"Glad I met you, Reegan. I don't feel as much a Goddamn heel."

Mike got a little tight that night on the host's best old brandy.

Mike had gotten into the habit of dropping in on Dr. Sontag. The doctor was just finished with his clinic patients and was in his office, lighting a heavy cigar.

"I saw Gene last night. A very fine guy."

The doctor puffed his cigar into life and grinned. "Why not? You expected a monster?"

"I guess my ego did."

"You mugs are all alike. Mollie is the mother bonellie of you all. You think you're free-acting agents. You're just male bonellie."

"What the hell is a bonellie, Myron?"

The doctor went to a pile of old scientific magazines, found one, blew dust off it, flipped its pages, and held it toward Mike—a section of it marked in red crayon. "Here, I thought of you when I read this. Marked it for you."

"Thanks." Mike took it and read the marked section:

"The bonellie is a marine worm found among coastal rocks in both the Mediterranean and the Atlantic. The male compares in size to the female roughly as a flea compares to a man. He leads a simple, healthy, somewhat restricted life, being little more than an apparatus for the convenience of the female."

Mike looked up, "Christ! As bad as that?"
"Read the rest of it."
"Why should I?"
"Scared?"
"Hell, no."

"Indeed, he hasn't even a digestive tube, and accordingly can live only by getting his nourishment, in true parasitic fashion, from his host, or, rather hostess, who thus provides him with both bed and board. Since the male bonellie is reduced to this single activity, he passes his life, appropriately, in the uterus of the female . . ."

Mike put down the magazine and picked up a dusty cigarette from the desk and lit it. "So that was my address with Mollie?"
"You feel lonely out in the daylight?"
"No, but it's a shock to find out I was a Goddamn bonellie."

Mike left, refusing a lunch. He needed a long walk. He ended up in the small bar at the Ship Café. He held a large martini in his hand and said softly, "To the male bonellie, the poor lousy bastard . . ."

24

THEY took the finished picture on its first sneak preview. They put the cans of film on the floor of the car and they drove sixty miles inland, Mike at the wheel, John and Mandy in front, and Walter wedged in among the cans of loose film in the back. The cutter and editor and the man who had written the music followed them in another car. Mike was keyed very high. He had a pint of whisky in a paper bag and every once in a while he took a long pull on the bottle. Mandy had to take over the driving before they were past Glendale.

They stopped for another pint on the way and about seven they came into the town of Riverdale. The movie house was low and of peeling stucco. Walter lugged up the cans of film to the projection room and they sat in a roped-off row. Mike inspected the paper bag for the last time and gave it to John who pushed it under the seats in front of him—among the peanut husks and candy wrappings and the forgotten popcorn. They sat through a jungle picture of apemen and white hunters, and women who had beautiful shaved legs and behinds, none of them scratched up at all by the evil-looking, spiny jungle.

Suddenly it was over and a card went up on the screen. STUDIO PREVIEW. The kids whistled. The titles flashed on the screen, the music began, the picture started. Mike sat very still and John sat well back in his chair and held Mandy's hand. "Screen Play by John Fennel." He didn't know if the picture was good or bad. He had no idea as to its merits. He had seen so much of it, in so many forms. The customers laughed in the wrong places, but John knew by now this always happened at the first sneak. Stuff that looked fine in the projection room often got a laugh in a theater.

He thought Mollie came off very well in several key scenes, but her performance seemed fuzzy toward the end, where she got several bad laughs in the wrong places. A baby cried and several people left before the end of the picture. Before it was over Mike went out and they found him in the lobby, when the showing was over, seated on a sofa, topcoat collar up around his face. He was pretty drunk. Walter got the film cans, and the fat little manager kept bouncing around and saying, "Mr. Zelsmith, I always liked your pitchurs. We broke the house record on all of 'em. That river pitchur . . . we had lines four blocks long. Yes, sir, Mr. Zelsmith, always liked your pitchurs."

"Buy the crud a cigar," Mike mumbled when they lifted him to his feet.

Mike recovered in the car, the cold shock of desert night air bringing him back to life.

"Well, not bad at all," he said. "Gotta cut those laughs out in the morning. The music stinks, gotta get a new score under it. And that process plate from the island (oh my aunt's piles) gotta get rid of that. What do you think, John?"

"I can't tell. I've seen it too often."

"What do you think, Walter?"

"It has some very good scenes. Lots of it doesn't come off."

"We'll recut it. Get all the uncut shots we haven't used so far, and we'll rerun the stuff and see what we can use in place of the bad stuff in it now . . . Mandy?"

"Don't ask an actress about any picture she's in. She never sees any of the rest of it. I was just wonderful."

"Wanta drink, M.Z.?" Walter asked.

Mike shook his head. "I wouldn't take a drink for a thousand dollars . . . not for a thousand dollars."

When John went in to see him before turning in, Mike was lying on the bed, his shoes off, two quarts of whisky open on the night table. He looked up, his head rolling as if attached to his shoulders by only a string, and then he fell flat on his back and lay there looking at the ceiling while John emptied the bottles into the toilet bowl.

"That's right, Johnny," said Mike, from the bed, "solve the dilemna of a modern Hamlet in baggy pants—you listening, chum? The problem of a life fixed in a world of no external symbols for the inner values, filled just now with booze. I said I wouldn't take another drink, didn't I? We carry built-in lies, don't we, Johnny, like a lover carries his love inside himself like fruit does its kernel. Oh my aching head. I don't feel so good, I feel terrible, I can't move. I couldn't get out of this bed now, not if they offered me million bucks a reel to shoot a picture.

"Wasn't very good picture tonight, you think? Hell, it was a doll, a real doll. I don't fool easy over the futility of aspiration, the vanity of lousy endeavor; mustn't say lousy so much. Alice says it's my lack of formal education . . . Dames all want you to be a hairy sonofabitch in bed and a gent in public. Ever figure it out, Johnny, that loss of appetite, happiness, and sleep serves no Goddamn useful purpose in love? Nope, none at all. It's all a ball. A real ball.

"The way I see it, kid, we mistake a morality of love for an attitude of love. Any two-buck whore can tell you an attitude is only adequate to a personal experience—but a morality, that includes everybody in, as Sam Goldwyn puts it so well. Give me a drink, Johnny, and I'll go to sleep. Give

263

me two fingers, a snort, half a pony. You sonofabitch, you cold New England codfish, if I loved you any more I'd kiss you . . . Wouldn't touch it anyway, not for . . ."

Mike was suddenly snoring, flat on his back, and John turned out the lights and went back to his room. He was very tired.

Mike was dead drunk before morning, in his pajamas in the hotel bar. He had bribed the night man to open it for him. John put him to bed and he stayed there all day. At dinner he ate a little and said he was all right. He wasn't going to touch a drop. "Not for . . ." John took his clothes away and locked them up and put Mike in his own bed. He ordered the hotel not to sell Mike a drink. Then he went to sleep in Mike's cottage. He was awakened by the phone ringing. Mike had bought the bellboy's suit and shoes and was at the Black Witch drinking. He had just offered his solid gold Swiss wrist watch to pay his bill.

The joint wouldn't take the expensive watch for the twenty-two dollars in drinks he had treated people to. John went and got him in a cab.

Mike promised to stay in bed and Dr. Sontag gave him some pills. He got away naked as a jay bird's rump before morning, stole a raincoat from a parked car, and was promising the madame of a whorehouse on Fairfax a part in his next picture for a quart of whisky.

John bought him a case of Haig and Haig and let him drink for a week. Mike was a pretty sick man, but when they shaved him and pumped some food into him, he lay back on the pillows and slept very well. When he woke up and looked at his shaking hands he trembled. He sat up to drink his coffee, and he shook so he spilled the scalding stuff all over himself. His mouth was loose and baggy. But the next day he sat up in slippers and robe, listening to Debussy on the radio. John was reading in the next room. Mike got up and turned off the radio. John came in and he looked at him.

"Big drunk, huh?" Mike asked.

"Pretty big. Biggest I ever saw."

"Don't flatter me. Look, get Walter to set up the showing of the uncut film stock. I'm going to recut the whole picture again. It's all right. I can look at her again, without going back on the sauce."

It was now a time of turmoil and of frenzy for Zelsmith Productions. Mike was recutting the picture, trying to bring to it all he could, and lamenting all he didn't have, and needed. He couldn't put a new music score on it, he lacked the money. He was bothered by many things. The beach house stood empty now, and the real estate people demanded the rent. His lease still held, and lawyer letters lay unopened on his night table.

He hired—anyway signed a lease for—a fancy theater in Beverly Hills, the Fine Film Arts, for the grand première of his picture. Walter worked on publicity, sending out press items, handing out interviews, making all the arrangements of ballyhoo and weirdness that attracted attention to a picture. Mike himself called up stars, and what were known as stuffed shirts, trained seals, and chowderheads— the so-called impressive and important people of the town —to accept tickets to his great opening.

Walter, hamstrung by lack of cash (although he did run up staggering charge accounts at Romanoff's and Chasen's and the Beachcomber and the Cock 'n Bull) got a lot of attention focused on the coming picture. Most of it to the good.

A strange thing had happened. Mollie had suddenly become famous. She was written of as the new Garbo, the freshest, greatest personality in twenty years. No one of those who boosted her had seen a foot of film with her in it. But it was one of those things that begin as publicity, break away, and become a flood of interest and excitement. Walter tried to sidetrack this attention to the picture, but the demand for stills and biogs of Mollie Binning continued.

It was Walter who dared to talk to Mike about an idea that would help the picture. Mike was shaving, moving his old-fashioned long razor across his red face, peering dimly into the mirror of his cottage bathroom as Walter talked at him from the doorway, leaning a little too casually against the door frame.

"We didn't expect it, M.Z., and we didn't do anything to make it play, but there it is. The public and the fan press and the legmen of the columnists are clamoring for stuff on Mollie."

Mike shaved under his big ears, pulling them out of the way skillfully. Walter went on. "I know you're going to leap down my throat, but suppose we gave a big cocktail party three days before the picture opens."

Mike grunted. "We may swing the credit for it."

"And give it for the star, Mollie Binning. Present her to the press."

Walter looked down at his white shoes and Mike wiped the razor carefully on a hotel towel and placed the razor back in the big ebony case lettered *Isadore Zelsmith*. I held six other razors; the set had belonged to his father and he was careful with it. He turned to face Walter.

"You expect me to be against it?"

Walter shrugged his well-bred shoulders. "I expected screaming, M.Z. I wouldn't bring it up only we're going to have trouble enough getting a release without kicking something as good as this in the kisser."

Mike said, "Find out where she is in Mexico. Wire her money and plane tickets, and send along explanation as to why she can help us out of a bad spot. She will."

Walter nodded. "I'll sign it myself."

Mike grinned. "You can sign it with my name, Walter. You know where she is in Mexico?"

Walter said, "Bertie Ironspinner has her address. I'll get it. I'm going over there this afternoon."

Mike nodded and drenched himself with aftershave lotion.

Walter Chase, John saw, was putting on weight and there were lines on his face that no longer went away after lunch. John was sorting out his sport jackets; he was not going to take much of his tropical wardrobe with him when he left for Boston.

"You're invited to a special party," Walter said.

John sat down and lit his pipe and shook his head. "I don't want any more parties. This is the most party-giving town I have ever been in. Everybody is always giving parties. They must have trouble finding guests to go around."

"It's a problem, but this party is special."

"No, *no* more parties. I must have been to hundreds. My whole life out here can be measured by the parties I've attended."

Walter grinned. "Bertie Ironspinner is giving this one around the pool in his garden. It's for Highpockets—he's four years old."

"Who the hell is Highpockets?"

"Bertie's French poodle. He asked me to invite you."

"I'm not a French poodle."

Walter smiled. "He'll overlook it. Also we have some business to do."

Bertie Ironspinner lived in a huge, ugly old house built years ago by a retired meatpacker with no taste but a great deal of money. It had a beautiful garden, and Bertie had done the house over several times; every time he met a new inspiration in the form of a well-built interior decorator. He lived with his mother, whom he told everyone he hated, and a sister who looked just like Bertie.

The afternoon sun was making deep violet shadows in the Ironspinner garden and there was the sound of barking. The drive had been decorated with paper lanterns and on some of the trees were gay little signs reading: Reserved for the Host's Leg; For the Boys in the Back Room; Tail-waggers Number Three; Joyce Kilmer's Own Sweethearts; and other wordings by some of the most elegant screen-writers.

John and Walter were among the few dogless people there; everyone else had a dog or two, French poodles, naturally, on silver or leather straps. A huge birthday cake was by the pool side, set in a dog bed, and around it a group of shrill, excited people stood with their dogs posing for cameramen from national magazines. "Bertie," Walter explained, wasn't "one to overlook a good press item."

Bertie broke away from the table, wiping sweat from his face, and shook hands hard with John. "Good of you to come."

"Sorry I haven't a dog," John said.

"Damnedest party. Come meet the guests."

"I can see them from here."

"Important people. Do you a lot of good in the studios. Oh, that Highpockets—he's an only dog, and spoiled."

John and Walter were dragged to meet producers, directors, song arrangers, stars, actors, and just enough high-bracket screenwriters to make it, as Bertie put it, "literary."

The dogs were amazing creatures, all wearing gay paper hats. There were two white poodles who had been dyed blue-pink and yellow. They were all snarling at each other or pissing on the table legs, and they had rhinestone collars, and the really fancy ones had golden bobbie pins in their curly hair. They were all tailored and curried and curled

267

and smelled, John noticed, of Chanel No. Five instead of good old healthy dog. Only in their sniffing and dripping habits were they at all doglike.

Two little Japanese houseboys were lighting the candles on the cake, and Bertie excused himself as the cake glowed, and he ran into the house. Someone sang out, "Happy Birthday, dear Highpockets, Happy Birthday to you!" and the dogs barked and some of the people began to sing louder. Bertie appeared leading a magnificent French poodle, its curls clipped and shaved into a Dutch bob, with hairy pants and a fringe of hair tailored just above its gleaming eyes. Bertie was weeping with joy and excitement and Highpockets snarled at a blue poodle and looked brightly about him.

Walter grinned and handed John a martini from a passing tray.

John said, "Bertie could do something special, like barbecuing a Christian for the mutts."

The singing ended, the cameramen took more shots, faking it as Highpockets was supposed to blow out the candles on the cake. A little Japanese houseboy, with two gold front teeth, appeared before John and bowed and held a small pencil over a small pad of pink linen paper.

"Sir, rare, medium, or well done?"

"What?"

"The ground sirloin."

"I always have it medium."

"You misunderstand, sir, for your dog, we're cooking each one's special—Mr. Ironspinner's orders."

"I haven't got a dog."

The little Japanese bowed and moved off. John sat down behind a hedge and finished his martini. The barking grew louder and someone whipped a dog with baby talk.

Bertie came around the hedge. He was carrying a small nest of packages. He smiled at John and Walter and handed each a package.

"Each dog gets a gift."

"But . . ." said John.

"Oh, you haven't a dog, keep it yourself."

The jeweler's box contained a golden pin of a fire plug with a red ruby set in."

"Clever?" asked Bertie.

"Clever," John said.

Bertie sat down and wiped his face with a silk handkerchief smelling of Tweed. "Highpockets is pleased as hell. He's a smart dog. There aren't many members of the Screen Writers' Guild have his I.Q., now that we've driven out the Reds."

"Does he act in pictures?" Walter asked.

Bertie lifted one well-shaped eyebrow. "Does *anybody* I like ever work? No, I have to slave for anything I ever admire."

"I hear Beppo is painting a picture of Highpockets for you," Walter said.

"Yes, I can hardly wait. It was a birthday gift for High-pockets, but it isn't finished."

"Where are Beppo and Mollie living in Mexico?"

Bertie lifted an eyebrow and rolled an eye at John. "Scandal, scandal! They're shacked up in Tuxpan, Jalisco. At the Casa Real. D. H. Lawrence lived there, you know, while working on *The Plumed Serpent*. But keep the address to yourself, they're kind of hiding away for a while. I hear that . . ."

There was mad barking and shouting and a human voice yelping loudly in pain. Bertie spun around and said, "Oh, damn, Highpockets has bitten someone! He's so full of beans, and he's bright enough to understand I wouldn't punish him, today of all days."

John went into the house to see if he could find his top-coat which a small Jap had peeled off him. It was Bertie's white period; the rare old Chippendale and Regency furniture had been scraped down and had some legs cut off and were now a dull white. The drapes were a blue-white, and the wallpaper was a modern version of Second Empire brothel decorating. The paintings were in plastic frames and were of muscled young men tearing lions apart or pulling big fish from a sea or walking high wires, as seen from below.

John turned to go as Bertie and Walter came in, leading a sobbing, balding man wearing blue-stoned finger rings.

Walter was smiling. "Got George right in centerfield with the full set of teeth."

The man called George groaned, and Bertie pulled a first-aid kit from a pearwood desk and Walter bent George's head over a potted plant. "Half-mast, George."

Bertie opened the bottle of iodine and George opened his belt and lowered his tailoring. John excused himself and went out. He heard the yelp as iodine bit into flesh.

The dog's birthday party made no impression at all on the town, as a female star gave a party on horseback for her race horse, who had almost been entered in the Kentucky Derby. But John had not been considered important enough to be invited to that one.

Walter sent off the long wire and money order to Tuxpan, Jalisco.

25

WALTER came awake slowly, tired and feeling as if he had been dropping great stones into the sea for days on end. The phone was ringing and he picked it up. It was Mandy Rye's well-modulated voice. He expected it to be very witty in a moment, like in her films. It blasted into his ear.

"Listen, Walter, Mollie isn't on the plane! The plane, remember? I'm at the International Airport. No, she isn't here. The gal on the plane said she got off at San Diego. That's right. And the press party planned at four this afternoon at the Biltmore!"

"Why did she get off, Mandy?"

"Didn't say. Wake up, Walter!"

"Adrian J. Christ," said Walter slowly. "Let's keep this from M.Z. When's the next plane?"

"In an hour. But she most likely's going the other way. Heading back to old Meeheeko."

"What?"

Mandy repeated her idea of how to say Mexico in Spanish.

Walter said a feeble thanks and hung up. He decided to have a very large breakfast. He would worry later. Boy, would he worry later . . .

The cottage that Mike lived in hadn't been made up or cleaned for two days. It was full of sketches for press books, roughs of movie posters, tickets, mailing lists, and empty bottles that had soothed the thirst of the fan magazine press. Mike was looking down at some legal papers as Walter walked in. He lifted his head, slowly reading trouble in Walter's effort to act like a gentleman—that grace under pressure, something he had gotten out of reading Hemingway.

"What's *your* bad news?" Mike asked.

"Mollie got off the plane at San Diego."

Mike nodded. "That means she's changed her mind." He threw a paper at Walter. "Another kiss from Cinderella. Alice is boiling mad at Mollie's press notices. She's tearing all hell apart. In other words, she's acting like a woman. Those are her lawyer's papers."

Walter studied the paper. "What does it say, M.Z.?"

"She's attaching my interest in the big house, demanding an accounting of her money in my bank accounts, giving me the works legally."

Walter said, "Do any good to talk to her?"

Mike shook his head. "Let it ride. Nothing is working out anyway. I may lose the theater for the opening. Need five grand, cash."

Walter said slowly, "Alice isn't like this. Maybe if someone else talked to her?"

Mike got up and walked to the window and looked out into the bright sunshine. "Better think up some good reason why Mollie isn't going to be at the cocktail party. Also why we may not open in three days."

"We're not licked yet," Walter said.

Mike waved an arm at him. "You act cheerful, Walter, and I'll kick your teeth out."

Mandy hadn't minded signing the check for five thousand dollars for the theater, only saying, "I should have my head examined." But she did not like the idea of John and her talking to Alice. As she drove up the long paved drive by the still unfixed radio-controlled gates, she turned to John and said, "Here go a couple of cat's paws."

John, feeling none too sure of their mission, nodded.

The butler, needing a shave, said they could wait in the red study, and they stood there looking at each other. Mandy lit a cigarette but didn't smoke it, rather held it like a weapon of defense in front of her.

Alice came in, looking very smart in hunter's green and matching jade, her face stern, her jaw set, her arms folded —showing very red fingernails on long brown fingers.

She said, "I knew he'd send somebody crawling!"

John said, "It was Walter's idea."

She called Walter a very dirty name in a very depraved vice. Then she said, very low, "Mike is a low sonofabitch and it's time I admitted it. He hasn't got it any more and

271

that's it. Premières, grand openings, all the damn publicity setup, for what? To star a broken-down little tramp that isn't even a good lay any more. No, I'll not withdraw my attachments, my legal boys. I'm going to run Mike out of town, I'm going to bust Mike Zelsmith so wide open we'll see the color of his guts. Have a drink?"

"Yes," said John.

Alice moved over to a small red leather bar and they soon all held a glass of cold whisky and watched each other sip. Alice rattled her ice cube in her glass. "I'm sorry I popped off like this. But I'm real mad. I've been the patsy long enough. Mike uses everybody, even you two goons. What the hell are you getting out of it? What am I? What is anyone? If it's a hot picture he's living high off the hog again. If it's a flop you'll be to blame because you screwed up a genius."

"Ice?" said John holding up his drink.

Alice dropped a fresh cube into his glass, then she turned and threw herself into a deep yellow sofa. "He's no good, never was any good. Once he could make great pictures and he used us as rugs. Now we don't have to stand for it, none of us. You hear me? I'm not standing for it. Plaster that little tramp all over town, all over the whole United States. Who the hell is she? Ethel Barrymore? Duse? Hell, she isn't even Hepburn or Shelley Winters."

"Darling," said Mandy, "it's all for the picture."

"I don't care what it's for! Another drink?"

"I don't think so," said John.

"Sure, sit down. I'm lonely as hell." She rang for the butler. "Let's have tea. I haven't eaten for two days. My insides are all sandpaper. And as for sleep . . ."

They ate a very good tea, and Alice had two chicken wings, eating them in her fingers with enjoyment. She had calmed down and was telling them her troubles. There was no money. The damn estate lawyers, and Papa's stock and the trust fund all shot. And everybody she never heard of wanting a handout. And the taxes—estate, inheritance, death, income, surtaxes, state, city, county—nothing to pay them with. She looked up and said, "Papa's hundred million doesn't exist. This house has to go. Poor Papa, at the end there, we didn't know how broke he was. Neither did anyone else. I've become a gabby old witch." She wiped her fingers and had more whisky. "Let's not spoil it now. Let's not talk about money or Mike. I'm cutting him out of my life. I've cut him out. It's done, finished, accomplished. How you two doing?"

"We're getting by," said Mandy with great dignity.

"I know, I know, it's awful when you have it and awful when you haven't got it. How about dinner tonight?"

"Work to do," John said. "Things are pretty mixed up."

"Call me tomorrow, kids. I'm having some stuffy English people over. But the music will be good and the cook is the real stuff. Might as well use it all before the banks move in. Is it a date?"

They said they would see and they left, true-blue friends it seemed. Alice went back to the tray and began to hunt among the debris in the plates for another chicken wing. She was going to cry and maybe if she ate again she wouldn't. But it had only been a two-wing chicken . . .

The cocktail party was, of course, a dismal failure. The press hadn't liked the announcement by Walter that Miss Binning was so shy, "such an elf," she just couldn't face the press. Mike hadn't gone to the party but sat in his cottage writing out wires to exhibitors about how fine the picture was, and that they should bombard their exchanges for a chance to book it.

He did not think the picture would ever open. He was a little tired of his luck. He had never believed in luck in the old days, but now he was numb with effort. There was nothing more he could do but sit back and let the fates kick him around. He hadn't believed in the fates either, once. Well, there was no whisky to toast luck or fates. Walter and John had seen to that, and it would be a hassel if he tried to get a drink at the hotel bar. That, too, had been denied him. Besides he didn't really want a drink; drinking appeared such a fancy romantic escape from reality.

Thinking back, he wondered why he had not quit on the top. The box-office champ, winner of six Academy Awards, the greatest maker of pictures the town had ever seen—now to piddle out like this in a corner, with a quickie shot on peanuts. He decided to get some sleep, and lay down on the unmade bed. He remembered his father sleeping a lot just before the big bust-up. How he used to sleep two or three days at a time, escaping from his troubles in that short, bedded death, escaping from everything. Lately Mike noticed he had been doing the same. Curling up like some damn lump in a womb and sleeping a lot.

It was already dark outside and the hotel orchestra was playing dance music. It was effective corn—really the solid hoke. He used to like to lie in bed when a boy visiting relatives in Asbury Park and listen to the dance music come across the water from the big pier. What the hell did they play in those days? "I Can't Give You Anything but Love, Baby," the one about finding a four-leaf clover, and, Chicago . . . Chicago, that wide-open town . . .

The invention of the saxophone and the silver-plated derby had made Hollywood great. The town had been a pretty wild place when he was a young punk promoting short reels. It had been fun in those days with all the bootleg liquor and all the babes in short skirts and rolled stockings. Dog stars, Tom Mix's horse, Mack Sennett's bathing beauties, the big parties on the big white boats, and if somebody got shot or tossed overboard—well, that was part of the fun too. They doped a lot and spent their money foolishly—Valentino's "Falcon's Lair"—and they all died young and left beautiful bodies. A lot of them took sleeping pills or figured out how to attach the vacuum cleaner hose to the Dusenberg's exhaust. And their friends put radio music into their tombs at Forest Lawn.

Mike grinned and rolled over on the bed. If he had a sense of humor he'd take that bottle of pills in the bathroom cabinet, but no one ever said Mike Zelsmith had a sense of humor, so he'd just hang around and see how it worked out.

There was a knock on the door and John came in. He crossed to the bed, and Mike wondered what was the matter now.

"Mike, Dr. Sontag just called."

"What does he want?"

"He had a call from a valley motel on Ventura. They found Mollie out there. She's pretty sick, she insisted they call Dr. Sontag."

"She *didn't* go back to Mexico?" Mike sat up on the bed.

"No, something about being taken sick on the plane and getting off at San Diego. She came up from there by bus it seems and had another attack, and somehow got to this motel."

"What's Doc doing?"

"He sent an ambulance for her. He's taking her to his clinic. Thought it best to avoid publicity."

Mike picked up the phone and asked for the clinic's number.

A waiter came in with Mike's breakfast. Mike took a quick sip of scalding coffee. He smiled a tight-lipped smirk at John and the waiter and signed the tab. "Dr. Sontag is busy at the clinic," the nurse's voice said. Mike gave his name and begged she deliver it to the doctor. He waited, looked at his fingernails that he had forgotten to file down. He looked at John and shook his head.

The phone rang. "Hello, Zelsmith."

"Hello, Doc. Where is she?"

"Here."

"Is she . . . How is she?"

"Come over and look."

"I'll be over, Doc."

"Good boy."

Mike asked John if he minded if he didn't go with him.

The clinic looked more rat-eaten than ever. The shabby palms over it were shedding yellow fronds. A small delighted colored child marked up the sidewalk with a bit of chalk, and then got up on its roller skates and went through some intricate pattern of play in front of the clinic.

Dr. Sontag looked tired but fatter. He shook Mike's hand limply and led him down a dark hall and opened a door painted a battleship gray. There was a transparent hood over the bed and a hissing tank of oxygen. The stone-faced nurse looked at her wrist watch.

"That's all right, Miss Conroy. Take ten minutes."

The doctor lifted the transparent hood and Mike walked over to the bed. She was still beautiful. Mollie was flushed and damp and her breathing was troubled.

The doctor said, "It's pneumonia now on top of malaria. And a few other complications . . ."

"What's going to happen?"

"We'll see. It's a form of lung inflammation, however, that we can't use any wonder drug on." He pulled back an eyelid and looked at a bloodshot eye and frowned. "Let's go into the office. Lots of malaria in Mexico—must have hit her suddenly on the plane."

Mike looked back. She was sunk in on the pillows. Her face was expressionless. The face was that of a bright child's. It was also, Mike felt, damn mortal.

The doctor's office was dark, the blinds drawn against the white sun. Mike took a cigar and let the doctor light it for him, but he did not smoke it.

"Well, Zelsmith, perfect artistic tragedy, isn't it? The Greek fates have caught up with Mollie. And yet we are not amused or entertained, are we? Real drama is too much for real life. It belongs safely on the stage and screen, far off."

"What has been happening to her?"

"The horror of imagining that dirty village is enough."

"Sick as she was, she tried to make it . . ." Mike said.

"Pneumonia before you could turn around."

"There isn't much to say."

"If you want tragedy, Zelsmith, this is it up to the hilt. Want ironic comedy? Want a heart story? Take the true down-beat out of it, schmaltz it up, and sell it to pictures. A wonderful girl: maybe it's her fault, maybe it's her father's. I don't know."

"Maybe it's my fault," Mike said.

"If it flatters you to think so, take it away."

"Don't be so tough, Doc. Not today."

"I'm not tough." The doctor sat low in his chair and rubbed his eyes. "I'm not really hard. I'm just Goddamn sorry."

"Did you call her sister?"

"Can't get her sister. She's off with the whole family visiting her husband's relatives in the Middle West."

"Any idea where?"

"None. The husband went along."

"So there is nobody but us?"

The doctor nodded. He pulled a case of index cards to him and began carefully, with a large pen, to fill in the forms with a series of marks that looked like nonsense, but Mike was sure they had vital scientific purpose. He wanted very much just then to believe in the power of science.

26

MOLLIE was back under the transparent tent again when Mike left the clinic. He ate a simple dinner with John and Mandy, and later sat alone through two features at a movie. Everyone around him enjoyed them very much. He called Dr. Sontag, who said there was no change, either for the worse or the better.

Mike went to his cottage and looked out at the traffic and put on his coat and went for a walk. The elm leaves were still falling in the streets, and the ripe olives were staining the walks purple. He walked bent over, not really thinking, not even trying to avoid thinking, just feeling numb. It was late at night.

Suddenly a globe of light hit him in the face. A police prowl car stood there and the cop was fixing the light to keep him in range. Beverly Hills was very well patrolled.

"You," said the cop, as an order.

"What is it?"

"You live around here?"

"At the hotel."

"Not much walking done this late at night."

"I'm sorry, officer."

"Got any identification?"

The light never left his face. "I don't know." He put his hands in his pockets. The cop said, "Say, you hung out a lot at the Plume Café at Cortez this summer?"

"Yes, I've been there."

"Yeah, I remember you now. Came in a lot with the beautiful little dame with the beautiful legs."

"I guess so."

"I thought that was her picture in *The Examiner* this morning. What do you know! A babe like that. Sounds like she was on the junk. She certainly gave all the boys a thrill down there on the beach, kicking the juke box tunes around. Hop in, I'll give you a lift back to the hotel."

So the papers had sniffed something out.

The car picked up speed and the radio gave off a growl and began to speak. "Section Three calling. Woman just shot a man on Stanley Drive, right above Hollywood. Back studio apartment, one flight up."

The cop turned it off. "Not our district. That's on the Strip. Crazy things happen there."

The town was like a small village. Everybody seemed to know everybody else.

The cop said, "I could tell you things make your hair stand on end. Things that happen in any house you wanta pick out on this or any other block. Wait a minute."

The car had stopped and its searchlight picked out a large colored woman carrying a well-packed paper bag.

"Hold it. What's in that bag?"

"My cleaning stuff."

"A little totin'?"

"Just the usual totin'. Some cold pork chops and half an apple pie. Wanta look, officer?"

"No, that's all."

The car started again. "You gotta watch them day workers, or they'd tote the house out from under you if you don't watch 'em."

"Isn't it a little late for a day worker?"

"She's been baby sittin'. That house they come home late there all the time. Who'd have thunk it, huh, the times we sat around with beers in our mitts at the Plume this summer watching the girl whoop it up that she'd be in this spot? We used to sit there all of us and . . ."

"I'll walk the rest of the way, thanks."

"Sure. I hope she comes out of it all right."

Mike slept till noon and called Dr. Sontag. It was the same. He went out after lunch, avoiding Walter and John, and sat with the doctor and then went in and saw Mollie. Her breathing seemed worse. Dr. Sontag was pushing a big needle into her naked ribs and a yellow liquid was flowing out in the glass cylinder. The little breasts hung tired now; they no longer seemed able to bear their own slight weight.

"About a pint and a half of fluid I've taken out of the lungs so far," said the doctor, watching the nurse prepare to let some drip bottles down from the ceiling into an opening made in Mollie's arm.

"We're giving her stuff through the veins to keep her going. Most of it's going right through her. No controls left."

"You're not giving up, Doc?"

"Since when is it up to me? I'm just directing traffic. I didn't build the car."

They sat in the doctor's office and smoked and talked about many subjects that had little bearing on Mollie. Mike sent out for food and they ate, and then they sat again listening to classical music, mostly Bach, on the radio. Mike left the clinic at ten. Mollie was breathing better and the lungs seemed drained of their fluid. The doctor refused to be pleased.

Mike went down to the hotel bar and had some brandies. Ed, the old-time motion picture director, came over to him and pressed his arm and shook his head.

"The world has kinda come apart at the seams for you now, hasn't it? I been watching you drink and I've been saying to myself, you boring old bastard, leave him alone. Nobody can do anything for him and he doesn't want anything done. But at least I can help him drink. I still have the power."

"Thanks, Ed. I don't want to be alone."

"And you don't want to talk about it. I know that too. In fact, I know everything. I wish I'd known when I was a young man what I know now. That's the trouble with knowledge, you get it so damn late that you're a broken-down wreck before you're able to use it. Now the heart inside us is an odd thing. When you're young and full of juices, it has all the answers, and yet one blow and it's shattered like it was glass. Listen to me, it's going to be a time getting over, and then it's going to be gone, like it never was.

"Looking at me, would you think I followed a woman from Chicago to South America and from there to the dogs and back to Hollywood? She was ten years older than I was and a faithless creature, but you couldn't tell me. I learned something from it. You never give the heart in vain, as the poet says. Whatever it is, it builds up in you something of the understanding of human pain and human sadness on earth, and before you know it you can face everything, old age and being forgotten and getting ready for the last leap under the daisies. Shall I shut up now?"

"What did you say, Ed? I was thinking of something else."

"I bet you were. I was giving you the gift of knowledge. I was telling you the secret of eternal wisdom. But it's all right. You didn't miss a thing."

"Huh?"

"Say, I got an idea for a great picture—take your mind off things."

"I'm out of pictures."

"Bring back the real stuff. A picture shot all in sound, but no talkin'. Great universal art form once. Christ, I remember when we were bigger heroes in Bombay and in Budapest than in West Lung, Ohio, or North Hernia, Texas. Now you listen to this idea."

"I've got to go, Ed."

He took a cab to the Galla. It was early yet and couples were still eating out on the terrace overlooking Sunset

Boulevard. The manager, who always carried a gold-headed cane, showed Mike to a table.

"Walter been in?"

"Not yet. It's a little early for the gang."

"Can I get some whisky sours?"

"Naturally."

He sat drinking the sours, and a fancy character with long hair played the piano; all the sad popular songs, the weepy clap-trap that customers call for. Around twelve Walter came in with a party of gay friends, and he saw Mike and came over.

"Drinking alone, M.Z.?"

"Yes."

"I'm with a party."

"Walter, why don't you go out to the clinic and see Mollie?"

"I broke with Mollie some time ago."

"She's dying."

"Bad as that, huh?"

"Yes. She doesn't know anybody, so if you go you'll not lower your pride in her eyes."

Walter said, "We were really friends, weren't we? The three of us. No sticky attachments—real friendship. Those summer days on the sun deck and all the daffy talk about life and books. I'll go see her in the morning."

"Thanks, Walter."

Walter stood up. "M.Z., you still in love with her?"

"I can't remember all of it. All that's left to me with any feeling is a bruised ego; the vulgarity of it, Walter, the hurt vanity in me."

"Gotta go, we're making the rounds. Be seeing you."

"Good-by, Walter. No matter what happens, the picture opens tomorrow night."

The piano player began to play some blues. Mike paid his check and left. As he came into the lobby of the hotel, the cop from the prowl car stood there reading tomorrow's paper at the clerk's desk.

He waved to Mike. "Hiya! Been out on the town?"

"A little elbow bending."

"Oh, how's Miss Binning?"

"Doesn't look so good."

He called the clinic and got the usual yes-and-no report.

HE was drinking in the darkness of a little bar. If she would only die and get it over with. Couldn't she even do this thing properly? His head ached and felt too light and tender to touch.

Someone was talking to him at his elbow. Someone who must have been talking a long time, in a small shrill voice.

"We never did get together, Mr. Zelsmith, did we? All our plans."

"What the hell you talking about?"

"You were going to write some adventure comic strips for me."

"Who said so?"

"We talked it over on the phone. You remember me, Henry Matt."

It was too dark to focus, to see in the barroom, or he was too drunk to see. "Look, Matt, don't you know you don't exist, you're an invention of my brain when I'm low or tired. A projection of something inside me. No one else ever heard of you, no one else has ever seen you. Go creep away."

"That's not bad, Mr. Zelsmith. We could create a great comic on the idea; a superman projected by an active mind, a sort of Einstein, see, and . . ."

The voice drifted off after a while and he found himself in his cottage.

He called the clinic and they said he better come right away.

Dr. Sontag said Walter had just been there and left crying.

"I guess Walter has let Mollie back into his exclusive social club," the doctor said.

"Walter's all right," Mike said.

"I suppose he felt like a Catholic letting a backslider return to the faith."

"Did Mollie know him?"

"No, she's been raving a lot. The little dog, her father. I think he's always with her now, her father."

"How long can this go on, Doc?"

The doctor looked at his milk-white hands as if he hated them. "A long time, a short time."

"What's it like to her?"

"Why fool you, Zelsmith, nobody really knows. We have a lot of fancy labels for things. We call it art, or music, or love, or destiny. In the end it's a dirty corner to crawl in and die."

"You sound like a poet, not a doctor."

"Ha, what do you know about poetry, the real stuff that Job shouted to the Jews and lamented at God with. 'Let the day perish and the night be blotted out in the hour that I was conceived.' That's true poetry, doctors' poetry."

Mollie began to cough and the doctor went in to give her a drink. Mike followed and stood at the bedside and he said, "It's me, Mollie."

Mollie suddenly stiffened and began to talk in a high, young girl's voice: "It's such a fine day. I've walked miles, Father. You're not angry at me again, are you, Father? I know what you wanted. A good, quiet child, a real born lady. But I do try and I am getting better. Don't be so stern with me."

She began to laugh and ended in a giggle.

"I love Atlantic City and you smoking big cigars. You're the best-looking man on the boardwalk. I've been to the pier with the big pickle on it. All those pictures and all painted by hand. I met a boy there. You mustn't object to him, my boy. His name is Mike."

Mike felt cold blows on his spine. Mollie giggled again.

"He, Mike, was standing looking at the pictures and I loved him the first time I saw him . . . I'm sitting polite and neatly, Father. I'll make you proud of me yet. I'm bright and I know it and I'll study hard. No, I don't want to ride the big horse, and that dreadful groom . . . Oh, I can't talk about it. I know the riding habit costs money . . . I hate you! I hate you when you give orders . . . I don't care if you're tall and handsome and give me the bands off your cigars . . . Where did I put Gene's ties? Did he wear his raincoat? I like men like Beppo who have dirt under their fingernails and make vulgar sounds when they eat soup. I like a man who's a beach bum and doesn't work and lets women keep him. Kiss me, Beppo, here comes Father . . . Have a good look, Father, isn't Beppo a de-lightfully slimy object?"

Her face was dry and hot, but she had stopped talking.

The doctor motioned to Mike and they went back to his office and sat there.

The doctor shook his head. "The old man doesn't leave her for a minute."

"What a bastard he must have been."

"No, just a stern old moralist. What a revenge she's having on him. Maybe on California, too."

Mike lit a cigarette. "California: everybody living stripped in the sun, all the children growing too tall and the fruit has no taste and the flowers no smell. The olive trees bear fruit and no one picks it, and if they took away the lousy water you could give it all back to the desert toads."

The doctor shook his head. "Maybe Mollie would have been better off if her family had stayed in Upstate New York. She would have rejected all the young men because they weren't good enough in her father's image and taken up charity work and retired to the white salt-box house of her father's when he died, and she'd have orgies of hard cider with the hired men in the barn, and one day they'd have put her in a bag and locked the iron door and thrown away the key."

Mike turned away from the doctor and clasped his hands and unclasped them and listened to the late street traffic and the brown dried-out palm fronds (that no one ever bothered to cut off the palm trees) rattle as the rats that nested there moved in their sleep.

He had been sitting a long time and everything was out of focus. He was suddenly very alert . . .

The nurse came in—there was some unseen signal between them—and Dr. Sontag got to his feet and moved quickly out of the room. Mike followed.

Mollie's breathing was now a nerve-shattering rattle. The doctor pushed a needle into her arm, listened to her heart, and stood up and pursed his lips. He moaned softly to himself and swayed as if in ritual prayer.

"Oy, oy."

"What is it, Doc?"

Mike went close to the bed. The doctor pushed back one eyelid. "She's blind," he said. "It's the complications that have hit the optic nerves, it's in the brain soon. You can look now, Zelsmith. You'll need a real deathbed scene some day. Note the pious grace and the mumbled forgiveness and the easy, noble death. Look at it, this is the McCoy."

Mike leaned over the bed and took one thin arm.

"Mollie, baby . . ." he said softly.

The eyelids rose but the blind stare did not focus. She was so beautiful now. Really beautiful. The skin tight and pink on the well-formed skull, the lips drawn away a little from the teeth, the wonderful neck taut and held like a work of art.

Her voice was blurred and burned. "Mike? We're in each other's blood always."

"Sure, kid."

She tried to lift his hand to her face, and he put it to her lips. She had no strength left to finish the gesture. Her teeth grated and she was trying to smile.

"Love you, Mike."

He didn't answer. Didn't want to answer. He couldn't. The face on the bed frowned, then the smile again, the dead blue eyes wildly open, seeing nothing.

To his horror, Mike found he was not pitying the suffering flesh on the bed, but professionally, like a film director, he was trying to see and feel things from inside the girl herself—wondering, imagining what it must all look like to her now, there below him. Did she know now after the agonizing journey that the public person she had identified herself with all her short life was nothing much, was only perhaps a figment of the imagination of people who saw her? Was she now letting go her hold, drifting off to the presence of the dark and finishing mystery? What the hell good were consolations of Mrs. Henry's religion and Mike's philosophy to her now? The greater, bigger maw of the final desolation was closing in. Darkness in deep, under-lit, never-ending space.

Mike could only stare and be the director on his chair, the viewer of the final performance inside the hot fever-filled mind. Physically, she was alone—suffering in solitude, laughing perhaps in solitude, incapable now of pulling another swimmer into the private pool of her aloneness. Had she found calm acceptance? The corny happy ending, the old formula, the peaceful end that movies often filmed? A rigid, sleeping ecstasy of coma and catalepsy?

Mike shook himself, sonofabitch, what fancy stuff was he thinking now? It was enough to tear you apart and he decided all love is a matter at the end, not of feeling, but of the will. Yes, he would force love out of himself the way he did the toothpaste out of the tube every morning. He would make for her now, here, a little garden, perfect to grow flowers in and dig her grave . . .

The girl stirred. "Love you, Mike," the burned voice repeated again.

"Love you, too," he said, and dropped the hand.

"It's all over," Dr. Sontag said. The jaw had sagged open into a beautiful, contented smile. The doctor closed it and pushed down the eyelids over the blue stare as the nurse briskly pulled the sheet over the delicate, wonderful face.

From the sidewalk, Mike thought he heard the rattling sound of roller skates.

It was very still just before morning. They sat in Dr. Sontag's office drinking gin, the only thing they had without sending out for it. Through the open door they could look down the hall and see into the little gray room. The nurse had finished washing the body and plugging with cotton all the body openings, and now she pulled down the shades and turned out the overhead light. The nurse went out quickly nodding to them as she passed, carrying the pan of soiled soapy water.

"Anybody to notify?" Mike said.

"Her sister someplace, that's all."

The doctor went to the window and looked at the morning sun coming in over the ridge of cliff. The light crept along the ground, hunting details.

The doctor rubbed his red eyes. "It's going to be good weather to be buried."

28

THEY buried Mollie that afternoon, hid her away like a well-kept secret, on a slight rise among the tall grass of a rather neglected graveyard. Mike had arranged it. They had not been able to get in touch with Belle and there were few people at the graveside.

John, Mandy, Walter, Myron Sontag, and Mike stood looking at the black clay clods, and beyond the grave the hill ran steeply down toward a road and beyond it was the sea, and Mollie, Duty's Child now, was buried. They buried what they had, what was in the polished dark wood casket with the bronze handles.

Mike stood there and the young man with the clerical collar folded his hands and nodded and the gravediggers began to fill the grave quickly, the sunlight on their rough weathered hands. Mike felt nothing, he merely stood and sensed John at his side looking at him.

It was a clear day of washed blue shadows and clouds of brushed wool overhead, a common enough day, but one somehow cheerful, even here. The young man in the clerical collar opened a small Bible and took out a slip of paper on which John Fennel had typed out for him some lines of Donne, and which Mike had approved. The young man looked at Mike, and Mike nodded, and the young man began to read slowly:

Though in the ways of fortune, or understanding, or conscience, thou have been benighted till now, wintered and frozen, clouded and eclypsed, damped and benummed, smothered and stupified till now, now God comes to thee, not as in the dawning of the day, not as in the bud of the spring, but as the sun at noon . . .

They all hurried away to dress for the première.

Alice tried to get Mike on the phone. He refused the calls. The newspapers made a holiday of it:

DEATH TAKES NEW STAR
ON EVE OF HER FIRST SUCCESS

MOLLIE BINNING BURIED AS LIGHTS FLASH FOR HER PREMIERE; GRIM REAPER WRITES NEW ENDING TO ZEL-SMITH EPIC; THE SHOW GOES ON; SHE WANTED PREMIERE HELD AS PLANNED.

No one knew how the news had gotten out, but the town was built on half-guessed and half-secret stories. There were old pictures of Mollie, and stills from the picture on the front pages of the evening newspapers.

That strange mob of people who only appeared at macabre events was present in front of the Fine Film Art Theatre. Scabby, rancid old women in sun-faded tweeds pinned together, moronic old faces bitten by wind and gin.

Feeble-minded boys with open mouths and soiled auto-
graph books. Fat, white-faced schoolgirls, their large wet
eyes sucking everything in. Old men who smelled stale and
showed snags of teeth in leering smiles as they pushed
against everyone. The ropes had been put on the sidewalks
and police fought the crowd. Revolving white searchlights
had been towed into place earlier, to the curb, and their
shafts of light crossed aimlessly in the dark sky.

Frightened baby rats crept deeper into the fronds of the
palm trees over the theater.

The afternoon burial had helped the showing. Many of
the important people, or at least the people who were supposed to be important, came after all. The big black cars
were emptied and a smooth young man talked into a portable mike and smart people made smart remarks, several
claiming to have known Mollie before, and they had always
predicted she could do it. "Too bad she has passed over,"
said the eternal female star with the bony face, who never
mentioned death, or dying.

The mob broke out of the ropes twice and soiled borrowed mink and a bald producer lost his top hat. It
all seemed ghastly to John and Mandy when they drove up
very late, after the picture inside had already started. The
mob still milled around and the overgrown youths with
faded hair were tearing down huge cardboard figures of
Mollie that had stood in the lobby. It seemed indecent, this
paper rape of her painted, varnished body. The hoodlums
and morons handed each other parts of her flat anatomy.
Mike and Walter stood in the inner lobby, hands in pockets,
listening to the sound of the picture behind the ornate walnut doors.

Two young men in torn raincoats, long hair worn to their
shoulders, suddenly appeared in the lobby and tore a huge
picture of Mollie out of its frame. From the theater itself,
behind the doors, came Mollie's voice as if protesting from
someplace what was being done to her image. Walter and
John pushed the youths out of the lobby, and a few ushers
locked arms across the scarlet rug scarred with old wads of
chewing gum that from where Mike stood had lettered on
it: FINE FILM ART

Mike stood in the middle of the lobby, his head down,
looking at his shoelaces. John and Mandy stood beside
Walter who lit a fresh cigarette every two minutes and

mashed it out in a bowl of dirty white sand before it was fully smoked. No one said anything. A rasping warm wind had come up and smelled of oil sumps. The dust and torn paper on the lobby floor whirled across the rug until an usher closed the big glass doors to the street.

They knew the picture was a failure when sharp-looking little men escorting tall blonde women with puffy eyes, chewing gum, began to drift out of the theater. They ignored Mike, as if he were transparent and went on their way, the men smoothing back their oiled heads or hunting cigars near their hearts, the women walking tenderly on their high heels as if, John thought, they carried large glass balls between their thighs. One of the ushers picked his nose and lit a cigarette. A little old man came along with a brass dust-pan on a stick and began to gather up the candy wrappings and butts.

Mike had not moved. There was stillness in the theater now as the score faded out and the music marked time for the voices in those scenes that should have stirred the people, have made them move, sigh, laugh, wonder, and even applaud . . .

John felt Walter at his side putting an elbow into his ribs. "Come on, they repealed the law you have to stay to the bitter end, John."

The doors opened.

The lights did not go up after the last fade-out. A newsreel bumbled brassily across the screen. Mike turned to face the escaping crowd. John and Walter stood in the lobby smelling of buttered popcorn, and watched Mike wipe his face with the back of his hand.

"You got a picture there," said the short man from the Morris Office.

"You can put it in the can as she stands and ship it."

"It's low key, but they'll eat it up in the big bergs. Another *Open City*."

Walter walked off saying nothing. His friend with the big nose was waiting for him. They left quickly.

John followed Zelsmith to the big black car. The lobby was now packed with people holding dirty bits of paper and short pencils, hoping to see a motion-picture star to torment. Someone shoved a popcorn bag and a ball-point pen at Mike. He brushed it aside. Outside someone had set fire to dried fronds of a palm tree.

When their car had gotten clear of traffic, Mike turned to John.

"The kiss of death, John, the kiss of death. I know it."

"You sure, Mike?"

"I'll never get a release for it in this country."

Mike sniffed and blew his nose. A big man with a hurt face behind black-rimmed glasses. "They broke me, John. Busted me. All the great pictures I gave them, all the credits I brought to this town, and they put a knife into me. They couldn't even let me quit with a winner. They couldn't help me with enough dimes to get a good director and build some decent sets. I'm going out a flop."

John said nothing.

"D. W. Griffith stood around for years in bars, a lonely guy picking up little talks with strangers. He lived in a lousy hotel room and couldn't get enough money together to fix a parking ticket. But he's the giant of the early screen. Chaplin fooled them, he saved his money. But people not fit to shine his shoes avoid him, cross the street when they see him coming. But he'll make whatever history this place had. Remember when F. Scott Fitzgerald died? There was nobody in the undertaker's parlor where he lay. The man there asked me if Scotty had any friends in this town. They stole his smart young people and his sad young men and his schools of flappers a million times, and they wouldn't come, even to toss a dog turd on his grave."

"It doesn't matter," John said.

"They named a street after my father. Lasky has a street, and Ince has one, and you can't raise a dime on those honors . . ."

John felt something cruel and banal would help Mike out. He said, "You had your big success, Mike, stop beefing."

"Sure . . . who said, 'Success is a poison that should be taken only late in life, and then only in small sips'? Me, I had it as a kid. Now when I could use a little of the poison . . . Hell, stop me before the self-pity sets in. What hurts isn't so much the big flop—that's like getting a leg cut off, I'm not going to feel that till later. It's the way the town had to do it, the way it had to hang me up out in the open . . ."

John noticed again how Mike spoke in images, how very often he made picture scenes out of his emotions. He didn't answer, he didn't think Mike wanted any answers, just wanted to talk.

"The town is a medieval hangman," Mike said. "You know about those characters? The medieval hangman put the noose around his victim's neck, pushed him off the ladder, then leaped on his back as he swung free, wrapping his arms around him. The hangman's weight making the rope taut as a Goddamn drop. There the hangman hung, arms around the victim like a lover, feeling the body shudder in his arms like a love's climax. When the last shake of life was gone, he relaxed his love hold and let go. That's what this town did to my talent. Maybe it didn't do it to me, just my talent. But I felt their arms around me tonight. The kiss of death, Johnny, the full-flavored, sixteen-jeweled Swiss movement kiss of death.

"I hate to admit it, I liked it here, Johnny, working here, living here, beating them on their own grounds. I felt easy and I felt sure here. Where the hell do I go now? You know what it is to me? Don't laugh, pal, an expulsion from the womb. Or is that too corny?"

John said he didn't think it was *too* corny.

Mike turned the car up a side street. "I can't go back to the cottage. Somebody will be waiting there to ask how it feels to have a flop, or ask me what I'm going to do next. Try and answer *that* one. Do you mind, John, if we drive to the shore?"

"Of course not, Mike."

"We'll go to the beach house and hide out. It's all right. I'm feeling no pain about it. Feeling no pain about anything. Just numb."

"The beach house, if you say so."

"It's quiet down there this time of the year. Jesu, I'll never be able now to pay up the back rent."

29

THE beach house as they drove up looked dusty and uncared for. The garden in the glare of the car's headlights was yellow and leprous white. The front door was no longer left open and Mike hunted on a loaded key chain, pulled off a key, and the door opened at last after a heavy push.

The place was airless, heavy, and warm, and smelled of seepage and pine wood and kitchen rust. Mike opened the big windows on the sea, and found a light switch. They looked over the living room. The good drawings and paintings had been removed, some effort had been made to cover the furniture, but not much. The table used as a bar held only empty bottles and dead flies and old newspapers already turning the yellow of Egyptian tombs. Some moths beat dusty noses against the light fixtures.

Mike walked around the room and then looked at John. "Maybe I shouldn't have come here. But I wanted to. I don't know why. Yes, I do." He walked to the fireplace, opened the woodbin door set into the wall, put his hand way in, and brought out a bottle of whisky. "I stashed it here to keep the beach bums from getting it. Prime twelve years old."

They sat drinking out of two kitchen glasses with nursery rhymes printed on them. Mike said, "I'm going to Europe. I have some frozen money owing me. In France and Italy. I can live on it, always hoping I'll run across something to do. But I wouldn't. I'll be like all the characters you meet over there taking on a lot of liquor and telling you how lousy things are back in the states for people who are extra-sensitive. But no more self-pity, Mike. No self-pity. You had it. You had a lot of it. It was good, John, don't let them ever tell you it isn't good up there. It's wonderful, only you're going so fast you never stop to look at the view. AND THE COW RAN AWAY WITH THE SPOON," he read off his glass.

John refilled the glasses. "I never was up there, Mike. I'm not the type. I do my best work on a low level. I'm going back to Boston and work on a new book."

"A book about this fink town?"

"No, I never got to know it very well."

"What about Mandy?"

"I don't know. It's up to her. It's going to be a long, long talk and a lot of crying, I suppose, on genuine antique furniture."

Mike said softly, "I wish I could get drunk again. Could stay drunk until I land in Southampton. But I can't take the booze any more, don't even want it, you see."

The front door opened with a bang and Alice walked in. She looked *chic* (a word Mike hated) in a knitted yellow dress with cut steel jewelry, her hair worn in a tight swept short cut. She looked different with this almost boyish hairdo. Thinner, her eyes larger.

"Hello, Mike," she said. " 'Lo John."

They returned the greeting and John stood up.

"I knew you'd be here," she said. "I knew you'd hole up here after what the bastards did to you tonight."

"You see the picture?" Mike asked.

"No, but everyone I saw told me—were happy to tell me how bad it was and what a phony you had always been. Oh, the lice, the scum! It couldn't be that bad."

"I guess so," said Mike. She came up to him and took his head in her hands and looked at him, and then she leaned over and kissed him earnestly on the mouth. Then she smiled. "I know you're hurt, Mike. I know how it is. But you're not alone. I'm here, and maybe it isn't what you planned or how you say it, but we still have each other . . ."

Mike looked at her, saying nothing, his face expressionless till he frowned.

Alice said, "And no cracks about deserving each other now. I guess we do. We survived. That's the only victory these days—to survive."

Mike said, "You can do better than me. I'm a marked-down bargain."

"I don't want to do better. Lightning only strikes me once."

"I'm broke, Alice, not even enough dough to get out of town."

"So am I. Papa really went down the drain in the last few years. He never let on, but he died without a pot, living like an emperor till the end."

John said, "I think I'll go back to the hotel."

"We're going too, John." She looked over the room. "Poor bitch, I'm sorry for her. They gave her loaded dice. This place smells unlucky, Mike. Let's get out of here."

Mike stood up and finished his drink, corked the bottle with his fist, and walked to the firebox and put the bottle away. Then he turned back to them.

"The next tenant has a dividend coming. Alice, you think you can stand Europe with me?"

"Sure, Mike."

"Good, I'll promote some train and boat tickets, somehow."

Alice said, "I'm selling our shore house. There will be

enough left after the mortgage is paid for first-class tickets all the way. I'll even pay some of your bills."

Mike nodded. "Make it three tickets. I owe John a first-class trip East."

John said, "You forget I'm a frugal Yankee. I still have the return half of my ticket."

"Velvet," said Mike, "everything is velvet." He took Alice's hand and patted it. "I keep thinking of what that old frump, Emerson, said: 'Beware of what you desire. You'll get it.'"

"That's not very complimentary . . ." Alice said.

Mike looked over the stripped beach house walls. "I wasn't thinking of you, honey . . ."

They walked out of the beach house after snapping off the lights, and Mike slammed the front door. Then he turned and threw the key in the direction of the sea. The thunder of the winter surf sounded like barking.

30

THE chilly seas were tearing away at Redondo Beach down the coast. John could see the pictures of it in the morning *Los Angeles Times*, the big breakers coming in and washing away the beach and hurling tons of water against the walks and walls of shaking houses. Huge sheets of spume and scud tore into the sky, and when it let up for any little time at all, people went out quickly to hunt the moonstones that the high seas brought in from the deep holes offshore.

John read every bit of news about the heavy seas and looked at the pictures of the waves angry and heavy, attacking the land. The winter sun was white but gave little heat till noon. He bought a topcoat with raglan sleeves, a heavy patterned English tweed, and he had a hat now. A snap-brim hat. They had their reservations East on the Super-Chief.

It was cold now in the night and John turned on the room heater first thing in the morning. In Beverly Hills those streets that had Eastern trees were full of falling leaves. He walked down Elm and Maple Drives and kicked at the brown leaves and felt he was back at prep school for the first time. He was very lonely then and writing brave, misspelled letters home (they had promised him some musk-rat traps and the complete works of Mark Twain for Christmas).

The sea continued to pound at the Redondo Beach front and the pictures in the newspapers grew dramatic. That morning he put on his new topcoat and his new hat and went down to the beach. He stood on the shaking sidewalks and watched the walls of a stucco house fall in as an old lady came howling out, skirts up, showing her varicose veins, and carrying a cage of love birds. He walked down on the beach and watched the moonstone hunters hurry along, bent over into the wind. A boy found one as big as the end of his small finger and John bought it for Mandy—a going-away present.

For their last time on the town, John and Mandy went to one of those low, smoky joints on Central Avenue where the food was bad, the liquor strong, and the music the pure New Orleans barrelhouse jazz that Walter admired so much. Walter had taken them to this dive and they sat there now around a small table with a dirty tablecloth, strangers' fingerprints on the glasses of scotch in their hands.

Walter was very pleased. "This is the real solid stuff for cats. You like it, Mandy?"

Mandy always sat very straight in this kind of dive, like a good sport who went along with a thing but remembered her manners. She always appeared cool and collected at such times, and now she nodded at Walter while the heavy colored woman, looking purple under the small spotlights, moaned:

> "Leave me be your sidetrack, poppa,
> Till your main line comes,
> I can do better switchin'
> Than your main line ever done . . ."

Neither Mandy nor John understood fully what this prime number-one boogie was about; they looked at Walter and nodded, not wanting to hurt his pleasure in the solid beat. They were both a little tired, a little worried, and in a kind of pain.

> "Baby, see that spider climbin' on the wall
> He's goin' up there for to get his ashes hauled . . ."

Walter grinned. "The old nympho-kick shouting. Listen to that second bar on the skins. They don't horse around with the corny Dixieland stuff, that's only for squares, that's not real jazz. This is the kind you got from Zutey Singleton, Pops Armstrong, King Oliver, Tubby Hall, Johnny St. Cyr. This the real Storyville jive. Your head hurt, Mandy?"

"It's so smoky in here."

John felt empty and futile.

"Just a little longer," begged Walter. "Listen to how they play it. That seventh that appears in the key of B-flat, making that abrupt change. What a riff! There's nothing like gutbucket playing."

John ordered another round. He wanted to talk to Mandy alone, but he decided he was a coward and the longer he delayed tonight the better.

> "Oh, tell me how long how long must I wait
> Oh, can I get it now or must I hesitate
> You're playing in my orchard now don't you see
> If you don't like my peaches stop shakin' my tree.
> Oh, tell me how long how long must I wait
> Oh, can I get it now or must I hesitate . . ."

The place was getting very crowded, the whole joint seemed to breathe in at the same time, and exhale its smoke in big clouds of white and blue smoke. Mandy began to get ready to leave, but Walter had turned away and was following the music, eyes closed. It was, he heard, a straight thirty-two bar number with a release and no introduction. The clarinet solo was more like a fiddle style, daring in not using arpeggios. Then the solo took a South Side inflection, then a two-bar flare. Walter was turning around to face the table on the rhythmic riff as it went into a shuffle rhythm, when he opened his eyes and saw that Mandy had risen and was leaving. He and John followed her to the door through the heavy traffic.

> "It's a hell of a note said the Queen of Spain
> Three minutes' pleasure and nine months' pain
> Two weeks' rest and you're back at it again
> It's a hell of a life said the Queen of Spain . . ."

They were alone later at Mandy's beach house and they had it out in a polite, civilized, and rather cozy session.

Mandy Rye in her blue robe sitting under her framed Grandma Moses, her long legs tucked under her on her Regency chair that had once belonged to Mrs. Jordan at Bath, in the days of George IV.

"I couldn't live in Boston, John, and I couldn't give up my acting. It isn't that I don't love you. It's just I'm adding it up and that's the way the figures read."

John kissed her cheek and smiled just enough to bend his mouth. "You don't want to be Mrs. John Fennel?"

"I wouldn't fit in. You know that."

John repeated, "You don't want to be Mrs. John Fennel?"

"All right, dear, I don't. I've got a life I like here. When I get baggy and wrinkled, there is always radio or road companies of Coward and Behrman."

"Yes, there is."

"I never cared much for a man around the house at an age when it meant most. It never took or cracked the ice until you came. I love you, darling. I wish I could say how much I do."

He wanted to tell her, "I'll write you some witty dialogue," but he didn't.

"It was fine," she went on, "but it never set the world exploding, and maybe I was lucky. Look where it got poor Mollie."

"We're pulling out tomorrow. Mike and Alice and myself."

"Good luck, John. I'm going on location tomorrow for Fox. I feel terrible I can't see you off."

"We'll say a sane and safe good-by right here."

"I'm going to cry . . ."

"And I'm going to miss you, Mandy."

"Yes."

"Good-by, Mandy . . ."

"I'll have the moonstone set in a ring . . ."

Belle came in. The long stride, the head so like Mollie's, in many ways. She sat down and faced Mike and they looked at each other closely for a moment, as if trying to see how much the other had been affected by events and how much of their wound they should exhibit to each other.

"You should have wired us sooner," said Belle. She looked uncomfortable in black. From the back yard came again the bark of dogs as some hounds played among the fallen fruit.

"Yes," said Mike, "we should have. But we weren't very bright. We didn't call Henry's boss for a forwarding address until it was all over."

"You were too upset to think."

Mike nodded. "What the hell—it was all my fault."

"It has to be somebody's fault."

"I came to her with too many strings. I should have kept hands off."

"Could you?"

"If I had let her alone, she'd be alive today."

"You think so, Mike?"

"Sure. She'd be taking care of Gene; he seems a pretty fine guy. Her life wouldn't have been so exciting, but she'd have managed. I'm the heel in this whole thing."

"Maybe you are, Mike," Belle said.

"Forgive me, Belle."

"I can't say how much of it all was wrong with Mollie, or how much was wrong with you. Anyway, it didn't work out."

Mike stood up.

"Good luck, Mike," she said calmly, then she bent over and began to weep. "Mollie! Mollie! My sister Mollie!"

31

THERE weren't many good-bys. The taxi taking them to the Pasadena railroad station was moving in among the parked cars. Mike had decided to get on the train here, rather than in Union Station in Los Angeles. Alice counted the bags. John watched the landscape. He had come in here to the new Pompeii, and it seemed fitting to leave from here, why he didn't know.

The porter took their bags and said the Super-Chief was due in a few minutes. A wedding party was all over the station. A tall, handsome groom, the standard type groom that they had seen in all the beauty soap ads, and a small, pretty bride with all her family and all the bridesmaids and all the wedding party. Someone was flinging rice and flash bulbs took last pictures.

Their wedding baggage was all new, linen covered, a pale blue. They could see the crisp leather tags that held

297

their name. Somebody still had a few bottles of champagne and people were drinking it out of paper cups on the platform as the train came in. The wedding party went charging down the platform to their car and a middle-aged woman wiped an eye and kept saying: "Remember Uncle Charles in Kansas City. He sent the silver creamer."

The porter put the Zelsmith baggage into their compartment and told them the diner was three cars forward and the club car two cars to the rear.

Alice was writing a letter, frowning over the spelling. It was to the estate lawyers. They were moving again, gathering speed for the long climb to the blue ridges above San Bernardino. In the failing light the orange orchards dropped quickly away.

Mike sat watching the tracks pass in the blue gloaming. The sun was setting in the west, a big inartistic smear of red; setting on the ocean there, setting over the beach houses and the sun decks, setting over all the fine hills, and the dry hills that would some day be fine hills if real estate values held. Setting over the Sontag Clinic and the pink baby rats bedding down in the dry palm tree fronds. Setting on the tar-stained beach where the suntanned bums lived and where the birds stood now at nightfall all facing the same way, their feet in water and the last seagull swooping down on the flickering moths. Setting, Mike knew, on the low beach house, the low pinewood walls, and the low-pitched ceiling with the resin boiling out in the rafters, and the empty heated rooms, silent now and the windows closed and the drapes lying dead against the window sashes. Setting and making shadows where he had lived life more than he ever had elsewhere.

The sun was a thin razor edge of orange now, and the pitch and lurch of the speeding train was a shaking rhythm rocking him as he and Alice climbed up out of California in a hurry.

A fat man in gray took the seat next to John in the club car, put a cigarette into an amber holder, and lit it. He lifted a highball glass the waiter had just set down and held it against his face and smiled at John and took a big swallow.

"Really going, aren't we?" the fat man said.

"Yes," said John, "we'll go a lot faster than this tomorrow."

"Great state, California. Hate to leave it. Live in Tarzana, but have to go East twice a year. Hate to do it."

"Lots of people like that."

"I guess so. My great-grandfather came out by wagon train. Took four months. You a visitor?"

John nodded. "Yes, a visitor."

"Coming back some day?"

"No plans."

"Care for a drink?"

"No, thank you, haven't had any dinner yet."

John Fennel got up and went back to his bedroom and washed his hands and face and stood looking at himself in the small wall mirror. He had a feeling that none of it had ever happened on that sun-drenched coast, that the coast itself did not exist, there was no California. He could remember, but he could not swear any of it was true. It had dropped away like a hasty dream and nothing could ever have been like the things he thought he remembered.

He couldn't blame it all on the climate or the sun or the empty circling of the parties and the sterile work, and the lack of rain, and the strong drinks in the weak hours of the cold nights—nights like living in the craters of the moon.

There was no season and no changing to seasons, and even the leaves did not fall. The people cast no real shadows but only shapes black and odd from modern art, and their skin was always the color of theater make-up. A far land, a silent land, locked away from the cities of the East and the tumult of Europe and the agony of people in terror. No strong noise that jarred the sunlight, no great voices to trap the mind into thinking; a remote wasteland lost to the things that one felt and was hurt by. Yes, that was it, he felt. There were no wounds, no hurt, and that was the sad part. Mandy hadn't even left a scar, no pain; he didn't give a good Goddamn if she had ever been. The bite of existence did not cut into one in that land the train was climbing out of . . .

That was it; nothing had looked real; the fruit had no taste, the flowers no smell, the land no savor. The memory lacked barbs to catch and hold onto one's flesh. It was all play-acting to phantom cameras, to invisible directors. To grab and love and make little deaths in this listless sunshine was to fail on a small stage that no one came to see. There were even no acoustics so one could scream and be heard. It was like a silent film with a big black mouth open and the darting tongue in agony, and the throat knotted with words and nothing coming out; just the tinny rattle of a piano playing the blues in bad time. There is no charge of energy, no piling of thunder in the mind and marrow to discharge in human rage, in human passion; only the slow grind of bodies to the draw of a white sun, no vibrant passages to record and mark on the memory.

Love had been after all only a negation, had left no marks, he now saw; had no more existed than the dreadful night moistures that passed for summer rains on the yellow grasses of the landscaped hillside. It was all the parties, all the record-playing, all the strong drinks in what the film people called a *montage;* one of those artistic arrangements of objects: bottles, faces, train wheels, clouds, all pumped full of music to take the place of real action, to advance the plot without telling anything true and honest in detail. Mere symbols of life, like Chinese characters that once were pictures, but no longer. Life elsewhere was real and slippery and struggled in the arms like a big fish dying in real air, drowning with every flap of its gills.

He wanted to bang his head against the train windows, he wanted to feel something, hate someone, remember the hurts, the bites, the close, tumbling moments of sensual nihilism, but the devil with it; it was better perhaps that it had not happened in a place that did not exist. Somehow he would never be able to account for that void even in his journals, those months in his life. He would only be able to say, "I once was in California." Maybe they would understand what the hell he was talking about . . .

The train was going too fast, too fast to write with comfort. Alice put the letter aside and took out a cigarette and lit it herself. Mike was looking out into the landscape. She felt close and cozy, she felt the end of the last round and was thankful she didn't have to get up at the bell any more and slug.

It wasn't going to be all she ever dreamed, but it was going to be what she had wanted. They would mellow and grow together, they would see places from travel posters and be bored. They would go away from old and sacred things and hope for something exciting on the horizon. Together, the two of them, the big days of the past, and the full days forgotten, or just walled up inside, where they couldn't cry too loud in the walls.

She would never let him know how much she had disliked Mollie alive or dead. And in the end, even Mollie would fade out of the sensitive film in the back of Mike's eyeballs and he would forget for long periods of time what she had ever looked like.

In the end Alice would win, she would have him alone, and he was Mike. Maybe not what he had once been. She had no dream in her that he would not deteriorate; all the artists did when they lost it, and couldn't go on creating. But that, in a sad way, was good, too, for he would be easier to live with and if he were grouchy or ill, she would baby and serve him, wean him from his dreams, and pad him against the sharp hopes that would only hurt him more.

Mary pity women, as the poet said. This being a woman was nothing you asked for, or wanted, but there it was and if you were alive you sweated and you fought for what was yours—and if you won, there he was sitting across the way from you, not pitying himself any more. Mike was pretty tough, but soaked in the last of the native air. Soon they would be out of California, the two of them, and into middle age. She yawned, like a cat satisfied. She admitted to herself she had always been so greedy for him it still frightened her at times.

The train gained power, increased its speed, and the sun was all set now in the west. A waiter passed outside their door, banging his chimes, reminding all men that man must eat, and that all flesh is grass. Alice felt hungry, suddenly, and decided they would have dinner at once. A medium-rare steak (damn the California habit of a salad first) and then apple pie and black coffee. She felt cheerful as she relished the idea of the steak. The food, Alice remembered, was very good on the train. It was a beautiful train and she was very happy to still be able to travel in such comfort and style.

THE END

301

What Every Teen-Ager
Should Know

FACTS OF LIFE AND LOVE FOR TEEN-AGERS
(REVISED EDITION)

EVELYN MILLIS DUVALL

From handling the physical changes of puberty
to fulfilling the emotional needs of
marriage—here is the frank, realistic advice of
a well-known family and marriage consultant
who has helped thousands of young people meet
every demand of life and love.

"This sane, sound, reassuring book for
young people gives not only the
facts of sex and growth, but also an
understanding of how these facts
are related to life, from etiquette to
ethics. It minces no words in its
descriptions of growing up and all
the attendant problems of sex."

—New York TIMES

A Popular Library
Non-Fiction Giant • **35c**

An Explosive Novel Of
The Liberation Of Paris

TEN DAYS IN AUGUST

BERNARD FRIZELL

---

*"The narrative unfolds in terms of a
thriller that should move the
sardonically sentimental heart of
Alfred Hitchcock . . . And Mr. Frizell,
a first novelist, who served with the
American psychological warriors in
France, has made the most of a
chaotic and compelling drama . . . I read
this story with unflagging interest
far into a recent spring night."*

—New York TIMES

A Popular Library
Giant Bestseller • **35c**

He Sold His Soul
For Another Man's Wife

THE EMPTY TRAP

JOHN D. MACDONALD
Author of BORDER TOWN GIRL

Lloyd Westcott's love for the beauteous
and tempting Sylvia was a force over which
he had no control.

She was a demanding woman. She wanted love
and money—and Lloyd was expected to
supply both on her demand. And so he became
a cheat and a thief for her—for Sylvia—
his boss' wife!

This is a piercingly honest story about an
overpowering emotional obsession that
drove a man to take dangerous risks with
everything he held dear.

A Popular Library
Fiction Bestseller • **25¢**